Dear Reader,

Autumn is nearly up[...] longer evenings wh[...] *Scarlet* novels. Wha[...]

There are three fabulous titles this month for you to enjoy, including our second hardback *Finding Gold* by Golden Heart Award winner, Tammy Hilz: Jackson Dermont is on the trail of a thief and the mysterious Rachel Gold is high on his list of suspects. Is she guilty or innocent? In Kathryn Bellamy's novel, *A Woman Scorned*, we have a secret baby plot spiced up for the nineties, and in Vickie Moore's third Scarlet novel *Seared Satin*, security firm boss Tess Reynolds doesn't need any man's help until gorgeous Ethan Booker joins her to solve a deadly mystery.

By the way, is your collection of *Scarlet* novels complete, or are you longing for a certain title that sold out before you had chance to get hold of it? If so, feel free to drop me a line and I will ensure that your letter is passed on to the relevant department.

Till next month,

Sally Cooper

SALLY COOPER,
Editor-in-Chief – *Scarlet*

About the Author

Kathryn Bellamy was born in 1953 and educated at Queen Elizabeth's Grammar School in Horncastle, Lincolnshire.

After gaining excellent examination results, she worked in a bank until ill health forced her to resign. Since then, Kathryn has worked for her husband John, a chartered accountant, on a part-time basis, and has been able to spend more time writing fiction, which has always been a much-loved hobby.

Kathryn still lives in Lincoln, and her hobbies include reading, tennis and yoga.

We are delighted to bring you Kathryn's fourth *Scarlet* novel, featuring characters we know you will love.

Other *Scarlet* titles available this month:

SEARED SATIN – Vickie Moore
FINDING GOLD – Tammy Hilz

KATHRYN BELLAMY

A WOMAN SCORNED

Enquiries to:
Robinson Publishing Ltd
7 Kensington Church Court
London W8 4SP

First published in the UK by Scarlet, 1998

A copy of the British Library Cataloguing in
Publication data is available from the British Library

ISBN 1–85487–899–9

Printed and bound in the EC

10 9 8 7 6 5 4 3 2 1

CHAPTER 1

'Mummy! Why is that man staring at you?' Abby tugged at her mother's arm but Tessa Grant didn't even bother to look up.

'Ignore him,' she said absently. She was frowning over her shopping list and the pile of bills to be paid, checking the total amount against her available cash. As usual, the outgoings exceeded her income, and she was far too concerned about that to be remotely interested in any stranger whose attention she might have caught.

'Mummy!' Abby repeated impatiently, and Tessa reluctantly glanced up, totally unprepared for the shock which awaited her. Her eyes widened in disbelief and she put a hand to her mouth to stifle the involuntary gasp of dismay that sprang to her lips. Matt Stafford! After one painful jolt, her heart resumed its beating, but at a much faster pace than before, and her large brown eyes widened even further as they locked on to the steely blue-eyed gaze from the man standing not twenty feet from her.

Tall and broad-shouldered, as darkly handsome as ever, he dominated the coffee-shop – the place Tessa had chosen at random merely to while away the half-

1

hour before Abby's dental appointment. Matt was standing just within the doorway, his feet planted firmly on the floor, legs apart and arms aggressively akimbo as if he dared her to try and pass him by. Oh, no! Why had he appeared here and now? Tessa thought, in considerable panic. She'd had no contact with him since passion had briefly flared between them in Cyprus, six years before.

Involuntarily, her gaze flew to her daughter sitting beside her, and she was suddenly relieved that Abby had inherited her own small frame and that, out of school uniform, she looked younger than her years. Surely Matt would assume she had married upon her return to England and borne her husband a child? He had no reason to suspect the truth, yet still Tessa trembled and she had to use both hands to place her cup carefully down on to the saucer, concentrating on the small task lest she betray her agitation by spilling the contents.

'Who is he?' Abby demanded, but Tessa merely shook her head by way of reply, interlocking her fingers tightly together and lowering her ringless hands to her lap, out of sight. Frozen into immobility, she could only sit, as if mesmerized, and watch him approach.

He moved slowly, stiffly, as if he desired this confrontation as little as she, so why hadn't he simply turned and walked away? she wondered resentfully. There had been a time when she would have welcomed him back into her life, but no longer. She had managed, alone, for six years, had built a new life for herself and her daughter, pushing memories of Matt Stafford so deep that now he only appeared occasionally, unbidden and unwanted, in dreams; vivid, haunting dreams which left her heavy-eyed and listless upon awakening.

'Tessa.' Matt came to a halt beside her table, effectively blocking her escape. Quite unable to respond, she gazed up at him, noting how little he had changed over the years. He'd be thirty-four now, and still looked tanned and fit, his body hard and lean, the strong muscular frame evident even beneath the pale grey suit he was wearing. His hair was still as black as a raven's wing, his eyes the same piercing blue she remembered, although now there were laughter lines creasing attractively at the corners. But he wasn't laughing now: he regarded her steadily, betraying no emotion, neither pleasure nor dismay at this unexpected meeting. Tessa licked her suddenly parched lips and cleared her throat nervously as she forced a slight smile.

'Hello, Matt,' she replied coolly. 'I hope you are well?' She was pleased that she at least sounded composed and hoped she could sustain the tone of casual politeness for as long as was necessary.

'You do?' His mouth twisted and he raised one disbelieving eyebrow at her query. 'I'm sure you really couldn't give a damn,' he drawled, and she flushed hotly. She tried not to squirm in her seat and fervently wished he would move his too-perceptive eyes from raking her face and figure and turn his attention elsewhere. Then, to her consternation, her wish was granted and he did just that. Abby had been regarding him with wide-eyed interest and he lowered himself easily until he was sitting back on his heels, his face level with hers.

3

'Hello, sweetheart,' he said softly. 'What's your name?'

'Abby Grant,' she replied promptly. Tessa suppressed a groan, wishing, far too late, that she had forestalled her daughter and provided only her first name. Now Matt would know she was still single . . . Maybe not, perhaps he won't realize, she thought hopefully.

'Grant?' Matt shot a puzzled glance at Tessa. 'You've never married?' he asked slowly.

'No,' she replied tersely, then turned her attention to Abby. 'Finish your milk,' she instructed her, 'we have to go now.' She stood up and rooted in her bag for cash with which to settle the bill, indicating the meeting was over, but Matt didn't budge an inch.

'Why not?' he persisted. 'Where's her father?'

'That's none of your business!' Tessa snapped sharply. Too sharply, and she realized her error at once, for his eyes narrowed as he scrutinized Abby's small features, and Tessa was sure he was searching for a resemblance to himself.

She held her breath, standing motionless and silent as if any movement or word from her would betray the truth, although common sense told her she had nothing to fear. Abby's dark hair could have been inherited from either herself or Matt, but the brown eyes were definitely Tessa's legacy, as was the delicate bone structure.

He remained absorbed in the child, and Tessa allowed her own gaze to rest on him, and was appalled to find herself having to fight a sudden yearning in her for him to guess the truth; for him to take them both into the strength and protection of his arms . . . Oh, get

4

a grip, Tessa! she admonished herself sternly: it was far, far too late. If Matt had really wanted her as much as he had once claimed he had, he would have sought her out long ago.

'I'm very pleased to meet you, Miss Abby Grant,' Matt said politely, and with a broad smile that elicited a grin from Abby. 'How old are you?' he continued softly, and Tessa's heart almost stopped beating, for she knew Abby would respond with the too-precise five-and-a-quarter with which she answered all such queries, thus giving Matt the opportunity of pinpointing the date of her conception with some accuracy.

'She's four,' she lied quickly, forestalling Abby, who looked up at her reproachfully and was about to correct her, Tessa knew. 'Eat this last biscuit,' she said, pushing it unceremoniously into Abby's mouth to hopefully prevent her from speaking or, at the very least, render her indignant objection unintelligible to Matt. 'You'll have to excuse us, Matt; we have an appointment,' she told him firmly, for he still barred her exit.

'Can I get past you, please!' An irate, plump middle-aged woman, laden with shopping bags, demanded loudly, coming unwittingly to Tessa's rescue. With a muttered apology, Matt moved aside to let her pass and Tessa grabbed her opportunity, propelling Abby ahead of her, slapping down their bill and the money by the till and then hurrying out of the coffee-shop. A brief glance over her shoulder told her Matt had followed her outside and she desperately scanned the busy traffic, searching for a cab to provide a quick getaway and to hell with the expense.

5

'Look out for a taxi,' she instructed Abby and the little girl, fired by her mother's urgency, looked and then nodded eagerly, pointing to one of London's black cabs.

'There!' Without waiting for Tessa, and forgetful of her road-safety schooling, she darted towards the cab which had drawn up on the opposite side of the road to disgorge its contents.

'No!' Tessa screamed. Heedless now of Matt's pursuit and concerned only with the danger to her child, she dashed out into the road, grabbing Abby's collar and pushing her back to the safety of the pavement. But then Tessa stumbled, half falling to her knees, and she was powerless to do anything but watch as a huge red double-decker bus bore down on her. She clearly saw the driver's contorted features as he fought to halt the heavy vehicle, heard the frantic screech of brakes but, after one brief second of agonizing pain, felt nothing more . . .

As if from a great distance Tessa heard the insistent sound of an approaching siren, seemed to hear Abby sobbing in distress, and was vaguely aware of Matt bending over her and talking urgently, but she was frighteningly incapable of speech or movement, quite unable to comfort Abby and reassure her she wasn't hurt. Even opening her eyes fully or lifting her hand proved impossible and soon it was too much effort even to try and she sank into a bottomless well of sleep . . .

Matt had reached her first, impatiently elbowing his way through a crowd of onlookers which had quickly gathered, using his broad shoulders to good effect.

'Don't move her!' he warned one would-be helper sharply. He stooped over her, feeling for a pulse with one hand while unclipping his mobile phone from his belt with the other and punching out 999.

He breathed a huge sigh of relief when he found a steady, strong beat – she looked so . . . lifeless, a crumpled, immobile, broken figure. Why did you run away from me, Tess? he wondered silently, staring intently down at her as if she could answer his unspoken question. The wary tension that had been etched on her face during their brief confrontation had gone and she looked as young and pretty as the nineteen-year-old he remembered. Her body was still as small and slender as a young girl's and he found it hard to believe she was twenty-five and a mother. An unmarried mother at that: life since he had known her had not been good to her, he thought regretfully. The Tessa he had known deserved better.

A slight but insistent tugging on his jacket finally caught his attention and he turned to see Abby's tear-drenched face only inches from his own. Unable to find the nice waitress who had given her extra biscuits, Abby had decided to go to Matt, the only other person present who wasn't a complete stranger to her.

'Don't cry, sweetheart.' Matt forced a smile and hugged her tiny frame closer. For some inexplicable reason, he felt he was to blame for Tessa's mishap; certainly for her hasty departure from the coffee-shop. Therefore, despite an almost complete lack of experience in caring for children, he felt the least he could do was to look after her daughter until the father or some other relative could be found.

7

Tessa's bag had fallen open where she had dropped it and the contents littered the road. Matt pointed to the various objects.

'Will you pick those up for Mummy?' he asked, to give her something to do. Abby nodded and began collecting up the assorted letters, keys, lipstick and coins. When she had finished the task she clutched the bag tightly to her chest and once again held firmly on to the edge of Matt's jacket.

The ambulance arrived only minutes after Matt's phone call; Tessa was quickly but carefully transferred inside. Matt made as if to follow, but the paramedic stopped him, glancing at Abby.

'It might be better if you followed us, sir. Rather distressing for your little girl,' he said quietly, jerking his head slightly to indicate the paraphernalia inside the ambulance. Matt hesitated, then murmured his agreement and stepped back.

Abby began to sob again as the ambulance left the scene, blue light flashing and siren blaring. Matt scooped her up in his arms and tried to comfort her as he hailed a cab and sat her down beside him.

'Don't worry; she'll be all right after she's been to the hospital,' he said, forcing a cheery smile. 'But she might have to stay there for a little while,' he continued carefully. 'Who else looks after you besides Mummy?' he asked. Abby stared at him and shrugged slightly.

'Just Mummy,' she said finally.

'Where does your father live?' Matt asked next.

Abby considered that for a moment, then, 'He's in Heaven,' she said solemnly. Oh, God, Matt thought despairingly. Poor child. Poor Tessa, too.

'Your grandparents?' he tried, with not much hope. He knew Tessa's parents were dead: when he had met her, they had only recently been killed in a car accident and she had been staying with her aunt before returning to teacher-training college in the autumn. The father's parents might still be in contact, though, but his question merely elicited a rather bewildered shake of Abby's head and Matt suppressed a sigh.

'May I have a look inside her bag?' he asked, putting his scruples aside as he rifled the contents, searching for a diary, perhaps, one of those with a page listing personal information such as a next of kin, or an address book. What he found was a sheaf of bills, which at least provided him with Tessa's address and seemed to indicate that she was the sole householder. He also found that month's salary slip which included the name of her employer. There was also a dental appointment card for that day and he was about to dismiss it as being unimportant, then glanced at Abby.

'Have you had toothache?'

'No.'

'Just a check-up, then,' he mused. 'You're supposed to be going to the dentist – do you want to go?' he asked. 'Stupid question,' he muttered, even as Abby shook her head vigorously. 'Okay, we'll leave that for now. But tell someone if you get toothache,' he told her, and resumed his perusal of Tessa's belongings. 'Who looks after you while Mummy's at work?' he was suddenly inspired to ask.

'Nobody; I'm at big school now,' she informed him proudly.

'You are? You must be a clever girl to go to big school when you're only four,' he told her, smiling.

9

'I'm not four! I'm five and a quarter,' she said, which stunned him into momentary silence. Why had Tessa lied to him? He gazed searchingly at Abby, even more intently than he had in the coffee-shop, his earlier suspicions, allayed by Tessa's deceit, returning in full force. She could be my daughter, he thought dazedly, seeking a resemblance. She began to fidget under his scrutiny and Matt realized he was making her feel uncomfortable, so he sat back and began asking casually about her schoolfriends.

When they arrived at the hospital, he put aside thoughts of Abby's parentage and hurried inside the Accident and Emergency Department, making his way to the Reception desk.

'Tessa Grant?' he asked urgently.

'Are you her husband?'

'No.' Matt shook his head, then realized he would receive no information at all if he weren't careful. Worse, Abby would be handed over to Social Services. He glanced down at her tear-stained, woebegone expression and knew that, his child or not, he couldn't stand by and see her passed on to foster parents, however kind they might be, nor into the impersonal care of a children's home.

'Tessa's my fiancée,' he said firmly, praying Abby wouldn't recognize the word and contradict him. Luckily, he was able to rattle off Tessa's address as if he had known it forever instead of a mere five minutes. 'I'll stay here until there's news of Tessa, but I'll phone Abby's grandmother and ask her to come and collect her. It will be quite all right for Abby to stay with her for as long as necessary,' he added, even more firmly, his tone brooking no argument. The receptionist nodded, too busy to be anything but grateful that the problem had been solved so easily.

'If you'd like to take a seat, someone will be out to talk to you in due course,' she said, already turning to deal with another query.

'Thanks.' Matt turned, took Abby's hand in his and steered her over to a row of chairs. She sat down, a tiny disconsolate figure whose feet didn't reach the floor. She had stopped crying but her lower lip trembled ominously.

'I want my mummy,' she whispered, and Matt's heart twisted with sympathy for her. Matt Stafford was seldom at a loss, but he felt useless in this situation.

'I know you do, sweetheart. The doctor is looking after her now.' He hesitated, wanting to assure her Tessa would be well again soon, but he daren't raise her hopes while there was a possibility he might have to dash them again later. He felt it was important that she learned she could trust him.

He took out his mobile phone and began punching out the number of his parents' house before realizing this was one conversation Abby ought not to overhear.

'I'm just going over there to make a phone call,' he told her, pointing to a public phone on the far side of the waiting area. 'I won't be long,' he promised her. She nodded slightly, but kept her gaze fixed unwaveringly on him as he walked over to the booth. Matt smiled reassuringly at her as he fished out change from his pocket and again stabbed out the numbers. Fortunately, his mother, Evelyn Stafford, answered.

11

'Mother, I need your help,' he began without pre-amble. Evelyn felt a stab of pleasure at the words, fleetingly wondering just how many years had passed since Matt had needed her. Or, indeed, any of the children who had absorbed most of her time, thoughts and energy for so many years . . . She was jolted quickly out of her reverie when he briefly explained what had happened.

'Matt! You can't simply take the child!' she exclaimed. 'You could get into a great deal of trouble.'

'I realize that. Abby's too upset to talk to anyone right now.' He cast a glance and another forced smile at the little girl who was still watching him intently. 'But if she lets slip that she's never seen me before today, the staff will call the police and hand her over to Social Services. Even if she's not my daughter. . .' He paused, struck by how much that hurt, then continued urgently, 'She's Tessa's child and I want to take care of her.' Evelyn hesitated, common sense warring with the desire to help him and her longing for a grandchild. This little girl might not even be Matt's, she reminded herself, and this was the first time she had heard him mention Tessa Grant. Who was she? If she had been important to Matt, surely he would have told his family about her? And what would happen if the mother died of her injuries? They couldn't keep the child indefinitely, but nor could they hand her back as if returning damaged goods to a store!

'I'm on my way,' she said finally, grateful that her husband was not at home. She shuddered to think what George Stafford would have to say about this little cuckoo in the nest.

Evelyn drove quickly to London, deciding that the whole idea was insane and she would tell Matt so just as soon as she arrived; then the excitement at the possibility of having a grandchild would bubble to the surface of her mind and she realized she was grinning idiotically. She had to keep reminding herself that Matt himself wasn't even sure he was the child's father, and that Tessa Grant had shown no desire to share her daughter thus far and would probably take the child away as soon as she recovered from her injuries; might even press criminal charges against Matt . . .

However, as soon as she saw Abby, her heart and her reservations melted. Poor little mite, she thought, as she hurried over.

'Ma! Thanks for coming.' Matt stood up and kissed her cheek. 'This is Abby – Abby, this lady is my mother,' he told her.

'Hello, Abby.' Evelyn smiled gently, and received a whispered 'hello' and a wan smile in return. The smile revealed a small but definite dimple in Abby's cheek, and Evelyn caught her breath, glancing up at Matt to see if he had noticed. Of course not, she thought at once; he'd had just such a dimple in babyhood, but neither she nor anyone else had dared remind him of it for around thirty years!

She sat down and took Abby's hand in hers, and quickly realized the child was suffering discomfort other than the more obvious upset over what had happened to her mother.

'Oh, Matt, really!' she said, exasperated, before turning to speak softly to Abby. 'Shall I take you to the bathroom?' she asked, thereby earning herself a

13

heartfelt nod and undying gratitude from the little girl who had been too embarrassed to tell Matt of her need.

'She didn't say anything,' Matt protested, rather uncomfortably. Evelyn shot him a quelling look, then stood up and took Abby with her. A passing nurse directed them to the nearest cloakroom and Evelyn waited outside the cubicle after being assured that Abby could manage alone. She watched approvingly as Abby, without being prompted, carefully washed her hands, noticing, with a slight smile and a tug on her heartstrings, how she had to stretch on tip-toe to reach the taps. However, the hot-air drier was fixed too high on the wall for her and Evelyn pulled out tissues from her capacious bag and bent to dry her hands.

'Thank you,' Abby whispered, her large brown eyes locking on to Evelyn's blue ones. Evelyn momentarily tightened her hold on Abby's hands and resisted the impulse to hug her. It was too soon . . . or was it? She gathered Abby loosely into her embrace, ready to retreat if there was any resistance. But Abby pressed closer, tiny arms going around Evelyn's neck and almost strangling her. Evelyn held her closer.

'Cry if you want to, little one,' she told her. 'I know you're frightened, but I'm here to look after you until your mummy's better.' She repeated the offer when they returned to Matt, looking at him questioningly over Abby's shoulder for an indication of how long that might be. He interpreted the glance correctly and shook his head slightly.

'Coma,' he said quietly. 'They're going to do a CAT scan and can't tell me much until then. I've told them she's my fiancée,' he added, even more quietly. Eve-

14

lyn's brows rose sharply. 'I want to hang on here for a while, but I think Abby would be better at home.'

'Yes, she's worn out,' Evelyn said, glancing down at Abby, who was leaning against her, her eyes half-closed, her thumb firmly in her mouth. 'Carry her out to the car for me,' she told Matt. Abby barely stirred and certainly didn't protest, for which both Matt and Evelyn were grateful.

'I feel like a kidnapper,' Evelyn said nervously. 'Are you sure she has no close family?'

'Well, Tessa's parents died some years ago. There was an aunt, but I can't even remember her name now. I have Tessa's address and keys so I'll go and check her house tomorrow, talk to her employer and neighbours, see what I can find out,' he said, rather wearily.

'You will come home tonight?' Evelyn asked, as she climbed behind the wheel, for Matt divided his time between his flat in London and the family estate in Hampshire. 'I'm not explaining this to your father!' she added feelingly.

'I'll be there,' Matt assured her.

'Good. Oh – Matt?' she called, as he turned to begin walking back into the hospital. He swung around and looked at her enquiringly. 'I don't think we should tell your father there's any doubt about Abby's paternity,' she said meaningfully. A slight smile flitted across Matt's features.

'I agree. Thanks, Ma, I appreciate your help.' He stood back and watched her leave before squaring his shoulders and striding back inside.

George still hadn't returned when Evelyn arrived home, and, feeling like a smuggler, she whisked Abby upstairs. The Staffords' housekeeper, Molly Bailey, had been with the family since Matt was Abby's age and she accepted the child without reservation, helping Evelyn get the tearful tot fed, bathed and into bed before George could even know of her presence in the house.

'There's a casserole in the oven for dinner,' Molly told Evelyn. 'I'll stay with Abby for a while,' she offered, both from a desire to look after Matt's daughter and to be out of George Stafford's way when he heard the news.

'Thank you,' Evelyn said drily, well aware of the dual reason behind the suggestion.

She hurried away to her own suite, needing to look her best to boost her courage before facing her husband. Nearing sixty, Evelyn Stafford looked younger than her years, admittedly with the help of cosmetics, an excellent hair-stylist and a strict exercise and diet regime. Her hair, now artificially blonde, was swept back from her face in two smooth wings, her bone structure and skin were both good, her eyes still the bright sapphire blue of her youth.

She showered quickly and dressed, as always, simply and elegantly, choosing a blue dress – one of George's favourites – to match her eyes and added a pearl necklace and ear-rings. As an afterthought, she exchanged her comfortable shoes for high heels – the added height, making her almost as tall as her husband, would give her more confidence. She hoped. George Stafford was a formidable opponent, always forthright in his views – bloody rude, Matt called it – and the onset of arthritis in recent years had made him exceedingly short-tempered and implacable – if he decided against Abby, there would be little she could do to sway him.

Evelyn returned downstairs to wait for him in the drawing-room and sipped at an exceedingly large – and very necessary – gin and tonic as she pondered the best way of dealing with her husband. An ex-military man and former magistrate, George tended to treat everyone as though they were subordinates or criminals, or both, but he was basically a decent and kindly man. He would probably feel Abby should have been handed over to Social Services, of course, and might insist they take that course of action in the morning, but . . . there's always a 'but', Evelyn thought hopefully. But . . . George dearly wanted Matt to come and live permanently at Drake's Abbot and take over running the estate full time. And Matt had often said he would only do that if he had a wife and family; that, as a bachelor, he preferred London . . .

She jumped as she heard George's voice outside in the hall and took a huge gulp of her gin before hurrying to greet him with the whiskey and soda she had already poured for him. Tall and lean, his hair grey now, he was still a distinguished-looking man in his late sixties and they made a handsome couple.

'Thank you.' George took the drink she offered and kissed her cheek. He eased himself into his favourite leather-upholstered high-backed chair and asked, 'Had a good day?'

'Interesting,' Evelyn said, finishing off her gin and thinking longingly of another. 'We have a house guest for a few days,' she went on brightly, as if she had nothing unusual or disturbing to impart. 'A lovely little girl; her name's Abby Grant and her mother

17

was involved in a road accident today,' she went on quickly, 'I told Matt I'd look after her until he can contact her family.'

'Matt?' George frowned. 'What the devil has Matt got to do with it?'

'Well, I don't really know any details,' she said vaguely. 'He'll be here soon to explain.' I hope, she thought, casting a despairing glance in the direction of the driveway. She took a deep breath. 'The thing is, George, well, apparently the child is Matt's daughter . . .' His brows shot up at that and she rushed on, 'Wait until you meet her, darling, she's just beautiful and so sweet. And dreadfully upset about her mother, naturally. I had to say we . . . I would help,' she amended hastily. 'I'll keep her out of your way; I'm sure she'll be no trouble . . . George?' she crossed her fingers, waiting for the explosion. He sighed as he regarded her eager, anxious face.

'I know how much you've wanted a grandchild,' he said finally – and quietly, much to Evelyn's relief. 'But the mother hasn't wanted us to be involved so far, has she? She can stay here, but don't let yourself get too fond of her,' he warned gruffly.

'You make her sound like a stray puppy!'

'Quite,' he muttered, then, 'How old is she?'

'Five,' Evelyn told him, and he nodded.

'Grant, you said? Did we ever meet the mother?' He frowned.

'Er, no, I don't think so,' Evelyn admitted.

'Hmm!' He said nothing further, but the glint in his eyes and the tone of his voice were hard as he confronted a weary-looking Matt when he duly arrived.

'I think you owe your mother and me one hell of an explanation!' he barked.

'Later,' Matt replied briefly and just as brusquely, shrugging off his jacket and heading for the tray of drinks. He was in need of a stiff Scotch. 'How has she settled down?' he asked his mother.

'Fine. There were a few tears, which is only to be expected, of course, but she was exhausted and soon fell asleep. Molly is sitting with her in case she wakes and I've arranged for Christine Cooper to come and live in for as long as necessary. I've put Abby in the turret room – there are two beds in there and Christine has no objections to sleeping in the same room.' Matt nodded his satisfaction: Christine lived locally and often helped out in the house when they had guests: she was a cheerful, sensible girl and well used to caring for small children as she had several younger siblings.

'What's the news on Tessa?' Evelyn asked next, watching in concern as Matt slumped in a chair, his face etched with lines of tension and weariness.

'Nothing,' he replied bleakly. 'We just have to wait.'

'Let's go and eat,' Evelyn suggested. 'And you can tell us all about Tessa,' she added. Matt nodded, finished the rest of his drink and stood up.

As Molly was still upstairs with Abby, Evelyn served the casserole herself, and they sat down to eat in the cosier breakfast-room instead of the large dining-room. At first Matt merely picked uninterestedly at the food on his plate, but his body needed the sustenance and he began to eat automatically as he talked, forking up pieces of chicken and vegetables as he recounted when and where he had met Tessa Grant. His parents listened avidly, saying little.

'I was in Cyprus on holiday, six years ago,' he began. 'Tessa was staying with her aunt – her parents had

19

recently died and she had gone over there for a break before returning to teacher-training college in the autumn.' He paused and Evelyn noticed a distinct softening of his features as he recalled his first encounter with the girl who was to conceive his child. 'She was only nineteen then, and very sweet . . .' A slight smile curved his mouth. 'We met by chance – her hire car had broken down in a rather remote spot. Actually,' he grinned again, 'she had only run out of petrol and I had a spare can in the boot, so I could easily have sent her on her way in two minutes flat. But I didn't tell her that was the problem and tinkered with the engine for several hours. Finally I said I couldn't fix it and offered to drive her back to where she was staying –' He stopped speaking, his thoughts too private and personal to share. 'That was how it started,' he added, more matter of factly.

'And now we know how it ended! With a child!' George barked at him. 'Bloody irresponsible!'

'I know,' Matt agreed quietly. 'We only had a few days together – it was just before I went to Bosnia. All leave was cancelled unexpectedly and I had to return to barracks sooner than I'd expected. As soon as that tour was over, I tried to find her, but I couldn't. As I said, her parents had recently died and the family home had been sold. Tessa promised to write and let me know her new address, but she didn't,' he said bleakly. 'I received two letters from her posted from Cyprus, but then nothing.' He shrugged slightly. Evelyn stared at him, remembering several urgent phone calls from him around that time, demanding to know if there were any letters, had been any phone calls . . . Matt took a deep breath, then continued quietly. 'Finally, I let it go. She was only nineteen, I figured she'd had second thoughts, had decided she was too young for a steady relationship or had maybe found a boyfriend of her own age at college. It never occurred to me that she might be pregnant.' He sighed, looked down at the food on his plate as if seeing it for the first time, then pushed it away. 'I never saw her again, until today – and then she ran away, right under the wheels of a bus!' He grimaced.

'What does she look like?' Evelyn finally broke the silence. Much to her amazement, he reached for his wallet and, by way of reply, took out a rather dog-eared snapshot and passed it to her.

'You've kept this for six years?' she asked slowly, glancing across at her husband, hoping this would alter his opinion of events somewhat – obviously the relationship had been rather more than a brief holiday fling. Actually, George was wondering cynically just how many more photographs of ex-girlfriends Matt kept in his wallet – useful things, old snapshots; the ability to produce one always banished any grievances a discarded girlfriend might be harbouring.

'It wasn't just a holiday romance,' Matt echoed his mother's thoughts. 'That was just the beginning; we both felt that. At least, I thought we both did. I can't imagine why Tessa didn't contact me when she knew she was pregnant.'

'Pride, I expect, or fear of rejection,' Evelyn said, still studying the petite bikini-clad girl in the photograph. A cloud of black hair framed a very pretty face which was dominated by the large brown eyes that she had bequeated to her daughter. 'She's lovely,' she commented, before handing the snapshot to her husband, who looked at it briefly and without comment before returning it to Matt.

'What –' George began, then broke off, frowning, when Matt's mobile phone rang.

'Sorry, I gave the hospital my mobile number,' Matt said apologetically, knowing how his father loathed mobile phones, particularly when they disturbed his meals. He quickly unclipped it from his belt. 'Yes? Oh, Belinda.' His voice went flat, and his heartbeat returned to its normal pace. 'Did we have a date for this evening? I'm really sorry, but I forgot all about it,' he said, getting up from the table to speak in private.

George and Evelyn exchanged glances of amusement, neither at all sorry he had upset the lovely Belinda Croxley. Now that Matt was in his mid-thirties, they tended to view each new girlfriend as a potential daughter-in-law and Belinda had made it patently clear that she never wanted to live in the country, nor did she want children. However, if the enraged squawking they could hear from the other end of the phone was anything to judge by, Miss Croxley could be safely crossed off the list!

'I can't talk now; I'm expecting an important phone call; I'll explain later,' Matt snapped and abruptly disconnected.

'What do you intend doing about the child now?' George asked, ignoring the interruption.

'Take responsibility for her, of course,' Matt retorted.

'You're a stranger to her, Matt,' Evelyn pointed out gently. 'If this aunt of Tessa's is still on the scene, Abby would probably be happier staying with her while her mother's in hospital.'

'I realize that. I'm going to Tessa's house tomorrow, see if I can find an address book, or talk to the neighbours . . . Excuse me, I want to go and check on Abby and then I'm going to turn in.'

He entered the turret room quietly: Christine was already there, reading by the light of a table lamp. Matt nodded to her and went to stand by the side of the bed where Abby was lying, so small and defenceless, but thankfully fast asleep. The distress she was suffering hurt him deeply, and he knew there was more in store for her when she awoke, unless a miracle occurred overnight and Tessa recovered consciousness.

He hated the feelings of uselessness that swept over him; there was so little he could do to alleviate her pain. His daughter's pain. Unexpectedly, a great surge of anger against Tessa overwhelmed him; anger and a deep sadness that he had missed so much of Abby's life; might never have known her at all if not for the quirk of fate that had caused him to pause and glance inside the coffee-shop.

'If she wakes during the night, come and fetch me,' he said quietly to Christine. He stretched out a hand to touch Abby's cheek, then pulled back, fearful of disturbing her. She looked peaceful, obviously happier in Dreamland than in the real world which had so suddenly and horrifyingly disintegrated around her. Why did you shut me out, Tessa? he wondered, with a mixture of pain and fury as he turned and made his way to his own separate suite of rooms.

CHAPTER 2

Why did you shut me out, Tessa? It was a question that remained, unanswered, uppermost in his mind, never more so than when he surveyed the small flat she and Abby called home. The locality was certainly not one of the best; in fact, he was reluctant to leave his Mercedes parked outside unattended. Only his need for information urged him indoors, that and a slight brightening of Abby's expression at the sight of familiar surroundings. She had been upset and disorientated upon awakening and inconsolable when he'd had to tell her that her mother was still 'asleep'.

'We live upstairs,' she told him, once he had unlocked the front door of the red-brick terraced house with the one of the keys he had taken from Tessa's handbag, and she scampered ahead of him, waiting impatiently for him to unlock the second door at the top of the stairs.

Matt followed her inside and looked around – the whole flat would fit in just one of the dozens of mostly unused rooms at Drake's Abbot. It comprised a combined sitting-room with a dining area and tiny kitchenette, two small bedrooms and a bathroom. His lips tightened as he noted the shabbiness and poor quality furnishings, but his smile returned when Abby reappeared in her bedroom doorway, clutching a stuffed monkey in her arms. From the look on her face it was a much-loved toy.

'Would you like to take that home?' he asked unthinkingly, and her face clouded.

'I live here,' she told him, enunciating clearly and slowly, as if he were dim-witted, Matt thought, with an inner grin.

'I know, but you're staying with us at Drake's Abbot while your mother's in hospital. In fact,' he went on, 'I think it would be nice if you lived at Drake's Abbot all the time. What do you think?' he asked casually. Abby considered that carefully for a moment.

'Mummy too?'

'Of course,' Matt confirmed.

'You'll have to ask her.' She frowned again. 'But who would bring me to school? It's a long way and Mummy doesn't have a car,' she said.

'Well, you'd have to go to a different school, a much nicer school,' Matt told her, then realized he would have to contact her headmistress, or questions would be asked. He also made a mental note to speak to Tessa's employer. There had been a heart-stopping message earlier – the police wanted to speak to him, presumably only about the accident but he was taking no chances and intended knowing every detail of Tessa's life before submitting himself and his actions to police scrutiny.

He moved inside Tessa's bedroom and glanced around: it was obvious Tessa's spare cash was lavished on her daughter. Abby's room was bright and pretty, with matching bed linen and curtains, a collection of toys and books. The small wardrobe and chest of drawers contained more clothing than he had expected, certainly more than he discovered hanging in Tessa's wardrobe.

'Collect up whatever you'd like to take back with you,' he told Abby. 'I need to look through Mummy's papers – do you know where she keeps them? Letters, bank statements, things like that,' he added. After a long moment, during which Matt wasn't sure if she didn't know, or was wondering whether to trust him, Abby nodded and pulled out a small case from the bottom of Tessa's wardrobe.

'Thanks, sweetheart.' Matt sat down on Tessa's bed – too small to share with a man, he found himself thinking with some satisfaction, then he shook his head slightly to clear his thoughts and began rifling the contents of the case.

He quickly discovered that her employer and landlord were one and the same – a local estate agent. The bank statements – he rarely bothered looking at his own – had scribbled sums on them, showing how Tessa painstakingly worked out her available cash after bills had been paid each month. Again, Matt felt a surge of mingled pain and anger as he realized how much she struggled, mostly down to her last few pence before her salary was credited to her account.

He could, and willingly would, have doubled, trebled her income without even noticing the loss. Why had she not trusted him? Was this lone, penny-pinching near-poverty really preferable to having him in her life? Obviously the answer to that was 'yes', he thought bitterly. Well, no longer. And, if Tessa proved stubborn, he decided he would go to court, prove the paternity of which he was becoming more sure with every minute spent in Abby's company, and demand his parental right to provide for and spend time with his child.

A few moments later, he made a discovery that convinced him he was indeed Abby's father. Her birth certificate – father unknown, he noticed with a tightening of his lips – with its date of birth confirmed she had been born exactly nine months after he and Tessa had been lovers. But even more conclusively, he felt, was the photograph inserted inside the folded certificate: a photograph of him and Tessa, one they had asked another tourist to take.

He studied it for a while, letting memories of a happier time sweep over him, then he put it aside and continued searching, for what he was not sure – a will, perhaps, naming a guardian in the event of Tessa's death or incapacity. He found nothing; he had remembered the name of Tessa's aunt, but Abby merely gazed at him uncomprehendingly when he questioned her, so he dropped the subject and decided to leave.

He had tried, not very hard admittedly, to locate someone else to take care of Abby, and failed; therefore, she would have to return to Drake's Abbot with him. He knew his mother was right in claiming the child needed to be with someone familiar at this time, but he was secretly relieved that there appeared to be no one.

He watched Abby carefully placing toys, books and clothes into a suitcase and wondered if knowing he was her father would reassure her while she was feeling so lost and alone without her mother, or if it would add to her confusion. He silently weighed up the pros and cons, then decided to tell her; at least she would know she belonged with him. He took a deep breath, then he asked casually.

'Abby? What has your mother told you about your father? Do you know his name?'

'No.' She shook her head. 'She said she'd tell me all about him when I was old enough to understand.'

'Don't you know anything about him?' Matt persisted gently.

'Yes. He was a soldier,' she said, and Matt caught his breath.

'And?' he prompted calmly.

'He was very brave and he died before I was born. He had to go and help some poor people who had no houses or food in . . . Boz . . .' She frowned.

'Bosnia?' Matt supplied.

'Yes,' she nodded.

'Abby, sweetheart . . .' he hesitated '. . . I've no idea why your mother thought I was dead,' knowing full well Tessa had thought no such thing. 'But I came back from Bosnia. I tried to find her, but she had moved away and no one knew where she was living.' He paused, looking at her intently for a reaction, but she just stared back at him solemnly, apparently neither pleased nor displeased. Or perhaps she didn't understand what he was trying to tell her. 'I didn't know you were going to be born, sweetheart; if I had, I'd have knocked on every door in England until I found you,' he told her earnestly. 'I'm so sorry I haven't been here to look after you until now, but I didn't know I had a daughter. I didn't know,' he repeated, rather helplessly. Still she stared at him silently and he saw, with a sinking heart, her thumb move slowly upwards and into her mouth. Oh, God, that was a bad sign, wasn't it? He should have left this until later, until she knew him better.

'Do you understand what I've been telling you?' he asked desperately. 'I'm your father, Abby. If I had known about you, I'd have loved you and looked after you from the day you were born. And your mother, too,' he added belatedly, although he wasn't exactly feeling loving and compassionate towards Tessa right now, coma notwithstanding.

He stretched out his arms tentatively, wanting to hug her, but dropped them when she made no move to come into his embrace. But she hadn't backed away, either, he consoled himself. He only hoped he hadn't added to the turmoil she was already suffering.

'Did Mummy think you were a ghost?' she asked suddenly, and Matt blinked.

'A ghost?' he said uncertainly.

'Yes. She didn't want to talk to you yesterday and she ran away – did she think you were a ghost? Was she frightened?'

'Oh, I see! Yes, I expect that was it,' Matt agreed, relieved. 'She never used to be frightened of me. She loved me, once,' he said quietly.

'You're my daddy?' she asked next, but rather doubtfully, he felt.

'Yes, I am,' he said firmly. 'And I'm going to look after you from now on – and your mummy,' he added hastily.

'I 'spect Mummy will be pleased you're not a ghost,' she commented, then returned to the subject uppermost in her mind. 'Will she wake up soon?'

'I hope so,' Matt said encouragingly.

* * *

29

He felt he was letting Abby down during the days that followed when there was no improvement in Tessa's condition: it hurt that he was helpless to do the one thing his daughter wanted of him – make her mother better.

However, he was busy making plans and decided to present Tessa with a fait accompli when she did recover consciousness. He told her employer she would not be returning to work, or to her flat, which he had stripped of all personal items and shipped to Drake's Abbot.

He also talked to Abby's headmistress, explained glibly that she was staying with her grandmother during Tessa's hospitalization and would be enrolled at another school nearby.

His interview with the police went better than he had feared; they were more concerned with the actual accident and accepted his explanation that he and Tessa had been having a slight disagreement and she had rushed off, too upset to register the danger posed by the approaching bus. He emphasized that the driver was in no way to blame for what had happened to his fiancée.

Fiancée; that was the magical word that made him, and his explanations, acceptable wherever he went – only one of Tessa's workmates had expressed surprise, but she lost her misgivings when she saw how comfortable Abby was with Matt. The more he uttered the lie, the more he became convinced that marriage to Tessa was the best course of action he could take to ensure Abby remained permanently in his care.

Apart from her natural bouts of distress over her mother, she had settled happily at Drake's Abbot. She still called him 'Matt', but readily addressed Evelyn as 'Grandma'. George Stafford she was a little wary of, having overheard him bellowing at one of the staff, but summoned up the courage to approach him one morning when she saw him surreptitiously slipping pieces of sausage to the dog lying under the table. Abby, never having had a pet, already loved the dog, an Irish Wolfhound called Flynn. She bent to pat his huge head, then peeped up at George.

'Are you my grandpa?' she asked shyly.

'So they tell me,' he grunted, then put aside his newspaper and surveyed her thoughtfully. She certainly was a pretty little thing. 'Have you had your breakfast?'

'Yes, thank you,' she said politely. Hmm, nice manners, he approved.

'I hear Matt's buying you a pony – ever ridden before?'

'Yes,' she said proudly, having twice ridden a donkey on daytrips to the seaside.

'Would you like to come and see my horses?'

'Yes, please.' She smiled, revealing the dimples, and her large brown eyes lit up with pleasure. George, after having repeatedly wasted his breath telling his wife not to become too fond of her, was smitten.

'Come along then.' He hauled himself to his feet and held out one gnarled hand towards her. Abby reached up and, hand in hand, they began walking towards the rear of the house, towards the stable block.

'Good Heavens,' Evelyn said faintly, when she spotted the ill-matched duo. George had practically ignored Abby's presence until now, insisting Tessa would probably take her away again when she recovered. 'George! It's chilly outside this morning; she'll need a coat,' she called after him.

'I know that. I'm not stupid, woman,' George growled at her, and Abby giggled, then clapped her hand to her mouth, not sure if Evelyn were angry or not. She looked from one to the other, then held out her spare hand towards her grandmother. 'You come too, Grandma?' she asked.

'Of course I will, sweetie,' Evelyn agreed at once, despite having just donned an extremely expensive suede suit for a shopping trip. Matt, returning to change after an early morning ride, watched Abby chatting happily to both grandparents as she walked in the middle, one hand to each, and resolved to do everything in his power to keep his daughter.

More than a week had passed before he received the phone call he had almost despaired of. It was two a.m. but still he went straight to Abby's room, feeling that she deserved to know. She stirred a little when he switched on the bedside lamp.

'Abby,' he said quietly. She sighed, then opened her eyes and regarded him sleepily. 'The doctor has just phoned – your mummy's going to be all right now. She woke up a little while ago. You'll be able to talk to her tomorrow, tell her everything you've been doing.'

'Go now?' she asked eagerly, sitting up as if about to clamber out of bed. Matt cursed himself for not anticipating her reaction. 'Tomorrow' was a dirty word to a five-year-old, especially when they wanted something as badly as she wanted to be with Tessa.

'No, it's the middle of the night,' he said, gently but firmly. 'You have to go back to sleep until morning.'

And have some pleasant dreams for a change, he thought, instead of the nightmares from which she had awakened in tears several times. She pouted a little, but obediently lay down again, albeit reluctantly. Matt bent and retrieved the stuffed monkey which had fallen to the floor.

'Here.' He tucked it in beside her. She clutched it to her then reached up and twined her tiny arms around his neck.

'Thank you, Daddy,' she said drowsily, using the word for the very first time. Matt almost cried.

'Goodnight, sweetheart. Sweet dreams,' he said huskily.

Tessa's first period of consciousness was brief, and she was barely aware of her surroundings before slipping quickly back into the dreamworld of holidaying in Cyprus. She had been so happy and excited after meeting Matt Stafford, falling in love for the very first time. She had gone to the island after her parents' death, a young girl feeling lost and alone, but she had returned to England a woman, still grieving for her loss, of course, but eagerly anticipating the adult life that awaited her.

Several hours passed before she finally opened her eyes fully and realized her body felt weak, yet leaden. She tried to move her arm, but couldn't and, glancing down, saw the drip-feed that had been attached. At the same instant she became aware of the bleeping noises from the bedside monitors and of more tubes, all over her body, and she panicked, trying in vain to rise. The sudden movement brought a white-clad nurse hurrying to her.

'Lie still,' she instructed, placing gentle but firm hands on Tessa's shoulders. Then she smiled and unobtrusively pressed a buzzer to summon a doctor. 'Hello, Tessa. I'm Nurse Fellowes. How do you feel?'

'I'm not sure . . . my head hurts . . . I'm in hospital?' she asked, somewhat foolishly, she realized at once.

'Yes. You were involved in a road accident – don't you remember?'

'No.' Tessa shook her head, feeling as if she were mentally groping her way through thick, impenetrable fog.

'What is the last thing you do remember?' Nurse Fellowes asked her.

'Cyprus. He had to leave . . . no, that was just a dream; it all happened long ago, before . . . oh, my God! Abby! My daughter!' The memory rushed back and again Tessa tried to rise. 'She ran out into the road. It was my fault. Is she all right? Where is she?' she demanded.

'She's fine; she wasn't hurt. She's being looked after by her father,' the nurse said soothingly, but the information agitated Tessa even more.

'Her father!' she repeated, in tones of horror.

'Of course – who else?' Nurse Fellowes asked, puzzled.

'I don't want her to be with him. She's my daughter, just mine!' Tessa insisted fiercely, and Nurse Fellowes guessed there had probably been some differences regarding visitation rights.

'Well, you can't look after her while you're ill, can you?' she pointed out reasonably, then turned in relief at the approach of a portly middle-aged man. 'Dr Stevens . . .' A low-voiced conversation ensued,

34

which Tessa was too upset to attempt to eavesdrop. Abby with Matt! What was he playing at? He couldn't possibly have known Abby was his child, she reasoned, since she could clearly remember telling him she was only four years old. She winced, wishing the pain in her head would subside enough to allow her to think clearly.

'Can I see my daughter?' she interruped the medical discussion going on at the foot of the bed, and Dr Stevens turned to her with a kindly smile.

'Very soon,' he promised her, and she tried to be content with that. Besides, she felt too weak to remonstrate with them and submitted to a thorough examination, then lay quietly while the various tubes were removed. She at least felt more like a human being and less like a piece of meat when she had been washed and helped into a nightdress. She didn't notice that the garment was not one of her own, but new and expensive, a gift from Evelyn Stafford. The sight of her own body appalled her, however, for a mass of ugly yellow bruises covered her left side.

'Yuk!' she grimaced. 'Now I know why I ache all over!'

'What do you expect, if you will pick a fight with a double-decker bus?' Dr Stevens asked cheerfully. 'You'll be good as new soon. There are no broken bones – you're not as fragile as you look, young lady. You had a nasty crack on the skull, though. How does your head feel now?'

'Awful,' Tessa admitted, and he nodded.

'Yes, that's to be expected, I'm afraid. But it will gradually ease off.'

'How long have I been here?' Tessa asked, suddenly realizing from the colour of the bruising that it wasn't recent.

'Nine days,' he told her, and she gasped.

'Nine days! Oh, poor Abby, she must have been frantic. We've never been apart before, not for a single night,' she said in anguish, more concerned about Abby than herself.

'Stop worrying about the child,' Dr Stevens admonished sternly. 'Lie still and rest, or that headache will worsen,' he warned, and she subsided back against the pillows. 'I'll be in to see you again later, when you've settled into your room,' he added, patting her lightly on the back of her hand before leaving.

'Am I being moved?' Tessa asked the nurse.

'Yes, this is the Intensive Care Unit – we need that bed for patients who are really ill!' she said brightly. Tessa tried to smile, but she wished they would stop speaking to her as if she were Abby's age. However, she cheered herself with the thought that she must be in better physical shape than she felt if they were transferring her to another ward.

Before long, two orderlies arrived and she was wheeled along the corridor and into an enormous lift, which carried her to an upper floor. There, a pretty blonde nurse, who introduced herself as Marianne Harper, helped her into bed. Tessa leaned back against the pillows, exhausted and giddy from even that minimal exertion. Slowly, she took stock of her new surroundings, noting the TV set, the phone beside the bed, the adjoining bathroom . . .

'Is this a private room?' she asked incredulously.

'Yes, Mr Stafford arranged it,' she was told.

'Huh! Mr Fix-it,' Tessa muttered ungratefully. She settled back to wait, with as much patience as she could muster, for Matt to put in an appearance with Abby – how dare he tell everyone he was Abby's father and take control!'

She fervently wished she had not dreamed so vividly of that time in Cyprus, reliving the passion and bright hopes for the future. She had suppressed those memories successfully for six years and now it was as if it had all happened yesterday. In fact, she could recall, more clearly than she could the scene in the coffee-shop, how desolate she had felt when his leave had been unexpectedly cancelled and he'd had to cut short his holiday.

They had known she would be back in England long before his tour of duty in Bosnia was completed and she had promised to write to him with her new address. Clutching a piece of paper containing both his home address and that of his barracks, she had waved good-bye at the airport, watching, through a haze of tears, as he climbed aboard the plane.

However, before she enrolled at college, she was sure that the one passion-filled night with Matt Stafford had resulted in a pregnancy and a visit to her doctor had confirmed her fears . . .

Tessa stirred restlessly against the pillows as she recalled those dreadful months. She had sat for hours in the small bed-sitter which was her temporary home, trying frantically to work out what she should do, missing her parents desperately and alternately craving and then despising Matt Stafford.

Eventually, she had decided she had no right to burden Matt with herself and a baby. Each time she considered telling him, she would have a mental picture of the look of horror and dismay with which he would greet her news. Worse, he might even question her assertion that he was the father. The very prospect made her flesh crawl, yet she had only known him for a few days before succumbing to his sexual advances: they had had no relationship as such and she supposed he couldn't be blamed if he doubted his paternity.

No, she simply couldn't bear the possibility, probability, of his rejection or disbelief, and resolved to cope alone. She would pretend to herself, and to the baby when it was old enough to ask questions, that Matt had died while helping refugees in a war-zone. That was the best and cleanest way for all concerned.

Determinedly, she ripped into tiny pieces the slip of paper containing his address – a somewhat futile gesture since the words were indelibly printed on her mind, but, as she burned the scrap of paper, it was as if she purged herself of all memories of those fun-filled, happy days and that one, wonderfully sensual night in his arms.

It wasn't as easy as that, of course. There had been countless times when, lonely and afraid, she had craved his comforting presence, needed his strength. But, as their baby grew inside her, she began to feel resentful, both of the child and its father. Matt had surely returned to England by now – why hadn't he traced her whereabouts, she thought, somewhat unreasonably since she had carefully covered her tracks.

Her Aunt Dora, with whom she had been staying in Cyprus, was appalled by her condition and, afraid of being burdened with Tessa and a child indefinitely, had decided she wanted nothing more to do with her. Her condemnation and assertion that Tessa's parents would be ashamed of her caused Tessa to shed many bitter tears. Dora's scornful attitude left its mark in another way, too – she so clearly felt Tessa had been used by Matt, stupidly falling for one of the oldest lines in the book: the I'm-off-to-war-and-might-not-be-back line of persuasion.

Once Abby was born, after a long and difficult labour, Tessa had loved the little girl the instant she held her in her arms, but the resentful feelings she harboured for the child's father only intensified as time passed.

The legacy from her parents was dwindling at an alarming rate and she knew she had to forget her plans to continue her teacher training and get a job, no easy task with a new baby. However, she had been lucky, spending two years happily employed as a live-in housekeeper and companion to an elderly lady who loved children and doted on Abby. With an eye to the future, Tessa learned secretarial and computer skills in her spare time and, when the old lady died, moved back to the London area and worked as a 'temp' in various offices.

However, her social life was practically zero: she had quickly discovered that, as an unmarried mother, she was considered easy prey by many of the men, mostly married, who employed her. By the time Matt Stafford walked back into her life, Tessa had learned from bitter experience to mistrust and dislike the entire male sex in general and Matt Stafford in particular.

Tessa looked up eagerly when the door opened, expecting to see Abby hurtling into the room.

Instead, her visitor was Matt – alone. Tessa was too angry and fearful to notice how careworn and haggard he looked, as if he'd had little or no sleep in recent nights.

'You . . . you kidnapper!' she blazed at him. 'Where is she? What have you done with my daughter?'

'She's outside.' Matt looked, and felt, taken aback. 'I came in first to make sure you were up to seeing her –'

'Of course I want to see her. Bring her in here. Now!' Tessa's voice rose and she winced involuntarily as an intense pain stabbed at her temple.

'All right, I will. Just calm down, will you?' Matt disappeared and returned almost immediately, carrying Abby in his arms.

'Mummy!' Abby strained to reach Tessa and Matt lowered her gently on to the bed. She flung her arms around her mother, almost strangling her. 'I've missed you.' Her voice was muffled against Tessa's neck, and she gathered her close, squeezing her eyes tightly shut so Abby shouldn't see and be upset by her tears.

'I'll come back later.' Tessa barely heard Matt's words, or registered his departure. She hugged and kissed Abby, revelling in the touch of the baby-soft skin against her own, the tiny arms clinging to her as if they would never let go.

'You've been poorly for ever such a long time!' Abby finally pulled back a little, staring almost accusingly at her mother.

'I know; I'm sorry,' Tessa said apologetically. 'Have you been all right?' she asked anxiously. 'What have you been doing?'

'I'm living with Daddy now,' Abby announced, and Tessa felt as if someone had dashed a bucketful of ice-cold water in her face. She licked suddenly dry lips and strove to keep calm. This was worse than she had expected. And how easily she called him 'Daddy'!

'No, you don't live with him, you've just been staying with him while I've been ill,' Tessa corected her, but Abby shook her head confidently.

'No, I've got my own room and Grandma says I can choose some new wallpaper,' she informed Tessa happily. 'It's a nice house, Mummy, ever so big, and I 'spect you can have new wallpaper, too,' she added encouragingly, as if sensing Tessa's lack of enthusiasm. 'And there's lots of horses and Daddy bought me a pony, just for me to ride, and there's a doggie . . .' She rattled on, telling a dumbstruck Tessa about trips to the seaside and amusement fairs, about the new school she was to attend and the new toys and clothes she had been given.

At length, Abby's voice faltered, her eyelids drooped and she snuggled contentedly against Tessa before quickly falling asleep. Tessa remained motionless, fear and anger warring in her for supremacy. What Matt and his family had been doing was monstrous! Obviously they were trying to buy Abby's affection, giving her all the things that she, Tessa, had been forced to deny her through lack of money. The Staffords, it would seem, had bottomless wallets!

Her grip on her daughter tightened unconsciously – had they also been trying to alienate her from her mother? Just as soon as I'm out of hospital, I'm taking Abby far away, she decided grimly. They would disappear from Matt's life as abruptly as they had entered it. And the law is on my side, she reminded herself, fighting down waves of panic that threatened to overwhelm her. However much money Matt has, he can't simply take Abby against my will; it's ridiculous to even think that he can, she told herself firmly.

However, fear was not so easily banished and she looked up warily when Matt re-entered the room; her heart beginning to thud painfully with dread. There was such a palpable strength about the man, not just the physical height and muscular frame, but the aura of self-confidence, almost of arrogance, as if he were a man accustomed to getting what he wanted.

She motioned to him to be quiet and he closed the door softly behind him before coming over to sit on the edge of the bed. Tessa glared at him, edgily noting the unmistakable tenderness in his gaze as he glanced down at the sleeping child, the gentleness with which he smoothed back a baby-soft curl from her cheek.

'I'm glad she's asleep,' he said quietly. 'We've managed to keep her occupied during the days, but she's been fretting for you at night.' His words did nothing to placate Tessa or eradicate her fears – what did he want her to do? Apologize for spoiling his game of Happy Families by being on Abby's mind?

'How dare you try and buy my child?' she hissed at him. 'She doesn't belong in your home. I've half a mind to call in the police and have you arrested for child abduction!'

'Well, that's all it would take – just half a mind,' Matt drawled sarcastically. He hadn't expected, or wanted, gratitude but he was damned if he was going to take all this hostility. 'If I hadn't stepped in she would have been handed over to Social Services and placed in a children's home with a dozen others.

42

Would you have preferred that to have happened?' he demanded.

'You had no right to take my child,' Tessa insisted, ignoring his reasoning and refusing to consider that he had acted altruistically.

'Our child,' Matt corrected and, in a flash, Tessa knew how to extricate herself from this nightmare.

'No.' She forced herself to meet his hard blue gaze unflinchingly. 'You are not her father.'

'I think I am,' Matt said, after a short, emotionally charged pause. He was shocked by the intensity of the disappointment and pain her words of denial had caused him. 'You lied to me about her age,' he reminded her – and himself – and felt a surge of renewed confidence. 'I found her birth certificate,' he said, with a note of triumph that was not lost on Tessa.

'So?' She feigned nonchalance. He had been to her flat? Poking around? She tried desperately to recall anything other than the birth certificate he might have discovered, but her brain felt as if it were wrapped in cotton wool. 'She was premature – you can see how small she is for her age,' she improvised wildly. 'I met her father weeks after you and I were together,' she said, and felt her cheeks suffuse with colour at the memory of how intimate she had been with this man who now posed such a threat to her happiness. 'It was someone at college, a guy my own age,' she was suddenly inspired to say, for Matt had made a great deal of the difference in their ages, fearing he was too old for her. So why was he now looking so smug?

'Oh? At college? In England?' Matt smiled slightly, but there was no amusement in his eyes. 'I found the photograph with the birth certificate,' he said softly.

'Photograph?' Tessa faltered.

'Yes. And you told Abby her father was a soldier who died in Bosnia. Sorry to disappoint you, Tessa, but I came home safe and well,' he said harshly.

'I . . . her father *was* a fellow student!' Tessa insisted desperately. 'He didn't want to know when I became pregnant. I lied to Abby. When she began asking why she didn't have a father like her friends, I told her something that wouldn't hurt her; something she could be proud of, not ashamed. I didn't want her thinking he had abandoned her,' she mumbled.

'I did *not* abandon her!' Matt gritted out. 'Stop playing games, Tessa! I'm certain I'm her father and it can easily be proved if you persist with this idiocy. In any event, surely it's irrelevant until you're able to take care of her yourself again? She has settled down with us very well – are you really so stubborn and selfish that you'll insist she be uprooted and go into foster care until you're better?' he demanded. Tessa hesitated, sorely tempted to do just that, but Abby's welfare won.

'I suppose she can continue to stay with you,' she conceded grudgingly. 'But you have no rights over her, Matt. None at all.'

'We'll discuss this again later; you're looking tired,' Matt said, and, before Tessa realized what he was doing, he stood and lifted Abby from her arms, waking her at once and thereby effectively silencing any further protests from Tessa. She could only blaze her hatred and resentment with her eyes, something to which he seemed totally impervious, when he should have been lying dead on the floor, she thought savagely.

'Time to go, sweetheart.' Matt kissed Abby's cheek. 'Mummy needs to rest now, but you can come again tomorrow,' he told her.

'Aren't you coming with us?' Abby's eyes filled with tears and she held her arms out towards Tessa.

'I can't, not today.' Tessa choked back her own tears. 'I have to stay here for a while. You go with . . . Matt.' She could not, would not, call him 'Daddy'.

'All right. I love you.' Abby reached to kiss her and Tessa hugged her fiercely.

'I love you, too. We'll soon be together again, just the two of us,' she said firmly.

'And Daddy,' Abby contradicted her. 'We're going to live with him.' Tessa met the gleam of mockery and triumph in Matt's eyes and bit back a retort. She wasn't strong enough to fight him, not yet anyway. For now, perhaps it was better if he thought he had the upper hand; if she allowed him to become complacent and over-confident, he would be off-guard when she disappeared with Abby.

'I'll see you tomorrow,' was her only reply to Abby and, after a final hug and a kiss, she had to watch Matt carry her from the room.

CHAPTER 3

Matt drove Abby back to Drake's Abbot with the intention of then returning to London to spend the evening with Belinda Croxley, his girlfriend and lover of several months. She had been remarkably patient with his new-found status and responsibility as a parent, for while Tessa had been so ill and Abby so distressed, he had spent most of his time at Drake's Abbot, feeling it would be grossly unfair to let his mother and the staff cope with the child's bouts of weeping.

However, he felt sure Abby would be content with her grandparents and Christine for company now she had been reunited with her mother and was confident of her recovery. He phoned Belinda and arranged to meet, and told his mother he would probably stay at his flat in London overnight. Evelyn accepted his announcement calmly and bit back the hope that this was to be a farewell dinner with Belinda.

'How is Tessa?' she asked instead. 'Did you speak to the doctor?'

'Yes, I did. They want to run a few more tests, but they're hopeful she'll be well enough to leave hospital in a few days.'

'And then what happens to her?'

'She'll come here – if that's all right with you?' he added belatedly, aware he was taking a lot for granted.

'Of course.' Evelyn inclined her head in acquiescence. 'She's the mother of my grandchild; naturally she'll come here to recuperate. But what then, Matt?'

'I'll provide a home for them both. The Dower House is empty: I can't see the old man having any objection to them living there. Structurally it's in good order; it needs re-decorating, but Tessa can choose her own colour schemes and furnishings,' he said carelessly.

'I see.' Evelyn hid her disappointment. 'And you'll visit Abby as and when you feel like it, I suppose?' she enquired, rather tartly. 'Has it occurred to you that Tessa might not actually want to live at the Dower House? She's a city girl – what will she do out here in the country, especially when Abby's at school?'

'Er, I've no idea,' Matt admitted.

'Quite,' his mother agreed drily. 'I suggest you get some ideas – fast,' she advised him. 'Even if Tessa agrees to stay here, you'll have no hold over her – or Abby,' she pointed out.

Matt frowned; Tessa had already said as much.

'Tessa can move on just as soon as she feels fit enough – or bored enough,' Evelyn continued. She had yet to meet Tessa, but would miss Abby dreadfully if she were taken away. Despite her husband's repeated warnings, she had indeed become too fond of the child for her own peace of mind. She had discussed the situation with her husband and they both agreed there was only one solution – marriage, even if it were six years too late. However, she was too shrewd and knew her son too well to actually suggest such an outcome.

She would have been delighted to know that Matt, albeit reluctantly, had already arrived at the same conclusion. And, as he drove back to London to meet Belinda, he decided, with some regret, that he would have to end the affair.

The feelings of regret intensified when Belinda opened the door of her flat clad in nothing but a skimpy towel and high-heeled shoes.

'Darling!' She wrapped her arms around his neck and purposely let the towel slide to the floor. Matt groaned and, for a moment, held her voluptuous body close against his own, burying his face in her long, golden hair. 'I thought we'd order food to be sent in,' she murmured. 'We have such a lot of catching up to do!' she added meaningfully.

'I think we'd better eat in a restaurant,' Matt said firmly. Belinda pouted her displeasure.

'Spoilsport. What's wrong, darling?' she asked, sauntering over to pour him a drink, perfectly at ease with her nudity. 'I thought what's-her-name was back in the land of the living?'

'She is,' Matt confirmed, ignoring the sarcasm. After the way he had messed her around recently, she was entitled to be feeling aggrieved. 'Thanks.' He took the glass she held out to him and took a large gulp of neat Scotch.

'So, what happened? Lovey-dovey reunion?' she asked edgily. Matt's lips twisted in a wry grimace.

'Hardly – she threatened to call the cops and have me arrested for kidnapping Abby,' he told her.

48

'Really? Has she always been insane or shall we be charitable and suppose the blow to the head has rendered her temporarily unbalanced?' Belinda enquired sweetly, neither sounding nor feeling particularly charitable towards Tessa Grant. Matt smiled slightly. He really would miss Belinda . . .

'She doesn't want to share Abby, that's for sure. She was very quick to remind me that I have no legal rights over how and where my daughter is brought up, no right even to see her if Tessa decides to keep her from me,' he said bitterly. 'It's going to be harder than I thought to win her over – Tessa is nothing like the girl I remember . . .' He frowned and shook his head slightly, lost in thought. His memories had always been of a sunny-natured, sweet and loving girl. The Tessa he had met in the coffee-shop, the woman and mother, no longer a girl, had looked the same – he had recognized her at once; she was still beautiful, but hard and cold. Perhaps he had carried a false memory, an idealized picture in his mind, for all these years, one that had made him see flaws in other women, never able to find one that matched what he had thought he had found in Tessa Grant. He drew a deep breath and looked at Belinda, trying, with difficulty, to ignore her lush, sexy beauty.

'I'm sorry, Bel, but I intend doing whatever it takes to keep my daughter. And, the way I see it, I can only have her if I marry Tessa,' he said flatly.

'Marry her?' Belinda repeated. She moved to refill her own glass, then, feeling suddenly vulnerable, fetched a robe from her bedroom and belted it tightly around her waist. Her full breasts pushed against the thin fabric, and it was somehow even more tantalizing

49

than her naked splendour. Matt stared resolutely down at the contents of his glass.

'You really intend marrying her?' Belinda asked again.

'Can you think of any other way I can keep Abby?' Matt asked harshly. 'I don't want to go through the courts, but, even if I do, what visitation rights can I hope to be granted after all these years? One weekend a month? That's not nearly enough; I've missed out on too much already, I don't intend losing any more time with her,' he said firmly. 'Besides, if I don't marry Tessa, there's nothing to stop her marrying someone else and moving far away. I just can't bear the thought of some other guy bringing up my daughter,' he finished, quietly but implacably. Belinda bit her lip.

'You've obviously made up your mind, so I won't try to talk you out of it. Or make a scene,' she added, much to his relief.

'Go and get dressed and then we'll go and paint the town red,' Matt suggested.

'Okay.' She stood up and dropped a kiss on his cheek before going to dress.

Despite her stated acceptance of his decision, she purposely left her bedroom door open and took her time over dressing, sitting on the edge of the bed while smoothing sheer black stockings slowly up her long slender legs. She didn't bother with a bra, and slipped into a short, figure-hugging black dress, leaving her blonde hair wantonly loose around her face and shoulders in a I've-just-got-out-of-someone's-bed look.

Matt watched her, torn between amusement and desire, and mused on the physical differences between her and Tessa; Belinda so tall, blonde and buxom, Tessa so petite, dark-haired and brown-eyed. Only now did he recognize that, since he had met and lost Tessa, he had avoided women who looked like her, as if he could save himself pain by so doing.

He became aware of his growing arousal, and, with an acute sense of shock, realized that it was caused by memories of the aching sweetness of initiating Tessa into the glories of love-making, and not by the sight of Belinda's teasing display of her body.

'Are you sure you want to go out, darling?' Belinda purred, noticing his obvious discomfort as soon as she re-entered the room.

'I'm sure.' Matt resisted the temptation, aware that he would be slaking his lust for another woman on her body if he accepted her unspoken invitation.

'Okay.' She shrugged, and dropped the subject of Tessa for the duration of the evening, but returned to it once more when he took her home in the early hours of the morning, and refused to stay with her for the rest of the night.

'Thanks, Bel; it's been fun, but this has to be goodbye,' he told her.

'It can still be fun,' she insisted. 'This arranged – no, deranged marriage of yours doesn't have to change anything between us.'

'Yes, it does.' Matt gently disentangled her arms from around his neck, stepped back and then turned and walked determinedly away.

Belinda watched him go, only closing the door when his car had disappeared from her sight. If it were any other man, she would be confident that he would be back once the novelty of having a child had palled. But then, no other man she knew would be prepared to marry an ex-, very temporary, girlfriend who had been stupid enough to get pregnant. Matt Stafford was too honourable for his own good, she thought disgustedly, and wished she had a cat to kick.

Tessa, meanwhile sedated, slept peacefully throughout the night and felt much better when she awoke. She managed to breakfast on orange juice, toast and coffee but, when she tried to climb out of bed, she quickly discovered just how weak she had become, and needed the help of a nurse to totter into the adjoining bath-room.

'I feel as if I'm recovering from a bout of flu coupled with a horrendous hangover,' she tried to joke, sitting on the loo cover while the nurse ran the bath for her.

A long soak – watched over as if she might pass out and drown! – did much to ease the aches and stiffness caused by both the bruises sustained in the accident and also by her enforced rest in bed. Her hair felt awful, her scalp dry and itchy, but the task of sham-pooing and drying it daunted her and she sat quiescent, feeling the same age as her daughter, while the nurse brushed it until it recovered some of its usual sheen. Even that small exertion had exhausted Tessa, and she readily agreed to be helped back into bed.

'This nightdress isn't one of mine.' She looked questioningly at the nurse as she realized the silk garment couldn't possibly be hospital issue.

'No. Your future mother-in-law sent it in for you,' she was told.

'My – what?' Tessa asked faintly.

52

'Mrs Stafford,' Nurse Harper said loudly and carefully, clearly puzzled. Tessa bit back further protest, afraid she would be thought insane if she persisted. She allowed herself to be settled back into bed, grateful for the comfort and support of the pillows. How tired she felt! And confused. Not at all equal to thwarting whatever plans Matt Stafford had made while she had lain, unconscious and unaware, for nine days.

She lay back and tried to relax but numerous questions were buzzing around her brain, intensifying her headache. She fingered the obviously expensive silk nightdress, her gaze resting on the matching negligee draped over the back of a chair. And the private room must be costing a small fortune . . .

And Matt had evidently lied to the hospital staff, leading them to believe they were engaged to be married. But why? A cold finger of fear feathered her spine as she considered his motive – he wanted Abby; he'd already made that clear. Did he, in his arrogance, believe he could bribe her into granting him custody? If so, he would quickly learn that some things just couldn't be bought, she thought angrily. However, fear wasn't so easily banished, and she began to make plans for her and Abby to disappear from his life just as soon as she had recovered her strength.

She waited impatiently for the object of her anger and fear to appear, but her first visitor was Dr Stevens, who examined her thoroughly and finally pronounced himself pleased with her progress.

'How soon can I leave here?' Tessa asked anxiously.

'In a couple of days,' he told her, to her relief. 'You'll need plenty of rest, though, but I gather that won't be a problem. Mr Stafford assures me he has adequate staff to take care of you.' he smiled at her.

'Mr Stafford!' Tessa almost spat. 'I won't be staying with him,' she declared adamantly.

'Oh?' Dr Stevens frowned. 'You have other family you can go to?'

'No, but I'll be fine by myself,' Tessa assured him, but he pursed his lips and shook his head.

'Oh, no, I'm sorry, but I'm afraid I can't agree to that,' he said firmly. 'You won't be fit enough to cope alone, especially with a young child, for quite some time.'

'Oh.' Tessa digested that for a moment: she was determined to be reunited with Abby as soon as possible, to negate the influence Matt and his family were exerting over her, so, if that meant accepting Stafford hospitality for herself too, well, so be it.

'Very well,' she agreed reluctantly. 'I'll go to . . .' she hesitated.

'Drake's Abbot,' Dr Stevens supplied, frowning again, this time at her apparent memory loss.

'Yes, that's right; Drake's Abbot,' Tessa repeated slowly, recalling the address Matt had written down for her so long ago.

'You get on well with the Staffords?' Dr Stevens asked, but obviously only out of politeness. Tessa wondered briefly what his reaction would be if she told him she had never met them, nor had her daughter until Matt had abducted her. She resisted the sudden impulse to blurt out the truth, afraid he would think her insane or suffering from amnesia. No doubt Matt, if challenged, would assure the staff that they had been engaged for some time. And no prizes for guessing who would be believed.

'I'm sure I'll be fine,' she said instead.

'Good. That's settled, then,' he said, obviously relieved, patted her hand and took his leave. Tessa looked rather despairingly at his retreating back. But the most important thing now was to get out of hospital, back with Abby, and she would only be able to do that if Dr Stevens believed she would be looked after by Matt and his blasted family.

She was drinking a mid-morning cup of coffee and nibbling on some biscuits when Matt finally deigned to put in an appearance – alone.

'Where's Abby?' Tessa wasted no time in greeting him and Matt's lips tightened at her rudeness and hostility. Briefly his thoughts flashed back to Belinda; her sexy, blonde beauty and ever-eager welcome . . . He sighed.

'Where *is* she?' Tessa repeated loudly. Matt raised one eyebrow in silent rebuke for her tone, sauntered over to the bed, hooked a chair round with his foot and sat down to face her.

'You look much better today,' he commented. 'I'm sorry to see your temper hasn't improved though. Or your manners. How's the headache? And what did Stevens have to say?'

'Oh, never mind all that! I asked you where my daughter is!' Tessa ground out.

'She's with my mother, choosing some flowers for you,' Matt finally condescended to enlighten her. 'I wanted a word with you alone first. What's the matter, Tessa? Don't you like being deprived of her company?' he snarled, his anger and bitterness surfacing even though he had cautioned himself to

55

save the reproaches until much later, when Tessa was better. 'She'll be here in five minutes – thanks to your selfishness, I've been deprived of more than five years of her life!'

'How could you be deprived of someone you never knew existed?' Tessa retorted, rather unwisely, she realized at once, and she shrank back from the blazing fury in his blue eyes. She felt particularly vulnerable, in bed, and wearing only a somewhat transparent nightdress. Not that she feared a sexual assault – Matt looked as if he had strangulation in mind rather than seduction. He glared at her for a moment longer, then made a visible effort to calm down.

'What did Dr Stevens say?' he asked again, speaking more quietly.

'I can probably leave here in a couple of days, but he won't let me go home alone,' she admitted unwillingly. 'I had to agree to convalesce at your wretched house.'

'How gracious of you to accept my invitation,' Matt drawled sarcastically, and she only just refrained from throwing the contents of her coffee cup in his face. He seemed to guess her temptation and removed the cup from her hand, placing it out of reach before continuing. 'Actually, you'll be staying at my parents' house. I have a flat in town, although I do keep a suite of rooms –'

'I'm really not interested in your domestic arrangements,' Tessa interrupted bitingly. 'I'll only be there for a week or so, then Abby and I will return home,' she finished defiantly.

'Oh? And where might that be? Not that poky little flat, I hope?' Matt asked casually, sitting back with his arms folded across the breadth of his chest and looking altogether too . . . complacent, Tessa thought, with a fearful lurch to her heart.

'It's adequate,' she said defensively. 'And only temporary. I shall soon be able to afford something better – now that Abby's at school full-time, I'll be able to work longer hours –'

'You no longer have a job,' Matt informed her coolly. 'Nor a flat, actually,' he added. 'I took the liberty of terminating both contracts on your behalf.'

'You did – what?' Tessa hissed at him, too furious at that moment to wonder where she was going to live or how she would pay her bills. Took the liberty indeed! Damn right he had!

'You heard me,' Matt said coolly. 'I went to the estate agent and told your boss you wouldn't be returning, either to work or to your flat. Your personal belongings were packed up and delivered to Drake's Abbot last week.'

'You . . .' Tessa could only gape at him, the wind taken completely out of her sails.

'Speechless? Good. Now you just listen to me.' Matt leaned forward, aggression and determination apparent in every line of his powerful body. The very expression on his face made Tessa feel even weaker and more vulnerable than she had previously, and she had to make a conscious effort not to cower away from him and thus betray her fear. 'Abby has settled happily at Drake's Abbot and I intend to see that she stays there,' Matt ground out. 'I'm prepared to turn my life upside down to accommodate the two of you, to provide a home and security. I've decided we should be married as soon as possible,' he finished. Tessa stared at him, and bit back hysterical laughter.

57

'You must be mad,' she said finally. 'I guessed you'd told the hospital staff we were to be married, but I assumed that was to allay any objections they might have to your taking Abby.'

'It was, originally,' Matt confirmed. 'But I've come to realize that marriage is the best solution; I'd have married you six years ago if I'd known you had conceived my child.'

'Whether I was agreeable or not?' Tessa asked edgily. 'Personally, I've never thought a mistaken pregnancy was a good enough reason to tie oneself to the wrong person,' she added, and Matt's lips tightened in annoyance. 'Apparently I have no alternative but to accept your hospitality, but it's only temporary, Matt. Just as soon as I'm well enough I shall look for another job – and another home,' she finished.

'Don't do this, Tessa,' Matt said quietly – almost pleadingly, she thought. He sighed heavily at her mutinous expression, then continued, 'If you refuse my offer of a home, of marriage, then you will have to face me in court for custody of our child,' he said, still quietly, but so implacably Tessa knew he meant every cruel word. Matt saw the shock and fear in her large brown eyes and hardened his heart: unfortunately, it was necessary that she believed his threat.

'You wouldn't win!' she gasped at last, fighting down the waves of panic which threatened to overwhelm her. 'I admit you can give her material things that I can't, but no judge would grant you custody on that basis. You were a stranger to her until a few days ago.'

'Whose fault was that?' Matt countered bitterly. 'And don't be too sure about winning, Tessa. Possession is

58

nine points of the law, remember, and you are home-
less, jobless and, I presume, almost penniliess? How
do you intend supporting her? You won't be fit
enough to return to work for some considerable time
and by then Abby will be happily settled into her new
school and with her new family. And, once my lawyer
– the very best, I do assure you,' he added, lest she
harboured any doubts about that, which she didn't.
'When he explains the circumstances in which you
were living, well, I imagine any right-minded judge
would be shocked.'

'What the hell are you talking about? What circumstances? Okay, I admit that flat wasn't Buckingham
Palace, but it was a good enough place in which to live,'
she said hotly.

'Was it? With two hookers occupying – and plying
their trade – in the flat downstairs?' Matt asked
softly.

'Two . . . you're mad! You can't go around saying
things like that!' she spluttered. 'It's libel –'

'Slander,' Matt corrected calmly. 'Except it's
neither, because it's true.'

'It is not! Janey and Linda are very nice girls,' Tessa
told him indignantly. Really, was there nothing he
wouldn't stoop to, in order to get his own way?

'They are common prostitutes,' Matt said evenly.

'No way.' Tessa shook her head.

'My God, you really didn't know, did you?' Matt
asked incredulously.

'N-no, of course I didn't,' Tessa faltered, beginning
to be afraid that he wasn't lying to frighten her; he
seemed so sure of his facts. 'I told you, they were both
nice girls, polite, friendly . . .'

'Very friendly,' Matt agreed drily. 'The blonde one even propositioned me! I knocked on their door, trying to discover if you had relatives living nearby, and she thought I was a client!' He gave a mirthless laugh. 'You must have realized, Tessa.'

'No, it never even occurred to me. Why should it? I knew they were popular –' She broke off when she saw the look of utter incredulity on Matt's face. She fell silent, biting on her lower lip as she mulled it over. If it were true – and she had a horrid feeling that it probably was – it might well appear to a judge that she was an unfit mother, exposing a small girl to such behaviour. Moreover, Janey, the blonde who had, according to Matt, offered him her services, had also on occasion volunteered to babysit for Abby. Tessa shuddered to think what Matt would do if he had that particular piece of information in his armoury.

'Did I mention that my father is a magistrate?' Matt put in, ultra-casually.

'No, you did not.' Tessa glared at him, well aware of his reason for mentioning the fact now. She eyed him uncertainly: would he really take it to court? Try to take Abby away from her? We're strangers, despite having a child, she thought; she really had no idea if he would carry out his threat.

'Would you really take her away from me?' she whispered.

'No. But if I win a custody battle, then I will have the legal right to have her living in the home I provide, and you would be breaking the law if you tried to disappear with her. You would naturally be invited to share that home,' he said dispassionately. 'I'm not cruel enough to deprive the child of her mother,' he added coldly, and the implication that Tessa had cruelly deprived Abby of her father was not lost on her. Her headache had worsened during the course of their argument and she knew she was too weak to fight him. At least she had his word that he would not part her from Abby, even if she were to lose the court case. For now, it was better to let him believe a legal battle would not be necessary.

'You've had plenty of time to think it over.' Matt broke into her thoughts. 'Are you prepared to come and live with me at Dtake's Abbot, or would you prefer to face me in court?' he demanded.

'I'll come to Drake's Abbot,' Tessa said promptly. 'But . . . marriage? Even a marriage of convenience – that's such a huge step: can't we put that idea on hold, at least for a few weeks?' She tried a placating smile but feared her face might crack with the effort. Matt's too-shrewd blue eyes bore deeply into hers for a moment before he relaxed slightly.

'Very well,' he agreed finally, but privately resolved on an early marriage. Anything less would not prevent Tessa from removing Abby at some future date, unless he really did take the matter to court. And, despite his confident manner, he was well aware that merely being the biological father counted for very little – only by becoming her legal guardian would he have rights over where his child lived.

'But who said anything about a marriage of convenience?' he asked softly. 'We do make beautiful children, Tessa . . .'

'Oh, no!' she said sharply. The memories of her lonely pregnancy and difficult labour hadn't dimmed over the years. 'I'm not going through that again!' Oh, yes, you are, my darling, Matt thought: he had missed so much of Abby's babyhood, her first words, first faltering steps, and he was impatient to experience the wonder of watching and nurturing a child from the moment of its birth. However, he wisely refrained from pursuing the subject, feeling he had gained as much ground as he could, for now.

Surely a few weeks recuperating at Drake's Abbot would convince Tessa she would be happier with him than continuing to struggle alone? After all, they had spent a magical few days together in Cyprus – admittedly six years ago – but hopefully they could recapture and build on the powerful attraction that had produced Abby. Even if Tessa remained hostile to him, he was confident she would come to realize that Abby would benefit from their marriage – a comfortable home, a mother who needn't go out to work, grandparents and an extended family.

'We'll see,' was all he said to her vehement refusal to have another child, and the accompanying slight smile warned Tessa that the subject was far from forgotten. She opened her mouth to reiterate her views on the horrors of childbirth, but, at that moment, the door burst open and Abby, holding on to the hand of a tall, elegantly dressed woman, dashed forward.

'Mummy!' She gave a shout of delight and ran over to the bed, thrusting a bunch of carnations at her mother.

'Thank you, sweetie, they're lovely. And so are you.' Tessa reached to hug her but Matt forestalled her, lifting Abby easily onto the bed and into Tessa's ready arms, then deftly unbuckled and removed her shoes.

'The nurses will have your guts for garters if you dirty the sheets,' he told her, with a twinkle in his eyes. Abby giggled, instinctively knowing a vulgar remark when she heard one.

'Guts for garters,' she repeated happily. 'You are funny, Daddy.' Abby grinned at him and Tessa had to avert her gaze from the look of adoration in her daughter's eyes. Obviously Matt had won Abby over completely; perhaps it was already too late for her and Abby to resume their old way of life, just the two of them.

For the first time, she faced the unpalatable fact that maybe Abby had lost out by never knowing her father, but was distracted by the sight of Abby's shoes, new shoes, shiny and red, almost identical to a pair Abby had seen and asked for barely two weeks earlier. Tessa had been forced to refuse her, truthfully claiming lack of cash. A spurt of resentment flooded over her – did Matt or his mother realize how much it hurt, to have to deny her child the things she wanted? Of course they didn't, she thought bitterly, then took a deep breath and looked across at Evelyn Stafford, Matt's mother, whose sapphire blue eyes, so like her son's, were regarding her with interest and curiosity.

'Thank you for taking such good care of her,' Tessa said, rather stiffly, not knowing what to expect from Matt's mother. She must have been utterly taken aback, to say the least, by the sudden knowledge of Abby's existence. Would she be a friend or foe to Tessa, if Matt carried out his threat to challenge her for custody? Would she support her son, right or wrong, or, as a mother herself, try to persuade him against an attempt to remove a young child from its mother's care?

'It's been my pleasure. I'm glad you're so much better.' Evelyn advanced to shake Tessa's hand, then impulsively bent to kiss her cheek.

'Tessa will be leaving here in a couple of days,' Matt put in.

'Oh, that is good news! And you're coming to stay with us, of course.' It was more of a statement than a question and Tessa felt sure Evelyn Stafford knew of Matt's plans.

'I don't want to impose, but I'm afraid the doctor won't let me return alone to my flat. Not that I have a flat to return to,' she added, with a baleful glance towards Matt, who only grinned unrepentantly.

'It's no imposition,' Evelyn assured her, ignoring the last part of her statement. 'We have a huge house and plenty of staff. Now then, Matt, I'm sure Tessa and Abby would like to be alone for a while. I have some shopping to do – you can come and carry my bags,' she said briskly, to his evident disgust. Abby giggled at the expression on his face and even Tessa suppressed a grin.

'Sorry, I have some business to attend to in town,' he said quickly. He paused on his way out of the room, glancing from Abby to Tessa, so alike, the child he already loved and claimed for his own and the woman – well, he had been crazy about her once before. If only he could rediscover the old Tessa, or, to be more accurate, the young Tessa he had known, then the future could be bright indeed.

Before Tessa realized his intention, he stooped and bent his head to hers. His hand moved to the back of her neck, holding her gently but firmly, while his mouth sought a response from hers. With Abby

64

sitting so close and Mrs Stafford standing at the foot of the bed, Tessa could do little but submit to his caress and hope her displeasure communicated itself to him.

She remained motionless under the onslaught of his kiss, using every ounce of willpower not to yield to the beguiling demands of his lips and tongue, determinedly – and appalled by just how much determination she had to summon up – suppressing the frissons of pleasure she experienced from both the kiss and the light touch of his fingers stroking her skin.

'Hmm.' Matt straightened slowly, his blue eyes narrowing as they regarded her. Tessa stared back defiantly, but saw neither the anger nor the disappointment she expected. Instead, to her consternation, he suddenly grinned and inclined his head slightly, as if he were acknowledging – and accepting – a challenge.

CHAPTER 4

'Can I bring you anything back from the shops, Tessa?' Evelyn enquired blandly, breaking the spell.

'Huh?' Tessa, with difficulty, tore her gaze – and her thoughts – from Matt. 'Um, something to read, perhaps? Nothing too heavy; my head still aches abominably,' she said.

'Right. I'll see you later. Goodbye, Abby, I won't be long,' she told her, giving her a hug.

'Bye, Grandma.' Abby happily returned the embrace, Tessa noted; noted, too, the way her face lit up when Matt casually ruffled her hair in farewell.

When the door closed behind Evelyn and Matt, Tessa sank back against the pillows, her thoughts and emotions in turmoil. She hated the way in which her traitorous body had wanted, ached to respond to him. She despised all men, but especially Matt Stafford – he was the most overbearing, arrogant bully she had ever had the misfortune to meet! And, as for marriage? Hah! She would never agree to that ridiculous idea, never in a million years, particularly as he seemed only to want her around as a nanny to Abby and a brood mare to produce his future children!

However, the child she had already produced clearly adored Matt and chattered on excitedly, fortunately not requiring any answers or comments from her mother, which was just as well considering the condition of Tessa's mind and temper!

'Is Matt still in the Army?' Tessa asked suddenly, thinking longingly of him being sent on a two-year posting to the Falklands or somewhere equally remote, to give her the opportunity of disappearing from his life once again.

'No.' Abby shook her head, promptly dashing that particular hope of escape. 'Grandpa's retiring, and Daddy runs the state,' she announced.

'Runs the State?' Tessa echoed: surely that was a little high-handed, even for Matt Stafford? she thought bemusedly. 'Oh, do you mean an estate?' she questioned. 'A big farm?'

'Mmm.' Abby nodded vigorously. 'It's ever so big. I sat on Daddy's horse and we rode for miles and miles. I saw the cows and the sheeps –'

'Sheep,' Tessa corrected.

'No, sheeps. There were lots, hundreds and hundreds,' Abby insisted solemnly, and Tessa let it go, hiding a grin.

'And Daddy took me to see our new house . . .' She shot Tessa a suddenly uncertain look and Tessa forced a bright smile.

'You like him, don't you?' she asked softly.

'Yes.' Abby nodded again, even more vehemently, the, 'I wish he had always been my daddy,' she murmured, and Tessa bit down on her lower lip, the words cutting her to the quick. Had she made a dreadful mistake by not contacting Matt to tell him of

67

her pregnancy? It was painful to admit that she had been wrong, that Abby had been deprived, and not only of the material things he would have provided. It was as if the years of struggling to provide for her child alone counted for nothing, and weak tears of self-pity and reproach welled in her eyes. She blinked them back furiously lest Abby notice them and be upset.

'Tell me about everything else you've been doing,' she urged brightly. Abby needed no further prompting and continued her happy chatter until Mrs Stafford – 'Call me Evelyn, dear' – returned, bearing an assortment of magazines, fruit and chocolates for Tessa.

Evelyn noticed immediately that Tessa looked pale and tired, and bore Abby away to let her mother rest. Tessa protested, but rather half-heartedly as she did feel unwell, and she quickly drifted back to sleep.

She awoke several hours later feeling refreshed. She raised herself from her pillows and stretched experimentally, pleased to discover that some suppleness and strength had returned to her limbs and muscles; she no longer felt so much like a rather battered and bedraggled rag doll as she had earlier.

She paused in mid-stretch when she became belatedly aware of Matt's presence, and felt herself blush as if he had caught her in some intimate act. She felt uncomfortable with the knowledge that he had been watching her while she slept and hoped she hadn't talked in her sleep – if she had, Matt certainly wouldn't have heard anything in his favour, she thought.

'How's the headache?' Matt left the window ledge on which he had been perched and sauntered over to the bed.

'Much better, thank you.' Tessa avoided his gaze and reached for the carafe of water on her locker.

'I'll do that.' Matt poured her a glass and handed it over, his hands warm as they brushed against hers. Warm hands, cold heart, Tessa suddenly recalled the old adage heard in childhood – was it true?

'How long have you been here?' she asked, sipping the cool, refreshing water.

'Not long; I'm on my way back to Drake's Abbot.' He stood and walked away, as if needing to place some distance between them, then turned and faced her.

'Why didn't you tell me, Tessa?' he asked abruptly.

'Tell you what?' she prevaricated, the water she was drinking suddenly settling heavily and too cold on her stomach. Matt flung out one hand in a gesture of impatience.

'That you were pregnant, of course!'

'Isn't it obvious? I thought you wouldn't be interested.'

'Not . . . ! We're not all bastards, hiding from the Child Support Agency,' he said roughly. 'You should have told me; I had the right to know, the right to be her father –' He broke off, cursing himself as Tessa visibly shrank away from his anger. 'Okay, okay, recriminations are pointless now,' he said, more quietly. But, dammit, it hurt unbearably that she hadn't trusted him. 'Was that the only reason you kept quiet – fear of rejection? Or –' he swallowed '– didn't you want me in your life?' he asked harshly.

'I was afraid of rejection, yes,' Tessa said slowly, reluctantly remembering the emotional turmoil she had suffered during the early months of her pregnancy. 'If you had been around, maybe I –' She broke off and tried again. 'You were already in Bosnia when I discovered I was pregnant. You have no idea how scared I was, particularly as my parents had so recently died . . .' She shuddered as the memories of the darkest days swept back; the days, weeks, of panic and uncertainty. She had even, briefly, considered an abortion. Now, she felt physically ill at the thought of how close she had come to taking the easy way out of her dilemma. She shook her head slightly and cleared her throat.

'It just wasn't the sort of news I could tell you in a letter; after all, I hardly knew you . . .'

'You knew me well enough to conceive my child,' Matt said bluntly.

'Yes, well, that was nothing to be proud of, was it?' Tessa shifted uncomfortably, recalling her aunt's scornful and disapproving reaction to her one night spent with Matt Stafford.

'As I said, I didn't feel I could write and tell you what had happened. You said you expected to be back in England in the New Year, four months away, and by then I'd decided you had probably forgotten all about me, and would be horrified if I turned up on your doorstep, uninvited and pregnant!' She paused. 'I also thought you would find me if you had meant everything you had said to me while we were together,' she added softly. Matt stared at her, unwillingly to admit how desperately he had tried to find her.

'Do you know how many listings there are for "Grant" in the London directory?' he asked instead.

'No – how many?' Tessa queried, and he smiled slightly.

'A lot. I did try, Tessa,' he said quietly, prepared to admit that much. 'But, as you just said, more than four months had passed. You were only nineteen – when you stopped writing to me and didn't send me your new address, I concluded you had met someone else after you returned to England. I wish I had known,' he muttered: she would never know how much, but regrets were futile; it was the future which mattered now – a future, he resolved, that was going to include Tessa and Abby.

'How did you manage?' he asked. 'Did your aunt help?'

'No,' Tessa grimaced slightly. 'She was . . . horrified,' she admitted. 'I wasn't too badly off financially – I had the proceeds from the sale of my parents' house and, after Abby was born, I got a job living in with a lovely lady, as a sort of companion and housekeeper. She was very good to both Abby and me, and the work wasn't hard. She employed a "daily" as well as me and she wasn't an invalid, just elderly and lonely. But then she died suddenly, when Abby was two, and her son inherited her house, so I had to leave rather quickly –'

'He threw you out? With a small child?' Matt interrupted, a dark scowl marring his features.

'Oh, no.' Tessa's lips tightened in remembered bitterness. 'He was perfectly happy for me to remain – provided he could come and . . . er . . . visit, whenever he could escape from his wife!'

'What's his name?' Matt asked, in a voice of steel. Tessa wasn't impressed.

'Oh, get off your high horse, Matt!' she scoffed. 'He wasn't aggressive, or bullying. He just made me a proposition, which I chose to decline. He was no

71

worse than you or any other man,' she said contemptuously.

'I find that comparison extremely offensive –' Matt began hotly.

'The truth hurts, huh?' she asked cuttingly. 'You'd have behaved differently, would you, if I'd asked you for support? Are you trying to tell me you wouldn't have expected me to sleep with you in return for your help?'

'I –' Matt cut short his indignant denial, realizing uncomfortably that there was more than a grain of truth in her accusation. Before he had concluded that only marriage would ensure his keeping Abby, he had indeed envisaged placing the two of them in a house conveniently on the Stafford estate, a house he would be free to visit whenever he chose. His main concern had been to keep his daughter, not a mistress, but, if he were honest, he knew he had expected Tessa to welcome him into her bed.

'You can't deny it, can you?' Tessa's lip curled derisively. 'And you wonder why I prefer a flat, however small, that I can call my own!'

'You are coming to live at Drake's Abbot. That is not open to debate!' Matt snapped, then strode towards the door. 'I'll be back tomorrow. I hope to find you in a better temper!'

'I wouldn't count on it!' Tessa called after his retreating back. Her only reply was the slamming of the door and the gradually receding sound of his rapid footsteps.

Tessa felt much better, physically at least, when she awoke the following day, and took several short walks along the corridor, resting as soon as she felt tired or dizzy before setting off again. She had recovered her appetite somewhat and could almost feel the strength returning to her as she ate.

Abby, accompanied by her grandmother, was overjoyed to see Tessa out of bed, and clapped her hands in delight when Tessa told her she would be leaving hospital the following day. Abby was wearing yet another brand new outfit and Tessa tried hard to feel grateful, but wondered what Evelyn had done with Abby's perfectly good clothes that she, Tessa, had provided – chucked them on the fire?

The two women talked only of Abby: Evelyn was consumed with curiosity about Tessa and Matt, but didn't quite dare probe. Tessa, for her part, was unsure of how much Evelyn was conspiring with Matt to take over control of Abby's future and was therefore careful to divulge nothing that indicated she was less than happy with Matt's actions thus far. Both were quite relieved when the visit was over.

Matt didn't put in an appearance until early evening, long after Evelyn had taken Abby back to Drake's Abbot – Tessa refused to refer to it as 'home', although Abby now did. Tessa put aside the magazine she had been reading and eyed him rather warily, wondering what new plans he had made since their last encounter.

'I stopped by to talk to your doctor – I hear you're coming home tomorrow,' he said pleasantly.

'I'm coming to Drake's Abbot,' Tessa amended coolly, and saw his lips tighten in annoyance. Good.

'I've put my flat on the market. It's very much a bachelor pad with only one bedroom. We can look for something bigger later, if you find living in the country too dull,' he continued evenly. Tessa merely shrugged, not at all impressed by this outward show of consideration for her wishes. Until very recently, she'd *had* a flat in London! Matt had already made it abundantly clear that his word was law, unless she wished to challenge him in the courts.

She had already decided to bide her time, to regain her physical strength before carrying out her plans to regain control of her life – and that of her daughter. For now, she was too weak – and broke – to fight him, but she was damned if she was going to pretend to like his high-handed attitude, even though common sense told her she would be wise to lull him into a false sense of security.

An opportunity to pretend to be won over was presented to her almost immediately.

'I also called in at my bank,' Matt continued, as he perched on the edge of her bed and produced a heart-shaped jeweller's box from his pocket. It obviously contained a ring and Tessa forced a smile when he held the box out to her.

'This is very kind of you, but it isn't necessary,' she said, with what she hoped was a credible mixture of appreciation and reluctance.

'It isn't kind, but it is necessary.' Matt smiled, so warmly she began to feel uncomfortable with her deception. 'It belonged to my grandmother and she bequeathed it to me in her will, with a request that it be passed on to my wife.'

'But . . .'

'Open it,' he insisted. Tessa hesitated for a moment longer, then slowly lifted the lid and saw an exquisite diamond and sapphire ring resting on a bed of velvet.

'It's beautiful,' she said truthfully, watching the light catch the stones. The ring was comprised of one huge diamond surrounded by smaller ones interspersed with sapphires and set in an intricate Victorian design of filigree gold. 'But I doubt your grandmother had this . . . situation in mind when she drafted her will.'

'You're the mother of my child – who else would I give it to?' Matt asked simply, taking the ring and placing it on the third finger of her left hand. 'And you will be my wife, Tessa,' he added sternly, thus banishing her burgeoning feelings of guilt over her acceptance of the ring.

'Matt . . .' She shook her head despairingly. 'We're almost strangers – we only knew each other for a few days, on holiday, long ago. Whatever there was between us just isn't there any more –' She stopped speaking abruptly, alerted by the gleam in his bright blue eyes, recognizing the smouldering desire she had last seen six years earlier and had never forgotten, reliving the memories in her dreams although she had always ruthlessly pushed his image away from her during waking hours.

She lay back against the pillows, staring at him as if mesmerized, and only resisted half-heartedly when he slowly tugged away the bedcovers and revealed her body, clad only in the clinging, almost transparent nightdress, to his gaze.

'Tessa,' he almost groaned, easing the narrow straps from her shoulders and placing his lips to the soft

75

hollow at the base of her throat. 'Stop fighting me,' he whispered, his breath a warm caress on her cheek. His hands, mindful of her bruises, moved gently over her body before cupping her breasts, his thumbs stroking each rosy nipple to an immediate hardening. He made a soft sound of triumph, lifting his head to look deeply into her eyes.

'How can you say there is nothing between us?' he asked urgently. 'There is such passion, Tessa, you can't deny it. That one night you spent in my arms was so special; I've never forgotten it.' Or matched it since, he thought silently, but held back from the admission. 'There are years ahead of us with many more such nights,' he told her huskily.

Tessa bit her lip and covered his probing hands with her own, trying to still their insistent stroking and teasing of her sensitive skin. She couldn't think properly while he was touching her so intimately. He spoke so easily and confidently of the nights they could spend together – but what of the days? How could they live together once passion had cooled, which it certainly would without the deeper and stronger emotion of love to fuel it and keep it alive. Nor was Abby enough of a reason to stay together – if sharing a child ensured marital harmony, there would be far fewer divorces.

'Matt . . .' she began, needing to put her doubts into words, to make him realize his marriage plans were ludicrous, but he cut off her protests, half lifting her off the mattress while he covered her face with soft, feather-light kisses before finally claiming her mouth.

Then he became more demanding, and her head fell back against his supporting arm, her lips parting of their own volition to eagerly accept his plundering tongue. Without conscious thought she twined her arms around his neck, catching her hands in the thickness of his hair and straining her body against his.

For six years she had ruthlessly subdued any stirrings of sexual desire; now her body was unexpectedly rebelling against her self-imposed celibacy, remembering the pleasures and delights this man could bestow. Tessa moaned, deep in her throat, as his hands began an almost lazy exploration of her body, now practically naked since the nightdress had snaked up around her thighs. She slid further down the bed until she was lying horizontally, then tugged at his shoulders until his body covered hers.

'Matt . . .' she said again, but this time the word was almost a plea, definitely a submission. Matt, suddenly aware that he was about to make love to an invalid in her hospital bed, pulled away abruptly. Tessa frowned slightly, puzzled, and watched him as he wordlessly picked up the pillows which had fallen to the floor. Then he lifted her, as impersonally as any nurse, and placed her carefully against them, even straightening the sheet and tucking her in as if she were Abby's age.

'Did that convince you?' he asked finally, as if he had only kissed her to gain her agreement to this impossible marriage, Tessa thought, hurt and confused. Yet she had been fully aware of his arousal when he had been pressed against her and he was still breathing rather heavily, she noted. As was she, she realized belatedly and reached for a glass of water with a shaking hand.

'Well?' he asked, when she didn't reply. Tessa continued sipping water, then smiled slightly and coolly – she hoped. It was time Matt Stafford realized she was no longer the gullible, naïve nineteen-year-old he had so easily won over with his experienced touch.

'That was just sex.' She dismissed it as nonchalantly as she could and had the satisfaction of hearing his indrawn hiss of breath.

'Then sex will just have to be enough for us, won't it?' he asked tightly. 'Because I have no intention of allowing you to marry someone else, Tessa! No other man is going to be a father to my child!' He stared at her implacably and it took an enormous effort of will for her to stare back defiantly. At least, she hoped it was defiance he read in her eyes, not apprehension . . . or longing. It was she who dropped her gaze first and she studied the diamond and sapphire ring on her finger. It *was* beautiful, but she would have preferred a brass curtain ring if it had been given with love.

'I have to go – I'm meeting a friend for dinner,' Matt said evenly. 'I'll come and collect you tomorrow morning; I'm not sure what time . . .'

'If it's too much trouble, I could always catch a bus,' she said sweetly, and he gave her a hard look.

'Do you need me to bring you any clothes in?' he asked politely, instead of the caustic remark she was sure had been on his lips.

'No, your mother brought some things in earlier,' she told him.

'Good.' He gazed at her moodily. 'If you would only stop being so stubborn and independent, you would realize that what I am doing is the best for all of us,' he said. Tessa merely shrugged and heard him sigh. 'Don't push me too far,' he warned her, and without making any further attempt to kiss her or touch her, he strode from the room.

Jack's Christmas List.

A. P. Webb PLANT HIRE LTD.

James Bond - QofS. PS2

Spider Man C on DVD

5 packs DJ Cards

crazy bones Yellom

pack X X X X

After he had gone, Tessa was unable to settle to watching TV or to reading, and gladly swallowed the sleeping pill offered to her at bedtime. It quickly took effect and she fell into a deep slumber in the darkened room.

She had no idea how long she had been asleep, or precisely what awakened her, first becoming aware of a musky, overpowering perfume and an inexplicable feeling of heartstopping fear. Groggily, she turned over and tried to force open her heavy lids.

Her door was slightly ajar, allowing a narrow beam of light into the room, and she sensed a presence by her bed, not one of the nurses, but a woman with diamonds sparkling at her throat and in her ears. Tessa was unable to make out her features, but the soft light glinted on blonde hair swept back from her face.

'You think you've won, don't you? You and that bastard of yours! Matt doesn't want you, just the kid. He wished you had died! If you know what's good for you, you'll disappear back to the gutter before –' She stopped speaking when Tessa gave an involuntary cry of alarm. Sure she must be hearing things, or be in the grip of a terrible nightmare, Tessa shook her head to clear it, then turned and fumbled for the bell to summon a nurse.

She felt as if the intruder's perfume was choking her and she struggled to breathe. Half expecting a physical attack, so malevolent and threatening was the voice, she tried desperately to clamber out of bed, to get away from the danger she felt sure she was facing. She caught her foot in the sheet and fell to the floor, sobbing for breath and panicking out of control.

79

The perfume was so overwhelming she felt as if she were choking and began to cough.

'What's the matter? Are you feeling ill?' The room was suddenly flooded with light and Nurse Harper stood in the doorway. There was no sign of anyone else.

'No, I'm not ill.' Tessa shook her head. She was bathed in perspiration and still fighting for breath, clutching at her bruised ribs which had begun to ache with the effort needed to fill her lungs with air. 'That woman,' she gasped. 'I thought she was going to attack me!'

'Which woman?' Nurse Harper moved swiftly to Tessa's side and took hold of her wrist, frowning at the rapid beat of her pulse. 'Get back into bed,' she ordered. Tessa obeyed gladly, her legs too weak and trembling to support her. 'There's no one here; you must have been dreaming,' she said soothingly.

'No, there was a woman in here,' Tessa insisted. 'And not a nurse. She seemed to be dressed for a night out, and was wearing diamonds.'

'Definitely not a nurse, then,' she agreed drily. 'I'm sure you must have dreamed it; all visitors left hours ago.'

'Are you certain?' Tessa was willing to be convinced. 'But can't you smell her perfume?' she asked, wrinkling her nose. She still could; it was filling her nostrils and making her feel sick.

'No . . . well, these flowers are heavily scented; I'll take them out of here,' Nurse Harper picked up the elaborate display which Evelyn has brought in earlier. 'You must have been having a bad dream – an outsider would have passed the nurses' rest room and I've been in there for the past half-hour.'

'It was very vivid,' Tessa shuddered; she was still shaking violently.

'You'll be all right now,' Nurse Harper said briskly, plumping up her pillows tucking her back into bed. 'Try to get back to sleep. Would you like some hot milk to help you settle?'

'No, thank you.' Tessa slid obediently down the bed, pulling the covers protectively around her shoulders. 'You . . . you won't be far away, will you?' she was ashamed to hear herself asking.

'No.' Nurse Harper leaned across her and unhooked the bell-push, then pinned the flex to the pillow next to Tessa's cheek. 'Just press it if you can't sleep, or feel frightened, and someone will be here within seconds. I'll explain to the other nurses, but I'm sure you were dreaming – only hospital staff are around at this time of the night,' she assured her once more.

'Thank you. I'm sorry to make such a fuss,' Tessa apologized, curling her fingers around the bell-push, ready to summon assistance if it were needed. But, very soon, her heartbeat returned to its normal pace, the sleeping pill again took effect, and she slept soundly.

In the morning, with sunlight streaming through the window, it was easier to believe she had indeed imagined the whole episode and she succeeded in pushing it to the back of her mind, and instead of dwelling on what might or might not have happened, looked forward to leaving hospital.

She ate breakfast, then bathed and dressed, and felt immeasurably fitter and healthier in normal daywear instead of a nightdress. She felt even better when she had applied make-up to alleviate her pallor.

She hoped Nurse Harper hadn't informed Dr Stevens of her disturbed night, and, as he made no mention of it when he called to examine her for one last time, she wisely kept silent.

'You'll be as good as new in no time.' He beamed at her. 'I'll make an appointment for you to come and see me in outpatients but, meanwhile, just make sure you rest as much as possible. As I've already explained, the headaches will persist for quite a while, and don't worry if you find you can't concentrate as well as usual, or if you're a little confused and forgetful,' he continued. 'That's all quite normal in cases like yours.'

'Thank you.' Tessa smiled at him, then, rather hesitantly, 'I was wondering if . . . could I start taking the Pill?' she asked, blushing slightly. Last evening's assault on her senses had proved to her that she might not be capable of saying 'no' to Matt Stafford if – when – he tried to get her into bed. And, whatever Matt's views on the subject, she was determined not to risk another pregnancy.

It was easier than she had expected: after a few routine questions about her medical history, he checked her blood pressure and then straightened up.

'I don't see why you should have any problems. I'll prescribe a pack for you now and, if they suit you, you can get a future supply from your GP or a Family Planning Clinic.'

'Thank you,' Tessa said gratefully. At least that would be one less thing for her to worry about.

After Dr Stevens had left, she sat alone and waited for Matt to come and collect her. Her thoughts drifted back to her nocturnal visitor, if indeed the woman had been real. Surely it was possible that a girlfriend of

Matt's was incensed by the arrival of herself and Abby into his life and had come to vent her spleen? She doubted very much if he had led a monastic existence for the past six years! But . . . to say Matt wished she had died? She shivered, despite the stuffy warmth of the hospital room. That couldn't possibly be true; could only be the rantings of a jealous and spiteful woman . . . couldn't it?

'Sorry I'm late.' Matt strode in, taking her unawares, and she caught her breath at the sight of him, so tall and strong, so fit and healthy, making her feel ill and wan by comparison, and also very weak and vulnerable.

'Are you ready to leave?' He regarded her quizzically, frowning a little when she remained motionless in her chair, gazing up at him and seeming almost, well, frightened, he thought, and his frown deepened. 'Tessa?'

'I'm ready,' she said shortly, tearing her gaze away from him, and struggling to rise. She shrugged off his helping hand with more force than was necessary and turned her attention to Abby who, after greeting her with a kiss, had gone to pick up the bag containing Tessa's belongings.

'She's eager to get you home,' Matt said easily, taking the bag away from her. 'She's been sitting in the car since breakfast!'

As they walked along the corridor Abby skipped ahead of them, then returned to Tessa's side, looking anxiously up at her before darting off again after receiving an assurance that Tessa was okay. Matt slowed his stride to match Tessa's and once again took her arm. It was a polite gesture only; his fingers gripped her just above her elbow, their bodies touched at no other point and Tessa held herself stiffly away from him. Matt sensed something was badly wrong and an uncomfortable silence fell between them. Both were relieved that they would have Abby's talkative presence on the journey to Drake's Abbot.

Tessa paused to say her farewells to the nurses on duty and noticed how the younger ones eyed Matt, patting their hair into place and colouring when he spoke to them in his deep caressing voice, adding his thanks for their care of her. Two of them were blondes, Tessa noticed: if Nurse Harper was correct in saying that only members of staff could have been in her room so late last night . . . oh, get a grip! she chided herself; of course it wasn't a nurse who had threatened her. But she still felt glad to be leaving the hospital.

'It's wonderful to be out in the fresh air again,' she said, breathing deeply as they emerged outside and walked across the car park. It was a beautiful morning, cool, but sunny and invigorating.

'You sound as if you've just been let out of prison,' Matt said drily.

'Yeah, out of one and on my way to another!' she snapped. He made no rejoinder, but threw her case into the boot of his car and slammed the lid down with unnecessary force.

The short walk from her room had exhausted her more than she cared to admit and she sank gratefully into the leather upholstery of the silver-grey Mercedes, closing her eyes for a few moments until the slight dizziness passed.

'Isn't this a great car?' Abby demanded eagerly from the back seat. 'Look, Mummy, it's got electrocuted windows!' she said, enthusiastically demonstrating the mechanism.

Tessa opened her eyes and involuntarily glanced at Matt as she suppressed her amusement and caught him doing the same. Briefly, they shared a moment's pleasure in their daughter, then Tessa recalled being told Matt wished her dead, and she looked away. He wouldn't have to share Abby, or fight for custody, if he were her sole parent . . .

Abby quickly lost interest in opening and closing the windows and leaned forward to wrap her arms around Tessa's neck, her over-eager grip threatening strangulation.

'I'm glad you're coming home, Mummy. I want you to meet Flynn and Lollipop, and –'

'Hold on – who's Flynn?' Tessa asked.

'I told you – he's the nice doggie –'

'Dog,' Tessa and Matt corrected simultaneously.

'Dog,' Abby repeated, with an exaggerated sigh. 'And Lollipop's my pony . . .'

'Pony!' Tessa wished her brain had been functioning properly when Abby had first told her of this . . . menagerie. She looked anxiously at Matt. 'How big is it? She's only ever ridden a seaside donkey.'

'Don't worry, Mummy. It's only a little shitty pony,' she thought, with the utmost horror, she heard Abby say.

'*Abby!*' she gasped, mortified.

'It's a Shetland,' Matt interrupted hastily, trying not to laugh at the expression on her face. 'My father calls them Shetties. I think that's what she meant to say. I hope,' he added, under his breath.

'Oh, I see,' Tessa said lamely. 'His name's Lollipop?' she asked Abby, who nodded. 'Well, just make sure that's how you refer to him in future,' she said firmly.

'Yes, Mummy,' Abby agreed meekly. Matt glanced over his shoulder and winked at Abby, who giggled delightedly. Tessa bit her lip and looked away, feeling absurdly excluded. Is this how it's going to be in future? she wondered sadly – I become the nasty disciplinarian while Matt indulges her and laughs with her, even when she's naughty? For Tessa had her doubts as to Abby's innocence regarding the mispronunciation; some of the language she had picked up since starting school had been deplorable. Trying to look on the bright side, she told herself that the school Matt wanted to transfer her to had to be an improvement . . .

CHAPTER 5

'That's the school I have in mind for her,' Matt said casually, just at that moment, and Tessa visibly jumped: it was as if he had read her mind! God, that was going to be inconvenient! She thought outwitting Matt Stafford was going to prove difficult enough without him being aided by a psychic ability!

She craned her neck and caught a glimpse of a large red-brick building as Matt drove past. They were travelling through a pleasant residential area, with well-maintained detached houses set back from the road in large gardens.

'Is this Drake's Abbot?' she asked.

'No, Ashminster,' Matt told her.

'It's not a boarding school, is it? Because I won't agree to that . . .' she began hotly.

Matt sighed impatiently. He had only just acquired a daughter; he was hardly likely to want to send her away to school. Surely even suspicious, doubting Tessa couldn't believe that of him?

'Of course it's not. Although I went to boarding school and it didn't do me any harm,' he added, and then suppressed a grin at the unmistakable expression on Tessa's face. It clearly stated: that's a matter of opinion!

'Drake's Abbot is about five miles from here,' he continued. 'Ashminster is the most convenient place for day-to-day shopping – my mother informs me there's a good selection of dress shops and so on,' he added drily. 'You should be able to find everything you need here, save you trekking up to London until you're fully fit.'

'Well, I want to go and talk to my boss –' Tessa began.

'Ex-boss,' Matt corrected mildly, and she gritted her teeth.

'Yes, quite. I still want to go and see him; apologize for letting him down,' she said firmly.

'You didn't let him down; you were involved in a traffic accident,' Matt demurred: he found he didn't want her returning to her past, not even for a visit.

'I also want to talk to Claire,' Tessa continued, ignoring his protest. 'I'm surprised she didn't offer to look after Abby. She has a son around the same age and we often babysat for each other.'

'Claire?' Oh, yes, Matt thought, the workmate who had indeed offered to take Abby in to her home while Tessa was in hospital. 'It must have been her day off when I called in at the office,' he said smoothly.

'How do you know she works in the same office?' Tessa frowned.

'You just told me so,' Matt said quickly.

'Did I?' Tessa rubbed her aching head, and Matt felt a stab of contrition. But he was doing the right thing, he assured himself yet again. However, his catalogue of crimes over the past two weeks was rising at an alarming rate – frightening Tessa into running into the path of a bus, kidnapping a child, lying to the police and the hospital staff; now he was lying to Tessa . . .

He forced himself to stop thinking about it lest guilt overwhelmed him and he turned the car around to take Tessa back to that godawful flat she had called home. It depressed him to realize that Tessa, if not Abby, would be delighted if he did just that, and he cheered himself with the knowledge that he had an ally in his daughter.

She already loved her new home, the animals, her grandparents, but hopefully not in that order. Now that she had her mother back with her, Abby would be blissfully happy. He only hoped Tessa would recognize that fact and accept that the changes he had effected in her life were beneficial to all concerned.

'This is Drake's Abbot,' he told Tessa, and she sat up straighter, looking around her with interest. They were entering a small village, of the kind fast disappearing, swallowed up as they were by encroaching new housing estates.

Drake's Abbot, however, had so far succeeded in retaining its character, with stone cottages clustered around the village green, the focal point of which was the public house with white-painted garden furniture and tubs of brightly coloured geraniums outside.

There was also a row of small shops, and a medieval church set back from the road. That was it: blink and you'd miss it, Tessa thought flippantly. She had never lived in a village, a place where everyone knew everyone else, and she became embarrassed when she realized the car was attracting curious stares from the people they drove past. The car – or her?

'I suppose everyone here is gossiping and speculating about Abby and me?' she ventured.

'Afraid so,' Matt confirmed cheerfully. 'This is Stafford House,' he said, a few moments later. How typically arrogant to name the house after the family, Tessa thought idly – what was wrong with 'Dunroamin'? she wondered sardonically, but refrained from comment.

Her eyes widened when she took in the splendour of the mansion – there was no other word for it – that they were approaching. Matt slowed the car and turned into a driveway, which was at least a mile long, flanked on both sides by a column of ancient oaks, their spreading branches almost converging overhead to form a leafy archway. Beyond the trees lay open countryside.

'At least you don't have to worry about problems with noisy neighbours,' she quipped, trying not to show how impressed she was with the actual house. It was huge, far bigger than she had expected despite Abby's tales of getting lost, built of pale grey brick, with gabled third-storey windows jutting from what looked like – could it possibly be? – battlements at the base of the roof.

'Do you pour boiling oil on intruders?' she asked next, trying to wind him up, but he merely grinned.

'There's a great view from up there,' he told her.

'It's like a castle,' she said.

'Mmm, and almost as draughty and cold as they were, I expect. I prefer my London pad – even if I am occasionally kept awake by noise from the next-door flat,' he added, with a sideways glance. Tessa flushed; she knew she was being snide about his family home, but couldn't help it. If she and Matt couldn't build a

90

relationship, and he did carry out his threat to take the battle for Abby to court, well, his wealthy background would help his case tremendously.

'That's my room – in the turret.' Abby pointed excitedly to a rounded tower as Matt braked to a halt on the gravel beside a massive iron-studded front door. Tessa nodded and tried to smile, wondering bleakly what Abby's reply would be if she ever asked her: do you want to come away with me, or stay here with Matt?

'Look, Mummy, here's Flynn!' Abby cried, scrambling out of the car. Tessa dutifully looked, then blinked in disbelief at the sight of the creature bounding to greet them. The 'nice doggie' Abby liked so much was the most enormous dog she had ever had the misfortune to come across. Tessa decided to stay inside the car.

'Shouldn't that horse be in a stable?' she asked Matt faintly, and he grinned.

'He's an Irish Wolfhound and as gentle as a lamb,' he assured her, almost forcibly lifting her out of the car.

'I'll take your word for it,' Tessa muttered, keeping him as a shield between her and the huge beast. Abby, however, had no fear of him and Tessa winced when the child hugged the animal enthusiastically, her face only inches from its open jaw.

'It wasn't necessary to buy her a pony,' she told Matt. 'You could just put a saddle on that dog.'

'Come here, boy.' Matt whistled to the dog, who sprang towards him, tail wagging furiously. 'Let him sniff your hand,' Matt instructed Tessa, and she obeyed, but not without some trepidation. Couldn't dogs sense fear? And didn't that realization make them more likely to attack? Which idiot had made that particular piece of information public knowledge?' she wondered lightheadedly.

'I'm rather partial to my fingers,' she said nervously, as she submitted to having Flynn learn her scent. Apparently he approved, for his tail began waving vigorously once more. 'Good boy,' Tessa said, weakly and insincerely.

The front door was suddenly flung open and Evelyn hurried outside to greet them.

'You've made good time – I didn't hear the car,' she said to Matt, then she turned to Tessa and enveloped her in a warm embrace. 'Welcome to Drake's Abbot. Your room is all prepared, if you want to rest after the journey, but first come and meet the household –'

'Oh, no, not a reception committee,' Matt said irritably.

'It's important,' his mother insisted. 'There has been too much gossip already and I want the news to filter down to the village that Tessa is a welcome guest, and a part of our family now.' She smiled at Tessa, who managed a rather weak smile by way of reply.

'Where's my father?' Matt asked, with a distinct edge to his voice, and Tessa glanced at him sharply. So, was Mr Stafford senior not quite so pleased by her arrival in Matt's life?

'It's his Rotary Club lunch today,' Evelyn reminded Matt, whose grim countenance didn't lighten at the information, but he curtly nodded his acceptance of her explanation for his father's absence.

They stepped into an enormous hall, dark with mahogany panelling. The stone-flagged floor was brightened and warmed by several gaily coloured carpets and there was a huge, open fireplace, big enough to burn whole trees, although today it was filled with an elaborate display of dried flowers and leaves.

Standing in front of a long, intricately carved sideboard was a line of people, waiting, with barely concealed curiosity, to meet the girl who had given birth to Matt Stafford's illegitimate daughter. Oh God, Tessa thought helplessly, as Evelyn took her arm and marched her determinedly towards them.

Later, she could only remember Molly Bailey, the housekeeper, and Christine Cooper, the two people Abby had already mentioned with affection. But she smiled and shook hands with a seemingly endless queue of people, expressing the hope that having Abby to look after had not caused them too much inconvenience.

'Oh, no, not at all,' she was assured, with beaming smiles. 'It's lovely to have a child running around the place again,' Molly added, with an obviously genuine warmth.

'Mummy!' Abby tugged impatiently at her hand. 'Come and meet Lollipop.'

'Can I do that later?' Tessa smiled down at her apologetically. 'I'm rather tired.'

'You do look pale,' Matt commented. 'Would you like to go upstairs and rest?'

'Well, yes, I would,' Tessa admitted miserably. 'It's ridiculous! I've only been sitting in the car and I feel absolutely exhausted!' She was both angered and upset by her weakness, hating to be dependent on others.

How long would it be before she was able to take care of herself and Abby? she wondered helplessly. Too long. Abby had already become accustomed to a more affluent lifestyle, and a loving family. How could Tessa remove her from all that? Yet it was equally inconceivable that she stay . . .

'Don't be so impatient; it's your first day out of hospital,' Matt said gently. 'Chris – will you take care of Abby, please? And bring Miss Grant some lunch in her room later,' he added.

'Oh, no, I –' Tessa began to protest.

'Shut up,' Matt told her, but even more gently, and she felt hot tears spring to her eyes. He was much easier to resist when he was being an arrogant bully; she couldn't fight him when he was being kind.

Matt noticed her rapidly increasing pallor and, guessing she was not far from fainting, swung her off her feet and began effortlessly carrying her across the hall and then up the wide, shallow stairs. Tessa automatically placed her arms around his neck and closed her eyes to fight the dizziness that assailed her, taking deep, steadying breaths and hoping desperately that she wouldn't throw up.

'Remember Cyprus?' Matt murmured, his breath warm on her cheek. Her eyes flew open and met the heat in his gaze. Yes, she remembered vividly. She had broken the heel on her shoe and Matt had carried her up the narrow, rock-strewn cliff path. It had been a warm, mellow evening, and later they had made love under the stars, with the gentle sound of the surf in the background . . .

'No, I don't know what you're talking about,' she denied flatly, but he only grinned.

94

'Liar,' he said softly, negotiating the last turn in the stairs and striding along a broad corridor.

God, he is so arrogant, so sure of himself! she fumed to herself. 'I can walk by myself now,' she said firmly. Her dizzy spell had passed, but now a giddiness of a different nature was threatening her senses, caused, she was afraid to admit even to herself, by being held so close to Matt.

'Nearly there,' he said, making no attempt to release her. 'Besides, you're so light, I'm hardly aware I'm carrying you,' he said, with an inner sardonic laugh at the blatant lie. Unaware he was carrying her? His whole body was reacting to her proximity! 'Exquisite as you are, my darling, I shall have to fatten you up a bit,' he continued, as if she were his Christmas dinner, Tessa thought crossly.

He shouldered open the door of a large, high-ceilinged room decorated in delicate shades of pinks and gold, and laid her gently down on to the four-poster bed. 'In fact, I shall carry you up here every day to make sure you're gaining weight,' he added.

'Wouldn't bathroom scales be more accurate?' Tessa asked, rather breathlessly, alerted by the gleam in his eyes.

'More fun my way.' He grinned down at her, his mouth near to hers as he bent over her. Too near, and Tessa turned her head away.

'Is this bed an antique?' she enquired brightly, gazing determinedly at the intricate carving on the headboard and posts.

'Yes, but the mattress isn't, you'll be relieved to hear . . . what is it? What's the matter?' he asked, frowning when she jerked suddenly away.

'What's that smell?' Tessa demanded sharply: surely there was a trace of the same perfume which she had noticed last night? The cloying musk of a woman she had hoped had only been part of a nightmare? Had the woman been in this room? she wondered, her flesh crawling with fear at the thought, or, perhaps even worse, had she been with Matt, and her scent had clung to his clothing?

'I can't smell anything,' Matt said, baffled by her reaction to such a trifling matter.

'Perfume,' she shuddered. 'Strong, musky . . .' Matt went and opened a window, letting a slight breeze into the room.

'So? I expect someone was in here this morning, making up the bed and so on,' he said reasonably.

'Where were you last night?' Tessa demanded suddenly, and his brows rose.

'I beg your pardon?' he said stiffly.

'You said you were going out to dinner – who with? Was it a blonde woman . . . ?' Her voice trailed off under Matt's look of incredulity, and she bit her lower lip. God, I sound like a jealous, shrewish wife, she realized. But the woman had said that Matt wanted her, Tessa, to die. She shivered, suddenly deathly afraid. What did she really know of Matt Stafford? They had spent a few days of fun-filled excitement together on a holiday island six years earlier, that was all.

'What's troubling you, Tessa?' Matt asked calmly, sitting down on the edge of the bed and reaching for her hand. He had watched the play of emotions on her face and sensed something was frightening her, but couldn't begin to imagine what.

'Nothing, I'm just tired,' she said dully, pulling her hand away. 'I really would like to get some rest.'

'Very well,' Matt said after a pause; obviously she wasn't about to confide in him. He got heavily to his feet and gazed down at her averted face. 'Try and eat your lunch. And don't worry about Abby – she's being well looked after.' He stroked her cheek gently with his palm, but Tessa turned her back on him, curling her body into a tight defensive ball until she heard the door close softly behind him.

Then she got to her feet and began pacing the room restlessly, sniffing the air to try and locate the source of the perfume. But, with the window open, the scent was no longer detectable, which proved absolutely nothing, she realized. She could have imagined it, or the fresh air could have dissipated it, or it could indeed have been clinging to Matt's clothing. But, if the latter were so, surely she would have noticed it earlier, either in the car or, more likely, when he was carrying her up the stairs?

She sighed heavily and ceased pacing, rubbing absently at her throbbing forehead. She had been warned at the hospital to expect some confusion, loss of concentration and maybe even lapses of memory – but no one had mentioned she might suffer from delusions!

In attempt to take her mind off her disturbing thoughts – and she couldn't make up her mind which was worse, a real live vicious woman or an hallucination – she began exploring her room and its en-suite bathroom which echoed the pink and gold colour scheme.

Her personal belongings, collected from her London flat, had been neatly laid out in cupboards and drawers, her clothes hanging in the wardrobes. She discovered yet more evidence of Evelyn's generosity – unless Matt had been clothes-shopping for her, which she somehow doubted! There was expensive lingerie, new dresses, skirts and sweaters, even shoes and handbags tooled from the finest, softest leather.

Tessa fingered the lovely garments, but wasn't sure she appreciated this gesture – okay, so she hadn't possessed an extensive wardrobe, but her clothes were certainly not tarty or unsuitable, and she had certainly never been reduced to wearing rags!

She told herself not to be so ungracious and turned to examine the array of cosmetics and toiletries laid out on the cream and gilt dressing table. Feeling somewhat foolish she nevertheless unstoppered all the bottles and sniffed the contents – like a demented bloodhound, she told herself derisively. However, there was nothing that even resembled that which she had smelled earlier – these were all light, delicate fragrances.

'Get a grip, Tessa,' she said impatiently out loud, only seconds before a knock on the door startled her. It was Christine, bearing a lunch tray and eyeing Tessa rather oddly, she thought, grimacing slightly. The girl must have heard her talking to an empty room!

'Thank you.' Tessa moved over to investigate the appetizing smells, lifting silver covers to discover a melon starter with roast beef and all the trimmings to follow. 'It looks delicious.' She smiled warmly at Christine, knowing she had done much to ease Abby's fears and raise her spirits when she had been missing her mother. She was also a brunette, so, unless she had gone to the unlikely bother of hiring a blonde wig, she could not possibly be the woman who had appeared in her room last night.

'Just ring when you're ready for coffee and dessert,' Chris told her, then, seeing her puzzlement, indicated an old-fashioned bell-pull beside the bed.

'Oh, I see, thank you,' Tessa said, rather awkwardly, uncomfortable with the notion of summoning servants to do her bidding.

'Can I get you anything else, miss?'

'No, but please call me Tessa,' she said quickly. Really, she was surprised Evelyn didn't deck the staff out in floor-length aprons and mob caps! 'Oh, Chris?' she called, as she was about to leave. 'Were you in this room earlier today?' she asked casually.

'Yes, I brought some clean towels. Why – is something wrong?'

'No, everything's fine,' Tessa assured her. 'Er, was anyone else in here?' she asked, even more casually.

'Well, Mrs Stafford came in to check the room was ready . . .'

'Mrs Stafford?' Tessa repeated slowly, and she frowned. Evelyn was blonde and, while there was no doubt she welcomed Abby into her family, her feelings regarding Tessa might not necessarily be as fond.

'Was Mrs Stafford here last night?'

'No, she went out for dinner,' Chris told her, looking decidedly uneasy. She thinks I'm mad, Tessa thought, and she could well be right.

'I see. Thank you.' She smiled weakly, and Chris made her exit – gone to tell the rest of the staff Abby's mother is off her head, Tessa thought ruefully, as she settled down to her lunch.

She enjoyed her meal but grimaced slightly at the solid silver cutlery and napkin ring, the Royal Doulton china; she was unaccustomed to such luxury and certainly unused to the almost servile manner of the staff. Stafford House was more like a five-star hotel than a family home – a pleasant place to visit, but one wouldn't want to live there.

Not only did she feel uncomfortable about being waited on hand and foot, but, even worse, was the feeling of never being sure of complete privacy. Even in a house as large as this, curious eyes and ears must always be near, witnessing conversations and quarrels, details of which were no doubt later repeated and discussed amongst the staff, and thence to their families in the village. *Perhaps I should stop pussyfooting around and simply ask Chris outright about any sinister blondes in Matt's life!* Tessa thought wryly as she dug into her roast beef.

After her lunch, she slipped out of her dress and lay down on the huge, comfortable bed, intending to rest for only a short while before going in search of Abby. Instead, she fell fast asleep and didn't even stir when Abby and Matt walked into her room some twenty minutes later.

'I want her to come and meet Lollipop,' Abby stage-whispered, disappointed.

'Shh, she can meet him tomorrow.' Matt propelled her back out of the room and quietly closed the door behind him. When they were out of earshot, 'I'll race you to the stables!' he called and Abby, screeching with laughter, her disappointment forgotten, set off at a run, with Matt careful to be always one step behind.

Matt saddled up Lollipop for her and they set off, Abby riding while he chose to remain on foot, much to the disgust and loud disapproval of his own horse, Prince. However, Prince had already proved himself to be even more disdainful when expected to accompany a Shetland pony, having on a previous occasion taken bites out of and aimed vicious kicks at poor Lollipop when he thought Matt wasn't watching.

'Poor Prince – he wants to come with us. Will I be big enough to ride him soon?' Abby enquired brightly. Matt shuddered at the very thought.

'No, not for a long time,' he said quickly, and her face fell. 'Think how upset and jealous Lollipop would be if he thought you preferred Prince,' he added, and watched her expression as she mulled that over.

'Mmm.' She slowly nodded her agreement. I'm getting good at this child psychology bit, Matt thought, complacently and far too prematurely. 'Sorry, Lollipop, I didn't mean it,' she told him, completely disregarding everything she had been taught about riding as she flung herself forward to give him a consoling hug. Matt, with lightning reflexes he hadn't even been aware he possessed, just managed to prevent her from falling and righted her in the saddle.

'Oops! Thank you, Daddy,' she said cheerfully, while Matt was still sweating over the mental image he had of her splattered, bloodied and broken, all over the cobbled stable yard.

He wondered if all kids had such lack of fear, rushing headlong into things without a thought for danger. Bloody difficult, being a parent, trying to be constantly one step ahead, he thought, having completely lost the confidence of a few minutes earlier.

But he already loved being a father, loved Abby: all he had to do now was convince Tessa she would be happy as his wife, that they would make a success of being a family, that more children would add to their happiness . . . God, the list was depressing! Oh, so that's all I have to do, is it? Piece of cake! he thought ruefully.

Tessa awoke suddenly to the sound of Abby's voice outside in the hall and then Christine's, reminding her to be quiet. She smiled slightly, then stretched luxuriously, feeling refreshed after her nap and was amazed to discover she had been asleep for the entire afternoon.

Her headache had lessened considerably and she felt even better after she had splashed cold water on to her face. Then she quickly changed into jeans and a sweater – her own, not one Evelyn had bought for her – and slipped out of her room.

She hovered uncertainly in the long corridor, wondering in which direction Abby's room lay; there was no longer the sound of voices to guide her.

'Abby?' she called out, but there was only silence and blank, closed doors. Unwilling to intrude into the other bedrooms, Tessa made her way to the top of the stairs, then stopped abruptly when Matt came into view. He, too, had changed into jeans and an open-necked shirt, blue to match his eyes – a gift from a woman, she guessed. As always, he looked to be bursting with health and vitality and she continued watching as he began climbing the stairs, two steps at a time.

102

He checked when he saw Tessa leaning over the carved bannister rail and smiled warmly. Tessa felt her heart flip over. Get a grip, she counselled herself sternly. The gentleman prefers blondes – remember?

'I . . . I heard Abby, but I don't know where she went,' she stammered.

'I took her riding earlier and then Chris brought her up here to get changed. We looked in on you before we left, but you were sleeping like a baby,' he told her. 'Would you like to see her room?'

'Yes, please.' Tessa nodded. Matt climbed the rest of the stairs, then took her hand casually in his as he led her back along the corridor to the room opposite her own.

Tessa glanced down at their clasped hands, hers pale and small, engulfed in his large, tanned grip. She wished he would stop touching her; any physical contact between them reminded her too poignantly of the nineteen-year-old Tessa falling in love with a handsome Army officer. But she didn't pull away.

'Chris must have taken her to have some tea,' Matt said, when he discovered the room was empty.

Tessa stood on the threshold and looked rather vaguely around the room, too aware of Matt standing close at her side to register much. One side was semi-circular, forming part of the turret and consisted of three large multi-paned windows which gave the room a light, airy atmosphere.

'Chris has been sleeping in here with her,' Matt told her. 'I'll ask her to continue for a few more nights, shall I?' he asked. Tessa nodded, and began to look around.

There were toys aplenty, a huge rocking horse, a whole host of teddy bears and dolls filling the window seat, shelves stacked with picture books and jigsaw puzzles. The wardrobe door was ajar and Tessa glimpsed racks of new dresses and coats. Once again she experienced a pained resentment at how easily the Staffords had given Abby all the things she had wanted to give her but had been unable to afford.

'I suppose we have gone overboard a bit.' Matt seemed to divine her thoughts. 'We were only trying to distract her while she was upset about you being in the hospital,' he told her. 'And, don't forget, there were five years of birthday and Christmas gifts to make up for.'

'I understand,' Tessa sighed. 'But I don't want her becoming spoiled, Matt. I –' She broke off, staring in dismay at the TV set and video recorder that had caught her eye when she moved further into the room. Several cartoon videos lay on the carpet.

'Oh, Matt! A TV!' she exclaimed in annoyance. 'I've never allowed her to watch TV in bed. She's allowed to read for a short time and then it's lights out,' she told him firmly.

'Yes, ma'am! Are you sure you never finished your teacher-training course?' he teased, but she only scowled at him by way of reply. His grin faded and he raked his fingers through his hair.

'Okay, so it wasn't my most brilliant idea,' he conceded. 'It can soon be remedied, I'll just take the set out –'

'No, you will not!' Tessa snapped, and he turned to her enquiringly. 'How is that going to look to Abby?' she fumed. 'You give her something she has always wanted, and I take it away from her! Nice Daddy, nasty Mummy.'

'Oh, for God's sake! Do you want me to leave the bloody thing here or not?' he demanded irritably.

'Do whatever you want – that's what you usually do!' she snapped back, then turned on her heel and stormed out.

CHAPTER 6

Matt hurried after her – minus the TV set, she noted – and caught at her arm, pulling her to a standstill.

'Tessa, I'm sorry. I'm new at this parenting thing and I'm bound to make a few mistakes along the way – okay?' He smiled winsomely, but Tessa stared coldly back.

'Yeah, but when you make mistakes it's other people who suffer,' she said bitterly.

'Tessa, that's not fair,' Matt protested, hurt. 'All I want is for you and Abby to be happy and healthy,' he said earnestly.

'Sure you do,' Tessa scoffed. 'Just so long as we live where and how you want us to, of course!' She wished she could believe he had their best interests at heart and, where Abby was concerned, she did believe him. Or did she? She shivered as she recalled the vicious words hissed at her in the darkness of her hospital room – did Matt truly want her dead? If so, he certainly didn't have Abby's best interests at heart, only his own, for he couldn't possibly imagine Abby would be happier without her mother.

'You're looking very pale again,' he broke into her thoughts, sounding full of concern. 'Would you like to go and rest a while longer?'

'No, I need some fresh air.' She headed for the stairs. 'You said Abby was probably having her tea – where will I find her?'

'I'll show you,' he offered, leading the way downstairs and then to the rear of the house, pausing briefly to point out the formal dining-hall, a huge room with high, ornately moulded ceilings. The walls were deep red except for one vast tapestry of a hunting scene which almost covered one entire wall. The carpet was red also, with an Oriental design in the centre and around the borders.

The dining-table dominated the room and would easily seat thirty people, Tessa thought. Her three-room flat, plus tiny bathroom, would have fit into this one room with space to spare. She wondered if Abby had yet disgraced herself by spilling milk on what was obviously a valuable carpet, or marred the mahogany-polished sheen of the table with sticky fingerprints. She was ashamed to find herself rather hoping that she had . . .

'The kitchens are through there.' Matt pointed towards the door. 'And this is the breakfast-room,' he said, pushing open the door of a much smaller and somehow friendlier room. The furniture looked more comfortable, and Tessa could imagine sitting over a leisurely meal in this room, whereas she knew that in the dining-hall she would feel self-conscious and ill at ease.

'Hello, Mummy!' Abby beamed up at her, a 'moustache' of milk on her upper lip.

'Hi, sweetie.' Tessa moved to hug her, and automatically reached for a napkin to wipe her mouth. 'What have you had for tea? Apart from milk,' she added, pleased to see only crumbs on the plate in front of Abby.

'I've had peanut butter sandwiches and scrummy chocolate cake,' Abby announced.

'Would you like a cup of tea, Miss Grant?' Chris asked, either forgetting to call her Tessa, or reluctant to do so in front of Matt.

'Yes, please.' Tessa smiled gratefully.

'And me.' Matt pulled out a chair for Tessa and then sat down beside her. 'And I'll have some of that "scrummy" cake, please, Chris.' He grinned at her. 'How about you, Tessa?'

'No, thanks, just a cup of tea,' she said. But, when the cake arrived, together with smoked salmon sandwiches, scones and raspberry tarts with cream, it all looked so delicious that she soon found herself tucking in ravenously.

'Chris? Do you mind stopping over at night for a while longer?' Matt asked her. 'I don't want Abby disturbing Tessa if she wakes up during the night,' he explained, quite reasonably considering it was her first day out of hospital, yet Tessa found herself blushing, as if he had another motive for not wanting Abby to burst into Tessa's room unannounced . . .

'No, I don't mind; she's no trouble,' Chris said, ruffling Abby's hair affectionately. 'In fact, I'd sooner be here than at home – it's bedlam there and I don't get paid for babysitting,' she complained good-naturedly.

'Thanks, we appreciate it.' Matt smiled at her, then, when she had gathered up the used crockery and left the room, he leaned across to speak to Tessa, keeping his voice low so Abby wouldn't hear.

'How would you feel about hiring Chris full time?' he asked.

'It won't be necessary when I'm fully recovered. Besides, I prefer looking after Abby myself,' Tessa responded, rather coolly. Abby would only need a full-time nanny if something happened to prevent her, Tessa, from caring for her. She gazed at Matt searchingly, wondering if he really did want her out of the picture . . . permanently.

'I know you like to look after her yourself, but the Dower House is quite large – you'll need some help and it might as well be someone Abby gets along well with.'

'The Dower House?' Tessa repeated.

'That's where we'll live after we're married,' he began, forgetting to speak quietly.

'Married!' Abby exclaimed, and clapped her hands in delight. Tessa sighed heavily. 'You're getting married! Hurrah! Can I be a bridesmaid, can I, Mummy? Can I?' she pleaded, dancing around the room.

'You had no right to mention that in front of her,' Tessa hissed at Matt. 'I told you I wanted to put that ridiculous idea on hold.'

'Our daughter doesn't think it's a ridiculous idea,' Matt pointed out, grinning. Then, 'We're a family, Tessa,' he said firmly. 'The sooner you accept that, the better it will be for all of us.'

'Really?' she sneered.

'Really,' he confirmed, ignoring her tone. They locked glances and it was Tessa who looked away first.

'Stop dancing around, Abby, you're making me feel dizzy,' she told her.

'Can I be a bridesmaid. Please?'

109

'*If* we get married, yes you can. But nothing has been decided, yet, so don't talk about it to anyone else – okay?'

'Okay, Mummy.' Abby leaned against her contentedly, and Tessa hugged her close to her side. Matt watched them, so alike, so perfect. His family, whether Tessa liked it or not. Which reminded him of another hurdle to be crossed.

'Do you feel well enough to dine with my parents this evening?' he asked Tessa.

She hesitated, then, 'I'd prefer not to,' she said apologetically. 'I'd rather just have a bath and an early night after I've put Abby to bed. Will they think I'm being rude?' she asked. It was obvious from his absence upon her arrival that George Stafford disapproved of her and she feared that eating in that huge formal dining-room would prove to be something of an ordeal; certainly it was something she didn't yet feel well enough to cope with.

'Of course they won't think you're rude. It's your first day out of hospital; they'll understand that you're tired,' Matt said equably. 'As for putting Abby to bed, Chris can easily do that – I know,' he forestalled her interruption. 'You prefer to do it yourself?'

'That's right; I do.' She smiled slightly, feeling as if she had won a small victory. Well, it was a start, she consoled herself. 'Bathtime, Abby.'

'Okay. Then can I watch my Disney video in bed?' she asked eagerly. Tessa avoided Matt's eye.

'Just for a short while,' she conceded.

'Make the most of that TV, young lady,' Matt put in. 'That is a treat just for the holidays – as soon as you go back to school, the TV will be put away,' he said

110

firmly, glancing at Tessa as if expecting approval for the compromise. She kept her face impassive, but notched up another tiny victory.

'Aw!' Abby pouted.

'Aw, nothing,' Matt said firmly. 'Now, you heard your mother – bathroom. I'll come up and say good-night later.'

'Okay.' Abby's frown vanished and she reached up to kiss his cheek before holding out her hand to Tessa.

Bathtime had always been a lengthy process. When Tessa had been out at work all day, she had really enjoyed the fun and chatter as she prepared Abby for bed. Abby never wanted to go to sleep until she had narrated every last detail of the day's events. She was such a little gossip, with her 'she said this and then I said . . .' and, 'you'll never guess what so-and-so did . . .'

Matt could hear the shrieks and laughter as he neared the bathroom and he paused on the threshold, unnoticed, and watched them play. Tessa was kneeling on the floor beside the bath and was almost as wet as Abby, with a blob of shampoo on her nose. She was laughing with Abby and looking as young and carefree as the Tessa he had known six years earlier. All traces of the hostility and cynicism with which she had been treating him recently had gone.

He felt a painful tug on his heartstrings – how many thousands of moments such as these had he missed over the years? He knew he would never stop regretting the lost years, the most impressionable of a child's life, but knew also that he had to stop resenting Tessa for depriving him of so much they should have shared.

111

He understood why she had kept her pregnancy secret from him and knew many men would have been relieved not to have a holiday indiscretion return to haunt them. However, knowing and accepting the facts on an intellectual basis was one thing, banishing the pain, anger and regret was something different and far more difficult.

'That looks like fun – may I join in?' he asked lightly, moving into the room. Instantly, the laughter died in Tessa's eyes and she edged away when he hunkered down beside her. Wasn't she even to be allowed a few minutes alone with her own child?

'I've told my mother you're too tired to join us for dinner. Chris will bring something to your room,' he told Tessa.

'Oh, that's not necessary,' Tessa said quickly. 'I ate a huge tea.'

'Hardly huge,' Matt demurred. 'You must eat. How about something light – soup and an omelette?' he suggested.

'Yes, that will be more than enough. I don't want to be a nuisance,' she stammered.

'You're not a nuisance,' he assured her. 'We want to look after you, so just relax, will you?'

'Okay,' she smiled.

Later, they both helped Abby complete a jigsaw puzzle, perched either side of her on her bed. On the surface it was a happy family scene – Abby, now that she had her mother back with her, was certainly enjoying her new life, Tessa acknowledged, but the tension between her and Matt was almost palpable. Why couldn't he just accept that she didn't want him to take control of their lives? He was behaving as if she were Abby's age and had neither the right nor the intelligence to choose her own path.

Her headache had been gradually worsening for some time, and finally she conceded defeat and kissed Abby goodnight.

'Don't have your bath water too hot,' Matt cautioned her. 'You might faint. In fact –' his eyes gleamed '– I think I ought to come and supervise . . .'

'No, thanks,' Tessa declined shortly. Really, this was intolerable! Wasn't she even to be allowed to take a bath in privacy? Was there no limit to Matt's interference? Apparently not, for he did indeed barge unannounced into her bathroom. Fortunately, Tessa had sprinkled bubblebath liberally into the hot water and was completely covered by foam.

'Go away!' she hissed.

'I'm glad you don't wear those dreadfully unflattering shower caps,' he commented, perching on the edge of the bath and gazing down into the frothy water as if hoping he would suddenly be granted X-ray vision. 'They're such a turn off.'

'I'll be sure and remember to buy one when I go shopping,' Tessa retorted, wishing she had more than one flannel to cover all strategic points. Matt merely grinned, not a whit perturbed, she thought crossly.

'Come on, get out of that bath. Your dinner's getting cold,' he said bossily. Tessa ground her teeth in anoyance.

'Go away!' she repeated loudly.

'Come on, Tessa, don't be shy. After all, I have seen you naked before.'

'Go *away*!' she yelled.

He went, but he was laughing his stupid head off, she fumed, as she quickly towelled herself dry and wrapped herself in a voluminous robe, tying its belt securely against his return.

After picking at her meal, she climbed into bed and switched out the light, but sleep was elusive. She tossed and turned for hours, half-expecting Matt to reappear and demand his pre-conjugal rights, if such a thing existed. If not, he would probably invent it, she groused.

But he didn't return: her only visitors were Chris, to collect the debris from her meal, and Evelyn, to enquire if she had everything she needed. To Tessa's dismay, her heart leaped each time there was a knock on her door, but she refused to admit, even to herself, that she was the least bit disappointed not to see Matt. It would be the utmost folly to allow him to seduce her into falling in with all the plans he was making for her future.

In the darkness and silence of her room, she conceded that it would be very easy for the flames of passion to be rekindled, but, until she had discovered the identity of the mystery woman and knew if she had spoken truly of Matt's wish that she had died, she must do nothing that would lead only to heartbreak.

Not for the first time, she wondered if she should confide in Matt, ask him outright – for surely he would know, or could guess – who bore her such ill will? But – could she trust him to tell her the truth? The question remained unanswered and finally she fell into a fitful sleep.

Her slumber was undisturbed by nightmarish visions of her unknown enemy and she awoke, feeling refreshed and looking forward to the day ahead. As she climbed out of bed, she was pleased to discover that the bruising and stiffness had lessened considerably and so, too, had her headache.

Pulling on a robe, she went to say good morning to Abby. Chris was alone in the turret room, tidying up, and told her Abby was with her father in the stables. Tessa declined her offer of breakfast, biting back the comment that Abby should be tidying her toys away herself, and returned to her own room for a quick shower before donning jeans and a sweater.

She had yet to explore the beautiful and extensive grounds of Stafford House, having caught only a glimpse of them from the car when she arrived, and later from her bedroom window. She asked Chris for directions and then made her way outside, breathing deeply of the fresh early morning air.

The sun was shining brightly, yet there was a distinct chill, heralding the rapid approach of autumn, more noticeable here in the countryside, where the trees were already changing colour and losing their leaves, than in London. The peace and tranquillity were also a far cry from the busy city streets to which she was accustomed.

She walked into the cobbled courtyard that housed the stable-block and then paused, watching the scene in front of her with a slight smile curving her lips. Matt, in jeans and a sweater, was grooming a huge black horse: at his side, standing on a box to give her added height, was Abby, her face a study in concentration as she tended Lollipop, faithfully copying Matt's every move. The Irish Wolfhound, Flynn, was lying contentedly on the cobbles at Matt's feet, his eyes bright with interest.

Tessa was about to move forward to join them when the sound of approaching hooves made her pause. She shielded her eyes against the low sun as the rider, a woman, reined in beside Matt, whipping off her hard hat to allow long blonde hair to cascade down her back, reaching almost to her waist.

Tessa frowned and stepped back slightly, into the shelter of the wall, instinct telling her she would learn more if she remained unobserved.

'You're up early, Matt!' the woman called out. 'I thought you'd still be in bed, now you've got what's-her-name installed in the house –'

'Shut up, Helen!' Matt interrupted, jerking his head towards Abby.

Tessa, realizing she would now hear nothing incriminating, began walking towards them with her eyes fixed firmly on the rider, trying to find a similarity between the girl and her hospital 'visitor'. But, apart from the blonde hair, she could find no resemblance, and surely the voice was higher, clearer, than the malevolent, low-voiced hiss of the intruder?

'Good morning, Tessa.' There was only pleasure in Matt's eyes and voice when he spotted her. 'Did you sleep well?'

'Yes, thank you. Hello, sweetie.' She hugged Abby, keeping a wary eye on Flynn. Big dogs always seemed to look hungry when they gazed at her! She was also trying, unobtrusively, to keep her distance from Matt's horse, who revealed a mouth full of wicked-looking teeth when he accepted some sugar from Matt. She knew she was being pathetic, afraid of his dog and now his horse, when Abby had accepted both without a trace of fear, but, unlike Matt, she had not grown up accustomed to such animals – in fact, the only pet she had ever owned had been a hamster!

'Hello.' She looked pointedly up at Helen, waiting to be introduced.

'Tessa, this is my sister, Helen Warrender,' Matt supplied, and Tessa felt almost dizzy with relief. 'She and her husband, David, own Grange Farm, a couple of miles from here.'

'Hello, Tessa!' Helen smiled broadly. 'Sorry we've not met before – David and I were on holiday and missed all the excitement!' she said gaily. Matt's brows rose.

'Hardly excitement,' he demurred. 'We were all extremely worried about Tessa.'

'Oh, I didn't mean that!' Helen said, with a dismissive gesture of her hands that set her horse to rearing. 'I meant discovering you had a daughter – you must be Abby.' She smiled down at the child, but Tessa thought it was rather a forced effort. Abby evidently thought so, too, for she merely nodded slightly and, most unusually, kept silent.

'Do you have children?' Tessa asked, thinking it highly unlikely, but wanting to know if Abby had any cousins.

'God, no.' Helen almost shuddered, reinforcing Tessa's impression that she didn't care for children.

'Helen won't have children because that would mean she would have to become an adult,' Matt informed Tessa.

'Not true!' Helen protested, aiming a kick at Matt. Her action caused her horse to rear again and Matt grabbed hold of the bridle.

'If you can't control that animal, you shouldn't ride him!' he snapped.

117

'Sorry!' Helen struggled to keep the horse at a standstill. 'I only collected him yesterday; I haven't decided what to call him yet – his previous owners called him Butch – can you imagine anything so awful?' she trilled. 'Any ideas for a suitable name?'

'Neck-breaker?' Matt suggested drily. Helen pulled a face at him, but she finally succeeded in quietening the horse and began scrutinizing Tessa with avid curiosity. Suddenly, she leaned forward in the saddle and her blue eyes narrowed to slits. 'That's Grandmother's ring you're wearing; I always wanted that,' she said petulantly.

'Helen!' Matt thundered, as Tessa gasped at such blatant rudeness.

'Oh, no offence meant,' Helen said quickly. 'Do forgive me, Tessa, what a tactless thing to have said!' Tessa nodded slightly, but said nothing to reassure her. Tactless, yes, and deliberate, she thought. Evidently so did Matt.

'It was also extremely bad-mannered!' He glared at her, clearly angry. 'Shouldn't you be at home cooking David's breakfast?' he growled, and Helen grimaced.

'See what a male chauvinist pig he is?' she asked Tessa, before turning back to Matt. 'My lord and master is away for a few days, so I'm off the leash!'

'Pity,' Matt said drily. 'You need a leash – or perhaps a muzzle,' he added, but Helen chose to ignore his sarcasm.

'As soon as he returns, you must bring Tessa over for dinner one evening. Of course, I had intended inviting you and Belinda . . . oops!'

'God, you can be such a witch at times,' Matt said disgustedly. 'Get out of here before I save that horse the bother of breaking your neck by doing it myself,' he added wrathfully.

'I didn't mean to put my foot in it,' Helen protested, not too convincingly. 'Oh, okay, I'm going,' she said hastily, when Matt made a menacing move towards her. 'See you soon!' With that, she jammed her riding hat back on her head, dug her heels into the horse's flanks and galloped off. Tessa had refused to give her the satisfaction of seeming to be upset by her mention of Belinda, but now she turned on her heel and stalked back towards the house.

'Tessa!' Matt called, and moved in pursuit, checking briefly when he realized Abby would be alone. 'Ned?' he beckoned to the groom. 'Keep an eye on Abby, will you?' he asked, and then hurried after Tessa.

'Tessa, wait! Let me explain about Belinda,' he began, placing his hand on her arm and pulling her to a halt. Angrily, she shook him off.

'There's nothing to explain. Your private life is none of my concern,' she said loftily.

'Of course it is. Just as yours is my concern,' Matt told her, eyes narrowing as it occurred to him that she might be planning to see another man. Abby had told him Tessa didn't have a boyfriend, but he realized Tessa might well have kept a liaison from her child. Tessa shrugged carelessly.

'If you say so,' she said blandly. 'Now, if you'll excuse me, I'd quite like to go and have some breakfast,' she added, although she felt food would stick in her throat.

'In a moment.' Matt blocked her path. Tessa gave a theatrical sigh.

'I really don't want to hear about your sex life,' she said coldly.

'I wasn't intending to go into details,' Matt said, and he was actually grinning, damn him! Then he became more serious. 'I admit I haven't been celibate for the past six years,' he went on. 'And Belinda Croxley was my girlfriend –'

'Don't you mean mistress?' Tessa interrupted.

'No, I didn't pay her bills. Girlfriend, lover, what's the difference?' he said impatiently. 'The only thing you need to know is that it's over. I've told her that I won't be seeing her any more. You and Abby are the only girls in my life now,' he added softly, and Tessa bit her lip, staring resolutely down at the ground, scuffing the cobbles with her toe. 'How can I convince you that I'm serious about our marriage, Tessa?' Matt continued. 'Don't you believe I'll be faithful to you?' he asked earnestly.

'I don't know what to believe,' Tessa said finally. 'It's Abby you really want, isn't it?' she asked painfully. 'No, don't answer that,' she added quickly, not wanting to hear the unpalatable truth. But Matt answered her anyway, slowly putting his thoughts into words.

'Abby is the main reason I want us to set up a home together as soon as possible,' he conceded. 'But, even if you had been alone in the coffee shop that day, I would still have approached you, would still have wanted to see you again,' he said quietly. 'Remember, I didn't realize Abby was my daughter at that point – it was you I was interested in.' He paused, knowing he was betraying too much of himself – letting Tessa know how much she had hurt him in the past was to lay

120

himself open to further pain. But Helen's crack about Belinda had undoubtedly hurt Tessa, he thought, so he continued opening his heart. 'Six years ago, I tried to find you, I even returned to Cyprus, but your aunt had left and the house was being rented by a couple who didn't have her address.'

'You went back to Cyprus?' Tessa's head had jerked up at that piece of news.

'Yes,' Matt confirmed, with a rueful smile. 'I was crazy about you, Tessa,' he said quietly. 'I hated that four months I spent in Bosnia, especially when you stopped writing. All I could think about was getting back to find you . . .'

'I'm sorry,' Tessa whispered, near to tears. What a fool she had been not to have trusted him.

'Don't be upset,' Matt said quickly, reaching out to stroke her cheek. 'I found you again, that's what matters now. The future, not the past,' he said firmly, and she nodded and smiled, albeit rather shakily. 'Good. Now – did you mention breakfast?' he asked briskly, and began guiding her towards the house.

'Matt? Belinda – is she a blonde?'

'What the devil . . . ?'

'Is she?'

'Yes, as a matter of fact, she is. She's also history, so let's drop the subject,' he said firmly.

'Okay.' Tessa resisted the impulse to ask him if Belinda wore heavy, musky perfume – he'd think she was crazy. 'I didn't know you had a sister – what's her husband like?' she asked, simply to change the subject, not because she was particularly interested.

'David? Nice enough guy,' Matt said casually. 'He's an Australian, some years older than Helen – and extremely rich,' he added.

'Is that why she married him?' Tessa asked, for there was something in his tone that suggested David Warrender's money was an important factor.

'That's a little harsh. Let's just say I doubt she would have married him if he'd been poor,' Matt clarified. 'My father's always spoiled Helen rotten and David has continued the habit. He would like to return to Australia, but she refuses to go. He only bought Grange Farm so Helen wouldn't have to move far from Stafford House. He's a businessman, not a farmer. I think you'll like him,' he added. Good, because I don't think I'm going to like Helen, Tessa thought silently.

'Are she and Belinda friends?' she said instead, suddenly realizing the probable reason for Helen's prickly attitude. Prickly attitude? Don't be prissy, Tessa – downright bitchy, she amended.

'Yes, they are,' Matt confirmed. 'That's how I met Belinda – at a dinner party Helen and David gave,' he explained briefly. 'Don't worry, Tessa. Belinda understands the situation and she's far from heartbroken. Her ego's slightly dented, but that's all,' he added drily.

'Good.' Tessa smiled, and wished she were as confident as Matt. Sometimes the nightmare that had invaded her hospital room seemed just that, a bad dream. But at other times the memory of that malevolent voice wishing for her death was terrifyingly real.

For a moment, she was tempted to confide in Matt, but her courage failed her. If the voice had spoken

122

truly, and Matt did indeed wish she had died . . . she shivered. He would deny it, of course, but something in his voice or expression would betray his true feelings.

She felt sure that Belinda – if it had indeed been her – would not have told Matt of her hospital visiting. It had been the act of a spiteful, vengeful woman, cast aside by her lover, however reluctantly, in favour of another whom he intended to marry, for whatever reasons. No, Belinda wouldn't have told Matt what she had done and his shock and anger would be obvious, if only for an instant. So she couldn't risk confronting him until she felt able, physically and emotionally, to face the truth and, if necessary, leave Drake's Abbot.

'Tessa? You're miles away,' Matt intruded into her dark thoughts and she summoned up a smile.

'I was just thinking . . .' She racked her brains for an alternative subject. 'Don't you also have a younger brother?' she asked, vaguely remembering him mentioning the fact six years ago. Only briefly – they had been too wrapped up in each other to waste precious time thinking or talking about other people.

'Yes, Ricky. He phoned a couple of days ago. He'll probably be dropping in, unannounced, when it suits him. He's in Italy at the moment, finishing off a project,' he added, and the final words were obviously a euphemism.

'Project?'

'Mmm, he's an artist, a very talented one. However, he decided to specialize in painting nudes.' He slanted a grin at her. 'Always female, young and married. He also always beds them – and somehow succeeds in

123

getting the husbands to pay a fortune for the portrait when he finally gets around to finishing it!'

'You sound jealous,' Tessa commented. 'And he sounds fun!'

'I'm not jealous, and yes, he is fun, the young devil. But don't let him talk you into posing for him,' he growled, placing a possessive arm around her waist. 'He always wants what I have. I've never minded before, but now I do. If he makes a move on you, I'll break his legs!'

CHAPTER 7

'You're not serious!' Tessa was shocked; the bantering tone of voice had become more than a little threatening.

'Let's just hope he doesn't put it to the test,' Matt said neutrally.

'If he's always wanted what you have, why didn't he follow you into the Army?' she asked. Matt smiled and seemed to relax slightly.

'He did. But he didn't even make it through Sandhurst. He walked out just before he was chucked out, much to my father's disgust. I wasn't here at the time, but I believe the bellowing could be heard for miles around! Here we are.' He ushered her into the house by yet another side entrance and they made their way to the breakfast-room.

'Sit down.' Matt pushed her gently into a chair and then began plying her with food, piling a plate high from an assortment of hot covered dishes on the sideboard. Tessa sipped at freshly squeezed, chilled orange juice and buttered some toast. The food looked and smelled delicious and she began tucking in hungrily.

'It's all home-produced,' Matt told her, when she commented on its wonderful taste. She paused for a moment, eyeing the eggs with bright yellow yolks, the beautifully browned sausage and crisp bacon.

'Just don't introduce me to your pigs,' she said finally, then dug her fork into her food once more.

'You city girls,' Matt teased, grinning at her. 'Where do you think the supermarkets get their meat from?' he asked, as he poured coffee for them both and then pulled up a chair and sat beside her.

'I try not to think about it,' Tessa said honestly. She had often considered becoming a vegetarian, but lacked the will to give up some of her favourite foods. 'Aren't you eating?' she asked, surprised to see him sipping only at coffee.

'Abby and I had breakfast hours ago,' he said, rather smugly, and she wrinkled her nose at him, trying to ignore the sudden glow of happiness caused by the knowledge that he had come indoors merely to keep her company.

'That was lovely, but I'm afraid I can't eat any more,' she apologized, pushing away her plate. 'I haven't eaten a cooked breakfast for years.'

'Don't worry; have some more coffee.' Matt refilled both their cups and then began forking up her leftovers. 'Do you feel fit enough to go and look over the Dower House this morning?' he asked casually. Tessa's heart leaped; this was their possible future home they were discussing.

'Well, yes, okay,' she agreed, rather awkwardly. 'Is it far from here?'

'Not really, but it's too far for you to walk there until you're fully recovered,' he said. 'There's a short cut cross country, but it's about four miles by road. If you've finished eating, I'll go and get the keys to the house and bring the car round.'

'I'll fetch Abby . . .'

'Not necessary. She's already seen the house and loves it,' he assured her.

'I didn't mean that. I can't leave her here.'

'Of course you can. Tessa, there are other people to help take care of her now,' Matt reminded her gently, and suddenly, Tessa found that a comforting thought, not a threatening one. 'She'll be quite happy and safe with Ned and her pony,' he added, and she nodded.

Tessa's first glimpse of the Dower House drew a gasp of pleasure from her. It was large, set in wooded, well-tended gardens: the house itself was three storeys high, with dormer windows jutting from the red-tiled roof. The walls were thickly covered with ivy, the front door set back in a colonnaded porch. The paintwork was white, seemingly freshly painted, and the window panes sparkled with reflected sunlight.

'I thought it had been standing empty,' she said questioningly; this was nothing like the rather dilapidated building she had been expecting to see.

'It has. No one's lived here since my grandmother died, five years ago. But we've kept it in a good state of repair,' Matt told her, braking to a halt on the sweeping drive.

He took her hand to help her out of the car and continued holding it as he unlocked the door and led her inside. Tessa looked around with interest; the hall was large, with panelled walls and oak flooring. Double doors opened on to a spacious, airy drawing-room which ran the width of the house. Downstairs there was also a dining-room, a smaller, cosy sitting-room, a large kitchen, utility and storerooms.

'Just say the word and the decorators can be here this afternoon,' Matt said softly, watching the expression on her face as she wandered through the rooms. At least she approves my choice of house, he thought ruefully, even if nothing else I've done recently has pleased her.

Tessa glanced at him and smiled, but said nothing. It was a lovely house, and had a welcoming, homely atmosphere – unlike Stafford House, she found herself thinking, and was instantly ashamed of her ingratitude when everyone had been so kind and helpful.

'Come upstairs, wench.' Matt leered at her, and she let him take her hand again as they clambered up the wide, shallow steps which led from the hall to a half-landing and then split into two further flights at right angles. 'There are eight bedrooms, three bath-rooms –'

'Eight bedrooms? Were you intending installing a harem?' she asked.

'I suppose that's out of the question now, is it?' Matt queried regretfully, and laughingly dodged the punch she aimed at him. 'This will be our room,' he said soberly, and tensed a little as he stood back to let her enter first.

'Might be our room,' she corrected, trying to ignore the flutter of excitement his words had caused. She walked over to the French windows, which opened on to a balcony, and caught her breath at the panoramic view spread before her.

A lake shimmered beneath her, stretching into the

distance, bounded as far as the eye could see by mature woodland. There would be no sound from up here other than the call of the birds and the wind rustling the leaves.

'Lovely,' she breathed.

'Yes,' Matt agreed, but he was watching her, not the view. He thrust his hands into his pockets to stop himself touching her, and moved away.

They continued their tour through the house; it had every amenity, and Matt assured Tessa the heating, wiring, etcetera, were all in good order. All it needed was the cosmetic repainting and papering to their own taste, plus the purchase of new furniture.

'Abby said she would like this room,' Matt told her, opening yet another door, and Tessa smiled slightly, instantly guessing its attraction. The ceramic tiling surrounding the Adam-style fireplace featured a collection of animals – including a Shetland pony.

'And how about this one for a nursery?' Matt suggested softly. Instantly Tessa's smile vanished and she tensed. How stupid of her to forget her main function was to provide Matt with more children!

'Matt . . . you're going too fast,' she warned him, shaking her head slightly.

'I know; I wasn't suggesting we try for a baby here and now,' he strove to speak lightly, but his disappointment was acute. 'To misquote somebody: to conceive one child out of wedlock is unfortunate, two smacks of carelessness!' He smiled, but the gleam of desire in his eyes told a different story. Tessa looked away and walked over to the cushioned window seat.

129

'Don't you dare call my daughter unfortunate!' she chided lightly.

'Our daughter,' Matt corrected her, moving to sit beside her on the rather cramped seat, his body pressed against hers. He took her hands in his. 'You're cold,' he noticed, frowning. 'I should have turned the heating on.' As he spoke, he shrugged off his jacket and wrapped it around her shoulders, keeping his hands on the lapels.

'Thank you. It is a little chilly in here.' Tessa smiled gratefully, and huddled into its comforting warmth: it smelled faintly of Matt, she thought, a little dazedly, a clean, very male scent.

'You're welcome.' He leaned and touched his forehead to hers, then drew back slightly so he could study her more closely. Tessa waited, rather anxiously, for him to speak for his expression had become suddenly serious.

They were both too absorbed in each other, sitting close together within the confines of the window seat, to be aware of the blonde woman who was sitting and watching from her car parked in the lane which ran alongside the wood above the house.

'So, it's just your daughter you want, is it, Matt?' she asked mockingly, her hands gripping the steering wheel so tightly that her knuckles gleamed whitely through her skin. 'You lying bastard! And as for that pale-faced bitch . . .' Unable to witness any more, she savagely gunned the car into life and roared off, her jealous brain plotting and planning. One way or another, Tessa Grant would very soon be history! If she didn't leave Matt voluntarily, well, a more permanent solution would have to be found . . .

* * *

130

Inside the house, Matt was dimly aware of the distant roar of the car engine, but took no notice; all his attention was on Tessa.

'Why are you so against the idea of having another child? Did you have a bad time when Abby was born?' he asked softly. Tessa sighed heavily and shook her head slightly. Matt guessed the reason for her reaction, or lack of one, and smiled slightly. 'I know I'm only a mere man and can never understand, but I'd really like you to tell me about it. Was it rough?' he persisted gently.

Tessa nodded, not trusting herself to speak. She remembered crying out for him in her agony; at the time it had seemed unbelievable to her that he could be unaware of how much she was suffering in giving birth to his child.

Wherever he was and whatever he was doing, she had expected him to know what was happening and magically appear at her side. Of course, he hadn't, couldn't possibly, but, however unreasonable, her feeling of being betrayed and abandoned by him had persisted through the intervening years.

'I think there's a worldwide conspiracy amongst older women,' she said finally, forcing a smile. 'All that rubbish about it not being so bad, and that you forget the pain afterwards . . .' She shuddered: she would never forget. 'I'm convinced they only say that because they figure that they've suffered, so therefore the next generation should suffer as well!' She paused and bit her lower lip. 'I thought I would be okay; I'd been fit and healthy through-out my pregnancy and, although I was a little apprehensive about the birth, I was more worried about how I would cope afterwards as a lone mother.'

'Tessa –' Matt grimaced '– you didn't have to worry about that. Just one letter, one phone call, and I would have been with you.'

'I know that now,' she conceded.

'And you wouldn't be alone a second time,' he said earnestly, lifting her hand to his lips and brushing her fingers with a light kiss. 'You would have the very best medical care and all the support I could give you,' he continued. Tessa refused to look at him, tried to not even hear him. She almost wished he would try to browbeat her into submission – she found it so much easier to fight him when he was issuing orders than when he tried to coax her into agreement. He was hard to resist when he was pleading for something that obviously meant so much to him.

'I know it would probably be easier a second time,' she acknowledged. 'At least, my brain knows it, but my body and my emotions recoil from the very idea. It was the most painful, degrading experience . . .'

'Degrading?' Matt frowned. Tessa just looked at him expressionlessly. 'Oh. Sorry, I'm being a mere, insensitive male again,' he said, and flashed a lopsided, rueful smile at her.

'Abby would be jealous of another baby – she hates it if I pay attention to other children,' Tessa went on hastily, shamelessly trying to heap some of the blame on her absent daughter's head, and thereby hopefully deflect Matt's enthusiasm for another child. Or at least postpone further discussions for, say, fifty years?

'If she's possessive of you,' he said – with a slight emphasis of the 'if', Tessa thought, as if he had seen through her subterfuge – 'I'm sure it's only because she's had no one but you to rely on until now. There would be plenty of time for her to adjust to the idea of having a brother or sister and she would be settled, both at home and in her new school, months before the baby was born.' He was at his most persuasive, his voice soft and caressing and Tessa made the mistake of gazing up into his eyes; the longing she saw there was hard to ignore. He doesn't love you, she reminded herself sternly. The marriage might not work out and then you would have two children caught up in an unhappy home.

'Tessa.' The word was an endearment as he cupped her face gently in his and bent to kiss her, a butterfly touch to her mouth, asking, not demanding a response. Tessa felt herself weakening: oh, if only he loved her . . .

'Daddy! Where are you?' The shrill call from downstairs made them both start.

'Oh, God, she's seen the car. I should have hidden it,' Matt muttered. Tessa laughed, a little shakily. not sure if she was relieved or dismayed by Abby's interruption. This was probably the first time Matt had shown a preference for her company over Abby's, she thought.

'You'll get used to it,' she teased him, as he reluctantly moved away from her.

'She doesn't wake up during the night, does she?' he asked, in tones of mock anguish. Despite the bantering tone, his meaning was clear, and Tessa flushed.

'Frequently,' she assured him, her eyes bright with mischief and, since Abby's arrival ensured her safety, added, 'And she usually wants to climb into bed with me.'

'She can wait her turn,' Matt said drily, walking over to the door. 'We're up here, Abby,' he called, and Tessa heard the clatter of busy feet.

She was somewhat taken aback by the picture Abby presented when she burst into the room; kitted out in formal riding clothes from the tip of her polished boots to the top of the hard, black hat.

'Well, don't you look a proper little princess,' she said, privately thinking that, apart from the protection of the headgear, the child would be more appropriately dressed in old jeans and a sweater. Evelyn again, she guessed, and tried to feel grateful.

'Hello, Mummy! I didn't know you were here, too!' Abby exclaimed happily. 'Isn't this a nice house? Are we coming to live here?'

'Maybe,' Tessa prevaricated, and Matt forbore to comment. That 'maybe' was preferable to the vehement refusals and downright abuse to which he had been subjected a few days earlier.

'I've just seen Rachel,' Abby continued excitedly. 'And she's got –'

'Rachel?' Tessa looked enquiringly at Matt.

'Christine's youngest sister – she's around the same age as Abby,' he explained.

'Yes, and she's got pierced ears, with real gold ear-rings,' Abby told Tessa. 'Can I have . . . ?'

'No,' Tessa said firmly.

'Aw, Mummy. I want to have ear-rings!' Abby pouted.

'No!' Tessa repeated, more loudly, then her jaw dropped with dismay and disbelief as Abby, most uncharacteristically, scowled and poked out her tongue at her before appealing to Matt.

134

'Can I, Daddy?' she wheedled.

In two strides, Matt crossed the room and gripped Abby's shoulder, towering over her.

'Your mother said "no", and I don't want to hear another word on the subject,' he said sternly. 'And if you ever poke your tongue at her again, I shall be extremely angry and punish you. Now go and wait quietly downstairs.' He pushed her, albeit gently, towards the door and Abby ran out, her sobs and retreating footsteps the only sound in the room.

Tessa moved over to stare unseeingly out of the window, stunned and desperately hurt.

'See how quickly she has learned that you can give her the things I won't,' she said bitterly to Matt, and he reached for her, pulling her unresisting into the shelter of his arms.

'If so, I think she has just unlearned it,' he said calmly. 'But I am sorry, Tessa. You were right – we have spoilt her, given her too much, too soon. I'll tell my parents not to indulge any more of her whims without consulting you first.'

'You'd better.' Tessa wasn't ready to be mollified, and remained stiff and unresponsive in his embrace. 'If she returns home from a shopping trip with your mother with . . . mutilated ears, I shall walk out and take her with me.'

'No,' Matt said, rubbing gently at the tense muscles in her neck and shoulders until she began to relax beneath his ministrations.

'I mean it,' she said, but with rather less conviction than before.

'No,' Matt repeated, still calm. 'I won't let you go. I can't let you go,' he murmured and realized, with a sense of shock, that it was as simple as that. His feelings for his daughter were an entirely different issue; he could not lose Tessa again, and would feel the same way about her even if she had not borne his child.

'We ought to go to her,' Tessa said, a few minutes later, knowing she was weakening against the gentle but insistent pressure of his hands.

'She'll be okay.' Matt didn't move an inch, and Tessa found it quite impossible to pull away. She felt strangely comforted, yet excited, too. Her anger towards Abby had quickly vanished – after all, the child could hardly be blamed for testing the extent of Matt's indulgence. And at least he had backed her decision.

'She ought to be in school,' she said finally. 'She's no longer upset about the accident and she needs more than her new toys and her pony to keep her occupied. She also needs the discipline,' she added.

'You're a hard woman.' Matt shook his head in mock sorrow.

'And you and your parents are too soft!' Tessa retorted.

'Point taken.' Matt nodded his agreement. 'I'll arrange for us to go and talk to the headmistress, see if we can get her enrolled before half-term. Come on, let's go, I think she's had long enough to contemplate her sins!'

Abby was hovering by the open front door, and she looked up uncertainly as they descended the stairs. Her tear-stained face smote at Tessa's heart, but she kept her own features impassive.

'I'm sorry, Mummy.' Abby's lower lip trembled and

she ran to Tessa, wrapping her arms around her waist and pressing her face against her.

'I know you are. It's over now; let's just forget it,' she said, giving her a brief hug of forgiveness. 'Now, where's Lollipop?' she asked. Abby's face brightened immediately and she grabbed at her hand, urging her outside.

The reins of the Shetland pony were being held by a middle-aged man of kindly appearance, comfortably dressed in old cords and a faded plaid shirt. Matt introduced him only as Ned.

'Thank you for looking after Abby,' Tessa said warmly, as they shook hands. She knew from Abby's chatter that Ned had frequently accompanied her on her rides. 'I hope she's not pestering you too much?'

'Not at all; it's my pleasure,' he assured her.

'Thanks, Ned, but we'll take care of her now,' Matt told him. Ned hauled himself back into the saddle of his own horse with an agility that belied his years and urged the animal into a canter. The Shetland whickered impatiently and made as if to follow, but Matt quickly caught the reins.

'I think you have a problem, Matt,' Tessa told him casually.

'Another one?' He sounded outraged and Abby stifled a giggle, not sure if he were still angry with her or was joking.

'Mmm. The car, Lollipop, Abby and me. How are we all getting back to the house? Abby can't go alone on the pony and you said it was too far for me to walk,' she reminded him.

'Lollipop can sit on the back seat with me,' Abby

suggested, desperate to make amends with Matt and finding the – to her – logical solution.

'No fear.' Matt gave her a fierce look before turning to Tessa. 'I'll go with Abby and you can drive the car back,' he decided.

'No fear,' she echoed his own words, eyeing the Mercedes as warily as if it might bite. 'I haven't driven at all for years, and never anything as powerful as your car.' Or as expensive, she added silently to herself.

'You'll be fine,' Matt said dismissively. Tessa watched, with mounting apprehension, as he locked up the house, then reversed the Mercedes until it was back on the road and facing in the right direction.

'Come on, get in.' He held the door open for her as she still hesitated. Tessa sighed, but did as she was told. Her confidence took a further knock when Abby backed hastily away from the car, evidently thinking it would be wise to give Tessa plenty of room to man- ouevre.

'Can you remember the route?' Matt asked.

'I think so,' she nodded, experimenting with the gears.

'You're so small, you can barely see over the dash- board,' Matt teased her, reaching in to adjust the seat. 'I must get you a car of your own,' he mused.

'Oh, no, that's not necessary,' Tessa said quickly.

'Of course it is. You're not in London now – there are no buses or Tube stations out here.'

'I know, but . . .'

'Tessa, you'll need a car,' Matt insisted patiently. 'Abby will have to be taken and collected from school each day and it will be a great help if you

138

can do some of the journeys,' he said, making it sound as if she would be causing a nuisance if she didn't have a car. Tessa guessed it was a deliberate ploy, but she also knew it was true, so she decided to accept his offer graciously.

'Thank you; a car would be lovely. But just a little runaround,' she added quickly.

'Okay, whatever you say. And I'll put a spare can of petrol in the boot,' he said, grinning knowingly as if the remark should have some significance for her.

'A – what?'

'Cyprus. You'd only run out of petrol, not broken down at all,' he informed her, six years after the event.

'You never told me that!' Tessa gasped. 'Why did you pretend I – ?'

'Why do you think?' Matt interrupted, regretting the confidence and stopping further questions by dropping a quick hard kiss on her mouth before stepping away from the car. 'Off you go,' he closed the door and moved away to lift Abby back on to Lollipop's back.

Tessa waved in farewell, ignoring Abby's will-I-ever-see-you-again expression. She set off, rather slowly and nervously at first, musing that, if she had only filled up with petrol on that day six years earlier, Abby might never have been born. She put the disturbing thought from her and concentrated on driving, and quickly began to enjoy herself. Wow! This was some car! She put her foot down on the accelerator and exulted in the immediate leaping response from the engine.

Too soon, she reached the crossroads not far from Stafford House. She braked and studied the sign-post; knew she ought to return straight home, but the desire to drive further was well-nigh impossible to resist. Besides, no one would miss her; it would take Matt some time to walk back with Abby, she told herself.

She swung right, away from the house, heading back towards London as she retraced the route of yesterday. She sped along, her spirits rising with every mile until, all at once, exhaustion swept over her and the nagging headache worsened with every passing moment.

She had driven further than she had intended, not fully realizing how quickly and smoothly the Mercedes ate up the miles. She slowed and cruised along until she reached a lay-by, then cautiously reversed and turned the car and headed back in the direction she had just travelled.

Long before she reached Stafford House she was thinking longingly of the comfort of her bed, remembering, rather belatedly, Dr Stevens's instructions about resting for the greater part of each day. Perhaps he wasn't just an old fusspot, after all.

She began to find it increasingly difficult to concentrate and slowed her speed even more until she finally pulled up outside Stafford House and dropped her head wearily against the steering wheel.

'Where the hell have you been?' Matt's voice, harsh with anger, Tess thought, dismayed, broke into her near-faint. Actually it wasn't anger, but concern; his heart had almost stopped beating when he had discovered that Tessa had not yet arrived. She should have been back at the house long before him and Abby. He hauled her bodily, and none too gently, out of the car.

'Where have you been?' he demanded, in a slightly more reasonable tone of voice now he knew she was safe. He had envisioned her passing out at the wheel and crashing into oncoming traffic.

'I went for a drive – isn't that allowed? I haven't pranged your precious car!' Tessa glared at him and tried to pull herself free of his grip on her arms, but the dignified exit she had planned was more than a little spoiled when she swayed, the ground seeming to move beneath her feet.

'What is it?' Both Matt's voice and his grip gentled as he caught her in his arms.

'I'm just tired, and a little dizzy. I'll be okay in a minute,' Tessa assured him, suddenly grateful for his stalwart support.

'Oh, well, I did say I would carry you upstairs every day.' Matt smiled down at her as he swung her off her feet and strode indoors.

To Tessa's mortification, they passed a tall, grey-haired elderly man of military bearing as they moved towards the staircase.

'My father, George Stafford,' Matt announced to her cheerfully. 'This is Tessa, as you probably guessed. She's not feeling too well,' he explained before continuing on his way. 'At least the colour's returned to your cheeks!' he told a furiously blushing Tessa as he deposited her on her bed.

'I'm sorry I yelled at you downstairs, I was worried you might have fainted at the wheel. You look so gorgeous I keep forgetting you're convalescent,' he added, and placed a gentle hand to her cheek before turning away and walking out of the room.

141

Tessa stared after him, feeling the by now familiar maelstrom of emotions he aroused in her. She still deeply resented the way in which he had taken over her life and Abby's, but more and more often she remembered why she had fallen in love with him in Cyprus. Even if he had misled and manipulated her over the reason for her car breaking down! she thought crossly, but with a reluctant smile. It had been a roasting hot day and she had sat in the shade by the roadside while Matt had toiled beneath the blazing sun for no good reason other than to stay in her company.

She lay back and closed her eyes, forcing herself, before she got too carried away by happier memories, to remember Belinda's visit to her hospital room. She was sure her nocturnal visitor must have been Matt's ex-girlfriend, although it seemed inconceivable now that Matt could have wished her dead, as Belinda had claimed. He wanted to give her so much: his name, a home. He was making plans for a future together, sincere in his desire for more children . . . *too* sincere! she thought, with a grimace, and put that particular plan of Matt's to the back of her mind.

She considered the way in which he had chastised Abby earlier; that seemed to indicate that he wanted a partnership, not just to take over and usurp her own role as a parent. Stop avoiding the issue, she chided herself, and reluctantly turned her thoughts back to Belinda's words. She, Tessa, had been so ungrateful and hostile to Matt when she had first recovered consciousness, so she could hardly be surprised if he had been somewhat irritated.

142

Perhaps, in an outburst of angry frustration he had said something along the lines of: it would be easier if she had stayed in a coma! And Belinda had twisted the words for her own use. Yes, it must be something of that nature, she finally convinced herself before drifting off to sleep.

CHAPTER 8

Christine woke Tessa in the early evening, bearing a pot of tea and a request that she join Matt and his parents for dinner if she felt well enough. With the memory of her first embarrassing encounter with George Stafford fresh in her mind, Tessa was tempted to take the coward's way out and plead tiredness. Instead, she accepted the invitation with as much enthusiasm as she could muster.

'Where's Abby?' she asked.

'In her room. She's already had her bath,' Chris told her.

'Thank you.' Tessa drank her tea and then went to check on Abby, discovering that, although in her nightie, she was still up and playing with the contents of a huge, elaborately built and exquisitely furnished dolls house.

'Hello, poppet.' She stooped and kissed the top of her head. 'Are you ready for bed?'

'In a minute,' Abby gave the stock reply. 'I haven't had my supper yet,' she said, rather reproachfully. 'Chris is bringing me some milk and biscuits.' Tessa bit back the retort that sprang to her lips. In her opinion, Abby was rapidly becoming too accustomed to having people fetch and carry for her. Just as soon as she felt fully recovered and could take care of Abby herself, she would tell Evelyn there was no need for Christine's services.

'While you're waiting, you could tidy these toys away,' she said, for the large expanse of carpet was littered with games and stuffed animals.

'Chris does that.' Abby barely looked up from what she was doing.

'No, Abby, you do,' Tessa insisted, quietly but firmly. Abby glanced up at her, opened her mouth to argue, then, much to Tessa's relief, decided to comply, albeit with rather more noise than was necessary.

Tessa watched her for a moment, then, having made her point, she began to help her and Abby's slight scowl vanished as abruptly as it had appeared.

'Come and keep me company while I take a shower,' Tessa suggested, when the tidying-up was complete. 'You can pick out a dress for me to wear for dinner,' she added. She was reluctant to wear something Evelyn had bought her, yet it seemed rude not to, hence her decision to leave the choice to Abby.

'Does your grandmother dress up for dinner?'

'Mmm.' Abby nodded. 'A long frock sometimes and jewellery – white beads,' she added helpfully, from which Tessa deduced Evelyn was fond of wearing her pearls.

The cool spray from the shower banished the last vestiges of sleepiness and, after applying a little make-up and blusher, Tessa felt and looked almost her usual self.

Abby had picked out a cherry-red dress made of the softest, finest wool for her to wear – one of Evelyn's purchases – and Tessa slipped it on. It fitted perfectly, clinging to her slender curves, and the colour suited her, too. It wasn't something she would have chosen for herself, even if she had been able to afford it, but, after stepping into high-heeled shoes and studying her reflection in the full-length mirror, she was pleased with her appearance.

'Mummy? Look, here's a picture of Daddy.' Abby had been rummaging through the drawers of the dressing-table and now held out a photograph to Tessa, who took it and glanced at unthinkingly.

Then her heart gave a sickening lurch as she gazed at the picture of Matt, his arm around the shoulders of a tall, blonde woman who was talking to him, and very amusingly, too, judging by the broad smile on his face as he listened to her, all his attention seemingly focused on his companion. In fact, it appeared to Tessa that neither was even aware of the photographer's existence, so engrossed in each other were they.

Tessa let the snapshot drop from her hands, then rubbed her damp palms with a tissue. It meant nothing, she told herself: the photograph could be several years old, for Matt had barely altered in appearance in the six years since she had first met him. This woman could be a very old flame indeed . . . But why did she have to be a blonde? she thought wretchedly, as all the fears she had experienced that last night in hospital returned in full force. Was this Belinda Croxley? But Belinda was a friend of Helen's, and this woman appeared much older than Helen, even older than Matt, possibly in her forties. There was no

146

reason why Helen shouldn't have a close friend who was a dozen years older, of course, she realized.

'Where did you find it?' she asked Abby.

'In there,' Abby pointed to the otherwise empty drawer. Perhaps the woman had been a guest in the house, slept in this room? Tessa picked it up again and turned it over. The printed words 'MATT & SUE' leaped out at her. Not Belinda. 'Sue' probably had indeed stayed in this guest room, and slipped the snapshot into the drawer, intending to take it with her when she left, but had forgotten it, or not deemed it important enough to keep, she thought hopefully.

But she couldn't quite dismiss the more sinister possibility that this could be the woman who had entered her hospital room in the middle of the night to spit out her poison. It was so difficult to tell; the woman depicted in the photograph was obviously enjoying herself, her face animated, so different from the hostility which had emanated from Tessa's nocturnal visitor.

Try as she might, all Tessa could clearly recall was the sheen of blonde hair in the darkness of the room, the hard glitter of eyes, the sparkle of diamonds, real or fake and, of course, the heavy perfume. The woman's features had been so indistinct in the shadows that Tessa doubted very much if she would recognize her again if they met under very different circumstances. That knowledge made her shiver with sudden apprehension and a skin-crawling premonition that she would indeed meet her enemy again . . .

She heard Matt's voice outside and tossed the photograph back into the drawer and slammed it shut. Out of sight and, if not exactly out of mind, well, she definitely was not going to question Matt about it, she resolved firmly. She looked up and forced a smile when he knocked and entered the room. The look of appreciation in his eyes as he gazed at her did much to banish her fears of a rival.

'You look wonderful,' he told her softly. 'Would you like to come down for a drink before dinner?'

'Can I come?' Abby demanded.

'No!' Matt swung her up in his arms and held her above his head, then turned her upside down, causing her to shriek with laughter as she clutched at his knees. Tessa watched the horseplay with a smile, realizing what Abby had missed in the first years of her life, and knew she could never deprive Abby of all Matt had to offer.

'If you don't mind, I'd rather settle her down,' she told Matt. 'Besides, I'm not supposed to be drinking alcohol at the moment.'

She was pleased when Matt elected to stay upstairs, too, reading to Abby while she ate her supper. Tessa supervised teeth-brushing before tucking her in, inordinately glad that Abby still preferred the rather scruffy stuffed monkey as a night-time companion over the newer and larger soft toys she had recently acquired.

'I'll look in on you later,' Tessa promised, giving her a last kiss and feeling the usual surge of protective love as Abby's tiny arms reached up to hug her neck and bestow a kiss in return.

'I love you, Mummy,' she murmured.

'I love you, too.' Tessa stood back, watched her for a moment, then turned and slipped out of the room.

It felt perfectly natural to have Matt's arm around her waist as they descended the stairs, and she peeked at him from beneath her lashes. He looked especially handsome in a dark suit and white shirt, his dark hair brushed back from his forehead.

Unconsciously she pressed closer to his side; he glanced down at her and smiled, a heart-stopping smile that made her catch her breath. He might not love her, but he desired her, she was sure of that; he was generous and loving to Abby. He would love the mother of his son, she found herself thinking, and was jolted by the realization of how much she craved his love. That, of course, could only mean she loved him . . . oh no, not again, Tessa! she chided herself sternly. Remember what happened the last time you allowed Matt Stafford to seduce you! She was uneasily afraid that her warning to herself was both futile and rather too late –

'Good evening, Tessa.' Evelyn's voice broke into her thoughts. 'How are you feeling now?'

'Much better, thank you.' Tessa returned her smile. 'I hope we haven't kept you waiting? We were putting Abby to bed,' she explained.

'We have servants to do that!' Tessa stared in dismay at George Stafford as he stomped past on his way into the dining-room, and she felt Matt tense at his father's irascible tone of voice.

'Tessa prefers to do it herself, and I heartily approve,' he said sharply. Tessa bit anxiously at her lower lip; the last thing she wanted was to cause friction between father and son. Apparently the unreserved welcome she had received from Evelyn had been too good to be true, after all.

'Hmph!' George snorted, but at least he paused and then moved back to shake Tessa's hand. 'Pleased to meet you finally,' he said, not sounding at all pleased. Matt was still glaring at him and he added, 'That child is a credit to you.'

'Thank you,' Tessa murmured.

'And I quite agree about the pierced ears; I'm afraid my wife has been spoiling her outrageously,' he said – as if he hadn't, Matt thought drily.

'You've all been very kind to her,' Tessa said neutrally.

'Let's go through to the dining room, shall we?' Evelyn suggested, and led they way into the large room Matt had pointed out to Tessa earlier in the day.

A fire was now burning brightly in the open hearth, lending more warmth to the room than that of merely raising the temperature, and subdued lighting added to the welcoming atmosphere.

Tessa noted again the polished mahogany furniture, the gleaming silver cutlery and crystal glassware, the Royal Doulton china and reflected silently that her London flat would have fitted quite easily into this one room. She was glad she didn't have to do the housework!

Matt held out a plush velvet chair for her to be seated and gave her shoulder a reassuring squeeze before taking his place beside her.

The evening continued badly, despite the luxurious surroundings and beautifully cooked food. As soon as the staff had served the main course of pheasant, they left the room and, almost immediately, George Stafford began firing questions at Tessa, wanting to know about her parents, her father's profession, where she had lived and been educated. He wasn't making conversation, she realized quickly – he was interrogating her!

However, she answered him in as pleasant a manner as possible, constantly reminding herself that he was kind and generous to Abby, which was far more important than his attitude towards her, Tessa. Also, she didn't want Matt to explode in anger, which she worriedly sensed he was about to do – he had stopped eating and an increasingly dark frown was furrowing his brow.

Evelyn apparently shared Tessa's concern, for she suddenly intervened.

'For goodness' sake, do stop it, George! Let the poor girl eat her dinner in peace. What does it matter which college she attended? Tell me, Tessa, what did you think of the Dower House? Do you think you'll be happy in such an isolated spot after living in a city?' she asked brightly.

Aren't I supposed to be eating my dinner in peace? Tessa thought, hastily swallowing a bite of pheasant.

'It's a lovely house,' she said, rather non-committally, and Matt cast a quizzical eye in her direction.

'Does it need much work, Matt?' Evelyn turned to her son and Tessa switched her attention to her plate; everyone else had finished eating.

'Not really; mostly cosmetic. Fresh wallpaper and a coat of paint,' he told her.

'Oh, good. So, how soon will it be ready?' she asked. Matt grinned and turned to Tessa.

'What's she is really trying to ask is when are we getting married,' he said conspiratorially. Evelyn flushed slightly.

'Well, yes, there's a lot to do, organizing a wedding,' she said defensively. A short silence ensued and Tessa realized everyone was looking at her for an answer. There was a tense stillness about Matt, a pained wariness in his gaze and she experienced a flood of emotion for him that was frighteningly akin to love.

Why was she even hesitating? Resentment for being told what to do? Yes, that stll rankled; she felt she had managed rather well bringing up Abby alone, yet, while she had been lying in a coma, Matt had destroyed her old life, dismissing her efforts and hard work as not being good enough for *his* daughter.

It hurt to acknowledge that there was even an element of truth in his claims, but she knew Abby was happier, and certainly more secure, now than at any other time in her short life. No way could Tessa remove her from her father and grandparents.

'Christmas?' she hazarded. Matt relaxed perceptibly; not as soon as he had hoped, but a helluva lot better than the 'never' he had been half expecting.

'Two and a half months,' Evelyn mused. 'Yes, a Christmas wedding will be delightful,' she decided. 'The village church is a gem, and is always beautifully decorated for the holidays.'

'Church?' Tessa glanced at Matt. She didn't feel that was appropriate, especially as they would have their daughter as a bridesmaid.

'We'll discuss it later,' he said, under his breath: as far as he was concerned, that was a minor point. The binding marriage vows were all important.

'We'll have the reception here, of course,' Evelyn was continuing happily. 'And there's a wonderful dressmaker in Ashminster –'

152

'Am I allowed to arrange the honeymoon?' Matt enquired drily. 'Or do you want to do that as well?'

'Oh, Matt!' Evelyn flapped a hand at him.

'Six years too late for a honeymoon,' George muttered.

'Do be quiet, George,' Evelyn said, with unaccustomed acerbity. 'After all, the dates on our wedding certificate and Matt's birth certificate don't bear too close a scrutiny,' she added. Matt choked on his wine and glanced in amusement at his father. George shifted uncomfortably in his chair.

'Hmm! By the way, Matt,' he hastily changed the subject, 'I saw Dan Ellis at Rotary yesterday. He reminded me I ought to change my will now that we have a new addition to the family. You ought to do the same.'

'Oh, how morbid!' Evelyn exclaimed.

'No, he's quite right,' Matt said thoughtfully. 'I'd completely overlooked that. Dan's the family solicitor,' he explained to Tessa. 'I'll phone him tomorrow and ask him to redraft my will.'

'If that's what you want,' she said quickly, feeling, as Evelyn evidently did, uneasy by the turn in the conversation.

'You'd better get him to sort out Tessa's will, too.' George spoke to Matt as if Tessa weren't in the room. 'If anything happens to her before the wedding, you would have one helluva fight on your hands to keep your daughter,' he pointed out.

'Tessa?' Matt turned to her. 'Would you be prepared to sign a will naming me Abby's guardian?' His tone was casual, but deceptively so, Tessa thought, and she sensed how much it meant to him. She frowned

153

slightly, more than a little perturbed, but she knew it was sound common sense to do as he asked. And there was no doubt in her mind that she would not want anyone other than Matt to care for Abby if she could not.

'Yes.' She forced a smile.

'Thank you,' he said quietly, and then changed the talk to a happier topic. However, it wasn't long before Tessa was fighting exhaustion and wondering how soon she could make her excuses. Matt quickly noticed the tired droop to her shoulders and interrupted his mother's monologue regarding wedding arrangements.

'Tessa should have an early night,' he said firmly, getting to his feet and helping her to rise.

'Oh, of course, I'm so sorry.' Evelyn smiled at her. 'Sleep well.'

'Thank you. Goodnight.' She glanced at both Evelyn and George, but received no reply from the latter.

'I don't think your father likes me very much,' she said ruefully, as she and Matt walked upstairs.

'Don't worry about it; he doesn't like me too much, either,' Matt said cheerfully.

'I'm sure that's not true,' Tessa protested.

'It is true. He brought Ricky and me up to think for ourselves and now doesn't like the fact that we do.'

'What about Helen?'

'Oh, he indulges her every whim; always has done and still does. I guess he doesn't feel character-building is so important for a girl. Like I said, don't worry about him; he'll come around in time. He did say Abby is a credit to you,' he reminded her.

'Yeah, but I bet he thinks her good qualities have been inherited from you,' Tessa said drily, and Matt grinned as they paused outside her room and he opened the door. Someone had lit the fire and it cast a rosy glow around the otherwise darkened room.

Tessa glanced at the flames and remembered a cool night in Cyprus, and a fire on the beach . . .

'You looked like a beautiful gypsy that night,' Matt said softly, his memories obviously matching hers. 'Your hair and eyes so dark . . .' He wrapped a strand of dark, silky hair around his fingers and then gently stroked her cheek. 'Your skin so soft . . .' He bent his head towards her and Tessa stared up at him, mesmerized, knowing he was about to kiss her.

'Don't you prefer blondes?' she blurted out, and he drew back, startled.

'No, I prefer petite brunettes . . . You asked me if Belinda is blonde,' he suddenly recalled her question. 'I told you; that wasn't a serious relationship and it's over.'

'I know,' she said, but without much conviction.

'Then drop the subject and kiss me goodnight,' Matt ordered huskily. Tessa relaxed and smiled, ready and more than willing to comply.

'Daddy!'

'Oh, God, who nominated her your chaperon?' Matt muttered, drawing back as Chris emerged from the turret room.

'I'm sorry; she's not asleep and she heard your voice,' she said, eyeing Matt and Tessa with avid curiosity.

'It's okay, I'll –' Matt began.

'Daddy? Will you read me a story?'

155

'I'll read her a story,' he finished resignedly, and Tessa grinned. 'You go and get some rest; I'll settle her down,' he told her.

'Thank you. Goodnight.' Mindful of Chris watching them, Tessa reached up and planted a chaste kiss to his cheek before turning and walking into her room.

She got ready for bed, then, refreshed by her shower and released from the tension of being in her future father-in-law's disapproving company, felt less tired and decided to delay trying to get to sleep.

She turned off the light and curled up in an easy chair by the fireside. The heat was relaxing and comforting; she felt safe, snug and content. However, instead of lulling her towards sleep, the flickering flames brought back vivid memories of lovemaking in front of another fire, six years earlier.

Suddenly, heat of a different kind suffused her cheeks and she felt a deep, aching need within her. She stirred restlessly in the chair as all thoughts of sleep vanished completely, and, after a moment's hesitation, she stood up and walked towards the door.

Her heart was hammering loudly, her legs shaking, her whole body trembling with excitement and anticipation as she moved slowly towards Abby's room. She heard Matt's deep tones before she pushed open the door; then, as she stood on the threshold, clad only in a white nightdress of satin and lace, his voice died in his throat as he gazed at her.

After a moment, he looked intently into her eyes and found the answer he sought. He had to resist a schoolboy impulse to yell 'yes!' and punch the air with his fist.

'She says she's still not sleepy,' he told Tessa, with thinly disguised frustration, his eyes devouring her curves, plainly visible beneath the thin material covering her. Tessa smiled.

'Neither am I,' she said, and Matt groaned. 'I told you she ought to be in school,' she reminded him sweetly. 'She'd be tired, then.'

'I'll arrange it first thing tomorrow,' he muttered, but good-naturedly continued reading at Abby's urging.

'You've missed a page,' she accused him, a few minutes later.

'Have I really?' Matt sounded amazed, and Tessa grinned broadly. She had tried that ruse herself when she had been tired after a day at work and wanted Abby to settle down. It had never worked for her, either.

Tessa moved across to the second bed and curled up against the pillows, content to wait. There were many hours ahead, many nights of loving and many days of being a family. Somehow, she was sure of that now. Belinda, and Sue, whoever she was, well, they were in the past.

Finally, Abby's eyelids began to droop and she vainly tried to suppress a yawn. Matt put the book aside and Tessa stood up to straighten the covers and then tucked her in securely.

' 'night . . .' abby was suddenly fast asleep.

Matt watched her for a moment and then moved swiftly to take Tessa in his arms, moulding her pliant body against his as his mouth hungrily claimed hers, his tongue probing the soft sweetness within.

Tessa responded gladly, exulting in the knowledge of his obvious arousal. Her head fell back as he began to nuzzle her neck, his lips trailing kisses of fire down the column of her throat and then moving to the soft swell of her breasts.

His hands were roaming deliciously over her body, rediscovering every inch of her curves, and they both gasped as his fingers found and began stroking naked skin. Her nipples hardened instantly into aching peaks and Matt bent his head to the round fullness of each breast in turn, teasing with his tongue and gently biting, listening with pleasure to the soft sounds his ministrations elicited from Tessa. He lifted his head to gaze at her, noting her mouth, slightly parted and swollen from his kisses, her slumberous eyes made even darker with desire.

'I have to make love to you.' His hold tightened. 'But not, I think, in our daughter's bedroom,' he said, with laughter in his voice. Tessa had actually forgotten that they were still in Abby's room and she glanced quickly and guiltily towards the bed, but Abby was sound asleep.

'You'll get chilblains,' Matt told Tessa prosaically, noting her bare feet, and he swung her effortlessly into his arms. There was nothing remotely matter-of-fact about the look of desire in his eyes, though, and Tessa lifted her face to meet his kiss, her arms curving up and around his neck to pull him closer.

Without breaking the kiss, Matt manouevred them out of Abby's room and into Tessa's, where he lowered her gently on to the bed. Tessa still clung to his neck, letting go only to begin tugging impatiently at his shirt, an unwanted barrier between them. She ran her hands over the hard-packed muscles of his chest and then fumbled at the buttons with shaking fingers.

'Let me do that.' Matt raised himself slightly: he had discarded his jacket while reading to Abby earlier and now pulled the shirt over his head in one fluid movement, ignoring the buttons which were torn off and scattered in all directions.

He tossed it to the floor and Tessa's nightdress followed it seconds later. She reached out and touched him, first lightly and delicately with her fingertips, then she scratched with her nails. She heard a sharp indrawn breath when she let her hands trail slowly down the length of his torso, halting at the waistband of his trousers.

'Not yet, darling. You excite me too much,' Matt said honestly, already battling with himself to curb his impatience. She was temptation personified; he had never had such a craving to possess a woman as he had Tessa, both in Cyprus six years earlier and again now, proving, if he had needed such proof, that she was indeed the only woman he could marry.

He removed her hands from his waist and held both slender wrists in one hand while his other passed sensuously over her body, until she was writhing and moaning with the desperate need for them to be lying, naked and entwined, soaring together towards ecstasy.

'I'd almost forgotten how exquisite you are,' Matt said huskily. 'Soon, very soon, you will belong to me again and this time I will never let you go!' He raised his head and looked fiercely into her eyes, almost frightening her with his intensity. 'You're mine, Tessa, and don't you ever forget it. This perfect little body of yours is for my pleasure, and mine alone!' His words hit Tessa like a dash of cold water between the eyes: that's all she was to him – a body, to slake his need and, she remembered with horror, to provide him with another child. And she hadn't even begun taking her contraceptive pills!

She jerked her hands free, the sudden movement taking Matt by surprise and he released her at once, lifting his body away from her.

'What's wrong?' he asked, as she pulled herself further up the bed and out of reach.

'My ribs are still bruised,' she stammered, by way of excuse, but she didn't have to pretend to the tears which sprang to her eyes. They were real enough.

'I'm sorry,' Matt said contritely, running his hands lightly over the still-discoloured skin. Tessa flinched away. 'Did that hurt you?' He sounded horrified, but Tessa hardened her heart against him and turned her head away.

'Don't cry, darling, please,' he begged, reaching out to hold her gently in his arms. This time she didn't resist him, but remained, tense and unresponsive, in his embrace. 'I'm sorry,' he whispered against her hair, 'I've waited so long for you, it's hard to be patient now that I've finally found you again.' Tessa stayed silent, burying her face against his shoulder to hide her expression. Waited so long? But not without some distractions along the way, of course! He had admitted as much himself.

Matt realized he was not going to receive an answer, nor, he suspected, the real reason for her sudden change of mind. He masked his disappointment and kissed her lightly on the brow before getting to his feet.

'You'd better get some sleep. I'm going to take a shower – a cold one.' He grimaced, half-smiling to show he wasn't angry, but still he received no response. 'Tessa? Talk to me, please.' He stood by the bed, watching her and frowning slightly, but in puzzlement, not annoyance.

'I don't want anything like that to happen again,' she blurted out suddenly. 'Everything is happening too quickly. I'm scared –' She bit the words off.

'So I didn't hurt you physically?' Matt asked, his suspicions confirmed by her words. 'What was it, then? You wanted me as much as I wanted you. You can't deny it, Tessa. In fact, you initiated it,' he said bluntly.

'I know.' She flushed. 'I'm sorry; you have every right to be angry.'

'I'm not angry and you don't have to apologize. But I would like an explanation. Did I come on too strong? Is that what frightened you?'

'A little,' she conceded. But mostly she was afraid she was falling in love – again, would she never learn? – with a man who didn't love her, a near-stranger who seemingly had a string of blonde ex-girlfriends, one of whom wished that she, Tessa were dead . . .

'You don't have to marry me,' she said quietly. 'I wouldn't try and stop you seeing Abby, truly I wouldn't.'

'I thought we had settled this?' Matt said tightly. 'We are getting married, Tessa! What is this nonsense about? Abby told me there was no man in your life, but, if there is, you can forget him. Right now!'

'You asked Abby . . .' Tessa could hardly believe what she was hearing. 'You had no right to do that! But no, there is no one else. Not for me,' she added unthinkingly.

161

'Nor me. Is that what this is about? Belinda? Are you jealous, Tessa?' he asked, smiling with relief.

'Of course not,' she denied crossly, but he noticed she couldn't meet his gaze. His smile broadened.

'I told you the truth this morning. Belinda and I were lovers, but it's over, with no regrets on either side. I'll be faithful to you, Tessa, and I demand your complete fidelity in return,' he added sternly.

'Everything is happening so quickly,' she said again, rather helplessly.

'On the contrary, everything is happening six years too late,' Matt contradicted her.

'I know so little about you.' She shook her head in confusion. 'And you know just as little about me – except what Abby has told you, of course,' she added tartly.

'I know all I need to know. And so do you, if you would only stop being so stubbornly independent and admit it,' Matt countered confidently. 'What do you want from me, Tessa?' he asked gently. 'You can have anything you want, except your freedom, for I don't intend to ever let you go,' he warned her.

Tessa stared at him, and the awakening knowledge that what she really wanted from him was his love frightened her more than the threat posed by Belinda, or Sue, or whoever else might have crept into her hospital room.

She might not have felt so dismissive about that threat if she had been aware of the blonde woman parked outside Stafford House at that very moment . . .

'You'll have all the time you need to get to know me between now and our wedding in December,' Matt said quietly, but implacably. 'Anything you haven't

162

learned about me by then will have to come as a surprise, hopefully a pleasant one. Now, you need to get some sleep – your headache's bad again, isn't it?' he asked, placing a gentle hand across her forehead.

'Yes, it is.' Tessa had been only dimly aware of the increasing pain, too preoccupied emotionally and mentally to register the growing physical discomfort. 'How did you know that?'

'I could see it in your eyes,' he told her, lightly caressing the shadows beneath them with his thumb.

'Oh.' She glanced away, not knowing how to respond. Matt dropped his hand.

'Do you need anything else?' he asked politely. Tessa glanced at the bedside cabinet; at the full carafe of water and a box of biscuits someone had placed there.

'No, thank you,' she replied, just as politely, resisting the urge to plead for his love. She wished she could be as open and uninhibited as Abby, demanding his time, attention and love, and being confident of receiving it.

'Good night, then.' Matt dropped a chaste kiss on her brow, and then left.

Tessa swallowed two of the painkillers she had been given before leaving hospital and switched off the light. The fire in the hearth had died down but still cast a soft, comforting glow around the room, and she turned on her side to watch the flickering embers as she drifted off to sleep.

CHAPTER 9

The following morning, Christine brought Tessa breakfast in bed, plus a message from Matt informing her that he had arranged for them to see Mrs Everett, the headmistress of St Hilda's school in Ashminster, and could she please be ready to leave by ten-thirty. That was quick, Tessa thought, wondering if it was Abby's need for discipline that had prompted his haste or the child's interruption last night when things were, well, getting interesting?

'Do you know if Abby is coming with us?' she asked Christine.

'Yes. Matt suggested she wear her school uniform,' Chris told her, grimacing slightly. 'She's not too pleased – she wanted to go riding this morning.'

'Tough,' Tessa said lightly, hardening her heart. Abby was in need of a regular routine and discipline, not the non-stop treats she had so rapidly come to take for granted. Besides, she knew she was a coward, but she wanted Abby there as a buffer between her and Matt after what had so nearly happened last night. At her instigation, too, which only made her ultimate rejection of him even worse.

Tessa wandered downstairs shortly after ten,

dressed in one of the suits she had previously worn for work; it was smart enough, she thought, even if obviously bought from a High Street chain store.

She heard Evelyn's voice and followed the sound, hoping to find with her an Abby resigned to her fate. But, when she pushed open the door of the drawing room, she realized Evelyn was talking to someone on the phone.

'Sorry.' Tessa started to back out of the room.

'No, come on in.' Evelyn smiled and beckoned to her. Tessa noticed her giving the suit the once-over, but Evelyn's face remained expressionless. 'It's Helen.' She pointed to the phone and listened briefly. 'She'd like to have a word with you,' she said, getting up out of the chair and laying the receiver down on a nearby table.

'Oh. Right.' Tessa moved, somewhat unwillingly, to take Evelyn's place. 'Actually I came in here looking for Abby,' she told her.

'I'll go and find her. And I'll tell Matt you're ready to leave,' she said, bustling off. Tessa reluctantly lifted the handset to her ear.

'Hello?'

'Tessa, hi! I'm going in to Ashminster this morning and I wondered if you'd like to come along so I can show you around and maybe introduce you to a few girlfriends?' Helen asked brightly. A few girlfriends? Helen's or Matt's? Tessa wondered briefly, but decided to take the offer at face value – Helen certainly sounded a lot friendlier this morning.

'That's very kind of you, but Matt and I are just about to leave for Ashminster anyway,' Tessa said, and explained exactly where they were going lest Helen think she was making excuses and revert to being the somewhat prickly woman of the day before.

'St Hilda's? Oh, I was very happy there. I'm sure Abby will love it,' Helen said warmly, which reassured Tessa somewhat: however good a school's reputation, it was always heartening to talk to someone who had actually attended the place, although it was, of course, some years since Helen had been a pupil there.

'We'll go shopping and have lunch some other day, then?' Helen continued.

'I'd love to, thank you,' Tessa said gratefully.

'Don't thank me – it's by way of an apology,' Helen said cheerfully, and with no discernible note of repentance in her voice. 'I was rather upset for Belinda – she is a good friend of mine, you know – but I saw her yesterday and everything's fine. She understands the situation perfectly.'

'Isn't she dreadfully upset?' Tessa asked, striving to sound casual.

'Well, no one likes being dumped, do they? But she doesn't take her relationships too seriously and has probably got a replacement for Matt already. Don't worry, Tessa!' she finished gaily.

'Are you sure she doesn't . . . well, hate me?' Tessa asked uncertainly.

'Hate you?' Helen repeated incredulously. 'No, of course she doesn't hate you. Whatever gave you that idea?'

'Well, I think she came to see me while I was in hospital,' Tessa explained lamely, beginning to feel like a complete idiot.

'You *think* she did?' Helen asked carefully. God, she thinks I'm off my head, Tessa thought, but there was nothing for it now but to relate exactly what had happened that last night in hospital.

'I see; how very odd. And you think it was Belinda? Would you like me to arrange a meeting with her?'

'God, no!' Tessa shuddered, remembering the malevolence that had emanated from her nocturnal visitor. 'It wouldn't really help, actually. You see, I doubt if I could recognize her anyway, unless she was wearing the same perfume as she was at the hospital.'

'Perfume?' Helen queried.

'Yes, it was very distinctive, very strong. I'm sure I would recognize it again.'

'I can't say I've ever noticed her perfume,' Helen said thoughtfully. 'She's not one of those over made-up women whose perfume arrives in a room five minutes before they do!' she laughed. Tessa smiled slightly; she knew the type.

'I smelled it again here in my room, when I first arrived,' she blurted out.

'Really? Well, that rather rules out Belinda as the culprit, don't you think? I'm sure someone would have noticed if she had been skulking around the house,' Helen said, sounding more amused than concerned, Tessa thought. However, she had made a valid point. Unless, of course, the perfume had been clinging to Matt's clothing and she had simply not noticed it until he had carried her up to her bedroom.

'Any other suspects?' Helen enquired brightly. Tessa bit her lip, not sure whether to confide in her further, but then she decided to take the plunge – Helen already obviously thought she was a suitable case for a Care in the Community project, so what had she to lose?

'Do you know if Matt ever had a girlfriend called Sue?' she asked.

'Sue. I can't think of anyone . . .'

'I found a photograph of them together. She's blonde, tall, quite attractive, but looked to be older than Matt – around forty,' Tessa told her.

'Mmm; it's hard to guess without seeing the photograph, of course,' Helen said doubtfully. 'Oh! I suppose it might be Susan Dalton, she's the estate secretary, but she's never been romantically involved with Matt so far as I'm aware. She was widowed about three years ago and works at the house two or three days a week,' she explained. 'Do you think she might be harbouring a secret passion for Matt and wants to scare you off?' she asked. She was evidently finding the whole thing a huge joke – and perhaps she's right, Tessa thought. It did all seem rather ridiculous in the clear light of day.

'I probably just dreamed the whole thing,' she said finally. 'Please, don't mention it.'

'Dreamed what?' came Matt's deep voice from the doorway. Tessa jerked her head in his direction, tensing and wondering if he were angry with her for leading him on and then rejecting him the night before. He seemed a little guarded, she thought, but not angry, and she offered him a tentative smile.

'Oh, nothing really,' she said vaguely. 'I'm sorry, should we be leaving? I was just chatting to Helen and forgot the time,' she said apologetically. 'Helen? I –'

'I heard. I take it you haven't spoken to Matt about any of this business?'

'No, I haven't, so . . .'

'Don't worry, he won't hear about it from me,' Helen assured her. 'I'll talk to you soon. Bye.'

'Goodbye.' Tessa replaced the handset and turned to Matt. 'She offered to show me around the shops in Ashminster – that was kind of her, wasn't it?'

'Thank your lucky stars you had to decline the invitation – you'll need to be fully fit before you undertake a shopping expedition with Helen,' Matt told her drily. 'Men have carried fewer parcels on an attempt to climb Everest than Helen brings back from the shops! That reminds me, though, you'll need some cash –'

'No, I don't,' Tessa interrupted.

'Don't be silly, of course you do. Don't argue with me about this, Tessa, please. You don't have a job and you need spending money. End of discussion,' he said firmly. 'We'll call in at my bank while we're in town and arrange for you to draw on my account.'

'But . . .' She found she was protesting to thin air: Matt had turned and walked out. His way of ending the discussion, no doubt. 'Ohh!' Tessa almost stamped her foot in vexation; was even more irritated because she knew he was right, dammit!

She had very little money in her own bank account and no salary cheque – thanks to Matt's interference. Yes, it was his fault she had no income, she thought, stomping in his wake outside to where a downcast Abby was waiting by the car.

He wanted her to spend his cash, did he? Fine. In that case, she would phone the apparently shopaholic Helen and insist on accompanying her on her next foray to the shops – armed with Matt's credit cards, naturally. The prospect afforded her such pleasure

169

that she was able to offer him a genuinely sweet smile as he opened the car door for her. Matt frowned suspiciously, but wisely decided to refrain from comment.

Abby was unusually quiet during the journey and she clutched her mother's hand tightly as they left the car and made their way onto the school premises. The mid-morning playtime was in progress and Tessa noted the watchful eye of an attendant at the gates, unfortunately a necessary precaution these days, designed to keep undesirable characters out rather than to keep the children in.

In addition, there were plenty of auxiliary staff patrolling the playground and supervising the games, she saw with approval.

'It's a nice uniform, isn't it, Abby?' she asked brightly: the kids, both boys and girls, were decked out in dark and pale blue, with red ties and red braid trimming on their blazers. Abby nodded slightly and pressed closer to Tessa's side, overawed by such a large number of new faces. When she had begun 'big' school in London, she had at least known some of her classmates from her play-school. These were all strangers.

The headmistress, Mrs Everett, was waiting for them, and straight away took them on a guided tour of the school which, as was only to be expected from the private sector, was far better equipped than the state school Abby had previously attended, and the class sizes were much smaller. In addition to the mandatory subjects, Abby would have the opportunity to learn how to play a musical instrument and to attend drama and dance classes.

'You'd enjoy learning ballet, wouldn't you?' Tessa asked, for that had been a frequent request in the past, one which she'd had to refuse through lack of funds. However, Abby now decided that she didn't want to learn, after all, and shook her head vigorously.

'Why don't we let her join her class for an hour?' Mrs Everett suggested. 'You'll like that, won't you, Abby?' she asked briskly, but it was more like a statement than a question, and Abby was too apprehensive to say 'no'.

Tessa gave her a hug of reassurance and had to harden her heart; she knew Abby would settle and make friends quickly, but it was so difficult throwing a child in at the deep end, even when one was confident she could swim. She glanced at Matt and realized he was also upset by Abby's obvious trepidation.

'Perhaps it would be better to hire a private tutor to teach her at home?' he suggested quietly. Tessa smiled, knew he was sincere, and also knew it would be a mistake – learning to interact with other children was almost as important as the facts and figures taught in class.

Absurdly, she found herself wanting to comfort Matt and only just managed to bite back words of reassurance – any pangs of conscience he was feeling for his high-handed attitude in uprooting Abby from familiar surroundings were both richly deserved and well overdue!

When Mrs Everett opened the classroom door silence fell and all the children got to their feet. God, they don't do that in state schools any more, Tessa thought, and made a mental note to remind Abby about it.

'Children, this is Abby Stafford. She'll be joining us soon, so please make her feel welcome,' Mrs Everett said sternly, before handing Abby over to the class teacher. She then firmly propelled the parents – more trouble than the children, she often thought – out of the room.

'Abby Stafford?' Tessa hissed at Matt, her feelings of sympathy for him vanishing as suddenly as they had arisen. 'What's wrong with Grant?' she added, glancing back to give Abby a reassuring smile and mouthing 'see you soon'.

'You'll soon be Tessa Stafford: she'll want the same surname as you, won't she?' Matt said calmly. 'Why confuse the other kids by changing her name after a couple of months?'

'You're impossible!' she said crossly. However she could, albeit reluctantly, see his point of view and so maintained a rather tight-lipped silence as he made all the arrangements for Abby to enrol the following week rather than wait until after the half-term holiday as he had originally planned. He also wrote out a sizable cheque to cover the fees for the remainder of the term.

As they left they sneaked a look at Abby through the classroom window to try and guage how she was getting along. She was sitting, slightly apart from the others, quiet and solemn, listening attentively to the teacher.

'That teacher's in for a shock when Abby's shyness wears off and she starts talking non-stop,' Tessa said, then she waved the long list containing details of the extensive uniform required at Matt. 'Still got your cheque book handy?' she enquired sweetly.

Only one shop in Ashminster stocked St Hilda's uniform and consequently prices were high. Tessa, knowing Matt would foot the bill, cheerfully ordered everything that was necessary and some items that weren't!

'Are you sure these are big enough?' Matt asked doubtfully, holding up a small pair of blue socks. 'They look so tiny.'

'You should have seen the ones she wore as a baby,' Tessa replied unthinkingly.

'Yes,' he said quietly. 'I should have.' Tessa looked at him quickly, and then away, unable to watch the pain and reproach in his eyes.

'Hindsight's a wonderful thing, Matt,' she said softly. 'I honestly thought I was doing you a favour by not contacting you.'

'I know you did,' he agreed, and forced a smile. Regrets were not only futile but could easily jeopordize his future relationship with Tessa, the woman he was determined would be his wife and the mother of all his children, not just Abby.

He had carefully considered Tessa's claim that Abby would be hurt by the arrival of another child – despite recognizing it for the excuse it undoubtedly was – and was prepared to wait until Abby was confident of his love and that of her grandparents, and secure in her place as the eldest child.

He had been six when his brother Ricky had been born and couldn't remember feeling threatened by him, merely bored! His interest in the new member of the family had quickly waned when Ricky had seemingly done nothing other than sleep and cry. Also, he had never once felt that his parents no longer had time for him, or that they preferred Ricky, and that, surely, was the key to avoiding sibling rivalry?

'Why don't I just buy the entire shop?' he enquired good-naturedly, as the pile of clothing continued to grow. Tessa just grinned happily; she still disliked the thought of spending Matt's money on herself, but was quite happy to let him foot the bill for anything Abby needed.

Finally, Matt carried the bulging bags out to the car, then, despite Tessa's embarrassed protests, propelled her into his bank and arranged for her to sign on his account and to be issued with cheque book, cashpoint and credit cards.

'Stop arguing, Tessa,' he sighed. 'You're not a child, and I refuse to dole out an allowance to you every week as if you're Abby's age. Nor do I want you to feel you have to come and ask me for money whenever you need to buy something.'

'I might go mad and bankrupt you,' she warned, only half-joking: she had never had unlimited funds at her disposal before.

'I'll risk it.' Matt smiled at her. 'Come on, let's go and collect Abby.'

The morning's lessons had just finished when they returned to St Hilda's. To Matt's great relief, Abby came out to greet them with a broad smile on her face. He was discovering that sending her to school was more nerve-racking than his own first foray into the world outside his home, thirty years earlier.

'I'm going to learn to speak French,' she announced happily as they set off back to Drake's Abbot. 'Did you know the French word for "yes" is wee?' she asked Tessa, giggling at what she perceived to be a vulgar

174

word – and the freedom to say it out loud as often as she liked.

'*Oui*,' Tessa replied, with a sigh. The slight difference in pronunciation was lost on Abby, or else she simply chose to ignore it.

'Talk about a little knowledge being a dangerous thing,' Matt muttered a short time later, when it seemed every question about school necessitated a reply containing that particular word.

'Don't make an issue of it,' Tessa advised. 'The novelty will wear off quickly enough if no one comments on it.'

Unfortunately, Evelyn was hovering, anxious to know how Abby had fared, when they entered the house.

'Grandma! Do you know the French . . .'

'Why don't you come and try on your new uniform?' Tessa suggested hastily.

'Well done.' Matt grinned his approval of her successful diversionary tactics as she led Abby upstairs. 'Quick thinking.'

'Oh, I'm still one step ahead of her. Just,' Tessa said ruefully.

The last few days of Abby's 'freedom' passed quickly. Too quickly for Tessa, who continued to use her as a buffer between herself and Matt whenever possible.

He, for his part, seemed to sense that she needed time and space, and made no further attempt at seduction, which was hardly surprising after she had led him on so shamelessly and then rejected him. He would have had every right to be angry about that, she acknowledged fairly, yet he had made no reproaches at all.

He continued to treat her with kindness and generosity, concerned for her health, which was thankfully improving daily. He had bought her a car, as promised, arriving home one day with a spanking new blue sporty number that Tessa loved.

The decorators were installed at the Dower House, repainting and hanging new wallpaper. Matt asked her opinion on all the changes, pleased to let her choose carpets and curtains, kitchen appliances and anything else he thought she might like to update. Some furniture had already been chosen and would be delivered once the workmen had finished the renovation.

Meanwhile Evelyn was happily occupied with lists of things to be done for the wedding: in her element, she urged Tessa to leave all the organization to her, which Tessa was content to do – the only contribution she was making was to select her own and Abby's dress for the ceremony. Tessa's future life as Mrs Matt Stafford was taking shape without much input from Tessa herself; in fact, she often felt as if it were happening to someone else.

She was drifting along, from day to day, still healing from her injuries, which perhaps explained her lethargy, her feeling as if she were in some sort of a limbo. She had almost forgotten her concern over Matt's ex-girlfriends and had convinced herself that the nocturnal visitor to her hospital room had been a product of her drug-induced sleep, brought about by her anxieties over the way Matt had taken control of her and Abby's life.

But then, on the Sunday afternoon before Abby was to start at St Hilda's school, Tessa was suddenly, shockingly, jolted out of her complacency, and forced to reconsider the wisdom of remaining under the Staffords' roof.

After lunch, Abby asked if she might go riding on Lollipop, and Tessa accompanied her alone, save for the Irish Wolfhound, Flynn. Tessa was becoming fond of the huge, hairy monster and was no longer apprehensive because of his size. He was so gentle with Abby, and long-suffering, too, giving only a pained sigh whenever she tripped over him or accidently trod on his paw. Abby would apologize profusely, giving him a big hug and he would wag his tail in forgiveness.

Abby was quite proficient at riding the Shetland pony by this time, and Tessa walked by her side, keeping only a guiding hand on the bridle and a watchful eye on Abby's balance. Flynn tagged along behind them, pausing occasionally to investigate any interesting scents as they crossed the paddock and headed for the wooded area beyond. It was all Stafford land and Lollipop was accustomed to the pathways by now and needed little or no guidance.

It was a beautiful afternoon, mild and sunny. Tessa was listening to Abby's chatter and enjoying the leisurely walk, revelling in her returning strength and vowing never again to take her health and fitness for granted. She knew now how quickly it could be snatched away.

She had hardly finished the thought when a loud bang startled her. Instinctively, she ducked. What on earth was that? Surely it was too early for someone to be messing around with fireworks?

'What's that noise, Mummy?'

'I don't know.' Tessa tightened her grip on the pony's bridle and pulled him to a halt. She glanced around her, not even sure of the direction from which it had come. Then it sounded again, seemingly nearer, and again she ducked then spun around to stare in disbelief as the branch of a tree behind her cracked all fell to the ground. A firework couldn't have done that! A gunshot?

'Hey! Stop that! There are people down here!' she screamed, grabbing Abby and pulling her off the pony's back, and then using Lollipop as a shield.

'Crouch down,' she ordered Abby. 'I think someone has a rifle, and they don't know we're here.'

Flynn had bounded forwards, presumably in the direction of the trespasser, or whoever, but he came back when Tessa called him, seemingly unconcerned.

Tessa waited, listening carefully. There were no more shots, if that indeed was what she had heard, but neither was there any sound of someone retreating. Surely a poacher would have been scared off when she had yelled and would now be making his escape?

'What's the matter, Mummy? Can I get up now?' Abby peered up at her, wide-eyed. Tessa forced a smile and gave her a hug.

'Don't worry. I think someone was shooting at rabbits and nearly hit us instead!' she said lightly.

'Someone's shooting the bunny rabbits?' Abby clearly found that a more terrifying prospect than that of someone taking pot-shots at her and Tessa. 'That's horrid!' she said indignantly.

'I quite agree. I think we've frightened them away, but we'd better go back to the house,' Tessa decided.

She felt she was probably being over-dramatic, but she daren't risk letting Abby ride home, despite her protests. She was much less of a target, on foot, sandwiched between Tessa and Lollipop.

Tessa, half-crouching, dragged Lollipop behind her, with a silent apology to the good-natured animal for using him as a shield between her and whoever had a rifle. Or a firework, she thought drily, and bit her lip hard to stifle near-hysterical laughter.

Flynn brought up the rear, occasionally stopping and glancing back into the heart of the wood before once again turning to follow Tessa. It was as if the dog sensed the presence of another human being, and Tessa's amusement fled abruptly and fear took its place; she felt as if malevolent eyes watched their progress and her whole body was tense, expecting another shot.

It seemed an age before they reached the solid safety of the stable block, and Tessa sank wearily down on to a bench, stiff and aching and in desperate need of a double brandy. Before she had time to collect her thoughts, Abby, full of excitement and sharing none of Tessa's alarm, had run to tell her grandmother what had happened.

Too late, Tessa wished she had asked Abby to keep quiet. If – and she acknowledged that it was a big if – someone had deliberately shot at her, the culprit might be a member of the household . . . oh, don't mince words, Tessa! You mean Matt, don't you?

Tears pricked at her eyelids and she bit down hard on her lower lip as she struggled for control. For the first time in days, she allowed herself to remember the woman who had come to her hospital room, the woman who obviously wished she had died in the accident, and who claimed that Matt, too, wanted her dead . . .

179

With a gasp of horror, Tessa suddenly realized the significance of something else – her will! Only last night she had signed the will that appointed Matt Abby's legal guardian in the event of her own death or incapacity. Matt didn't need her alive any longer. With her killed in a shooting 'accident', he would have his child and would be free to have the woman he truly loved.

I signed my own death warrant! she thought, in horror, and jumped to her feet, intending to go and rip up her copy of the will immediately . . . her copy. Quite. She came to an abrupt stop, her shoulders slumping in despair as she remembered the original was now locked away in Matt's bank safety-deposit box. Ripping up hers would be pointless.

I have to get away from here, she thought wildly, and began running towards the house. She bumped into Matt in the hallway and backed off so hastily his brows rose in astonishment.

'You've been outside,' she stated flatly, noting the jacket he had donned since lunchtime.

'Not yet, I was coming to find you and Abby. I hear you had a bit of excitement,' he said, sounding amused.

'Someone shot at us,' Tessa said firmly, watching him closely for his reaction.

'It was probably a car backfiring,' he said dismissively. 'Would you even recognize a gunshot if you heard one?' he asked. Tessa hesitated, then shrugged her shoulders and forced a smile. Why let him know she was on her guard?

'I guess not,' she conceded. 'Perhaps I overreacted.'

'I suppose there could have been a poacher, although they're not usually at work in broad daylight,' Matt said thoughtfully. 'But you had Flynn with you, didn't you?' he asked, and at her nod, continued. 'He would have gone in pursuit of a stranger, so I'm pretty sure it must have been a car on the Ashminster road.'

'I'm sure you're right,' she agreed flatly. Yes, the dog would scare off a stranger – but a member of the family? Someone he knew had a perfect right to be in the woods?

'Are you all right? You look very pale.' Matt frowned. 'You weren't really worried, were you?'

'No, of course not. Just a little startled. I'm fine now, but I would like to rest for a while. Excuse me.' She pushed past him and hurried upstairs to the familiarity, if not safety, of her room, and had to resist the urge to shove furniture in front of the door to keep out an enemy.

But who was her enemy? Matt? Her whole being rejected that notion. Matt's father? She couldn't, or to be more accurate, wouldn't believe Matt would harm her, but George Stafford was a different proposition altogether.

He was still rather unfriendly, disapproving, giving Tessa the distinct impression that she wasn't good enough to marry a Stafford. And it was George who had first introduced the subject of her and Matt making their wills, she remembered suddenly.

Oh, this was too ridiculous to even consider! she chided herself. Okay, so maybe she wasn't George Stafford's idea of the perfect daughter-in-law, nor perhaps, and even more painful to acknowledge, Matt's idea of the perfect wife, but there was no doubt both men had Abby's best interests at heart and that certainly did not include plotting to murder her mother!

However, fear wasn't so easily banished, no matter how many times she told herself she was over-dramatizing a couple of vaguely sinister events. She paced her room restlessly, trying to decide what she should do. Part of her wanted to run to Matt, pour out her concerns and let him deal with it, but a small part, that which had learned to cope alone over the past six years and trust no man, insisted she hold back.

If she harboured any doubts about her safety here at Stafford House, then she should leave immediately. Again, easier said than done. She couldn't uproot Abby, who was happy and safe, particularly as she had nowhere to go, no job and no money save for the small amount in her own bank account.

She had access to Matt's account, of course, but, if she fled, she couldn't use her cashpoint card, not unless she wanted to leave Matt a map! A check on his account would tell him when and where she had used her card.

She had the car he had bought, of course – a getaway vehicle? She smiled grimly at the thought. She twisted her hands tightly together and the diamond and sapphire ring rubbed painfully against her skin. She glanced down at it; it was a little too loose and had slipped around her finger. She righted it absently, then continued gazing at it. It was a valuable antique which Matt's grandmother had bequeathed to him to pass on to his wife. Surely he wouldn't have given it to her if he meant to do her harm? If he really didn't want to marry her?

The thought calmed her, as did the memories of all he had done for her in recent weeks. She remembered the day he had taken her to view the Dower House, his desire to please her, his trying to understand her feelings regarding another pregnancy . . .

'Tessa?' Matt's voice, and his accompanying knock on her door, jolted her out of her reverie.

'Yes.' She hurried to open the door, unaware that tears had been pouring down her cheeks.

'Darling! What's wrong?' he asked, frowning in what she was sure was genuine concern. She almost confided in him then, but noticed Abby following in his wake and shook her head.

'Nothing, really. I was just being silly.'

'I hate to see you upset. Tell me,' he said, reaching out and gently wiping away her tears. His touch and the tender look in his eyes banished the last of her fears and she smiled tremulously, holding his hand to her cheek.

'I'm fine, honestly,' she assured him, and meant it. Matt wasn't convinced and would have persisted, but then he, too, noticed Abby and stepped away from Tessa, catching Abby in his arms as she hurled herself at him and tossing her high into the air, making her squeal with delight.

'Go and put your best dress on – we're expecting visitors,' he said.

'Are you talking to me or Abby?' Tessa smiled.

'Abby. I'm not sure I shouldn't keep you locked away, out of sight,' he said, somewhat to her consternation. He grinned at her expression and quickly explained. 'My brother's just phoned to say he's on his way. That's your uncle,' he added to Abby, as he set her back on her feet.

'Another family person!' she exclaimed, and clapped her hands in delight. Matt grinned at her, then turned back to Tessa.

'Just promise me you won't fall in love with him,' he said fiercely.

'I promise,' she said happily, her earlier fears banished to the deepest recesses of her mind. 'That's Ricky – right? The artist?'

'Yep. He's just flown back from Italy; probably chased out by an irate husband. God, I hope he had the sense not to mess with a Mafia wife,' he said, in genuine horror.

'Are you going to collect him from the airport?'

'No, he already has a lift arranged. He's bringing a "surprise", apparently. My mother's in a tizz at the prospect of organizing another wedding,' he said drily. 'She's in cloud cuckoo land if she thinks Ricky will ever settle down.'

'Don't be too sure. You told me Ricky always wants what you have, so maybe he's decided he wants a family, too.'

'Could be.' Matt glanced down at Abby and ruffled her hair. 'He'll never be able to match this, though, will he?' he asked proudly.

'Mmm, talk about angels with dirty faces,' Tessa said, reaching for a handkerchief to wipe away a smudge on Abby's cheek. 'Come on, poppet, let's get you spruced up before the visitors arrive.'

'I'm going to shower and change, too,' Matt said, giving her a quick kiss before heading off to his own room.

Tessa helped Abby wash and change into one of her new dresses, and then returned to her room to put on a smarter outfit, adding make-up and brushing her hair. She wanted Matt to be as proud of her as he was of Abby! Besides, if Ricky was bringing a sultry, beautiful Italian girl home, she didn't want the brothers' roles reversed, with Matt wanting something of Ricky's for a change!

Evelyn was, as Matt had said, in a tizz, delighted at the prospect of seeing her younger son, and excitedly wondering out loud about the identity – and importance – of Ricky's companion.

'Do you think it's the girl whose portrait he's been painting? Her name's Francesca, I believe. Lovely name, isn't it?'

'She's married,' Matt reminded her.

'Oh.' Her face fell, but she wasn't downcast for long. 'Oh, well, he must have met someone else!'

'Yeah, probably on the flight over here,' Matt said cynically.

'Oh, Matt! He's not that bad . . . oh, there's a car now!' She hurried out of the room. There was a confused babble of voices, male and female, followed by a short silence, then three people entered the drawing room. Tessa's attention was diverted by the sharp sound of a sharply indrawn breath from Matt.

'Ricky, you bastard!' he hissed.

CHAPTER 10

Tessa glanced enquiringly at Matt, but his attention was fixed on the newcomers. She looked towards them, wondering what it was about their arrival that had obviously upset Matt.

Ricky Stafford was physically a lot like Matt; tall and broad-shouldered, with the same black hair, although he wore his much longer. His deep tan emphasized the Stafford sapphire eyes, thickly lashed, but, unlike Matt, Ricky had a sleepy indolent look about him that was in sharp contrast to Matt's military bearing and quick, efficient movements.

The woman clinging to Ricky's arm was tall and blonde with a lush figure that was now enviably curvaceous, but which would probably require strict diet and exercise in a few years time if she wished to avoid excess flesh, Tessa thought. Beside her, Matt sighed heavily, then he glanced down at her, his expression unreadable.

'That's Ricky. The girl with him is Belinda Croxley,' he said tonelessly.

'Oh!' Tessa jerked her head round so sharply, she feared she had permanently ricked her neck. Belinda Croxley! She remained rooted to the spot, frozen into immobility, and waited for the group to approach.

Evelyn had quickly recovered her composure after her shocked realization that Ricky's companion was Matt's ex-girlfriend and was pouring drinks with a generous hand – some evenings could only be endured with lavish doses of gin! George was still out; she dreaded to think what he would say when he returned. Ricky's mischief-making had gone a little too far this time. Her gaze slid to her eldest son; really, it was amazing how sometimes Matt looked extraordinarily like his father . . .

'Hello, Matt.' Ricky stood in front of his brother, grinning unrepentantly, but well aware of the consternation he was causing. Matt resisted the urge to hit him. Just. Ricky guessed at his temptation, though, and turned to great Tessa. His smile for her was warm, his gaze friendly and, perhaps because of the resemblance to Matt, she found herself liking him despite Belinda Croxley. Instinctively, she felt his action in bringing her was born of younger-brother devilry, a delight in winding Matt up, rather than an act of malice.

'You're Tessa,' Ricky stated, enclosing her hand in his. 'I once wore my fingers to the bone for you,' he confided, and her brows rose in perplexity. 'I was helping Matt phone every Grant listed in the telephone directory,' he explained, and Tessa's spirits soared.

'Shut up,' Matt sighed wearily.

'I am really pleased he finally found you,' Ricky said sincerely, raising her hand to his mouth and brushing her knuckles with his lips. Then he stepped closer and kissed her on both cheeks.

'Cut that out!' Matt snapped.

'Sorry; it's a habit I picked up in Italy,' Ricky told him, still keeping hold of Tessa's hand.

'It's probably not all you picked up,' Matt retorted, 'so keep your hands to yourself. Hello, Belinda,' he added curtly, annoyed with her for coming. He expected childish antics from Ricky, but Belinda should have had more sense.

'Matt, how are you, darling?' Belinda kissed him on the mouth, then, almost purring with satisfaction, remained clinging to his arm as she turned to Tessa, with a cool, rather disparaging smile on her face as she blatantly assessed Tessa's face and figure.

Matt effected the briefest of introductions, shook off Belinda with something less than gallantry and pulled Tessa closer to his side, keeping his arm possessively around her waist.

Tessa nodded and smiled stiffly at Belinda, aware of a recurrence of her demented bloodhound act as she tried to detect if Belinda's perfume was that which she remembered from the hospital.

She was certainly wearing scent, but it was one which was unfamiliar to Tessa. But, of course, she realized suddenly, she had confided in Helen – a friend of Belinda's – and told her the only distinguishing features of her nocturnal visitor were her blonde hair and distinctive perfume. Helen could easily have passed on that information to Belinda, either casually, or purposely. The latter possibility was somewhat disturbing to admit, but she would have to bear in mind that Helen's loyalty would be to her friend, not to Tessa.

She wondered if she could discover, without sounding crazy, just when Belinda had collected Ricky from the airport, and whose idea it had been. Although she had to admit that it was difficult to imagine Belinda, clad in a pale blue suede suit and matching high-heeled shoes, skulking around the woods, shotgun in hand. In fact, it was preposterous, she decided; there was no way Belinda or Ricky could have known she and Abby would be in those woods; they hadn't decided themselves until after lunch.

'Hello, there, you must be Abby.' Ricky hunkered down to her level. 'I've heard a lot about you. I'm your Uncle Ricky, but just call me Ricky – "uncle" makes me feel old and responsible,' he added.

'God forbid you should have to take any responsibility,' Matt remarked snidely.

'And I'm Belinda.' She bent towards Abby. 'I used to be your daddy's girlfriend,' she cooed. Abby scowled.

'Well, you can't be any more. He's going to marry my mummy,' she declared. Tessa refrained from applauding. Just. 'And I'm going to be a bridesmaid and wear a red dress. The wedding's at Christmas.'

'I'm not so sure about that,' Tessa demurred. Matt, Belinda and Ricky looked at her sharply. She paused and glanced round at the three of them. 'I think you'll look much prettier in pink,' she said calmly. Ricky laughed, Belinda flushed angrily and Matt found himself able to breathe again.

'Minx,' he growled in her ear. Tessa smiled sweetly.

'You have lipstick on your mouth,' she informed him. He rubbed it off hastily, looking rather shame-faced.

'How long are you staying, Ricky?' Evelyn asked.

'I have to be in Edinburgh tomorrow,' he told her. 'I've got a commission lined up, but I'll be in Britain for the next couple of months at least. I'll definitely be here for the wedding – I am going to be your best man, aren't I?' he asked Matt.

'I suppose so,' Matt agreed grudgingly.

'Great. That means I get to take out the chief bridesmaid,' Ricky said cheerfully.

'We're only having Abby. Admittedly she's the same mental age . . .' Matt began.

'Here's your father!' Evelyn exclaimed, in tones of mingled relief and trepidation. She hurriedly poured him a glass of Scotch and thrust it in his hand as soon as he entered the room.

'Am I going to need an anaesthetic?' George enquired drily, studying the almost-full glass. He quickly discovered he did, indeed, need the alcohol, his pleasure at his younger son's arrival short-lived, negated by his annoyance at Belinda Croxley's presence. He ignored her completely, and went out of his way to be pleasant to Tessa, making her feel more welcome than he ever had before.

Ricky kept them entertained with highly unlikely tales of his exploits in Italy. Belinda sat and fumed – literally – incessantly lighting one cigarette from another and wishing she hadn't agreed to come. Ricky's phone call had taken her by surprise, but curiosity about Tessa Grant, a desire to remind Matt of what he was missing, and also to show him she now had his younger brother in tow, well, it had all been too much to resist.

However, judging from the dark scowl on Matt's face, it had definitely not been a good move! At least it

190

had its compensations, she decided; Ricky was certainly cute – not as challenging as Matt, of course, but definitely cute.

'Why do you smoke so much? You'll get yellow teeth and wrinkles,' Abby suddenly informed Belinda loudly, when she reached for yet another cigarette. Belinda glowered at her. Brat. Tessa hid a smile, with some difficulty. Matt choked on his drink.

'Are you coaching her?' he hissed, out of the corner of his mouth.

'Who – me?' Tessa gazed at him guilelessly.

'Come on, Ricky.' Belinda stubbed out her cigarette and got to her feet. 'I told Helen we'd call in – remember?'

'Must we?' Ricky grimaced. 'I'd much rather have an early night; I'm suffering from jet-lag,' he said plaintively.

'From Italy?' Matt raised an eyebrow in disbelief. Ricky winked at Tessa, as if she hadn't already guessed that his desire for bed had absolutely nothing to do with his journey! She shook her head slightly, but couldn't help liking him.

Before he left, Ricky took an opportunity to draw Tessa aside.

'Matt's been giving me earache about bringing Belinda here,' he said ruefully. 'He thinks I've upset you, and that wasn't my intention, I assure you.'

'I believe you – Matt told me you always pinch his girlfriends.'

'Well, he has such exquisite taste,' Ricky drawled, his eyes showing his appreciation of her own beauty. 'I am sorry, though, Tessa. I didn't think it through

191

logically; I only got as far as thinking it would wind Matt up!'

'It's okay, really,' she said. 'But why do you want to wind Matt up?' she asked curiously. Ricky considered that for a moment.

'Because I can?' he suggested, with a grin, and Tessa laughed out loud, causing Matt to turn and scowl in their direction. Tessa didn't even notice. 'Don't get me wrong,' Ricky continued hastily. 'I've hero-worshipped Matt all my life; he's a much better guy than I'll ever be, but he does behave as if he's still in the Army! I'm surprised he hasn't built Abby an obstacle course in the paddock and turned the stable yard into a parade ground!' Tessa grinned at the mental image his words conjured up of Abby quick-marching around the yard.

'He *is* bossy,' she agreed feelingly. 'He's taken over my life completely.

'That's because he doesn't want to lose you again,' Ricky said seriously.

'Really?' Tessa's eyes lit up.

'Really,' Ricky mimicked, but kindly. 'He really did try to find you, Tessa,' he said quietly, guessing Matt hadn't admitted to her just how much he had cared. 'He was even going to hire a private detective to track you down, but then his pride got in the way. He figured you must have found someone else.'

'Only Abby.' Tessa's glance moved to her daughter, who, she noted, was becoming rather excitable. 'Excuse me, I really ought to put her to bed. She starts her new school tomorrow,' she explained.

'Sure; don't let me hold you up. Welcome to the family, Tessa. I'll see you soon, definitely at the wedding if not before.' He bent and kissed her soundly on the mouth, then, ignoring Matt's glower, sauntered over to speak to his parents.

Tessa told Abby to say her goodnights and then bore her upstairs, listening idly to her bright chatter as she prepared for bed.

'I like Ricky,' she confided sleepily, as Tessa tucked her in. 'But I don't like Belinda,' she added. 'She's not Daddy's girlfriend now, is she?' she asked anxiously.

'Of course not,' Tessa reassured her, and bent to give her a kiss. 'Goodnight, sweetie.'

When she left the room, Matt was approaching, intent on bestowing his own goodnight kiss on his daughter.

Tessa gazed at him rather wistfully, and wished she could reassure herself as easily as she had convinced Abby that Belinda Croxley was no longer a part of Matt's life.

'You're wearing Belinda's lipstick again,' she told him sourly.

'So? Ricky was wearing yours,' Matt retorted.

'Huh!' Tessa stalked past him, into her own room, and slammed the door behind her. Matt didn't try to follow her.

As Monday was Abby's first day at St Hilda's, Matt accompanied Tessa on the school run. She was keyed-up, more than a little nervous – and so was Abby!

It was hard leaving her, even worse than her first day at her previous school, Tessa thought. At least on that occasion, Abby had been one of many new entrants; today she was joining a class where the children already knew each other and had forged friendships.

Matt busied himself with estate work while Tessa spent the day in something of a daze. Ostensibly she checked on the progress of the refurbishment of the Dower House, ate lunch with Evelyn and discussed wedding plans, but mentally she was with Abby, hoping desperately that the day was proving to be less of an ordeal for Abby than it was for her mother!

Stiff with tension she suffered the worst headache since leaving hospital and drove her new car cautiously to Ashminster, arriving outside the school gates far too early, and biting her nails to the quick while she waited for the bell to signal the end of the school day.

When the pupils finally began to stream out into the playground she climbed out of the car and looked anxiously for a glimpse of her daughter.

'Mummy!' Abby skipped towards her, a broad smile on her face. Tessa sagged with relief and bent to hug her. 'I can do ballet now,' Abby announced happily. 'Shall I show you?'

'When we get home,' Tessa said, propelling her towards the car and buckling her into her seat.

She was delighted to hear that Abby had thoroughly enjoyed her day – even the lunch provided – but the child's high-pitched excited chatter did nothing to alleviate Tessa's headache and she was relieved to hand her over to Evelyn upon their arrival at Stafford House.

'If you're sure you don't mind, I would like to have a bath and rest until dinner,' she said apologetically, still not accustomed to having other people to help take care of Abby and quite unable to take such help for granted.

'Of course I don't mind,' Evelyn said at once. 'I'd have collected her from school if you'd said you were feeling ill,' she added. 'Come on, Abby; let's find you a snack and then you can demonstrate your ballet steps,' she told her.

'Thank you.' Tessa made her way upstairs, but halted abruptly when she came face to face with the blonde woman pictured with Matt in the photograph Abby had found. The woman smiled pleasantly and held out her hand.

'How do you do? We haven't met. I'm Susan Dalton, the estate secretary,' she introduced herself, confirming that Helen had correctly guessed her identity. Tessa nodded curtly but ignored the outstretched hand.

'Matt asked me to give you these brochures,' Susan continued, her smile fading in the face of Tessa's coldness. Tessa silently took the pile of leaflets and glanced at them briefly; they contained details of washing machines, dishwashers, etc etera.

'Apparently the kitchen fitters will be at the Dower House next Monday, so if you could decide which appliances you –'

'Thank you,' Tessa cut her off and walked past her and into her room.

She made a conscious effort to relax her muscles in the hot, soapy water, closing her eyes and listening to soothing music, forcing her mind away from the unexpected meeting with Susan Dalton. So she was Matt's secretary. Big deal. The photograph . . . forget it, Tessa, she told herself sternly. It could easily be several years old and, if Susan meant anything to Matt romantically, he would hardly have asked her to bring those brochures to the woman he intended marrying.

When the bath water became uncomfortably cool, she hauled herself out and, wrapped in a large towel, sat at her dressing-table to rub body lotion into her skin and then painted her toe- and fingernails before blow-drying and brushing out her hair.

Only then did she move across to the bed to pick up her watch and the ring she had removed before entering the bathroom. The watch was lying on the bedside cabinet where she had placed it, but the ring – the beautiful diamond and sapphire ring – had gone!

Frantically, Tessa dropped to her hands and knees, scanning the expanse of carpet and peering under the bed to check if it had somehow rolled underneath, but there was no sign of it. Beginning to panic, she pulled off the sheets and blankets, shaking them out and tossing pillows impatiently aside. The ring had to be here somewhere! A family heirloom, irreplacable, cherished by Stafford women for generations and she had lost it in a matter of days! Oh, God, how could she tell Matt she had lost it?

Abby! Tessa often allowed her to play with her inexpensive costume jewellery. Perhaps she had wandered in while Tessa was in the bathroom and had taken it, attracted by its beauty and sparkle, and unaware of its value?

Tessa wrenched open her bedroom door, belatedly realized she was still wearing only a towel and whipped it off, reaching instead for a warm towelling robe and wrapped it around her as she hurried into Abby's room. It was empty. She turned and dashed down the stairs, eventually finding Abby demonstrating her newly learned ballet steps to Evelyn.

'Abby, have you been upstairs in my bedroom this afternoon?' Tessa asked breathlessly.

'No.'

'She's been with me.' Evelyn looked up and noticed Tessa's agitation. 'What's wrong?'

'Er, nothing really.' Tessa managed a sickly smile and returned upstairs to make another thorough search before facing Matt.

As she entered the room, she noticed the stack of brochures which she had placed in a neat pile on top of a chest of drawers. They were now scattered all over the floor, as if swept there by an angry, jealous hand. Or had she done it herself, in her whirlwind search of the room? She was sure she hadn't; had not been near enough to have knocked them over. Only one person had reason to be angry . . . Without stopping to think through her action carefully – or consider its consequences – she again hurried down the stairs, this time encountering the housekeeper.

'Where can I find Susan Dalton?' Tessa demanded.

'If she's still here, she'll be in the office,' Molly said, and gave her precise directions.

'Thank you.' Tessa pushed past her and, moments later, burst into the room, her gaze going directly to Susan, sitting in front of a computer.

'My ring! What have you done with it?' she raged. Susan put a hand to her mouth and stared at Tessa in dismay.

'Tessa!' It was Matt, appearing from an adjoining office. He grabbed her roughly by her arm, swinging her round to face him. 'Why are you shouting at Sue? What's wrong?'

'My ring. It's been stolen,' Tessa told him, almost in

tears. 'And she's got it, I know she has.' She pointed a wavering finger at Susan, who stood up slowly, chalky white as she faced her accuser.

'I can assure you –' she began, but got no further.

'Of course Sue hasn't taken your ring. You're being ridiculous!' Matt snapped. 'Apologize. At once!'

'I won't!' Tessa wrenched her arm free of his grip. How dare he take the other woman's side?

'Shut up and calm down.' Matt picked her bodily off her feet and planted her firmly in a chair, towering over her. Tessa stared back at him rebelliously, unaware of how vulnerable she looked with wide, tear-drenched eyes and trembling mouth. Matt resisted, with difficulty, the urge to kiss her senseless before carrying her off to make love to her.

'If you've mislaid your ring, we'll find it,' he said, much more gently. 'But you cannot accuse someone of theft without a shred of proof. What possible reason could Sue have for wanting your ring?'

'It's not just the ring; it's what it represents. She wants you, too,' Tessa burst out, and heard Susan gasp. 'She came to see –' She stopped abruptly: she had been about to tell him of Susan's hospital visit. But Susan had also said Matt wished Tessa had died.

'Go on,' Matt said curtly.

'No.' Tessa folded her arms and glared at him.

'I think I'd better go –' Sue began.

'No, you won't. Tessa will be apologizing to you, very soon,' Matt told her, his eyes never leaving Tessa's.

'Huh!' Tessa snorted, then she shrank back from the blaze of anger in Matt's eyes. All at once, the energizing heat of anger deflated, leaving her filled with exhaustion and despair. She wilted visibly and Matt stepped back a little.

'Right. Now let's see if we can straighten this out. Where did you lose the ring?' he asked calmly.

'I didn't lose it! She –'

'Don't start that again!' Matt warned sharply. 'Where did you last see it?' he amended his question.

'I took it off while I had a bath. It was on top of the bedside cabinet with my watch,' she told him.

'Are you sure it didn't slip off while you were in the bath? Do you distinctly remember taking it off first?' Matt asked.

'Yes!'

'Are you positive about that? It's rather loose – could it have slipped off your finger earlier today without you noticing it?'

'No, I've told you – I took it off before I ran the bath and left it beside the bed,' Tessa insisted, through gritted teeth. Why was he interrogating her and not Susan Dalton? The woman had tried to leave the room, was even now clutching her handbag. She opened her mouth to insist Matt search the bag – the leather one, not Susan – but didn't quite dare, and closed it again.

'I'll go and have a look for it,' Matt sighed. He raked his fingers through his hair and looked rather helplessly from Susan, shocked and unhappy, to Tessa, furious and determined. Ah well, he'd never fooled himself this was going to be easy! But this was one complication he had never considered. 'Stay here,' he ordered brusquely, and strode from the room.

Tessa remained huddled in her chair, beginning to shiver in her dressing gown. How much time would

Matt waste on a fruitless search? she wondered, as her bare feet slowly turned into blocks of ice.

She couldn't look at Susan Dalton, who had apparently thought Matt's instruction to remain in the room included her as well as Tessa, for she made no further move to leave, but sat, staring out of the window as if entranced by the view she must have seen a thousand times before.

The silence in the room was almost palpable and, as Tessa cooled down, emotionally as well as physically, she began to feel amazed and a little ashamed of her outburst. She had been hiding her fears for too long, she realized, and an eruption had been inevitable.

She probably should have told Matt what had happened at the hospital and left it to him to solve the problem with his ex-girlfriend. Of course, if she told him now, it would seem to him that she believed the woman's assertion that he wished her dead, and would make him even angrier than he was already. At least, he would be angry if the woman had lied about his feelings . . . what if she saw guilt instead of anger in his eyes when she told him?

Finally, after what seemed an age – an ice-age, in fact – Tessa heard the sound of Matt's approaching footsteps, and she looked up warily as he entered the room. Then she stared in disbelief for there, lying on the palm of his hand, was her ring.

'Oh, my God,' Tessa whispered. 'Someone is trying to drive me insane . . .'

'From what I've seen of your behaviour, they won't have to try very hard!' Matt snarled at her. Tessa gaped at him; his face was taut with fury, his mouth compressed into a thin, cruel line and the blaze of . . .

hatred? . . . in his eyes made her feel more afraid than ever before. He seemed far angrier than when he had left on his errand and she didn't understand why. She licked her lips nervously.

'Where was it?' she asked hoarsely, automatically reaching out to pick it up, but Matt snatched his hand back and placed the ring in his pocket.

'Where you left it, I imagine. In the drawer of the bedside cabinet,' he said, with no discernible emotion in his voice. But the grip of his fingers on Tessa's arm when he hauled her to her feet was less than gentle.

'I didn't put it in there, truly I didn't,' Tessa said faintly, but she was beginning to doubt her memory. Had she put it inside the cabinet for safe-keeping instead of on top with her watch?

'Don't you have something to say to Sue?' Matt asked, deceptively calmly. Tessa bit her lip: okay, so Susan Dalton obviously hadn't stolen the ring, but Tessa was still not convinced this wasn't the woman who had spoken to her so viciously in the hospital. However, the grim expression on Matt's face brooked no argument, so she turned unwillingly towards Susan.

'Apparently I made a mistake,' she said coldly. 'I'm sorry I accused you of something you didn't do.' She held Susan's gaze for a moment, glaring her dislike and mistrust, and then she turned to leave, but Matt was blocking her path.

'Not good enough,' he said, folding his arms across his chest and leaning against the door post as if he were prepared to stand and wait all day.

'I've said I'm sorry!' Tessa hissed. 'I am not grovelling to that woman!'

201

'I see.' Matt nodded finally, and Tessa thought he was going to drop the matter. But then he turned to Susan and smiled warmly.

'It seems I must apologize on Tessa's behalf. She's . . . overwrought,' he said, obviously substituting whichever uncomplimentary adjective had originally sprung to mind. 'Let me take you out to dinner this evening as recompense,' he suggested. Oh, very clever, Matt; feed her fantasies as well as her stomach, Tessa thought, trying not to cry.

'Oh, that's not necessary,' Susan demurred.

'I think it is,' Matt insisted. 'Besides, it will be a pleasure,' he assured her. 'I'll pick you up at . . . seven-thirty?' Abruptly, his smile and pleasant manner vanished and he turned to walk out of the room. 'You, come with me.' He spoke to Tessa as he might to a recalcitrant dog, and half dragged her from the office and into a smaller study nearby, slamming the door behind them.

'My search of your room was more illuminating than I expected,' he said coldly, and, as Tessa looked at him questioningly, fearfully, he slowly reached into his pocket and pulled out her packet of contraceptive pills.

'Oh, no!' She dropped into a chair and held her head in her hands.

'How long were you intending taking these things?' Matt enquired harshly. 'A year? Five years? Knowing all the time that I would be hoping you would become pregnant? Is this your idea of a sick joke, or is it revenge against me because I've committed the unforgivable sin of forcing you to give my daughter a reasonable lifestyle instead of the miserable existence you had condemned her to?' he demanded furiously, his voice dripping sarcasm.

'That's not fair! Abby has always been a happy, healthy little girl,' Tessa said, indignation temporarily overcoming her fear of the stranger Matt had suddenly become. 'And I did tell you I wasn't ready to have another child. I'm not rent-a-womb!'

'Oh, get out of my sight!' Matt snapped, throwing the packet of pills at her. But not the ring, Tessa had time to think, before she fled.

Luckily, she met no one on her dash back to her room and, once she reached its sanctuary, she slammed the door closed and leaned against it weakly until her breathing became less ragged. Exhaustion swept over her and she sank to the floor, resting her head on the mattress, too weary to replace the bedding she had discarded earlier in her frantic search for the ring.

She reached for a box of tissues when the tears began to flow, then a sob caught in her throat and she glanced wildly around, as if looking for an escape. She was truly terrified now, for the horrible, cloying perfume was back, filling the room with its sickly odour.

Gagging, she staggered to the window, fumbling with the catch in her haste and then swinging it wide open to cleanse the room with fresh, cool air. Oh. God, she was really losing her mind. She must be! And she had no one to turn to, no one who would believe her or help her.

CHAPTER 11

Tessa came awake slowly, to find the room was in darkness save for the glow from the log fire, and to discover she was tucked up snugly in bed, although still wearing her bath robe. As she stirred she felt, rather than saw, a movement in the corner of the room and she cried out in alarm as all her earlier fears rushed back into her mind.

'Hush, it's me.' Matt switched on a lamp and emerged from the shadows, moving to sit on the edge of her bed.

In the subdued lighting he no longer looked angry, but so drawn and unhappy that Tessa wanted to throw herself into his arms, but she desisted, afraid of rejection. Perhaps he was going to tell her to leave Stafford House, after all? She had told him constantly that a hasty marriage was a mistake, so why was she feeling so wretched?

'How do you feel? Are you warm enough? When I came in the window was wide open and you were slumped in a frozen heap on the floor,' he said, his voice calm and polite, and certainly betraying nothing of the rush of compassion and love he had felt for the forlorn figure lying on the carpet.

204

'I'm fine.' Tessa sat up and bunched a pillow up behind her to rest against, and pushed her tangled hair back from her face. 'What time is it? And where's Abby?'

'It's almost eight o clock; she's in bed, wiped out after her first day at school. She came in to say goodnight to you, but accepted that you were just feeling tired and needed an early night.'

'Good.' She paused. 'Why aren't you having dinner with Susan Dalton?' she asked, ultra casual.

'I thought it was more important to talk to you, and hopefully have a rational discussion about what's going on. Do you have any explanation for that dreadful display of temper this afternoon?' he asked sternly. Tessa lifted her hand from the coverlet in a gesture of despair.

'It wasn't temper,' she protested defensively. 'Well, not really,' she amended, blushing under his quizzical gaze and remembering how she had shouted at Susan. She took a deep, steadying breath. 'I'm so frightened,' she whispered. Matt edged nearer, but didn't touch her.

'Tell me,' he invited. After a brief hesitation, Tessa haltingly told him what had happened that last night at the hospital – but she omitted to tell him the woman's assertion that Matt also wished she had died. She wasn't strong enough to witness the truth of that statement in his eyes.

'The nurse said I had dreamed it,' she admitted. 'She seemed so sure no one could have got into my room unseen, and when I asked if she could smell the perfume, she said it came from some flowers next to the bed.'

'Do you believe it was only a bad dream?' Matt asked quietly. Tessa frowned, for she still wasn't sure.

'It was so vivid,' she said slowly. 'I've never before awoken from a nightmare in such a blind terror. But I suppose I wanted to be convinced it wasn't real and I tried to forget it. I expect I would have done if I hadn't smelled the same perfume, here in this room. It was here the day I arrived and again this afternoon. And then the shooting brought back all the fears and doubts –'

'Hold on,' Matt interrupted. 'Let's deal with one thing at a time. Did you recognize the perfume on Sue?' he asked, sounding incredulous.

'Er no, I didn't,' she was forced to admit. 'Just here in the room.'

'So what on earth made you think Sue was responsible for any of this? You said you couldn't distinguish the features of whoever it was came to the hospital,' he reminded her.

'No, I couldn't. It was too dark; there was only a thin sliver of light from the doorway, just enough to show she was blonde.'

'So – why accuse Sue?' he asked again.

'Well, I knew she was in the house today when I lost my ring. She brought some brochures to my room, just before I went for my bath. But I was already suspicious of her because of the photograph . . .'

'Which photograph?' Matt asked patiently.

'I didn't imagine that!' Tessa sat up straighter. 'In fact, it was Abby who found it, not me. It's a picture of you and Susan; you have your arm around her and seem to be enjoying each other's company enor-

206

mously,' she told him. Matt detected – he hoped – a
definite note of jealousy in her voice.

'Where did Abby find it?'

'It's in one of the dressing-table drawers.' Tessa
pushed back the covers, eager to show him the one
small piece of tangible evidence she had.

'I'll get it; you stay where you are.' Matt restrained
her and then moved over to the dressing-table. 'Which
drawer?' he asked.

'It's the second one down on the right-hand side,'
Tessa said confidently, but then she watched, with
mounting dismay and apprehension as Matt searched
fruitlessly, first the drawer she mentioned and then all
the others in turn, but to no avail.

'Oh, God! It must be there!' She scrambled out of
bed to help search, but Matt caught her up in his arms.

'There's no photograph there,' he said gently.
'Come on, get back into bed before you catch a chill.'

'It was there, truly it was,' Tessa said desperately.
She slumped against Matt, once more afraid she was
losing her mind, and submitted weakly to being put
back to bed. 'But Abby saw it,' she insisted. 'Let's go
and ask her; she'll remember, I know she will,' she said
eagerly, once again pushing back the bed covers.

'She'll be asleep. I'll ask her about it tomorrow,'
Matt said, once again having to physically restrain her.

'It was there,' Tessa insisted. 'I certainly didn't
dream it. It had "Matt and Sue" printed on the back
and I recognized her as soon as I saw her this afternoon.'

'So? It's probably a photograph taken at a party
here. It means nothing, Tessa. Sue is an old friend of
the family, as well as being the estate secretary for

many years. But I have never had an affair with her,' he said firmly.

'Maybe that's what is upsetting her,' Tessa said slowly.

'Is that supposed to make sense?' Matt enquired, mentally couting to ten.

'Yes. She could be in love with you and thought she had a chance, working here in the house. Then, one day, you arrive with Abby and announce that you're setting up home with me, marrying me. If she loves you, that would have been a dreadful blow to her,' Tessa continued, warming to her theme while Matt sat in amazed silence in the face of feminine logic. Or illogic. 'She might have decided to come to see me in hospital, maybe just out of curiosity,' Tessa went on, 'but then her anger and disappointment made her lash out at me, and she's been snooping around ever since, and deliberately left that photograph of the two of you together for me to find,' she finished, almost triumphantly, Matt thought, as if she had solved a major crime.

'You really have been giving this a lot of thought, haven't you?' he asked slowly, realizing how upset and worried she must have been. 'But I'm sure you're mistaken, Tessa. I may be a bit dense, but I think I would have noticed if Sue were in love with me. But, even if she were, she's not a vindictive woman and I certainly can't imagine her sneaking her into a hospital room in the dead of night to try and frighten someone out of their wits.'

'Huh!' Tessa wished he hadn't used the word 'dead'. 'If it wasn't her, who was it?' she challenged him. 'It must be someone who thinks she has a prior claim on you.'

'*If* there was anyone at all,' Matt reminded her, but very gently. Tessa sank back against the pillows, defeated.

'You don't believe me,' she said dully. 'But thank you for listening.'

'I don't disbelieve you,' Matt said. 'I just think it's more likely that you had a bad dream.' He hesitated, then went on. 'Dr Stevens warned me you might be a little confused and suffer mood swings for a while. It doesn't mean you're going mad; it's a fairly common after-effect of an injury such as yours,' he assured her.

'I know; he explained that to me, too, but he said nothing about having hallucinations!' she said despairingly. Matt saw the fear in her eyes and reached for her hands, holding them tightly in his, as if he could thereby transfer his strength to her.

'Don't be alarmed, but I'm going to get someone out here to examine you, tomorrow if possible. I don't think we should wait until your check-up at the hospital.'

'You mean . . . a psychiatrist?' Tessa faltered.

'No! I don't mean that at all. You had a severe physical trauma – you are not going out of your mind,' he told her, then he frowned. 'There is one thing I don't understand . . .'

'Only one? I wish I was that lucky,' Tessa said bitterly and he smiled at her.

'Isn't Belinda Croxley a more likely suspect? Not that I'm suggesting she would so such a thing,' he added hastily.

'Well . . .' Tessa peeped at him from beneath her lashes. 'I did originally think it was Belinda,' she admitted. 'But, as Helen pointed out, she couldn't easily have been in this room the day I came out of hospital. Nor, presumably, this afternoon, unless you had a visitor I know nothing about?' she added questioningly.

'I haven't seen Belinda,' Matt assured her. 'You've confided all this in Helen?' he asked, surprised and a little upset.

'I knew Belinda was a friend of hers, so I asked her if she was very upset at breaking up with you, and then I told her about finding the photograph and asked her if she knew the identity of "Sue",' Tessa explained.

'Helen told you I'd had an affair with Susan Dalton?' Matt asked angrily.

'Oh, no,' Tessa said quickly. 'In fact, she said she was sure you hadn't – she was just guessing who a blonde woman named Sue might be.'

'I see.' Matt relaxed: he wouldn't put it past Helen to try and cause trouble – she was more than a little miffed at having to share George's attention with Abby!

They both looked up at the sound of a tentative knock on the door, and Evelyn popped her head round.

'Abby's awake, I'm afraid; over-excited about school, I think. She'd like you to read to her, Matt. I told her Tessa was too . . . tired. How are you, dear? Would you like some dinner?'

'Yes and yes,' Matt answered both questions.

'Actually, I'm not very hungry,' Tessa demurred.

'Try to eat something. Please,' he added, and she nodded.

'All right, I'll try. Will you ask Abby about the photograph?' she asked. 'I'd feel better if we can sort it out tonight.'

210

'Sure, I'll ask her,' he agreed, and touched her cheek lightly before leaving the room.

'What would you like to eat?' Evelyn asked Tessa.

'Oh, just soup or an omelette; nothing too heavy,' she said quickly.

'Right. I'll send Chris up with a tray.' Evelyn smiled and disappeared. If she had heard about – or heard, period – Tessa screeching at Susan Dalton earlier, she was certainly giving no indication of either annoyance or curiosity.

After a few minutes, Tessa scrambled out of bed and followed Matt into Abby's room, just as he was asking her, calmly and matter of factly, if she remembered finding a photograph of him in her mother's room. To Tessa's horror, Abby said nothing, but frowned uncertainly, her gaze flickering from Matt to Tessa and then down to her hands.

'You must remember! You were in my room while I was getting ready for dinner,' Tessa insisted, her voice rising a little as she was once more forced to doubt her sanity.

'It doesn't matter, Tessa. She's had a lot of changes in her life recently,' Matt said easily, then he turned to Abby once more. 'There's nothing wrong, sweetheart,' he told her gently. 'But I would like to see that photograph. Do you know where it is?'

After what seemed an age, Abby finally nodded, and Tessa expelled a huge pent-up breath of relief.

'I found it in Mummy's dressing-table – it's a picture of you and that lady who works in the office. You had your arm around her,' she added reprovingly.

'I know, but that won't happen again,' Matt assured her solemnly. 'Did you move it?'

'Mmm,' Abby nodded, after another pause. 'I put it in my book.

'Photograph album,' Tessa clarified for Matt.

'Yes,' Abby confirmed. 'I have lots of pictures of me and Mummy, but none of you, Daddy, so I wanted to put it in there,' she told him.

'That's okay,' Tessa reassured her, not understanding why she seemed so troubled. 'May we have a look at it?'

'All right.' With obvious reluctance, Abby got out of bed and rummaged for the album in a cupboard full of books and toys. Tessa shrugged helplessly at Matt's questioning glance but they both quickly realized what was amiss when Abby turned back to them. She had only half of the photograph; the other half depicting Susan Dalton had been cut away.

'Oh, Abby.' Tessa didn't know whether to laugh or cry.

'Daddy shouldn't put his arm around anyone else. And I didn't want her in my book anyway,' she added defiantly.

'Quite right,' Matt agreed, scrutinizing what remained of the photograph. 'I can't recall exactly when, but this was definitely taken in the ballroom here – I recognize the panelling in the background,' he said. 'My parents usually hold a huge party in there around Christmas every year. The entire village is invited, plus all the tenants and labourers with their families. This is meaningless, Tessa, honestly it is,' he assured her. He handed the picture back to Abby. 'If you ask your grandmother tomorrow, she'll give you dozens of snapshots to put in your book,' he told her. 'Now: are you sleepy yet, or do you want another story?'

'Story,' Abby said promptly.

'Okay.' Matt picked up the book that was lying beside the bed, then he glanced at Tessa. 'I'll settle her down while you go and eat your dinner. As soon as this one's asleep, I'll come and sort you out,' he said, feigning annoyance at the responsibilities being heaped upon his head.

'Ooh, promises, promises!' Tessa said lightly, pausing to kiss Abby before returning to her own room.

She changed out of the voluminous towelling robe and into a more becoming nightdress, then sat down to her meal, picking at it without much appetite and knew she was only attempting to eat it in an effort to please Matt. Really, how pathetic! she scoffed at herself, but she was smiling.

Her smile widened when he re-entered the room and she hastily compressed the remainder of her food into a corner of the plate to make it appear as if she had eaten more than she actually had.

'She's asleep.' Matt glanced at the contents of her tray and smiled his approval of the apparently near-empty plate. Then his gaze slowly wandered over her body, clad in the semi-transparent nightdress and Tessa sensed immediately that all thoughts of Abby or her own food intake were rapidly vanishing from his mind!

'Matt? Can I try and explain about the contraceptive pills?' she asked tentatively, reluctant to break this softer mood, but knowing the matter had to be resolved sooner or later.

'I don't think you need to say anything.' Matt made it easy for her; her denunciation of him for considering her to be 'rent-a-womb' had stopped him in his tracks

213

and given him food for thought. 'At a guess, I'd say you were angry, resentful and scared by my insistence that we have another child and you were determined, with some justification, I have to admit, to thwart me.'

'Not for ever,' she said quickly.

'That's nice to hear,' he said easily. 'But let's consider the subject closed for, say, six months?' he suggested. 'We can discuss it again then.' Tessa smiled and nodded her relief and agreement, but perversely found herself beginning to change her mind in the face of his capitulation.

'Are you sure you don't mind?'

'I'm sure,' he said firmly. 'I want you to enjoy making love with me, not worrying you might conceive.'

'I just need time to get used to the idea,' she said apologetically.

'I know; I understand. Subject closed – remember?' He reached into his pocket and took out her ring. 'Keep it safe this time,' he said, as he replaced it on her finger.

'Perhaps you ought to hang on to it for a while,' Tessa said, but with some reluctance. 'Just until I'm sure I'm in full possession of my wits! I could swear I placed it on top of the cabinet and not in the drawer.'

'No, you keep it,' Matt decided. 'I trust you,' he added, with a smile that faded when Tessa refused to meet his gaze. 'What have I said? Don't you believe I trust you? Or is it,' he said slowly, 'that you still don't trust me? You still think I'm having an affair with someone who sneaked into your hospital room and threatened you? Is that it?'

'No,' she said, but rather doubtfully, Matt thought. 'However, I do think someone wishes I . . . would leave here, leave you.'

'Tessa, that's nonsense. Everyone here wants you to recover fully from the accident and be happy,' he said earnestly. 'You're placing too much importance on a mislaid ring, some perfume you don't care for and a midnight hospital visit that could easily have been nothing more than a bad dream,' he said, oh so patiently, as if talking to a dim-witted three-year-old, Tessa thought angrily.

'What about the shooting?' she demanded. 'I suppose I imagined that as well, did I?'

'I thought we had agreed that that was probably nothing more than a car backfiring?' Matt sighed.

'Cars backfiring don't tear branches from trees!' Tessa retorted.

'What? You haven't mentioned that before.' He frowned. 'What exactly did happen?'

'There were two loud bangs and, after the second, I noticed that a small branch had snapped off a nearby tree, just above our heads.' She shivered at the memory.

'Show me tomorrow and I'll have a scout round,' Matt decided. 'If it was a shot, it must have been a poacher,' he said confidently, then, when he received no reply, 'Why are you so convinced it it was sinister? Do you really believe someone deliberately shot at you?' he asked incredulously. Still no reply. 'You had Flynn with you – he'd have gone in pursuit of a stranger.'

'Quite,' Tessa bit out. The silence lengthened unbearably; the tension was palpable and part of her was screaming at her to back down, to smile and agree with whatever he said, but a greater part was insisting she stand her ground; that she be strong enough to discover if Matt was her enemy.

'You think that someone in this house wishes to harm you? Why?'

'I didn't tell you everything earlier,' Tessa said, and took a deep breath. 'The woman who was in my room at the hospital – she said you only wanted Abby, not me.'

'You've already told me that. It's not true,' he said vehemently.

'She also said you wished I had died in the accident,' she whispered. Matt felt as if he had been punched, hard, in the stomach. He swallowed painfully.

'Do continue,' he said coldly. Tessa gnawed anxiously at her lower lip.

'The night before the shooting,' she began slowly, 'I signed my will, giving you guardianship of Abby if anything happened to me,' she reminded him awkwardly.

'I see,' he said, even more coldly. 'So I'm cast as the villain of the piece, am I?' he demanded harshly, hurt beyond belief that she could mistrust him so much. He'd give his life to protect her and Abby . . .

'Well, it was your father who actually suggested that we make our wills,' she said tentatively. 'He can shoot; he's ex-Army, isn't he?'

'Yes. So am I. But that doesn't mean we solve problems in civilian life by committing murder,' Matt said icily. 'I suppose he, or I, donned a woman's clothing and a blonde wig and sneaked into the hospital to warn you of this nefarious plan?' he

216

asked, his voice dripping with sarcasm. Tessa shook her head slightly. 'No? Perhaps there's a conspiracy afoot,' he continued. 'Belinda, or Sue, visited you in hospital, I took a shot at you, although I can assure you that I don't miss my targets, and my mother comes regularly into your room to spray perfume. Does that sound reasonable?' he enquired, in the tone of one about to phone for the men in white coats.

'No,' Tessa whispered. Matt studied her bowed head for a moment, then his eyes narrowed in suspicion.

'I wouldn't be surprised to find you had invented all this nonsense,' he said suddenly. Tessa's head jerked up in amazement.

'Why on earth would I do that?' she gasped.

'To persuade me to let you and Abby leave,' he said, feeling even more hurt, if that were possible. 'If so, it won't work. If you try to take my child away, I really will sue for custody,' he warned her. 'And your recent histrionics won't help your case at all, will they? I have witnesses to attest to your fragile state of mind. You're not fit enough to look after yourself, let alone take care of a five-year-old child. Think about it,' he advised her tersely, turning to leave.

As he reached the door, he halted and lashed out in his pain, giving in to the impulse to hurt as he had been hurt. 'Incidentally, it couldn't possibly have been Belinda who came to see you in hospital,' he lied, 'because she was with me that night – *all* night,' he stressed.

To add to his other woes, Matt also had an horrendous hangover on Tuesday morning when he awoke, stiff and cramped from falling asleep – or passing out, he wasn't sure which – in an armchair.

Evelyn found him morosely gulping strong black coffee in the breakfast room and bit back the comment which sprang to her lips. It was obvious from his dishevelled appearance that he hadn't been to bed all night, not his own and not, she felt sure, Tessa's.

She hadn't seen Matt in such a dreadful state since shortly after his return from Bosnia. At the time, she had attributed his moods to the pitiful plight of the people of the former Yugoslavia, but now she knew it was mainly his failure to locate Tessa Grant which had been eating away at him.

She sighed; she'd had such high hopes of his reunion with Tessa but something was obviously very wrong. Sudden fear gripped her as she contemplated the very real possibility of Tessa removing Abby from Stafford House. It would break George's heart, too, she knew, and being able to say 'I told you so' would be of no consolation to him.

'Would you mind taking Abby to school this morning?' Matt asked her.

'Normally I'd be delighted, but my car is in for a service,' she reminded him.

'Take mine. No, better still, take Tessa's,' he amended, deciding he had been an idiot to provide Tessa with the means to escape him. 'Tessa shouldn't be driving yet; she's still not well, suffering dizzy spells and headaches,' he explained hurriedly.

'Oh, I see. In that case, yes, of course I'll drive Abby to school,' Evelyn agreed.

Matt sent Chris up to Tessa's room with her breakfast, together with a request for her car keys and a message for her to meet him downstairs at nine o'clock. He intended checking the spot where she claimed to have been shot at, but forbore to mention that to Chris. Consequently Tessa became extremely anxious regarding the purpose of their meeting. She'd had even less sleep than Matt, alternately worrying about her position at Stafford House and weeping bitter tears over the information that Matt had slept with Belinda even after deciding to marry her, Tessa. What more proof did she need that Abby was the only reason he had contemplated marriage?

She descended the stairs in some trepidation, and then had to cool her heels waiting for Matt to put in an appearance. Finally, he arrived, having showered, shaved and changed into clean clothes and generally looking far better than Tessa felt.

'Sorry I'm late,' he greeted her coolly, sounding anything but apologetic. 'I had a busy night; there were several corpses to bury and the ground was as hard as hell after a frost.'

'Very funny.' Tessa scowled.

'No, Tessa, there is nothing remotely amusing about this.' Matt sighed. 'Come along, show me which path you and Abby took that afternoon.'

They walked in silence, several yards apart, accompanied by Flynn. Tessa led the way, confidently at first, then she paused and glanced around uncertainly.

'It was somewhere along here . . .' She looked up, checking the branches of trees and continued slowly on her way. 'There!' She pointed to where newly exposed wood showed clearly that a branch had broken off recently. Matt moved to study it more closely, then checked the ground, searching for the dismembered limb.

'From which direction do you think the noise came?' he asked neutrally. Tessa hesitated.

'I'm not sure; it all happened very quickly.'

'Make a guess.'

'Well, over there.' She pointed ahead of them and slightly to the right.

'Okay. I'm going to take a look around. You can go back indoors,' he said dismissively. Tessa stood her ground.

'Why did you want my car keys?'

'You're not fit enough to drive, are you? You can have them back when I'm confident you're not a danger to yourself and Abby, or to other road users.' It wasn't the whole truth, of course, but he wasn't about to admit his fears that she might just leave, disregarding his threats to take her to court.

He began striding off in the direction she had indicated, but then, for some inexplicable reason, turned round to look at her. Immediately he wished he hadn't; she looked so forlorn, he wanted to grab her up into his arms and never let her go. Yeah, great idea, you make a move on her and she'll think she's about to be strangled! he reminded himself bitterly.

'I want to talk to the nurse who assured you no one could have sneaked into your room – which one was it?' he asked abruptly.

'Marianne Harper.'

'Oh, yes, the pretty blonde . . . I'll enjoy interrogating her,' he said, with an evil smile.

'Bastard!' Tessa muttered, spinning on her heel to return to the house. Once indoors, she fled to the privacy of her room and stayed there. She felt as if everyone knew she had wrongly accused Susan Dalton of theft, and that she suspected her life and sanity were threatened by someone in the household.

Matt, meanwhile, ignoring the pounding in his head which intensified every time he bent to scan the ground more closely, continued his slow search. Eventually he found what he was looking for – a small clearing with flattened grass and a partial footprint. A further search resulted in the discovery of a spent cartridge shell.

Matt sat back on his heels and sighed. He didn't bother searching for the second shell; it wasn't necessary. So Tessa hadn't imagined a shot . . . He glanced down at the dog sitting patiently beside him.

'Poachers,' he murmured, but without much conviction. Tessa's fears were contagious. 'Why didn't you chase them, boy?' he asked Flynn. The Wolfhound was gentle as a lamb with those he knew, but extremely territorial and protective of the family, especially of Abby. She was the only child he'd ever had close contact with and, from the beginning, her small size and possibly her distress over Tessa's absence had endeared her to the huge animal, and he had watched over her most carefully. If Abby had been under threat, Flynn would have attacked the source of that threat – unless he knew and trusted the protagonist.

'God, this is intolerable, unbelievable,' Matt said out loud, wishing his hangover would ease sufficiently to enable him to think straight.

He pushed his way through the undergrowth and scrambled up the steep side of the ditch, emerging on the grass verge which ran along the Ashminster road.

He glanced back in the direction he had travelled: Stafford House was clearly visible in the distance – at least, the upper storeys were. However, no one standing where he was now could possibly have seen Tessa and Abby set out on their walk, he realized, with some relief. Even when he climbed up a tree, he was still unable to see the gateway from the stable yard. It could only have been a random act, probably poaching after all, but by one of the Stafford employees, someone Flynn had recognized. And the dog was no stranger to gunshots, and would have had no reason to go in pursuit.

Matt walked slowly along the verge and then re-traced his steps and eventually found the print of a tyre in the grass. Someone, tenant farmer or labourer who had attended shoots on the Stafford estate in the past, must have spotted a pheasant while driving past with a shotgun in the car, and decided to stop to catch his dinner.

That was a far more logical and likely explanation than Tessa having an enemy nearby. As for her hospital visitor, well, he would go and talk to Nurse Harper, he decided, and, whistling to Flynn to come to heel, he made his way back to the house.

He was still deeply hurt by Tessa's suspicions that he might want to harm her, so he didn't go in search of her, but quickly changed his clothes and set off for London.

CHAPTER 12

Matt would not have felt quite so easy in his mind if he had been aware of what had happened to his mother in Ashminster that morning.

After dropping Abby off at school, Evelyn, in Tessa's conspicuous bright blue sports car, drove the short distance to the town centre, found a parking space and went off to browse around the shops. She met, by chance, an old friend visiting Ashminster for a few days, and the two caught up on their respective family news over coffee and cream cakes. It was eleven-thirty before Evelyn returned to the car for the journey home.

'Oh, no, not a parking ticket!' was her first thought, when she saw the folded piece of paper tucked inside a windscreen wiper. Crossly, she snatched it up and opened it out and then stared uncomprehendingly at the printed words: I WON'T MISS NEXT TIME!

'How extraordinary.' Puzzled, she checked all round the car for dents or scratched paintwork, but it was immaculate. Besides . . . she glanced at the note again; the writer apparently had missed, but wouldn't in future . . . ?

She walked around the car once more, checking that she had parked it correctly, within the white painted lines. She had; she had inconvenienced no one, so how could anyone be so annoyed by her parking to threaten to damage the car if she transgressed again?

Perhaps the writer had followed her into Ashminster, and been irritated by her driving such a sporty number slowly and cautiously? Oh, well, road rage was usually pointless aggression, she thought, as she crumpled the note in her hands and looked around for a litter bin. She failed to spot one, so put the note in her bag, intending to dispose of it later.

She was more concerned with the deterioration of Matt's relationship with Tessa than the note, and put the unpleasant incident to the back of her mind and completely forgot about it until much later.

Matt waylaid Marianne Harper as she left the hospital at the end of her shift. She recognized him immediately, which he thought was a good sign, and he smiled warmly.

'Are you here with Miss Grant?' she asked, guessing Tessa had an appointment in Out-Patients.

'No, but Tessa is the reason I'm here. Do you have time for a coffee and a chat?' he asked easily, and thought he detected a slight wariness creep into her expression. 'Please?' he added, with another charming smile. Ricky would be proud of me, he thought drily, as she relaxed again and accepted his invitation.

She led the way into the hospital coffee-shop and Matt was reminded of the day, only a few weeks before, when he had come across Tessa and Abby in a similar place and his life had changed forever.

'May I call you Marianne?' he asked, as they carried their cups to a small table and sat down.

'Yes, please do,' she smiled. 'Has Miss Grant – Tessa – fully recovered now?'

'She is much better, thank you. But she is still rather anxious about several things,' Matt said slowly. 'That's why I want to talk to you, to clear up something that is upsetting her.'

'Really?' Marianne stirred her coffee, a somewhat unnecessary procedure since she had not added sugar, Matt noted.

'Mmm. I believe you were on duty the night before Tessa was released?'

'Yes, I was,' she nodded, sipping her coffee, her eyes lowered to the cup.

'Do you remember that she had a disturbed night; woke up from a bad dream?' he asked casually, and was sure he saw her shoulders relax a little.

'Yes, that's right. She was very agitated. She thought someone had been in her room, standing over her while she slept.'

'That's what she has told me,' Matt nodded, and sighed heavily. He smiled at Marianne and leaned forward, as if they were co-conspirators, the two of them against an unreasonable Tessa. 'I don't suppose there's a possibility that there actually was someone in her room?' he asked, his tone implying that he didn't believe it for a second and was only here to humour Tessa.

'No. I would have seen them, and it was way past visiting hours, so I'm sure I would have noticed anyone hanging around,' she said confidently.

'They would have to pass your desk – right?'

'Yes.' She nodded.

'Oh, well, thanks for the clarification.' Matt sighed. 'I thought you'd say that, but it was worth a shot. I suppose I'll have to take her to a shrink . . .'

'Oh, no, I shouldn't think that's necessary! It was only a bad dream,' Marianne protested, shocked.

'But Tessa is so sure it really happened. She's even accusing people of wanting to murder her,' Matt said, grimacing and tapping his head significantly with his finger.

'Oh, my God!' she eyed him uncertainly and gnawed her lower lip for a few moments. 'Well, I suppose it is possible that someone sneaked in,' she admitted slowly. 'I did leave my desk for a few minutes . . . five at most,' she insisted.

'Go on,' Matt said tersely.

'One of the nurses was leaving that night and there was a farewell party on the floor below. I just popped in to wish her good luck – all my patients were settled for the night and none was seriously ill. In fact, they were all due to be discharged in a day or two,' she excused herself.

'I see. So Tessa was asleep and alone in her room, with no nursing staff on the floor . . .' Matt prompted her.

'Yes. I checked on all the patients before I left. When I returned, Tessa was frantically pressing her buzzer and I ran into her room. There was no one there and I honestly don't think there ever was,' she said earnestly. 'If someone had been in her room, I would have passed them in the corridor.'

'Mmm.' Matt frowned, mulling it over. 'Isn't there a cloakroom next to the room Tessa occupied?'

'Yes . . .'

'So, if there was someone in Tessa's room, and she left when Tessa started ringing for help, could she have hidden in the cloakroom until after you had gone in to attend to Tessa?' he asked.

'I suppose that's possible,' she admitted. 'If whoever it was saw me approaching, well, yes, I guess that could have happened. I was looking to see which buzzer had been pressed so I would have had my back to the corridor, but only for a matter of seconds.'

'I understand.' Matt nodded. 'This won't go any further, I promise you. I'm not interested in causing trouble for you,' he assured her. 'But are you positive you didn't see anyone hanging around, perhaps before you left the floor?'

'I'm sure,' she said firmly. And truthfully, Matt thought, which meant he was no further forward in his investigation than when he had set out from Drake's Abbot that morning.

It was possible there had been an intruder, but not very likely. He hadn't been able to conclusively rule it out, but nor was he any nearer proving it had really happened. In a way, he was sorry Marianne Harper hadn't seen a blonde woman skulking around the corridors, for, although the possibility of Tessa having a vindictive enemy was terrifying, at least he would have had something, someone, to seek out and confront. It had been too much to hope Marianne would have been able to positively identify such a person.

'Thanks for talking to me.' He smiled as he got to his feet. 'If you remember anything else, however unimportant you think it is, will you give me a call?' he asked, handing her one of his business cards.

'Of course I will. Actually, it's a relief to have told someone,' she said frankly. 'It's been on my mind. But I'm still ninety per cent sure it was nothing more than a vivid nightmare.'

'I hope so,' Matt smiled again and took his leave.

He mulled over it as he drove home, but was no nearer a conclusion, let alone a solution, by the time he arrived back at Drake's Abbot. It seemed to him very odd that Tessa should dream of a strong perfume and then smell it again while she was awake. That seemed to him to indicate that it was not a dream, but if it had been real . . . He shook his head to clear his thoughts.

He didn't consider himself to be unduly modest, yet he certainly couldn't envisage Belinda being heartbroken and vidictive over the ending of their affair. And Belinda was not one for subterfuge – if she had wanted to confront Tessa, she would have done it openly.

As for Sue Dalton . . . she and her husband had been very happily married; it was difficult to believe she had developed a burning passion for him, Matt, since being widowed. The photograph of the two of them together could have lain in Tessa's dressing-table drawer for several years, could have been left there by anyone.

He sighed heavily as he climbed out of his car and sighed again when he heard Abby crying. Oh, God, now what? he thought despairingly, as he hurried into the house to discover what was wrong.

His mother, looking unduly flustered, was in the hall with Abby. Tessa was running down the stairs, her attention focussed entirely on her distressed child.

'What's the matter, sweetie?' Tessa knelt and held out her arms. Abby ran into her embrace so fast, Tessa almost toppled backwards beneath the onslaught.

'What the hell's going on here?' Matt demanded. To Abby's ears, he sounded angry rather than concerned, and her sobs grew louder.

'I called in on Helen after collecting Abby from school,' Evelyn began, her face flushed and anxious. 'I'm afraid Abby has broken one of David's figurines,' she explained. Matt groaned audibly. David and Helen had an extensive – and expensive – collection of rare, valuable porcelain.

'All this fuss over an ornament?' Tessa said incredulously. 'I'm sure she didn't mean to break it.'

'I didn't, Mummy! I didn't,' Abby wailed.

'I know, sweetie, don't cry.' Tessa kissed her hot, wet cheek and held her close.

'They're rather special "ornaments", Tessa,' Matt told her. 'David collects Meissen, Chelsea, Sèvres . . . Which figure was broken?' he asked his mother.

'The Harlequin,' she said heavily. 'Abby loved the bright colours . . .'

'She would.' Matt sighed. He knew the piece in question – or pieces, now, he thought with black humour. It was a recent acquisition and had cost upwards of five thousand pounds. Tessa paled a little when he passed on that little detail, but then hugged

Abby to her, suddenly hating all these people with their blasted possessions that apparently meant more to them than a small child.

'How is Abby supposed to know the difference between that and a toy? What sort of moron gives a valuable, fragile antique to a child to play with?' she asked crossly, without stopping to think.

'I'm afraid I did,' Evelyn said, rather stiffly. 'We warned her to be careful. I only took my eye off her for a moment . . .' she trailed off.

'I'd better go over there,' Matt said. 'With my cheque book.'

'Come on, sweetie, let's go upstairs.' Tessa rose and lifted Abby, but with some difficulty. Matt noticed how she almost buckled beneath the weight and he strode forward, intending to help.

'Let me take her; she's too heavy for you,' he offered, and was totally unprepared for the blaze of hatred in Tessa's eyes, so fierce that he took an involuntary step backwards. He had completely forgotten his lie, telling her he had spent the night before her discharge from hospital with Belinda. Tessa hadn't.

'Leave us alone!' she hissed, and turned towards the stairs. I can't do that; I won't, Matt thought, watching the two people he loved most moving away from him. Abby had buried her face in her mother's neck, arms and legs wrapped tightly around her, eyes squeezed shut so she needn't look at her grandmother or Matt.

'I didn't . . .' she whispered.

'I know, don't cry, darling,' Tessa soothed her, as she made her way slowly and rather awkwardly up the stairs to Abby's room.

* * *

230

It took Tessa a long time to calm Abby down, but eventually, when she was assured her mother wasn't angry with her, she relaxed a little and began reciting the events of her day at school. Tessa read with her and they played board games until Chris appeared with food on a tray, milk for Abby and coffee for Tessa.

'What's happening downstairs?' Tessa asked – she was beginning to feel like a prisoner! Chris grimaced and rolled her eyes heavenwards.

'Mr Stafford – old Mr Stafford,' she clarified, 'was raising hell for a while, but with Mrs Stafford for being fool enough to let Abby play with the bloody thing – his words, not mine,' she added hastily. 'Honestly, what a fuss! I bet it was insured. Imagine anyone paying that sort of money for an ornament,' she snorted disgustedly, echoing Tessa's sentiments exactly. 'My boyfriend and I could put a deposit down on a nice house for that amount.' She sighed.

'Are you getting married?' Tessa asked, surprised, glancing at her ringless hand.

'Next year, hopefully,' Chris nodded, then reached out to give Abby a hug. 'But we'll be living locally, so I'll be available to help look after this one. And any newcomers,' she added, with a sly grin.

'Don't hold your breath,' Tessa retorted: the likelihood of her and Matt having another child seemed extremely remote at the moment! 'Er, has Matt returned yet?' she asked casually.

'If he has, I haven't seen him,' Chris told her, heading for the door. 'I've some ironing to finish, but I'll come back and stay with Abby if you want to go down to dinner,' she offered.

'No, thanks; I'd rather stay here,' Tessa said vehemently. Chris grinned in sympathy before leaving the room.

Abby brightened up considerably as the evening wore on, chattered happily while taking her bath and then settled down with Tessa in front of the TV – the one in Tessa's room, since Matt had stuck to his guns and removed the set from Abby's room the evening before she returned to school, promising she could have it back during the holidays.

'We have to apologize to David for breaking that figurine,' Tessa said quietly, when she was confident Abby had regained her composure, but she was careful to appear to share the blame with the 'we'. 'I'll help you write him a letter, shall I?'

'No,' Abby said firmly, compressing her lips tightly together. Tessa frowned slightly, surprised by her attitude. Usually, after an act of naughtiness or disobedience – although Tessa didn't class the accidental breakage as such – Abby was all contrition and eagerness to make amends.

'Why not? We have to say we're sorry –'

'Not sorry. Not my fault,' Abby insisted stubbornly. 'Don't like Helen. She smacked me!' she said indignantly.

'She did what?' Tessa was outraged. She had very rarely punished Abby physically, feeling she was doing a bad job as a mother if she had to resort to violence, however minor, in order to exert her authority. 'Where did she smack you? Does it hurt?'

'Here.' Abby lifted her arm and pointed to the back of her hand. There was no bruising or even a red mark, but that did little to mollify Tessa. She kissed it better

232

and dropped the subject of an apology: she would have something to say to Helen Warrender, she thought grimly, but the word 'sorry' wouldn't feature in it at all!

'Can I sleep in your bed tonight?' Abby pleaded, when Tessa tried to persuade her it was time for her to return to her own room.

'Yes, all right. You can watch TV while I take a bath and then we'll both get some sleep,' Tessa decided. Despite having done very little – except worry – the entire day, she felt worn out.

It was only a little after eight o'clock when she switched off the main light and snuggled down with Abby, who quickly fell asleep. After a while, Tessa turned on the bedside lamp and began flicking through a magazine, trying to find something to catch her attention. Although she was physically very tired, she was too tense for sleep to come easily.

'Why didn't you come down for dinner?' Matt suddenly walked in, without bothering to knock first. Tessa didn't even look at him.

'I wasn't hungry. And I don't care for the company downstairs,' she said coldly. Matt's brows rose.

'Abby did break a valuable antique,' he pointed out, but quite mildly. 'You've been making a fuss about how much we've all been spoiling her, and now you're resentful because my mother rebuked her.'

'I'm not angry because your mother chastised her. I'm angry because Helen hit her,' Tessa said hotly. 'I don't care if Abby smashed the entire contents of the house, Helen had no right to smack her!'

'No, I agree –' Matt began, then broke off, his lips tightening as Tessa's exaggerated grimace showed

233

plainly how little she valued his agreement. Or even his opinion, presumably. 'I'll talk to Helen,' he continued evenly.

'Don't bother. I would prefer to do that myself,' Tessa told him, in a tone that boded ill for Helen.

'Very well,' Matt nodded slightly. Tessa and Helen would have to learn how to get along, members of the same family and living near each other's house. He wasn't surprised to learn Helen had exacerbated the situation: accustomed to being George Stafford's pampered little darling, she was somewhat miffed at being usurped by Abby.

He moved nearer to the bed and gazed down at Abby, who was still sleeping peacefully, undisturbed by the conversation going on over her head, and cuddling close to her mother.

'I'm jealous of her,' he said, and strove to speak lightly, but realized it was true. Would he and Tessa ever be able to live in harmony?

'Tough. Go to Belinda if you're in need of a bed partner,' Tessa snapped.

'Don't be ridiculous.' Matt sighed. 'You know that's finished.'

'Really? Only because your younger brother has stepped into your shoes. Or, should I say, your bed?' she enquired snidely. 'How dare you say it's finished when you admitted you slept with her after you had decided you wanted to marry me?' she asked bitterly. Matt stared at her, then groaned and ran his fingers distractedly through his hair.

'I didn't spend the night with her. I only told you that to hit back at you,' he admitted. 'It was incredibly stupid and childish, but how do you think I felt, knowing you suspected me of wishing you had died?' he demanded. 'That hurt almost as much as your keeping Abby a secret from me for all these years!' He paused and then continued more quietly. 'The truth is, I haven't slept with Belinda since the day of your accident, or, to be strictly accurate, the night before,' he amended. 'While you were in the coma, I spent my nights here as Abby was at her most distressed in the evenings. Then, after I'd set my heart on marrying you, I took Belinda out to dinner – that was the day you recovered consciousness, actually – and told her I wouldn't be seeing her again. But it was just dinner. I did *not* sleep with her,' he finished firmly.

'Oh,' Tessa said faintly, appalled by the heady rush of relief she felt at hearing that. 'So Belinda could have come to my room,' she realized slowly. 'That was only a couple of days after you broke up with her.'

'Yes, but, believe me, she wasn't that upset,' Matt smiled slightly. 'I went to talk to Marianne Harper today,' he continued.

'And?' Tessa asked sharply.

'I'm afraid it wasn't a very constructive conversation,' he admitted. 'She insists she didn't see anyone hovering around that night, and I think she was telling the truth. However, she did tell me that she was away from her post at the time you were disturbed. She claims she was only absent for a maximum of five minutes, but I would guess she was away for nearer fifteen.'

'Oh.' Tessa grimaced slightly, not sure how she felt about that. She couldn't decide which was worse – suffering from delusions or being threatened by a real, live person. 'So it is possible my "visitor" was not the product of a nightmare?' She looked at Matt, as if he held all the answers, he thought, and only wished that he had.

'Possible, but not very probable,' he said gently. 'As for the shooting, well, I did find a spent cartridge, and also the spot where the gunman entered the wood from the Ashminster road. But whoever it was couldn't possibly have seen you and Abby leave the stable. I'm sure it was a local man shooting at pheasant – there's nothing unusual or sinister about a farmer having a shotgun or rifle in his vehicle.'

'I'll take your word for it,' Tessa said lightly.

'Do you?' Matt knew it had been a casual rejoinder, but he had to straighten this out; her mistrust was intolerable to him. 'Do you really take my word for it?' he repeated. Tessa, hearing the intensity in his voice, looked at him searchingly. 'Do you truly believe I mean you no harm?' he persisted.

'I . . . yes, I do,' she said truthfully. She wasn't so sure about his parents, or his ex-girlfriends, but she did believe in Matt.

'Good.' He expelled a pent-up breath of relief. 'I also had a word with our family doctor today,' he told her, eyeing her rather warily. 'He's coming to see you tomorrow at eleven o'clock and, if he thinks it necessary, we'll consult a specialist.'

'I don't need to see your doctor,' Tessa objected, grimacing at the prospect.

'Please?' Matt smiled winsomely and, as always when he was asking instead of telling, Tessa found herself complying with his wishes.

'Oh, okay,' she agreed reluctantly.

'Besides, he's your GP now as well, not just mine,' Matt pointed out. 'Call it a getting-acquainted meeting,' he suggested.

What Tessa wanted to call it was unprintable, but she merely nodded.

'If he pronounces you fully fit, we'll take a trip to London and you can concentrate on something more important – like choosing a wedding dress,' he continued huskily. 'I haven't sold my flat yet so we could stay overnight, see a show . . .' He bent to kiss her mouth and left the rest of the evening's plans to her imagination. Tessa remembered that the flat only had one bedroom and she flushed slightly, then glanced down at the sleeping child beside her.

'I know; she's more effective than a cold shower!' Matt said ruefully, pulling away from her. 'I'd better leave. Sleep well, my love,' he said softly.

After he had closed the door behind him, Tessa returned to her perusal of her magazine, but quickly discovered she wasn't absorbing any of the story she had begun reading earlier.

She switched off the light and slid down in the bed and closed her eyes. A broad smile was curving her mouth as she drifted off to sleep: he had called her 'my love'.

Tessa's early-morning coffee tray also bore a silver bud vase containing a red rose – and her car keys. Smiling, she picked up the vase and wondered where on earth Matt had found the flower in late October.

Matt appeared as she was getting Abby ready for school. Abby's chatter ceased abruptly when she saw her father and she eyed him warily, obviously wondering if he intended punishing her for breaking David's figurine.

'Good morning.' He smiled at Abby and then turned to Tessa, slipping his arm around her waist. 'How are my two favourite girls today?'

'How should we know how Belinda and Sue are faring?' Tessa enquired sweetly.

'Ouch!'

'Sorry, I couldn't resist it,' she told him cheerfully. 'We're fine, aren't we, Abby?'

'Yes,' she nodded, still a little uncertain about Matt's mood. He reached out and drew her to him for a brief hug and immediately she relaxed against him, confident of forgiveness.

'Thanks for the rose, and for letting me have my keys back,' Tessa said.

'It's your car. I should never have taken them from you,' Matt said, regretting his hasty action. 'But promise me you won't drive if you feel dizzy or have a bad headache? There are plenty of people here ready and willing to run errands for you.'

'I know; I promise I won't drive if I'm not up to it,' she agreed readily.

'Would you like me to take Abby to school this morning? I have to go into Ashminster some time today.'

'No, thanks, I'll take her,' Tessa said: she had already decided she would call in at Grange Farm to talk to Helen on her return journey.

'Fine,' Matt nodded. 'It occurred to me that you might feel happier if –' he broke off, belatedly aware of Abby, listening avidly.

'Go and brush your teeth, sweetie,' Tessa told her, then turned enquiringly to Matt.

'An ex-Army friend of mine runs a security firm, hiring out bodyguards,' he explained. 'I thought you might feel better if there was someone always around to protect you.'

'Thank you, but no,' Tessa declined slowly, feeling a warm glow at pleasure at this evidence of his thoughtfulness and consideration of her. It was a tempting offer, but she had to overcome her fears by herself sooner or later. 'Maybe if anything else weird happens, I'll reconsider, but I'm feeling much better about everything.'

'I'm certainly glad to hear that. Okay, we'll leave it for now,' Matt said easily.

Later, they would both remember his offer, casually offered, and even more casually refused, and wish they had decided otherwise . . .

Tessa hadn't yet been inside Grange Farm, but Matt had pointed out the whitewashed building one day when they drove past, and Tessa located it without any difficulty.

David Warrender was leaving just as she arrived, and he climbed back out of his car when he saw her approach. They had met only once, at Stafford House; Tessa had forgotten Matt telling her that David was a businessman and not a farmer, and had been surprised by his appearance. He was much older than Helen, late forties, she guessed, very smartly dressed and well groomed, with only the merest hint of an Australian accent.

'Good morning, Tessa,' he greeted her with a smile, she was relieved to see.

'Good morning. Don't let me delay you,' she said quickly, noting he had left his car engine running. 'I'm really sorry Abby broke something so valuable,' she said, not altogether sincerely. Like Chris, she felt there was something almost obscene about someone being able to spend so much money on what was basically bric-a-brac. And collecting porcelain figurines didn't seem a particularly masculine pastime, somehow . . . but that was beside the point, she told herself sternly.

'Don't worry about it; accidents happen. Unfortunately, Helen and I just aren't used to having young children in the house,' he said, with discernible regret and sadness. Tessa found herself warming to him. 'I'm not angry with Abby; obviously Helen should never have let her touch it,' he added, and Tessa warmed to him even more.

'Is there any possibility it can be mended?' she asked hopefully.

'I'm afraid not. But please don't worry, Tessa. It was insured for the full value,' David the businessman said briskly. 'It is a pity, though; it was over two hundred years old,' he added.

'Oh, dear,' Tessa said lamely. The flippant retort: I'm glad it wasn't new! sprang to mind, and she had to bite down hard on her lip to prevent the words escaping.

'Tessa!' Helen leaned out of an upstairs window. 'I'm so glad you're here – I was going to drive over later. Bye, darling!' She blew a kiss to David.

'I'll leave you two girls to have a chat,' he said, and returned to his car.

Tessa walked towards the house, straightening her shoulders as she did so. She realy did want to get along well with Matt's family, but she would not allow any of them to smack Abby. However, Helen quickly took the wind out of her sails.

'Tessa, I am so sorry about yesterday,' Helen began as she ushered her inside. 'I don't know if Abby told you, but I did something dreadful,' she said, showing Tessa into the drawing-room and disappearing briefly before returning with a tray of freshly brewed coffee.

'I knew David would go ballistic when he found one of his precious figurines had hit the dust – literally,' she grinned, and then continued seriously. 'I know it was unforgivable, but, well, I smacked Abby. I regretted it at once – I do hope she's not upset with me?' she asked anxiously.

'She was extremely upset last night, but she seemed to be back to her usual self this morning,' Tessa acknowledged. 'But that is the reason I'm here – that, and to apologize to David, of course,' she added quickly, prepared to meet her future in-laws halfway.

'Oh, he's fine about it now.' Helen shrugged. 'He loves going to auctions and poking around antique shops. He'll claim the insurance money and enjoy spending it on another of the wretched things,' she sighed, glancing around at the numerous *objets d'art* scattered around the room. 'He does get so attached to them, though,' she sighed again.

'I'm sorry,' Tessa said lamely.

'Oh, forget it, please. Listen, why don't we go shopping and have a long gossip over lunch?' Helen suggested next. 'I'd really like to buy Abby a gift, to apologize for losing my temper.'

'It's not necessary to go that far,' Tessa demurred. Abby should have been more careful and certainly didn't deserve a reward. 'Besides, I'm seeing the GP at eleven o'clock this morning.'

'Harvey? Oh, he's an old duck; an old friend of the family – you'll like him. But why – are you feeling worse?'

'No, I'm just not getting fit again as quickly as I had hoped,' Tessa told her.

'I see. Well, how about tomorrow? Are you free for shopping and lunch? My treat. We haven't had much of an opportunity to get to know each other yet, have we? And I could invite a couple of friends to join us for lunch – it's time for you to meet some of our social set – but not Belinda, obviously!' she added, laughing. 'Please say yes or I shall think you've not forgiven me for slapping Abby. I really am sorry about that, Tessa,' she said earnestly. 'I'm just not used to dealing with small children.'

'And the havoc they can cause?' Tessa drily added Helen's unspoken words. 'Okay; I'd enjoy a shopping trip,' she decided.

'Great! I'll pick you up tomorrow at – ten-thirty?' she suggested.

'That will be fine.' Tessa finished the last of her coffee and got to her feet.

'Good luck with Dr Harvey,' Helen said, as Tessa climbed back into her car. 'And don't let him fill you up with "mother's little helpers"!' she warned.

'With what?' Tessa queried.

'Tranquillizers,' Helen clarified. 'He swears by them, and doesn't seem to realize that most women simply crush them up in their husband's dinner to

242

keep the brute docile! On second thoughts, take them if he offers and give them to Matt,' she added, with a grin.

Tessa laughed and shook her head slightly: the idea of Matt becoming docile ought to be an appealing one, but somehow it wasn't. As she was coming to realize more and more, she loved him just the way he was.

CHAPTER 13

Tessa loved Matt even more when she returned to Stafford House and found him waiting for her.

'I thought you were busy this morning?' she asked him, trying to subdue the warm glow of pleasure she experienced upon seeing him.

'I am, but your health is more important than any business meeting,' he assured her. 'I want to be here when Harvey arrives.'

'Thank you,' Tessa smiled happily. She had been feeling a little apprehensive, but no longer. However, it was a little disconcerting to realize just how quickly she was not only becoming accustomed to being cossetted, but was actually starting to enjoy it.

The doctor arrived punctually at eleven; a small, dapper man with bright blue eyes and a capable manner whom Tessa liked immediately. He told Matt affably, but firmly, that he would talk to Tessa alone. Matt told him, only slightly less amiably, but rather more firmly, that he intended staying. Harvey looked questioningly at Tessa, evidently happy for her to decide.

'I've no secrets from Matt,' she assured him. 'In fact, I feel a fraud, dragging you all the way out here. I could easily have come to the surgery – not that I even need to do that,' she added hastily.

'Mmm, well, I might as well have a look at you now I'm here,' Harvey said easily, and proceeded to carry out the routine checks of pulse, temperature and blood pressure and peered into her eyes.

'That's all satisfactory.' he smiled at her as he began packing away his instruments. 'I understand from Matt that you're still suffering from headaches – are they becoming more or less severe?'

'Less,' Tessa said promptly. 'They're only really bad if I overdo things. I'm still getting tired more easily than usual, but apart from that, I'm almost as good as new,' she told him.

'She still has dizzy spells,' Matt put in, with a stern look for Tessa.

'Yes, that's true, but again, it only happens when I'm overtired,' she explained quickly, with a mind-your-own-business glance at Matt.

'Physically, you seem to be making an excellent recovery. But you must rest more, not wait until you feel tired,' Harvey cautioned her. He paused and looked at her searchingly, his bright blue eyes rather too shrewd for Tessa's peace of mind.

She recalled Helen's warning about the tranquillizers and tried to appear composed and relaxed, clasping her hands loosely together in her lap and meeting his gaze squarely. She guessed he was about to turn to the subject of the feelings she had of being stalked and threatened. She tried not to tense up, but sensed it would be important to come up with a sensible, calm answer.

'I hear you're getting married soon?' he asked, to her surprise.

'Yes, at Christmas,' she said, with a sideways glance at Matt, who smiled and nodded.

'Do you still feel one of this young reporobate's old flames is trying to frighten you away?' Harvey put to her suddenly.

'Well, I . . . no, I don't think that,' she said firmly, but couldn't control the hot flush which suffused her cheeks. She felt a complete idiot.

'I admit I overreacted when I thought someone had stolen my ring. But nothing really sinister has happened since I left hospital and I'm prepared to concede that that was a nightmare,' she smiled slightly. 'They gave me some sort of sleeping pill,' she continued, trying to place some of the blame on the hospital staff, 'and it all happened very quickly. I was barely awake before it was over and the nurse came into the room. That was still on my mind when I heard gunshots while out walking here, but then, I'm a city girl and Matt assures me there is nothing untoward about hearing gunshots out here in the country,' she finished, and offered the doctor another cool smile. She had deliberately spoken slowly and calmly, playing down the events and her fears, not all of which had been completely allayed.

'Hmm.' Harvey regarded her steadily and Tessa gazed back, making a conscious effort not to fidget under his bright-eyed scrutiny. She had the uneasy feeling that he didn't quite believe her. That was confirmed when he took out a prescription pad from his bag and began to scribble.

'What's that for?' she asked suspiciously.

'Just something to help you relax,' he smiled at her.

'Not tranquillizers?' Tessa was glad Helen had warned her.

'Very mild and non-addictive,' he assured her. 'They'll ensure you get a good night's sleep while you're recovering from the trauma of what was a very nasty accident,' he said smoothly.

'I see. Very well.' Tessa smiled and took the prescription he held out to her, and decided she would rip it up as soon as he had left.

'I'll get that made up for you.' Matt reached over and plucked the form from her fingers and folded it into his pocket.

'Thank you,' Tessa said, through gritted teeth. Oh well, she'd just have to chuck the wretched things down the loo instead, she thought. But just one at a time – knowing Matt, he would probably check at make sure she was taking them. He had been looking at her rather quizzically while she spoke to Harvey, obviously not recognizing this calm and collected Tessa as the same woman who had ranted and raved at Susan Dalton a couple of days before!

'If you have any problems, or those headaches get worse, come and see me,' Harvey told her, as he got to his feet. 'How's George's arthritis?' he asked Matt, as he accompanied him to the door.

Tessa blew out a breath of relief. God, it was nerve-racking, pretending to be calm and serene! She wasn't even sure she *had* convinced Harvey, and certainly not Matt, that she wasn't nuts. But it worried her that Harvey – an old friend of George Stafford – might want to hospitalize her if he considered her paranoid about a secret enemy. And the will George had suggested be drawn up gave Matt custody of Abby in the event of Tessa's death – or incapacity.

She no longer feared Matt's father had taken a shot at her, but she was sure he would be quite pleased if she were out of the picture, tucked away in hospital somewhere. In fact, he had suggested several times that Stafford House was more than big enough for them all and that the move to the Dower House was unnecessary. And, if Matt had sole guardianship of Abby, no doubt he would keep to the current living arrangements whereby his parents were always available to help look after Abby.

'Oh, get a grip,' she muttered crossly, and walked over to where a pile of colour charts and swatches of curtain material were spread out on a table. She had almost made a choice some days previously after dinner, but had thought it best to wait and check the colours in a natural light before making a final decision.

'I can drop those off in Ashminster this afternoon,' Matt offered as he re-entered the room, glad to see her involved in the refurbishment of their future home.

'That's okay; I'm going shopping with Helen tomorrow, so I'll do it then,' Tessa said. Matt frowned.

'You're supposed to be resting more,' he reminded her. 'Shopping with Helen is definitely not a rest cure.'

'I remember you telling me that before, but, if I refuse, she will think I'm still angry about her slapping Abby,' Tessa explained. 'She wanted to buy me lunch by way of an apology.'

'I see. Very well, go if you want to, but don't let her drag you round every shop in Ashminster,' he cautioned. 'You won't be taking your car, will you?' he added, not wanting her to drive when tired.

'No, Helen's picking me up,' she assured him. 'If I feel tired after lunch. I'll get a taxi home and Helen can do the rest of her shopping without me – okay?'

'Okay,' Matt agreed. He moved closer and put his arms loosely around her waist. 'That was quite an act you put on for Harvey – or are you really convinced no one here means you harm?' he asked intently.

'I'm convinced you don't.' Tessa reached up to kiss him, partly because she wanted to and partly to end the conversation.

Her ploy worked and Matt's hold tightened, drawing her closer until she was pressed against the hard-packed muscles of his body. He bent his head and kissed her hungrily as his hands caressed her body, seeking the soft warm skin beneath her clothing.

'Oh, Tessa,' he groaned, pulling away with the utmost difficulty and reluctance.

'Why did you stop?' she asked, and her voice sounded plaintive even to her own ears. Matt smiled slightly and rested his head against her hair.

'I seem to spend half my time telling you to rest, and the other half wanting to rip off your clothes and make love to you until we're both too exhausted to move,' he told her ruefully.

'Well, I'm bored with resting,' Tessa murmured meaningfully, moving closer to him.

'Tessa, if it's all right with . . . oh! sorry,' Evelyn said, glancing at first Matt and then Tessa, and cursing herself for interrupting what had obviously been an intimate moment. 'I didn't realize you were still here,

249

Matt. I thought you were seeing Tom Rowlands at twelve?'

'Oh, hell!' Matt glanced at his watch, then looked at Tessa. 'Tonight?' he asked softly, his sapphire eyes hot with longing. She nodded wordlessly, sure her own eyes were reflecting the desire that blazed from his.

Heedless of his mother's watching presence, Matt kissed Tessa once more, briefly but with the promise of delights in store.

The prospect of those delights meant Tessa spent the rest of the day in a complete daze. Evelyn, tiring of her every question or comment receiving only a blank stare or a vague, 'Sorry – what did you say?', eventually left her alone with her thoughts.

'I'll go and collect Abby from school,' she said at three o'clock, having decided Tessa was incapable of concentrating on driving.

'Where's Mummy?' Abby asked as soon as she saw her grandmother; she was still inclined to be anxious whenever her mother was absent, fearful of another accident.

'In a world of her own,' Evelyn muttered, then she smiled brightly at Abby. 'She's at home, she's fine,' she assured her. Abby relaxed, but tensed again as she got into Evelyn's car.

'We're not going to see Helen again, are we?' she asked fearfully as Evelyn buckled her into her safety-belt, the memory of the previous afternoon's events still fresh in her mind.

'No, not today,' Evelyn said, and not until they've got all their valuables safely behind locked doors, she thought, sighing. She still couldn't understand how the figurine had come to be broken. Abby had been sitting down, holding it carefully in her lap, yet somehow she had dropped it, and not on to the sofa cushions or the deep pile carpet which would have softened the blow, but against the hard brass corner of the coffee table.

It was almost as if the child had done it deliberately, she thought worriedly, yet, until that incident, there had been no hint of temper or spite in Abby in all the weeks she had been living at Stafford House. Evelyn sighed again and put it firmly from her mind.

'What have you been doing today?' she enquired brightly, as she started up the car.

Abby, reassured that Tessa wasn't ill and that they weren't going to call on Helen, began her usual happy chatter and proudly showed Evelyn a rather garish painting in bright yellow and orange.

'I painted this for Mummy. It's a flutterby,' she announced.

'A what?' Evelyn looked in some perplexity at the the drawing. She doesn't seem to have inherited Ricky's talent! she thought.

'A flutterby,' Abby repeated.

'Oh. You mean a butterfly,' Evelyn hazarded. It was Abby's turn to look puzzled.

'Are you sure?' she asked doubtfully. Evelyn considered the way in which butterflies wafted through the air and had to concede, the child did have a point!

'I'm sure,' Evelyn assured her gravely.

'Okay.' Abby gave her a beaming smile and, stopping at a red light, Evelyn leaned over and hugged her.

'It's a lovely picture, darling,' she said warmly, and cast aside her doubts. The breakage must have been just a bizarre accident, nothing more.

Abby was allowed to stay up later than usual that evening, much to her delight. Little did she guess that her parents wanted to be sure she would sleep deeply throughout the night. Chris no longer stayed over but returned to her parents' home in the village after Abby had gone to bed, so, if she awoke during the night, she would wander sleepily into Tessa's room and, more often than not, clamber into bed with her.

Encouraged by Matt, Abby happily demonstrated her newly learned ballet steps for them before her supper and then played a boisterous game of hide and seek with Matt, running the length, height and width of the huge house.

'I don't know if she's tired, but I certainly am,' he grumbled good-naturedly to Tessa, who had taken a leisurely bath while the horseplay was taking place.

'Not too tired . . . ?' She arched one delicate eyebrow.

'Never,' he affirmed, reaching for her, then, remembering Abby, reluctantly pulled back. 'She's waiting for you to go and say goodnight,' he told her, contenting himself with just one kiss before leaving the room.

'Where are you going?

'To fetch us some food,' he called back.

'I'm not hungry,' she told him.

'I am. Besides, I need to keep my strength up!' He winked broadly and grinned before disappearing down the stairs. Tessa was smiling as she entered Abby's room.

'Why does Daddy need to keep his strength up?'

Abby asked curiously. God, she's got ears on elastic! Tessa thought ruefully.

'Um, there's a lot of furniture to be moved into the Dower House,' she explained, blushing.

'Oh.' Abby lost interest. 'I'm taking my rocking horse, aren't I? And my dolls house? And –'

'Everything,' Tessa promised hastily, and somewhat rashly. 'Put that book down; it's time you were asleep,' she told her. She bent to kiss Abby's soft cheek and received a bear hug in return. A day at school and running around the house with Matt had indeed worn her out and, within minutes, Tessa was turning off the lights save for a muted night-light, and tiptoeing out of the room.

She crossed swiftly to her own room, which was warm and cosy with flames crackling in the hearth and subdued lighting from a dozen candles placed on top of various items of furniture.

She dropped cushions and pillows on to the rug, deciding they would eat and talk in front of the fire, just as they had once before in Cyprus, then she sat down to wait for Matt, her heart beginning to pound rapidly with excitement.

'Molly's done us proud,' Matt said, entering with a heavily laden tray which he placed on a low table near the fireplace before settling himself close to Tessa.

Despite her claim of not being hungry, the aroma of freshly baked still-warm bread made Tessa's mouth water. There was also homemade soup, cold chicken and ham, salad and cheeses. For dessert there was a delicious blackcurrant tart and thick cream. Matt had also purloined a bottle of his father's best wine, he told her with a grin as he handed her a glass.

'I shall really miss Molly's cooking when we move out,' Tessa said, through a mouthful of crusty bread and butter. Then, 'Is everyone in the house gossiping about us?' she asked, suddenly realizing that news of this intimate supper would be spread amongst the staff.

'Probably,' Matt said, as if he couldn't care less, which he probably couldn't, Tessa thought, aware that he had grown up surrounded by staff.

'Do you mind?' Matt asked, equally aware that she was not accustomed to having other people in her home on a daily basis.

'No,' she replied truthfully. She was doing – about to do, she amended, with a thrill of anticipation – nothing of which she felt ashamed. In fact, she rather hoped people were talking about it. If knowledge that she and Matt were lovers once more spread through the house and then to the village, perhaps her enemy, if indeed she actually had one, would hear the news and finally come to terms with the fact that Tessa and Matt were reconciled and the marriage was truly going to happen.

'To us.' Matt raised his glass to her and she smiled, touching her glass to his.

'To us,' she echoed, but sipped only sparingly at the wine. She was already giddy with excitement.

They fed each other morsels of food, and, when Matt caught her hand and slowly licked her fingers, pulling each one deep into his mouth, Tessa began to tremble, liquid with desire. A few moments later, when he fed her a portion of whipped cream, a small blob fell on to her shirt, just above her already-erect nipple.

'You did that on purpose,' she accused him, rather breathlessly. Matt merely smiled by way of reply; a slow, seductive smile that made Tessa glad she was already sitting down, for it turned her legs to jelly.

And, when he leaned forward to lick the cream from her shirt, she thought she might swoon. It was incredibly erotic, the way the moist heat from his mouth plastered the silk material to her breast.

'Matt . . .' she moaned, pleading, clutching at his shoulders.

With one hand, he swept away the debris from their meal and laid her gently back against the pillows, kissing her eyes, her cheeks, her chin, before finally capturing her mouth.

Tessa returned his kisses with fervour, sliding down until she was almost horizontal and pulling Matt with her, revelling in the weight of his body atop hers. The buttons of her shirt came undone, displaying her naked breasts and jutting nipples to his hungry gaze and even hungrier mouth.

He suckled greedily, gaining even more pleasure from her soft cries of delight than from the act itself. Well, almost. It was becoming increasingly difficult for him to keep his own excitement and need in check, but his desire to make this first time after six years special for Tessa was even greater. He moved down, kissing, oh so gently, the faint bruising that remained along her ribs, then moved even lower, circling her navel with his tongue.

'Please . . .' Tessa moaned again, arching her hips towards him in an age-old gesture of invitation. She tugged feverishly at the zipper of her skirt, wanting to be rid of all her clothes. Matt smiled at such impatience and quickly discarded his own shirt.

Tessa put out her hands to touch the muscled breadth of his chest, with its covering of thick, black hair. Then, needing to taste him, she knelt and placed her lips against his racing heart.

Matt groaned and held her to him, crushing her breasts against his chest, entangling his fingers in her soft, silky dark tresses before running his hands caressingly down her spine. Then he caught her questing hands in his and pulled away slightly to gaze deeply into her eyes. Desire to match his own shone from her beautiful brown eyes.

'Have you taken your pill?' he somehow remembered to ask.

'Huh?' For a moment, Tessa thought he was referring to the dreaded tranquillizers, one of which had already been flushed down the loo. Then she realized he meant her contraceptive pills.

'Yes, I have,' she assured him. She thought that a strange question, coming from him, and told him so. 'I'd have thought you'd have preferred it if I forgot to take them,' she added lightly. Matt frowned slightly.

'No, darling, I would not. No regrets – remember? Right now, I want to make love, not babies.'

'Oh, yes!' she agreed, so fervently, he grinned at her, loving her eagerness.

He began shedding the rest of his clothes, aided by Tessa, but then she paused.

'There's never been anyone else for me,' she whispered. Matt caught her hand and kissed her palm, well aware that the surge of relief he felt was both chauvinistic and hypocritical, although he realized he could now no longer remember any of the women who had shared his bed, temporarily, over the past six years.

'I'm glad to hear that, which makes me a selfish bastard,' he said ruefully. Then he frowned. 'Were you very lonely?' he asked quietly. Tessa shrugged, considered lying, then decided to tell the truth.

'At times, yes, I was,' she admitted. 'But I was busy – and I had Abby.' She peeped at him, half-expecting to see a hint of anger or regret for the years he had missed. But she saw only concern in his eyes.

'I'm sorry,' he said, wondering if he would ever stop wishing he had not given up searching for her.

'No, I'm sorry,' she said quickly. 'It was my stupid, stupid pride! I just couldn't bear to have you look at me in horror, or to demand a paternity test . . .' She gave a shiver.

'Shush, we're together now, the three of us, and that's all that matters. But don't ever leave me again,' he said fiercely.

'I won't,' she promised, and he crushed her to him.

Naked at last, they fell back against the pillows, exploring and rediscovering each other, eager for consummation, yet, by mutual, unspoken consent, they willingly prolonged the exquisite agony of denial. Their anticipation and and excitement grew and intensified as they continued to hold back from the final act, teasing and arousing, touching and tasting until they could bear to wait no longer.

Despite the long years of celibacy, Tessa felt no pain; her body was hot and moistly welcoming when Matt finally entered her. She wrapped her slender legs around him and arched to meet his thrusts. Wave after wave of incredible pleasure swept over her until she was beyond coherent thought, clinging mindlessly to Matt, murmuring his name over and over.

She matched her movements to his as they soared together, higher and higher, towards a climax that was almost unbearable in its intensity. Spasm after drawn-out spasm racked her body and she cried out. Her orgasm triggered his and she heard his own answering cry of fulfilment, then there was no sound but that of their ragged breathing as they slowly drifted back down to some semblance of reality.

Matt eased his weight from her and turned on to his side, cradling her to him, smoothing back her hair and pressing his lips to her brow. Tessa lay in the shelter of his arms, blissfully content and utterly at peace. All the doubts and fears that had plagued her in recent weeks had vanished; all that mattered was what had just happened in this room, this oasis of loving. The outside world had no place in it, nor was it of any importance.

Sighing with happiness, her body still tingling with the afterglow of their loving, she snuggled even closer to Matt and closed her eyes, only opening them again sleepily when he rose, with her still in his arms, and deposited her in the bed. She pouted when he moved away.

'You're not going?'

'No.' He threw a couple of logs on to the fire and blew out most of the candles, leaving just one alight beside the bed before he climbed in beside her. He pulled the covers securely around her shoulders and settled her comfortably against his side.

'I suppose I'd better not stay all night, though,' he said, although without much conviction. 'It

258

might upset Abby if she finds me here in the morning.'

'She'll have to get used to it,' Tessa said sleepily, hanging on to him as if her puny strength could prevent him leaving if he really wished to go. Which he didn't. Matt smiled and hugged her close.

'Try to get some sleep,' he said, sliding down the bed a little further.

Tessa dropped off to sleep so quickly that he felt guilty for tiring her, and soon felt even guiltier when he became aroused by her soft curves pressing against him. What an idiot he had been to think making love to her once would slake his desire. She was like a drug to him; as in Cyprus, the more he had of her, the more he wanted and needed.

He drifted in and out of a light sleep throughout the night, tormented by Tessa's proximity, yet her deep sleep was surely testament that her body was still in the process of healing after the accident, so he resisted the temptation to wake her.

Unfortunately, he fell into a deep slumber just before dawn.

He woke abruptly when a draught of cold air from the open doorway hit him between the shoulder blades. He knew at once what had happened and turned slowly to see Abby standing on the threshold of the room. Unusually quiet, she simply stood and gazed at him before looking past him at her mother. However, she seemed more puzzled than upset, Matt thought hopefully, and he smiled at her.

'Hello, sweetheart,' he said casually. He moved to get out of the bed, then belatedly remembered he was naked and stayed where he was.

259

'I'm thirsty,' she announced. Thankfully, a carafe of water was beside the bed, well within Matt's reach and he poured her a glass.

She sipped it slowly, her eyes fixed unwaveringly on him. Matt wished Tessa would wake up.

'Have you been here all night?' she asked finally, but sounded more interested than accusatory, Matt thought.

'Yes, I have,' he confirmed calmly.

'Why?'

'Well . . .' Matt wished even more fervently that Tessa would wake up and help him out. He toyed with the idea of saying Tessa had felt ill, or had had a bad dream, but discarded it almost immediately. As Tessa had said last night, Abby would have to get used to them sharing a bed.

'Parents usually sleep together,' he told her. If she asks 'why?' again, I'll . . .

'Why?'

'Just because,' he said, grinning as he supplied the answer she often gave when she couldn't, or didn't want to, explain something. A brief smile curved her mouth and revealed her dimple. 'You've stayed overnight with friends before – didn't their parents share a room?' he asked.

'Yes.' She nodded, after a moment. 'But I thought that was because they didn't have enough rooms for everyone,' she said seriously. Matt bid down hard on his lower lip. I must not laugh at her! he reminded himself sternly. Beside him, he heard a hastily stifled noise from Tessa and he nudged her, none too gently.

'How long have you been awake?' he hissed.

260

'Longer than you have,' she replied smugly. Matt glared at her, then grinned and reached across to kiss her – she was too adorable to be angry with.

'You need a shave,' she told him.

'I need my trousers!' he retorted.

'Oh!' Tessa half sat up as she realized his predicament. She kept the sheet above her breasts as she looked at Abby. 'You're not wearing your slippers,' she scolded. 'Come round here and get into bed,' she suggested, pulling back the covers on her side of the bed to spare Matt's blushes.

Abby glanced curiously at the remains of their supper, and at their discarded clothing but, fortunately for Matt's peace of mind, made no comment. Also fortunately for Matt, she dozed off again and, after a quick kiss for Tessa, he took the opportunity to gather up his clothes and beat a hasty retreat, making a mental note to buy some pyjamas!

CHAPTER 14

Helen arrived promptly at ten-thirty, dressed in black leather trousers so tight Tessa wondered how she could sit down in them.

'Have you got a Harley Davidson parked outside?' Matt enquired, coming across her waiting in the hall just as he was leaving for a meeting with one of the Stafford tenant farmers.

'You can be such a bore,' she told him, with a disparaging glance at his conventional country attire of jeans and tweed jacket.

'Don't let Tessa become too tired,' he cautioned her. 'She's still convalescent.'

'Oh, God, we're only going shopping!' Helen said impatiently.

'Only,' Matt grimaced, and turned to greet Tessa, drawing her to his side and kissing her soundly. 'I've had a shave,' he murmured. 'Have fun today, and don't worry about the time. I'll collect Abby from school this afternoon.'

'Okay, thanks.'

'And I'll see you tonight,' he added softly. Tessa nodded and blushed, so clear was his meaning. Matt smiled; he thought it was wonderful that he could still make her blush. Despite being a mother, she was still much the same as the innocent nineteen-year-old he had fallen in love with six years earlier, especially now she had lost that hard veneer of independence and mistrust.

Helen's car was a sleek red Porsche, and Tessa quickly discovered that she drove as recklessly as she rode her horse. She sped along the narrow country lanes as if taking part in a Grand Prix race, approaching every bend far too fast, negotiating each with a screech of brakes and nifty gear change and then accelerating back into top gear.

'Is there anywhere in particular you'd like to go today?' Helen asked Tessa.

'Not really, although I have to drop off an order for curtains . . .' Tessa said, rather faintly. In fact, anywhere at all was fine with her, just so long as it wasn't the hospital, she thought, closing her eyes when Helen overtook on a blind corner and then had to swerve violently to avoid an oncoming car, blaring her horn as if the other driver were at fault.

'Actually, would you mind showing me where the Family Planning clinic is situated?' Tessa asked, a little awkwardly, suddenly remembering she would need more pills shortly.

Helen shot her a sideways glance, wondering if Matt knew about this. 'Sure,' was all she said, though.

Fortunately for Tessa's nerves, Helen had to slow down as they encountered heavier traffic on the outskirts of Ashminster, and Tessa slowly eased her grip on the car seat.

'Usually I'd go straight ahead here,' Helen pointed out, when they had halted briefly at a red light. Then she swung left. 'This is the way to the Family Planning clinic,' she explained, driving for a couple of miles before slowing in front of the building. 'Do you need to go in today?'

'No, I'll phone for an appointment. I just wanted to know how to find it,' Tessa told her.

'Okay. Do you think you'll remember the route?'

'Yes, thanks.' Tessa nodded.

'Fine.' Helen reversed sharply and headed back towards the centre of town and into a car park, where she screeched to a halt barely two inches away from the wall of a parking bay and scaring the living daylights out of an old woman with a shopping trolley. 'They ought to be banned!' she muttered, glaring at the woman.

Tessa chose to assume she was referring to the trolley, and offered a smile of apology to the pensioner who'd had to move faster than she probably had for at least twenty years to get out of Helen's way.

'There's a short cut from here through to the main shopping precinct,' Helen told Tessa, as she bought a parking ticket and then led the way towards the shops. 'That's the Swan Hotel – I thought we'd have lunch there. I've told a couple of my friends we'll be there around twelve-thirty – I hope you don't mind? I thought it would be a good opportunity for you to meet some people.'

'Yes, I would like that, thank you,' Tessa said, tottering slightly in Helen's wake, her legs still shaky after the hair-raising drive. Cowardly, she decided to plead tiredness after lunch and take a taxi home!

She quickly discovered that Matt had not exaggerated at all in his assessment of his sister's capacity for shopping. Helen barely spared a glance for the window displays of the High Street chain stores that Tessa normally patronized, but headed instead for the exclusive, privately owned boutiques.

In the first, she tried on three strappy, skimpy party dresses, couldn't decide which she preferred and so bought them all at – to Tessa, at least – mind-boggling prices.

'Are you looking for something for a special occasion?' Tessa asked. Helen looked at her as if she were mad.

'No, I just like them,' she shrugged. 'But we always have a lot of "dos" around Christmas,' she added. 'And one can't wear the same dress twice, after all.' This 'one' does, Tessa thought, hiding a grin.

'Don't you want to try anything on?' Helen asked next, handing her gold credit card to the assistant.

'No, I don't think so.' Tessa shook her head.

'Oh, come on,' Helen said, a little impatiently. 'You and Matt will be receiving lots of invitations too, you know. You want him to be proud of you, don't you?'

'Of course,' Tessa said defensively. 'But Matt likes what I wear already.'

'Oh, Matt!' Helen waved her hand dismissively. 'He doesn't know the difference between a dress that costs fifty quid and one that costs five hundred, but the other women will,' she said shrewdly.

'Well . . .' Tessa knew she had a point.

'How about this one?' Helen held up a simple shift dress, made of golden satin overlaid with gold lace. Tessa nearly fainted when she saw the price tag. 'Or this? The colour would look good on you,' Helen

265

enthused, reaching for a burnt-orange little number. 'Try them on,' she urged.

'All right.' Tessa did so: both suited her colouring and fitted as if made for her. Helen had a superb eye – no doubt a case of practice making perfect!

'Which one shall I take?' she asked Helen, and realized immediately what a stupid question it was.

'Both,' Helen said promptly.

'Oh, I can't do that,' Tessa demurred, although she was sorely tempted. Finally, feeling guilty and extravagant, she purchased the gold lace dress, using Matt's credit card. She had used it before for Abby or furnishings for the Dower House, but never for herself and it felt quite strange. No doubt she'd become accustomed to the feeling, especially if she spent much time in Helen's company!

'Great! Now, you'll need shoes to wear with it,' Helen told her, predictably. 'There's a terrific new shop recently opened just along here – they have shoes and bags to die for. Actually, if you can't find a match, they will dye a bag to match shoes or vice versa,' she went on enthusiastically, hurrying along, leading the way and clutching the purchases she had already made.

Helen's expression was one of animation and pleasure as she entered the portals of each different store, excitedly viewing the contents, her eager hands rifling the racks of clothes and adding to her stack of bags at each port of call. She was like a kid on Christmas morning.

The assistants greeted her by name and with beaming smiles – obviously on commission, Tessa thought cynically. This really makes her happy, she realized and, with an unexpected pang of sympathy, wondered

266

just how long the 'high' lasted; how soon before she felt the need of another fix.

She has too much money to spend and too little to occupy her time, she thought, and decided then and there that, if she and Matt decided not have another child in the near future, she would try and enrol at teacher-training college and pick up her studies again. The vacations would probably coincide with Abby's school holidays, so that wouldn't pose a problem.

'Tessa?' Helen's loud voice and impatient tone told Tessa this wasn't the first time she had spoken.

'Sorry? Oh, yes, that's lovely,' she said of the shoulder bag Helen was holding out for inspection.

'You were miles away just then, weren't you?'

'Yes, I was thinking of going back to finish my course – where's the nearest teacher-training college?'

'I've no idea,' Helen said blankly. 'Why on earth do you want to do that?'

'To qualify, of course. Get a job, a career,' Tessa explained, although she knew she was wasting her breath.

'But you don't need to work for a living any more,' Helen said, puzzled. 'Matt's very rich, you know. Our grandfather left us all very well off.'

'I know that, but . . .' Tessa gave up. 'It doesn't matter.' She forced a smile, wishing she had never begun this particular conversation. Helen was trying to be friendly and helpful, but Tessa suspected the gulf between them was too wide ever to be bridged.

They – or, rather Helen – had so many bags by lunch-time that they returned to the car park to lock their purchases in the Porsche before heading for the Swan Hotel to meet Helen's friends.

'We normally go to an Italian restaurant, but I wasn't sure if you liked Italian food,' Helen said, as she marched through the busy lunch-time crowd, casting impatient glances at those who dared impede her progress. 'The Swan has a more varied menu, so . . . oh, there they are.' she waved and smiled.

Tessa looked in the direction she indicated and saw two well-groomed, smartly dressed young women sitting at the bar. They were both very attractive – and blonde. They would be, she thought ruefully, suppressing the suspicion that one of them might be the woman who wanted Matt for herself.

They must put bleach in the water supply around here, she thought idly as she followed in Helen's wake, and wondered if she would emerge from the shower one day to discover her hair had turned blonde under the spray. Perhaps Matt would prefer her that way . . . no, of course he wouldn't, she decided firmly, and consoled herself with memories of what he had said and done to her the night before.

'Judy. Delia,' Helen introduced them briefly. 'And this is Tessa Grant, Matt's fiancée.'

'Hi.' They both greeted her with friendly curiosity, and with no discernible hint of enmity or jealousy. Judy made way for her to take a seat and beckoned to the barman to order another round of drinks.

The lunch, an excellent meal from the carvery, offering a choice from several roasts and an assortment of fresh vegetables, passed pleasantly. Tessa said little, as the three friends chatted mainly about people she didn't yet know, although they didn't exclude her from the conversation and were careful to take the time to explain briefly just who they were talking about.

The three young women obviously knew each other very well, and it was very relaxed, girlish gossip, mainly amiable enough, but with a definite bitchiness at times. Judy, in particular, had a very acid sense of humour and tongue to match. She had just finished shredding the character and reputation of someone called Lorraine when she turned to Helen and, without a hint of irony, said,

'Don't forget it's her birthday next week. If you're wondering what to buy her for a pressie, she said she adored that scarf you bought from Hadleighs.'

'Oh, right. I'll get her one.' Helen brightened at the prospect of more shopping. 'Do you mind, Tessa? It's quite a walk. You're not too tired, are you?' Without waiting for an answer, she turned back to Judy. 'I'm under strict instructions from Matt not to let her overdo things,' she confided.

'I wouldn't mind being under Matt . . . oh!' Judy evidently received a kick under the table from either Delia or Helen. 'No offence, Tessa,' she giggled, not a whit abashed. 'We're all frightfully jealous, you know. We've all been panting after Matt for years. Do you remember when we sent him naughty pictures of ourselves when he was away in the Army?' she asked Delia.

'Why don't you pant after Ricky instead?' Helen cut in edgily. 'He's not spoken for and he's just as handsome as Matt.'

'Oh, sure he is, but Ricky's not a challenge, like Matt,' Judy said. 'Absolutely anyone can get Ricky into bed.'

'You speak for yourself,' Delia told her.

'I am!' Judy giggled again.

269

Tessa smiled slightly, wondering if she would be as light-heartedly casual about relationships as these three seemed to be if she had not become pregnant when only nineteen. Somehow, she doubted it.

Maybe she was old-fashioned, but she was more than a little shocked to have realized during lunch that, though married, all three women thought there was nothing wrong in indulging in extra-marital affairs – even Helen, apparently. The only rule they followed seemed to be: do what you want but don't get caught.

It was strange, Tessa reflected, that her companions were the outwardly respectable, married women while she, with only one lover, had become the socially unacceptable single mother. But not single for much longer, she remembered dreamily, and began to feel sorry for Helen and her friends. Not a child or a career between them, and they all seemed dissatisfied with successful businessmen husbands who were too often absent from home.

Helen settled the bill for all of them, waving away Tessa's proffered cash and handing over yet another credit card to the waiter.

'This is on David's business card,' she said airily.

'Okay. Thanks.' Tessa smiled at her, and then excused herself to make a trip to the cloakroom. As she pushed open the door, she came to an abrupt halt when she caught a strong whiff of *the* perfume.

'Oh, no,' she muttered, and glanced wildly around. She even checked under the cubicle doors, but she was the only occupant. She leaned weakly against a washbasin and put a shaking hand to her forehead. The slight headache with which she had awakened had been gradually worsening all morning, and had intensified after an unwise gin and tonic before lunch.

She took some deep, steadying breaths and wondered if the she simply imagined the perfume whenever she was in pain or over-tired. She thought back over the occasions when it had disturbed her: apart from the first time in hospital – real or imagined, she no longer knew – there did seem to be a pattern of her only sensing it when she was under strain, either physical or emotional.

Trying to shrug off her feelings of unease, she returned to the dining-room and rejoined her companions. As she walked towards their table, she checked the other diners to see if she could spot a likely candidate, but they were mostly small groups of businessmen, or middle-aged ladies enjoying a gossipy lunch.

She passed closer to Judy and Delia than was strictly necessary as she took her seat, but they were both wearing much lighter fragrances. Besides, she would have noticed earlier if either of them were wearing the perfume she had come to hate and fear.

'Are you okay?' Helen asked her. 'You look a little pale.'

'I'm fine, just a bit tired,' Tessa said, rather apologetically, for she felt her continued ill health was a nuisance to others – it certainly was to her! 'I think I'll get a taxi and go home.'

'No, don't do that; I'll drive you back. I only have one more purchase to make and then we'll go,' Helen said. 'We've just been discussing a shopping trip to London next week – would you like to join us?'

'I don't think so, thanks,' Tessa declined, feeling exhausted at the very thought. 'It's Abby's half-term holiday,' she was relieved to be able to offer as an excuse, for she truly did not want Helen to feel slighted when she was trying hard to be friendly.

'Oh, yes, of course it is.' Helen nodded, satisfied with the explanation.

Tessa could no longer smell the dreaded perfume, but was glad to be outside in the fresh air. She lagged behind the other three a little as they all made their way to Hadleighs, the shop where Helen, inexplicably to Tessa, wanted to buy a special gift for a girl she apparently considered to be a slut and a moron!

Despite being the younger by several years, Tessa actually felt much older than the others, due, she supposed, to having a child and also needing to earn her own living until very recently.

As Helen had warned, it was quite a long walk to Hadleighs and Tessa felt extremely tired by the time they arrived. She said nothing, though; she hated the residual weakness from the accident and sometimes despaired of ever feeling fully fit and healthy again.

She leaned against the shop counter for support while Helen, Judy and Delia picked over the range of silk scarves and costume jewellery as they decided on a gift for their friend.

'Tessa, are you okay? You're not, are you?' Helen immediately answered her own question. 'You!' She beckoned imperiously to the security officer standing nearby. 'A chair, please,' she ordered crisply. She has all the Stafford arrogance, Tessa thought drily, as she smiled her thanks for the hastily provided chair.

'And a glass of water,' Helen continued, this time glaring at one of the sales staff. Then she bent down to Tessa. 'This is all my fault; Matt will be furious. Tell you what, Judy and Delia will stay here with you while I go and fetch the car,' she decided.

'I'll be fine in a minute,' Tessa protested, uncomfortably aware that she was attracting a lot of attention from staff and shoppers. 'Besides, it's a pedestrianized precinct,' she reminded her.

'So?' Helen's tone indicated that traffic laws were for peasants, not for her. 'This is an emergency – I bet they'd let an ambulance through,' she said loftily. God, do I look that bad? Tessa thought.

The dizziness passed as quickly as it had assailed her, but Helen insisted on going to bring the car to the door. To pass the time, Tessa began looking idly through the bracelets and ear-rings which Helen had been oohing and aahing over. At least I now have a good idea of what to buy her for Christmas, she thought idly – unless, of course, Helen hadn't by that time already bought the entire stock!

There were some pretty enamelled bangles, too, and Tessa thought of Chris, who had been so kind to Abby. And Abby would love these, she thought, and rifled through them, hoping to find one in a smaller size.

'Helen's here,' Judy told her.

'Oh, thanks. I'm sorry to have been such a pain,' Tessa said, getting to her feet.

'No problem. It's been nice meeting you – I'm sure I'll see you again soon. Give my love to Matt!' Judy said wickedly. Both she and Delia kissed her cheek – Tessa loathed social kissing – but she submitted to the embrace. The two of them left, waving goodbye to Helen.

Tessa followed them out, barely noticed a bleeping noise as she reached the open door, then found her passage being blocked by the same security officer who had earlier found her a chair. Did he expect a tip? she wondered.

'Excuse me, madam, but I believe you've forgotten to pay for your goods,' he said smoothly.

'What? I didn't buy anything,' Tessa stammered, rather idiotically, she realized at once. His face remained impassive, but the word 'quite' hung in the air.

'What's going on?' Helen demanded crossly, storming into the shop to discover what was delaying Tessa. 'I'm not supposed to park out here, you know,' she told the security officer, as if he weren't already well aware of that. He ignored her and continued to block Tessa's path.

'If you would just come back inside, madam . . .'

'He seems to think I've stolen something,' Tessa whispered to Helen, absolutely mortified.

'Oh, for God's sake! Call the manager,' Helen said curtly. 'Give me your bag,' she added to Tessa, more calmly, and upended it on to the counter. Coins, wallet, make-up, keys, tissues . . . and, Tessa saw, with horror and disbelief, one of the shop's bracelets, still complete with price-tag and, presumably, the security coding which had triggered the alarm.

'Oh, God. I've no idea how that got there,' Tessa said lamely, aware the staff must have heard that excuse a million times before. And not only the staff was watching and listening, but other shoppers had stopped to stare, with either curiosity or contempt in their eyes.

'Truly, I don't know how it got inside my bag,' Tessa protested miserably, weak tears of humiliation very near the surface.

'Of course she doesn't,' Helen declared loudly. 'Are you the manager?' she asked of a be-suited man who had arrived on the scene. 'I'm Helen Warrender and this is Tessa Grant, who is due to marry my brother Matt Stafford of Drake's Abbot. Tessa was involved in a bad car accident recently and was in a coma for over a week. She is still suffering from headaches and blackouts,' she informed the entire shop.

Tessa cringed inwardly but could see the change of expression on the manager's face, although whether that was due to news of her illness or to Helen's name-dropping was hard to tell.

'There has been a stupid misunderstanding,' Helen continued briskly. 'I trust that gorilla on the door will let us leave now?'

'Well, our policy is to prosecute . . .'

'Don't be ridiculous!' Helen snapped, sounding much like her father. 'You can't prosecute someone for being ill! Ask . . .' she clicked her fingers in the direction of the sales assistant who had brought the glass of water '. . . she'll confirm Tessa was almost fainting when we arrived. She hung her handbag on the back of that chair – obviously someone knocked the bracelet off the counter without Tessa noticing.' It wasn't at all obvious to the manager, but Helen Warrender and her friends spent a lot of money in his shop. He forced a smile.

'I understand. Would you like to purchase the bracelet, madam?' he asked Tessa, ultra politely.

'No, thank you,' she mumbled, blushing furiously. She didn't even like the wretched thing.

'Let's get out of here.' Helen marched towards the door, glaring at anyone in her path. 'Pompous little

275

prat,' she added, far too loudly but no doubt deliberately, Tessa thought, as, head bowed in shame, she followed meekly in her wake. She half expected to be stopped again, but the security officer stepped aside, and she breathed deeply of the fresh air outside as if just emerging from prison after a long jail sentence.

She slid into the Porsche, still keeping her head down, feeling as if everyone were watching, nudging each other and muttering that she had only got away with it because of the Stafford influence in the district.

Helen let in the clutch and the car shot forward, scattering the pedestrians who had far more right to be there than she. She drove in silence for awhile, shooting sidelong glances at Tessa.

'It's your decision, of course, and I'll keep quiet if you want me to, but I think you should tell Matt before someone else does it for you,' she ventured at last.

'Oh, God,' Tessa groaned: she hadn't thought the situation could get any worse but it just had.

'This isn't London. The news will do the rounds, I'm afraid. And, by the time Matt hears it from someone else, it will have been blown out of all proportion,' Helen warned her. 'They'll be saying you robbed a bank or something! I know it's embarrassing, but it's not as if you did anything wrong,' she added.

'I'll tell him myself,' Tessa decided, but with a marked lack of enthusiasm.

When they arrived back at Stafford House after another hair-raising drive, Helen accompanied her indoors. Evelyn had heard the unmistakable sound of Helen screeching to a gravel-spurting halt outside and put aside the book she was reading to greet them.

'Come and have some tea – oh! Are you ill, Tessa?' she asked anxiously, noting how pale and drawn she looked.

'She's a little tired and upset,' Helen said quickly. 'Why don't you go and lie down?' she suggested. 'I'll send someone up with tea.'

'Thanks . . . for everything,' Tessa said, and walked towards the stairs. She avoided Evelyn's gaze; she couldn't bear it if her look of concern changed to one of contempt.

As she climbed the staircase she heard a low-voiced conversation begin between the two, followed by a sharp exclamation from Evelyn. Then the drawing-room door closed behind them and she heard no more.

When Tessa reached her room, she quickly swallowed a couple of painkillers, for her headache had worsened over the past, horrible hour, and then she kicked off her shoes and lay down on the bed. She didn't even open her eyes when Molly brought her a pot of tea – she didn't think she would ever be able to look anyone in the eye ever again – and merely mumbled her thanks.

Only when she was sure she was alone again did she sit up and pour herself a cup of tea, and glanced at her watch. Matt would be back with Abby soon. Oh, God, would he believe it had been an innocent mistake? She wasn't at all sure that Helen was convinced. Oh, she had defended her and very effectively, too, but Tessa felt she had been protecting the Stafford family name rather than Tessa herself. For a split second, before she had begun her assault on the manager's ears, there had been a look of . . . Tessa frowned, couldn't explain it exactly, just a glimpse of coldness, almost dislike.

She had finished her tea and her headache, if not her trepidation, had lessened by the time she heard Abby's high-pitched chatter. A couple of seconds later, she burst into Tessa's room and clambered up on to the bed for a welcoming hug.

'You're not poorly again, are you?' Abby asked, peering at her anxiously.

'No, just a bit tired,' Tessa assured her. 'Tell me what you've been doing today,' she urged. As usual, Abby needed no further prompting and launched into an excited monologue which fortunately required only a minmal response from her audience.

A light tap on the door preceded Matt's entrance a short time later. Tessa couldn't bring herself to look at him, afraid of what she might see.

'Molly's been baking cherry cakes today and she's saved some for your tea,' he told Abby. 'Why don't you go down to the kitchen and ask her for some?'

'Goody!' Abby clapped her hands, and scrambled off the bed. 'Do you want one, Mummy?'

'No, thank you, sweetie.' Tessa shook her head. She waited until Abby had left the room and then reluctantly raised her gaze to Matt's, already flinching in apprehension of what she might see.

'I'm sorry,' she stammered, twisting her hands nervously in her lap. 'But I honestly don't know how that bracelet got into my bag. I suppose I must have knocked it off the counter, but I don't remember. I'm not a thief,' she finished, on a whisper.

'I know that,' Matt said gently, coming to sit on the bed beside her. Tessa choked on a sob and threw herself into his arms and felt immeasurably better, not to mention relieved, when he gathered her close.

'It was awful,' she confided, her voice muffled against his neck. Matt could feel her shaking and began to massage the tension from her shoulders and back.

'Everyone was looking, speculating. There will be a lot of gossip, won't there?' she asked fearfully. 'Matt Stafford's fiancée caught shoplifting!' She shuddered.

Matt was silent, not knowing what to say to comfort her. She was right – there would be gossip and malicious amusement at the slur on the Stafford family name. He had already had sharp words with his mother on the subject and knew there would be a far worse confrontation with his father once he heard what had happened.

'There isn't going to be a prosecution, so everyone will know it was a misunderstanding,' he consoled her, but knew it wasn't true. On the contrary, everyone would choose to think Tessa's connection with the Staffords – landowners, employers and George Stafford's years of service as a magistrate – had meant strings had been pulled to avoid the usual consequences of theft.

Tessa's thoughts matched his, but she knew he was trying to make her feel better, so she pretended to be convinced and managed a rather shaky smile of agreement as she pulled slightly away from him to look into his eyes.

'Abby and I are causing you so much trouble – I bet you sometimes wish you had never glanced into the window of that coffee shop and spotted us, don't you?'

'Never,' he said, fiercely and truthfully. 'All I regret about that day is frightening you into running away. God, seeing you go under the wheels of that bus took years off my life,' he said feelingly. 'I thought I had driven you to your death.' He paused and then, 'Why did you run away?' he asked quietly, but intently.

'I'm not sure I can explain,' Tessa began, pleating her skirt nervously between her fingers. 'Partly it was because I was afraid of what you would do if you realized Abby was your daughter. I had managed alone for so long, and . . .' She bit her lip.

'You didn't want me to interfere?' he asked, trying to hide the hurt he felt, and failing.

'No,' she denied quickly, and not altogether truthfully. At that point, she definitely hadn't wanted him back in her life. She took a deep breath. 'I didn't fully understand this at the time – all I felt was panic and the need to get away – but I think I was afraid I would fall in love with you all over again,' she admitted, so softly Matt had to strain to hear.

'Would that have been so bad?' he asked.

'Well, look at the trouble I got into the first time!' she joked, then she frowned slightly. 'For all I knew, you could have been married, with children of your own. You could have forgotten all about me, and thought Abby and I were just a nuisance you could do without. Loving someone makes a person vulnerable.'

'Only if that love is unrequited,' Matt said quietly. Tessa's head jerked up: the tenderness in his gaze set her heart pounding and her pulses racing.

'Matt . . .' She leaned towards him. Their mouths met and clung. Gently he pushed her back against the stacked pillows, and . . .

'I brought you both a cherry cake!' Abby announced brightly as she charged unannounced back into the room. Matt hastily drew away.

'I'm going to fix a lock on that door,' he muttered, but knew he wouldn't. Abby had never had to share her mother's love before and to lock her out of Tessa's room would be incomprehensible to her and therefore unforgivable. Her timing, however, left a lot to be desired!

He smiled at her and took the offering she held out to him. Unfortunately, she hadn't bothered to put the cakes on to a plate and had clutched them, one in each sticky hand, on her journey from the kitchen.

'Thank you, but I've already eaten some,' he lied quickly. Tessa shot him a look that clearly labelled him a coward, and he grinned. 'You can have mine,' he told her.

'How kind,' she bit out.

'You're welcome. But don't let it spoil your dinner,' he warned.

'Dinner?' she repeated faintly. Dinner, downstairs with his parents? Not bloody likely! 'Oh, I don't think I'll bother,' she forced a smile. 'I'm not very hungry, and I had an enormous lunch! I –'

'Dinner, Tessa,' Matt said firmly. 'You will come downstairs with your head held high. You have done nothing wrong.'

'I know, but –'

'Seven-thirty,' he said, and walked out to prevent further arguement. Tessa poked out her tongue at his retreating back, but she knew he was right. Dammit.

'You tell me off if I stick my tongue out,' Abby said reprovingly.

Tessa couldn't think of an answer to that, so, 'Bath-time,' she said instead.

CHAPTER 15

Tessa stayed upstairs with Abby until the very last moment, then, with her head held high as instructed by Matt, but quaking inside, she ventured downstairs.

Chris, her eyes alight with curiosity, had already told her that George Stafford had returned to the house, so doubtless he now knew what had occurred.

As she reached the foot of the stairs, her steps slowed and she halted completely when her courage failed her, for she could hear voices from inside the drawing room. Raised voices. Angry voices. Matt and George Stafford were obviously having a row, and Tessa didn't think there was much doubt as to what – or who – was the subject of their argument.

Evelyn was also in the drawing-room with her irate husband and even more furious son. George had, predictably, hit the roof upon being told of Tessa's, er, misunderstanding in town, and, as usual, was voicing his opinions in a forthright manner. Evelyn no longer knew or cared what disgrace Tessa had brought to the family name; her only concern was that Matt and George didn't come to blows.

'We'll be a laughing-stock!' George bellowed, his face red with fury.

'She hasn't done anything wrong!' Matt yelled back, for around the twentieth time.

'Pah! Face it, Matt, you know very little about the girl. One quick tumble on holiday . . .'

'Matt! No!' Evelyn cried out in alarm, placing herself in front of him and grabbing his arm. For one dreadful moment she thought he might actually knock her aside, but then, breathing heavily, he visibly forced himself to step back, away from the temptation of physicaly silencing his father. He thrust his hands, balled into fists, deep into his pockets, out of harm's way.

'George, that remark was uncalled for,' Evelyn reproached her husband, but knew better than to ask that he apologize.

'But true, nevertheless,' George insisted, although he had lowered his voice somewhat. 'We know nothing about her, or her family background. She could come from a long line of jailbirds –'

'She is *not* a thief!' Matt gritted.

'You don't know that,' George retorted. 'What we do know is that she has lived from hand to mouth for the past six years, never having enough money to properly support herself or her child. Shoplifting is a way of life to some of those people,' he added contemptuously.

'Not Tessa,' Matt ground out. 'You're not talking sense. Quite apart from the fact that she is not and never has been a thief, it's absolutely ludicrous to suggest she would steal when she has unlimited access to my bank account,' he pointed out. George wasn't convinced.

'Pah! Got into the habit years ago, I expect, and can't

284

break it. Kleptomania!' George almost spat the word. 'She's probably not even aware she's doing it.'

'Oh, sure! The flat she and Abby were living in was a veritable Aladdin's cave of nicked treasure!' Matt said sarcastically.

'Please stop it, both of you,' Evelyn begged, sorely afraid that, if George persisted in his accusations, Matt would simply take Tessa – and Abby – and leave. She couldn't bear to lose them. 'Calm down, George. After all, there was no real harm done,' she said placatingly.

'No harm!' he shouted, glaring at her, which, she had time to think, was a slight improvement on him glaring and bellowing at Matt. 'How can you say that, woman?' he demanded angrily. 'The whole county will get to hear of it. I won't be able to show my face –'

'Don't shout at my mother,' Matt interrupted, seeing she was near to tears. 'If Tessa's presence here is an embarrassment to you, I'll take her –'

'No!' Evelyn said desperately; she didn't even want to hear him say the words that would deprive her of her grandchild. 'Don't go, Matt,' she pleaded, then turned to her husband. 'George? We'll lose Abby if you don't stop this,' she said brokenly. He glowered for a moment longer and then sighed heavily.

'No one wants you to leave,' he said gruffly to Matt. 'Abby is your daughter and our grandchild. She's a Stafford; she belongs here.'

'So does Tessa,' Matt said edgily.

'She's not a Stafford yet. The wedding –'

'George!' Evelyn interrupted sharply, terrified of what he was about to say. Matt would never forgive him for trying to be rid of Tessa. George apparently hadn't realized, as she had, that Matt was deeply in love with Tessa and would want to marry her even if she had not given birth to his child. George still seemed to think Abby was the only reason for the marriage. Men! 'Stop this,' she said sternly. 'Tessa will be down for dinner soon – can we please start talking about something else before she arrives?'

Tessa had, in fact, heard more than enough and had fled after hearing the word kleptomania spat with such venom. Blinded by hot tears of mortification, she had stumbled and almost fallen as she reached the stairs, and had stayed there, sitting on the bottom step and sobbing her heart out as distant sounds of the vicious row assailed her ears.

The fact that Matt was defending her was only of meagre comfort, for she hated herself for having placed him in such an awkward, horrible position. She was too upset to hear the heavy front door open and then slam closed behind the new arrival, nor did she feel the blast of cold air he brought into the house with him.

'If the prospect of marrying my brother is upsetting you that much, I suggest you elope with me instead!' Ricky Stafford drawled. When he received no acknowledgement, he crouched down on the step next to Tessa and gently pulled her hands away from her face, wincing when he saw the ravages her weeping had wrought.

'God, even Matt's not that bad! What's he done?' he asked interestedly.

'N . . . nothing. B . . . but I'm afraid he might come to blows with your father,' Tessa told him, sniffing rather inelegantly and searching in vain for a handkerchief. Ricky silently handed her his and stayed silent, leaving her to regain her composure.

He glanced towards the drawing-room when he heard the raised voices and moved swiftly to the door. He pushed it open slightly, noted his mother's presence as referee and, thus assured that his brother and father would not actually resort to physical violence, returned to Tessa's side. He felt she needed his help more than the two protagonists in the drawing-room.

'Come with me; you need a stiff drink,' he decided, and hauled her to her feet. More than a drink, she needed to be out of earshot of whatever row was raging, he thought, and steered her to the dining-room on the opposite side of the hall. He pushed her gently into a chair, poured her a large brandy and insisted she drink it all down.

'Bit better?' he asked, and poured her a refill before perching on the edge of her chair. 'Right. So tell me what's going on?' he suggested.

'It's awful,' Tessa whispered, and took another huge gulp of brandy before beginning to talk, haltingly at first, but then with greater fluency as the constantly refilled glass loosened her tongue.

Somehow, she found it easy to talk to Ricky: perhaps it was because he was so like Matt, yet she wasn't in love with him and therefore wasn't trying to make him love her in return.

She began with the supposed shoplifting that had begun the row between Matt and his father, but then poured out all her concerns, beginning with the blonde visitor to her hospital room and the accompanying perfume that still seemed to be haunting her.

She also told him about the shooting in the woods that had so terrified her, and her conviction that someone resented her arrival in Matt's life, resented it so much that they were trying to drive her away, or, failing that, make Matt decide to send her away.

'I thought it might be Belinda Croxley.' She looked at Ricky for his reaction. 'Has she said anything to you about how she feels? You've been spending time with her recently, haven't you?'

'Yeah, and I've still got the backache to prove it!' he drawled wickedly. Tessa made a noise that was half-laugh, half-sob. 'Have some more brandy,' he said, and topped up her glass again without waiting for a reply.

He silently mulled over what Tessa had just told him, frowning slightly. He had the uneasy feeling that it ought to be ringing alarm bells, but couldn't quite remember why. He was also trying to recall something Belinda had said about Matt . . . He could remember thinking it was rather an odd remark, but, since he had been making love to Belinda at the time, he had not given it much attention, and certainly had not wanted to discuss his brother!

He glanced at Tessa; with her hair mussed and tear-stained face now devoid of make-up, she looked no older than Abby. He decided not to add to her suspicions, but to speak to Belinda as soon as possible and then alert Matt if there really was something going on.

'You don't have to worry about Belinda,' he assured Tessa, refilling her glass once more.

'This is good.' Tessa drained her glass, then licked her lips and beamed at Ricky as she held it out for more. Ricky raised his eyebrows but refilled the glass without comment. She would have one helluva hangover in the morning, but, right now, she had stopped crying and had visibly relaxed. In fact, she was so laid-back she was almost horizontal! The thought of Tessa horizontal conjured up some interesting possibilities and he hastily reminded himself she was due to marry his brother.

'You'd better eat something to mop up the alcohol,' he told her. But that only reminded Tessa of why she had not yet had her dinner, and she reached for the brandy again, seeking amnesia.

'I can't stay here,' she announced suddenly, getting awkwardly to her feet and visibly swaying as she sought to maintain her balance. 'Have you seen my car keys?' she hiccuped, glancing around vaguely in the hope of finding them. Ricky groaned.

'You can't drive – you have a flat tyre,' he was inspired to say.

'I do?' Tessa considered that for a moment, then swore with a fluency that had Ricky blinking with amazement and then trying to suppress his laughter.

'Never mind,' she said airily, finding the obvious solution to her problem. 'I'll borrow yours,' she informed him brightly. That wiped the smile from Ricky's face.

'Er, no, I don't think that's a good idea,' he said nervously, quickly grabbing hold of her arm to steady her when she appeared to be in danger of falling flat on her face. 'Why don't you go upstairs and lie down for awhile?' he suggested eagerly.

'You naughty boy!' Tessa wagged an admonishing finger at him. 'You can't have all Matt's girlfriends, you know,' she told him, then she frowned hideously as she tried to think. 'Well, actually, yes, you can. Take the lot of them,' she offered generously, throwing out her arm in an expansive gesture that almost sent a vase of flowers crashing to the floor. Only Ricky's quick reflexes saved it.

'Oops! Abby broke one of David's figurines, you know,' she confided, then, 'What was I saying?'

'God knows,' Ricky muttered, desperate now to sober her up before Matt saw her in this state. He'd never known anyone get so plastered so quickly.

'Ah, yes, Matt's girlfriends,' Tessa remembered. 'You can have them all. But not me. He said he would break your legs if you made a move on me. Wasn't that romantic?' she asked, smiling broadly.

'Yeah, sure. Someone should write a poem about it,' Ricky said dourly. Tessa struck a dramatic pose.

'There was a young woman called Belinda,' she began declaiming. 'Who . . . damn, I can't think of a rhyme. Hang on a minute . . . oh, yes. There was a young woman called Bel, who was really the bitch from hell, and who wore perfume with an 'orrible smell –' She broke off, laughing helplessly. Ricky shook his head in despair; he could swear his legs were beginning to hurt, as if in anticipation of the multiple fractures Matt would shortly inflict on them.

'I'm going upstairs,' Tessa announced next, after discovering the bottle of brandy was now empty. 'Who drank all this?' she wondered out loud as she headed, staggering, for the doorway.

Ricky heaved a sigh of relief and sank back into a chair. Thank God for that! Perhaps he would still be able to walk in the morning, after all!

'I'm going to pack my bags,' Tessa added, reeling out into the hall. Ricky leaped out of his chair as if he had been stung and ran after her.

'No, Tessa, you can't do that,' he said urgently, grabbing her arm.

'Course I can; I'm not that drunk!' she told him indignantly.

'I didn't mean that; I meant you mustn't leave the house,' he clarified.

'Why can't I?' she demanded belligerently. 'You're as bad as Matt, telling me what to do. I never wanted to come here in the first place. And this idea of marrying Matt, it's rilid . . . ridilic . . .'

'Ridiculous,' Ricky supplied.

'Glad you agree,' Tessa nodded her head, and then found she couldn't stop. 'Tell Matt, will you?' she asked him brightly.

'You must be joking!' Ricky shuddered at the thought, and then followed her up the stairs.

'Shh! You'll wake Abby!' Tessa hissed, making far more noise than Ricky.

'Yes. Abby,' Ricky said, pouncing on the child's presence as an excuse to divert Tessa from her plan of action. 'You can't wake her now, so you'll have to stay, for tonight, at least,' he said cajolingly. And, in the morning, she would be Matt's problem.

Tessa paused.

'You're right, I can't leave tonight,' she agreed, and Ricky relaxed. Too soon, unfortunately. 'But I'm still packing my bags,' Tessa declared, as she marched into her room.

She flung open the wardrobe and reached for a suitcase, one of her own shabby ones, not one of the expensive, matching set Evelyn had bought for her. Even drunk, she was somehow aware of which items belonged to her by right and which were Stafford charity. Or generosity. Whatever; it made no difference now.

She began taking clothes off the rail and folding them haphazardly into the case. As she did so, Ricky silently took them out and hung them up again. Tessa seemed not to notice, nor to wonder why her case remained almost empty, and so they continued – clothes out of the wardrobe, into suitcase, back into wardrobe.

'This is futile, and fast becoming tedious,' Ricky said finally, wishing Matt would come and rescue him. Ten seconds later his wish was granted and he cursed himself for being a fool – what was that old adage about being careful of what one wished for in case it came true?

'I do hope you have an explanation for being in Tessa's bedroom?' Matt's voice was soft, but as menacing as Ricky had ever heard it, and his heart sank.

Matt, still filled with fury after his encounter with his father, was quite glad to have someone on whom to vent his anger. Whatever the provocation, he would never stoop to hitting his father, but Ricky was another matter entirely, and finding him sniffing around Tessa had provided the perfect excuse.

'He doesn't think I should marry you and he wants me to elope with him,' Tessa informed Matt happily. Ricky groaned; his legs were now seriously hurting. Why does she have to remember that remark! he wondered.

'I see.' Matt's voice went from cold to positively glacial. 'You're helping her pack, are you?' he enquired.

'Of course I'm not!' Ricky said, exasperated and

more than a little nervous. 'I only followed her up here to stop her leaving you! Now that you're here, you can deal with it yourself!'

'Gladly.' Matt stood aside and pointedly held the door open for his brother to leave. Ricky strode forwards, more than happy to oblige. 'Don't push your luck, little brother,' Matt warned, as they faced each other in the doorway. Ricky had had enough.

'You ought to take better care of her,' he told him. 'The poor darling –' He checked when Matt's eyes narrowed dangerously at his use of the endearment. 'The poor girl has been scared to death while she's been living here and, from what I can see, you have dismissed her fears as being nothing more than hallucinations. You deserve to lose her.'

'Maybe. But I don't intend to.' Matt slammed the door behind him, and so, luckily for Ricky, missed the mocking military salute his brother sketched before leaving.

Matt turned towards Tessa, who had lost interest in packing and was sitting cross-legged on the bed. She had listened idly to the exchange between the brothers and was squinting hideously as she tried to focus. She had thought she was seeing double; Matt and Ricky were much the same height and breadth, with dark hair, and both were this evening wearing similar blue shirts.

'Hi.' She smiled happily at Matt, and tried to get up, but forgot she was sitting in a yoga half-lotus position and very nearly toppled off the bed and on to the floor. Matt leaped forward and caught her, and only then realized what was wrong with her.

'You're drunk,' he sighed.

'I only had one brandy,' she told him.

'Yeah, sure. One bottle,' Matt said, and she giggled, swaying towards him. But then her mood altered in an instant, and tears glistened in her eyes.

'I don't want to stay here,' she whispered. 'No one wants me here.'

'I want you,' Matt said softly. 'And I won't let you go. I can't.' His lips brushed away the tears on her cheeks. 'But I will take you away from this house. You've never liked being here, have you?'

'Well, your mother's always been sweet to me,' Tessa said carefully, trying hard to concentrate.

'And my father?'

'A bit sour!' she laughed. 'Sweet'n' sour. Get it? Sweet'n' sour,' she repeated, inordinately pleased with herself. Matt's lips twitched with amusement as he watched her. God, she was adorable. High as a kite, but adorable.

'Can we really leave?' Tessa asked, as his words finally penetrated the fog of inebriation.

'Yes,' Matt assured her, thinking busily about where he would actually take her.

The Dower House wasn't ready for them to move in yet; there was little furniture and it reeked of paint, which would hardly improve Tessa's health, especially as it was now too cold to leave the windows wide open for ventilation.

Besides, he had serious doubts whether Tessa even wanted to live in the place – rather late to have such doubts, he thought ruefully, but it was probably what he deserved for imposing his will on her after the accident.

At the time, he hadn't realized how important her

wishes would become; far more important than his own, in fact. He now knew he would do anything to make her happy – except let her leave him.

'Darling, do you think you can bear to stay here for just one more night?' he asked. 'Abby's asleep, and we don't want to upset her, do we?'

'No, course not,' Tessa agreed, yawning hugely. Matt watched her eyes begin to close and hoped she would quickly fall asleep.

'She's on half-term holiday next week,' he reminded her. 'We'll pick her up from school tomorrow afternoon and go to London. My flat hasn't been sold yet, so we can stay there. It's not really big enough, but it will suffice until we decide what to do – okay? Tessa? We'll spend next week in London, just the three of us.'

'Good ole London,' Tessa said mournfully, as if she had been in exile for at least fifty years, Matt thought, grinning down at her.

'I'll take that as a "yes",' he decided drily, but he was talking to himself. Tessa was out cold.

Tessa awoke with a raging thirst, a pounding headache and blissful amnesia. She sat up very, very slowly, clutching her head firmly in her hands to prevent it exploding, or perhaps falling off completely. Actually, the latter option was quite a tempting notion, since that would at least rid her of the pain, she thought, rather dazedly.

Fortunately, the carafe of water on her bedside cabinet was full, and she filled her glass time after time, gulping down the cool, refreshing liquid until her thirst was quenched. Only then did she feel able to totter into her bathroom and splash cold water onto her face.

The shower made a hideous noise when she turned it on . . . strange that she'd never noticed before that it sounded like Niagara Falls. Not that she'd ever actually been to Niagara Falls. God, I'm delirious, she thought, and wondered if she had a fever, or flu, perhaps?

She tried to block out the dreadful noise and stepped under the hot spray.

'Ouch!' The water that hit her head was as hard as hailstones raining down. Not that she could ever recall being hit by hailstones . . . oh, whatever's the matter with me? she wondered, beginning to be seriously alarmed. She felt almost as ill and disorientated as she had when she had first recovered consciousness in hospital.

She shook her head in an attempt to clear it, and immediately wished she hadn't as the thumping inside her skull intensified tenfold.

'Oh, good, you're awake finally,' Matt said cheerfully and far too loudly as he walked into the bathroom.

'Shh,' Tessa begged him, reaching blindly for a towel. Matt picked it up and purposely held it away from her for a few moments while he gazed appreciatively at her glistening, nude body. Finally he relented and handed it to her, and Tessa wrapped it around her body, fastening it over her breasts.

'I've taken Abby to school,' he told her. 'What would you like for breakfast?' he asked, with an evil little smile. 'Fried eggs? Bacon? Sausage?' he continued, while Tessa's face grew paler and paler. When she took on a greenish tinge, he stopped, but for his own sake as much as hers – he didn't relish the thought of her throwing up all over him, much as he loved her.

'Just coffee, please,' Tessa said faintly, staggering

296

over to her dressing-table to sit down and clutching at her decidedly queasy stomach. She looked rather balefully at Matt – couldn't he see she had suffered a relapse? Where was the sympathy she deserved after being knocked over by a bus and nearly killed?

'I don't feel very well,' she said plaintively.

'Good,' Matt replied callously. Tessa gaped at him, open-mouthed. 'I've got rather a lot on today,' he continued briskly, glancing at his watch. 'I won't be here for lunch, but I'll be back to pick you up around three o'clock. Okay?'

'Pick me up?' she repeated.

'Yes. Surely you haven't forgotten? We discussed this last night. Chris is packing for Abby, so –'

'Packing?'

'Yes.' Matt sighed. 'We're going to London this afternoon – remember?'

'London?'

'Tessa, please stop repeating everything I say.' He sighed again. 'It's Abby's half-term holiday next week,' he reminded her. 'We decided we'd spend it in London while we sort out our future.'

'Future? Sorry,' she said quickly, seeing him frown. 'But I'm afraid I don't have a clue what you're talking about. Are you –' she swallowed painfully '– are you saying you want to change our plans? That you don't want to marry me?' she whispered, her eyes large with fear and loss.

'No! Never!' Matt declared, moving swiftly to gather her in his arms. The jerking movement hurt her head abominably, but Tessa barely noticed and she wrapped her arms tightly around his waist, resting her aching head against his chest. 'Of course I'm not

297

saying that,' he assured her gruffly. 'It's not working for us, you, here, that's all.'

'It isn't?'

'Well, no . . .' Matt pulled away and gazed down into her eyes. 'How much do you remember of what happened yesterday?' he asked.

'Yesterday? Let's see . . .' Tessa tried desperately to dredge up memories that were shrouded in dense fog. 'Oh! I went shopping with Helen,' she said triumphantly, then she frowned slightly. 'And her two friends joined us for lunch. I can't recall their names at the moment, but I do remember they were both attractive blondes and half in love with you,' she told him accusingly.

'Really? Please try and remember their names!' Matt urged, laughing. She wrinkled her nose at him.

'Rat! I wouldn't tell you now even if I could remember,' she said loftily. 'Did you know Helen drives like a maniac? Has she ever passed her test?'

'Yes, to both questions, but Helen's driving is not the subject under discussion,' Matt said sternly, eyeing her with some suspicion, not entirely convinced by her convenient loss of memory. 'What happened after lunch?'

'Lunch? We went to the Swan . . .' She wrinkled her nose again, but for a different reason this time. 'I smelled that horrible perfume again when I went to the cloakroom, the one I first smelled in hospital.'

'Really? You didn't mention that to me yesterday,' Matt frowned slightly. 'Presumably it is an over-the-counter perfume which anyone can buy,' he added, which was something Tessa hadn't considered before.

'I guess so.' She nodded.

'Is that what upset you? You must have had something on your mind while you were in Hadleighs,' Matt continued.

'Hadleighs,' Tessa repeated thoughtfully. 'I had a headache and I felt a bit faint, so Helen went to fetch the car –' She stopped and groaned as the memories flooded back. 'Oh, God! That wretched bracelet! You and your father were yelling at each other . . . Ricky was here, he gave me a drink.'

'Just *a* drink?' Matt queried.

'Well, a couple,' she admitted. She paused. 'Is that why I feel so dreadfully ill?' she asked, sounding surprised. Matt's brows rose.

'Haven't you ever had a hangover before?'

'Yes, but only after sharing a couple of bottles of cheap plonk at college. I've never been able to afford that much brandy,' she said frankly, and Matt laughed. She bit her lip and looked up at him anxiously.

'I truly didn't do anything wrong yesterday, or, at least, I certainly didn't mean to, but your father doesn't believe that, does he? I clearly recall hearing him refer to me as a kleptomaniac,' she said unhappily.

'I'm sorry you heard that. Please try not to hold it against him – he's over-protective of the family name,' Matt said diplomatically.

Much of his fury towards his father had abated overnight: George Stafford was old, set in his ways, fiercely proud of his standing in the community. He was accustomed to being deferred to and respected, not ridiculed. However unfounded the gossip about Tessa, George would find it very difficult to cope with, although he had softened his attitude sufficiently to tell Matt that morning that he would defend Tessa if

299

anyone dared to make derogatory comments about her in his presence.

Matt had accepted the olive branch graciously, but had not changed his mind about taking Tessa and Abby away for a week to give them a breathing space in which to carefully consider a future life away from Drake's Abbot.

'Don't worry about the old man,' he said huskily, moving Tessa backwards until her legs hit the mattress and then lowering her on to the bed, his body covering hers.

'I thought you had a lot on today?' Tessa reminded him, but rather breathlessly, her hands already caressing his back beneath his shirt.

'That was before I became distracted by how little *you* have on,' Matt retorted, untying her towel and whipping it away in one fluid movement. 'I missed you last night,' he murmured, teasing her with quick, soft kisses. 'I want, need, to make love to you every night. You're like a drug to me, I can't live without you.'

'I am so happy to hear that,' Tessa arched towards him, impatiently tugging at his clothes. Then she paused briefly. 'Just where exactly were you last night?' she asked, rather accusingly.

'In my own bed. Alone. You passed out cold,' he told her. I undressed you and put you to bed and you didn't even stir, so I left.'

'Couldn't you have woken me?'

'I'm good, but I'm not that good!' he retorted, and she giggled.

'Mmm, you're very, very good,' she told him, and sighed blissfully when the last of his clothing was discarded and he rejoined her on the bed.

She wrapped her arms around his neck and pulled him closer, eager for consummation.

'Now,' she pleaded.

'You'll have to wait,' Matt teased her. 'Penance for getting drunk with my brother,' he added, before beginning a gentle, insidious assault on her body and senses, curbing his own desire as he slowly and skilfully aroused her to a fever-pitch of need.

When he finally yielded to her pleas and entered her, she was so hot, wet and welcoming, pulling him even deeper inside her, that he had to fight against climaxing too soon.

'Tessa,' he groaned, striving desperately for control. He was like a teenager with his first lover when he was with her, unbearably excited.

She was already so incredibly aroused that she climaxed after just a few, powerful thrusts, crying out loud, her nails digging into his back as she tried to draw him even nearer, to fuse their bodies together.

Matt felt the spasms of her muscles around his shaft and that prompted the wonderful, hot release of his own orgasm, deep inside her body. One day, we'll make a son, he thought, as he gazed down at Tessa's flushed face, her large brown eyes sparkling, her soft, sweet mouth slightly open as she panted for breath.

He bent his head and lightly brushed her lips with his, then, as always mindful of his greater weight, he turned so she was lying by his side, his arms holding her securely against him.

After a while, aware of the chill in the room, he reached for the quilt which had fallen to the floor and wrapped it snugly around her. Then, with the utmost reluctance, he eased away from her.

'I'm sorry to leave you, but I really do have a lot of people to see today since I won't be here next week,' he told her, as he gathered up his clothes.

'Okay.' Tessa snuggled sleepily into the softness of the quilt.

'Tessa?' Matt paused before leaving. 'Will you do something for me while I'm gone?'

'Of course,' she opened one eye.

'Go into the village today.'

'To do what?' she queried, assuming he wanted her to run an errand.

'Nothing in particular. Just show your face, chat to people,' he said.

'Oh.' Comprehension dawned. 'You mean, show them I'm not ashamed of what happened yesterday?'

'That's right.' He nodded. 'I think it's important, especially as we're going away for a week. Be sure and make it clear we're going because it's Abby's half-term holiday, that's all.'

'I see. Otherwise, it might look as if I'm running away?'

'Exactly.'

'Yes, all right. I'll go,' she agreed, somewhat unwillingly, then she grinned impishly. 'Can I ask Ricky to come with me?'

'No! Anyway, he's not here – he's gone pot-holing, hopefully without a guide or a map,' he added sourly. 'Ask my father to go with you instead,' he suggested, to get revenge for her mentioning Ricky.

Tessa picked up a pillow to throw at him, and he ducked quickly out of the room, and grinned as he heard it thud against the door panels behind him.

CHAPTER 16

After reflection, Tessa decided to ask Evelyn to accompany her to the village, since her company – barring that of George Stafford, which she wasn't even going to consider – was the best way to silence any gossip regarding trouble at Stafford House.

Evelyn agreed readily: Matt's decision to take Abby away for the half-term break had frightened her badly, and she dreaded hearing the news that he thought it best to remove his family permanently from Drake's Abbot.

It was his heritage to take over the running of the Stafford estates, but she knew he wouldn't hesitate to simply employ a manager, or even hand over the reins to Ricky if he felt Tessa and Abby were not happy to stay.

Consequently, she was even more gracious than usual, waving away Tessa's stammering apology.

'That nonsense is all forgotten and forgiven, dear. Not that we feel there is anything to forgive,' she said hastily. 'We know it was just an unfortunate misunderstanding – Helen explained how you were taken ill.'

They wandered around the village for almost an hour, chatting pleasantly to all and sundry. Tessa

303

began to feel as if she were a Parliamentary candidate canvassing for votes, and had to bite back giggles when Evelyn again stopped to pass the time of day with two old biddies who had obviously emerged from their cottage with the sole purpose of accosting the two women.

Actually, it was Evelyn who ought to stand for Parliament, or perhaps enter the diplomatic service, Tessa thought, admiring the skilful way in which she managed to convey the message that Tessa's illness was still causing temporary problems, but was nothing to be concerned about.

The shopping expedition, and its horrible conclusion, was never directly referred to, but the message of Tessa's acceptance by her future in-laws, and therefore her innocence, was made abundantly clear.

'We're all so looking forward to the wedding,' Evelyn said brightly, holding fondly on to Tessa's arm. 'It's such a pity she and Matt lost each other all those years ago – that dreadful conflict in Bosnia caused so much heartache,' she prattled on to the vicar's wife.

Tessa hastily turned a gurgle of laughter into a cough: it was the first time she had heard this version of events; that she and Matt were star-crossed lovers, cruelly torn apart by the vicissitudes of war.

But, perhaps it was true, she thought, as laughter vanished and unexpected tears pricked her eyes. If Matt's leave had not been cancelled so abruptly, if she had known him better and been more confident of his love, then she would have unhesitatingly told him of her pregnancy.

She could have had six years of happiness, sharing the joys and anxieties of first-time parenthood with him instead of struggling alone. She drew a deep, shaky breath and concluded, as Matt had already done, that regrets were futile and only the future was important.

Fortunately for Tessa's peace of mind, she didn't encounter George Stafford throughout the rest of the day. As she packed a case her spirits rose; she was really looking forward to spending some time back in London, alone with Matt and Abby. No family, no staff, just the three of them together.

Matt arrived back at Stafford House at three, to collect Tessa and then pick up Abby from school en route to London. The only awkward moment came when they were about to leave and Molly, the housekeeper, tried to press on him a cardboard box containing an assortment of grocery items.

'There are shops in London,' he told her, making no move to take the box.

'I know, but you won't want to go shopping today. It's just milk, bread and something for a meal this evening,' Molly stammered, taken aback by the coldness of his tone and accompanying gaze.

'Oh, Matt, please,' Evelyn begged, wringing her hands in agitation.

'Thank you, Molly.' Tessa stepped forward and took the carton from her. 'It was a kind thought,' she added, smiling.

Matt slowly took out his wallet and, still holding his mother's gaze, flung a twenty-pound note on to the floor at her feet.

'We'd hate to be accused of not paying our way,' he said coldly. 'Come along, Tessa, Abby will be waiting,' he added, turning on his heel and walking out.

Tessa couldn't bear to look at Evelyn and hurried after Matt. His expression was still rather forbidding when he helped her into his car, so she stayed silent, wretchedly sorry that she was the cause, however unwittingly, of putting him on the defensive against his parents.

Abby was as excited as Tessa about returning to London, and greeted them both with a kiss and a hug. Her only reservations were in leaving Lollipop and Flynn behind for more than a week.

'Did you give them both a kiss and tell them I'll see them soon?' she asked.

'Oh, yes, absolutely,' Tessa fibbed solemnly.

'Who'll ride Lollipop while I'm on holiday?'

'Grandpa,' Matt put in, deadpan, and Abby giggled at the thought of George Stafford riding the Shetland.

'Are we going to the flat we used to live in, Mummy?' she asked next.

'No, mine,' Matt answered her.

'Is it as nice as ours?' she wanted to know. Matt bit back the reply that sprang to his lips: it had, after all, been her home and had contained the most important factor in her life – her mother.

'I like it,' he said casually. 'But it only has one bedroom. How do you feel about sleeping on the sofa? It turns into a bed,' he added cajolingly, hoping desperately she wouldn't decide she wanted to sleep with Tessa.

'The sofa turns into a bed? How?' she demanded, intrigued.

'Magic,' Matt told her.

'Cool!' Abby clapped her hands. 'I want to sleep in it!' she decided.

'You're getting good at this,' Tessa murmured, admiring his strategy.

'Is that all I'm good at?' he asked, and the heat of his gaze caused her to blush.

'You know it's not,' she assured him.

Tessa liked Matt's flat as soon as she stepped over the threshold. It was, as he had said, very much a bachelor pad, but it was extremely well fitted out and furnished.

There was a large drawing-room, small dining-room and kitchen, with just the master bedroom and bath-room – complete with jacuzzi. She tried not to wonder how many women had shared that with Matt in the past. Or the king-size bed.

'Don't be jealous.' Matt had seen the shadow cross her features and divined her thoughts.

He came up close behind her and pulled her back against his chest. His mouth nuzzled her neck and unerringly found the ultra-sensitive spot above her collar bone. 'Now that I have you back, I can't even remember what any of them looked like.'

'Good.' Tessa twisted in his embrace and reached up to kiss him.

'Daddy! Come and make the sofa turn into a bed!' Abby called imperiously.

'Abracadabra,' he muttered, and reluctantly released Tessa as he went to do his daughter's bidding.

'What else can it turn into?' Tessa heard Abby ask, and she grinned, wondering how Matt was going to get out of that one!

After they had unpacked, they went out, did some window-shopping and then had pizza for supper, after which Abby was visibly tiring so they returned to the flat.

Tessa bathed Abby and prepared her for bed, then produced her favourite Disney video for her to watch in bed.

'Good thinking,' Matt said admiringly. However, the diversion wasn't needed, and Abby was quickly asleep.

Matt had opened a bottle of wine and carried it through to the bedroom, where he and Tessa talked in whispers, hardly daring to move until they were sure Abby had settled for the night.

'This is like being fourteen again, necking on the sofa and hoping the parents won't wake up and come downstairs!' Matt said ruefully.

Finally, after a last check on Abby, Tessa returned to the bedroom and, facing Matt, who was lounging back on the bed, she began to slowly remove her clothes, kicking off her shoes and peeling off each garment.

She held his gaze, determined to exorcise the ghosts of any other women he had bedded here before her. Matt, who could easily be aroused simply by looking at her clothed, let alone naked, reached for her but she danced back out of range and continued with her slow strip-tease.

Matt watched hungrily as each soft curve was revealed to him, then suddenly lunged again, this time catching her and pulling her down on to the bed on top of him. Tessa laughed down at him, knowing and exulting in his obvious arousal and she rubbed suggestively against him.

'Patience is a virtue,' she told him, in mock severity.

'It's not one I possess,' he admitted unrepentantly,

308

his hands moving swiftly and seductively across her back and buttocks. 'Certainly not where you're concerned. And I definitely do not need you to perform a strip-tease to turn me on. Maybe after fifty years of marriage, when I'm old and grey, but not now.' He tangled his fingers in her hair and tugged gently until she raised her head to look into his eyes. 'You're thinking of my past girlfriends, aren't you?'

'A little.' She nodded.

'Well, don't. Because I'm certainly not thinking about them.' He paused, then, 'Marry me,' he said urgently.

'Yes, of course,' Tessa replied, a little uncertainly: wasn't it all arranged?

'I mean now. As soon as we can. Get a special licence,' he explained. 'I don't want to wait any longer. You are sure you want to marry me, aren't you?' he asked, suddenly not the super-confident Matt Stafford whose high-handed arrogance could make her blood boil. Tessa loved him so much it hurt.

'Yes, I'm sure. I'll marry you tomorrow, if . . .' His kiss stopped any further words for many minutes. Finally, Tessa managed to continue speaking, albeit rather breathlessly. 'Have you thought how disappointed your mother will be? She's so looking forward to a big wedding – honestly, I'm sure a royal wedding takes less organization than ours!'

'She won't mind. We can still have a blessing in church instead of the wedding ceremony,' Matt decided. 'And the reception can go ahead as planned. That will be a public celebration; what I have in mind is more private,' he said, deftly turning her on to her back and covering her body with his.

He kissed her again, slowly and extremely thoroughly, until she was mindless with need, and would have willingly agreed to anything he suggested, just so long as he promised to continue kissing her.

'Make sure you tell your parents this was your idea, not mine,' was all she said before surrendering to the urgent demands of his body.

Matt was up and dressed before either Tessa or Abby on Saturday morning, although Abby soon awoke despite his effort to be quiet, and she came padding barefoot to join him in the kitchen.

He grinned at the sight of her: tousle-haired, yawning, and clutching her favourite stuffed monkey. She was wearing one of the nightgowns her grandmother had bought for her: it was adorned with a teddy bear and bore the legend, I AM 5. Tessa considered the purchase to be a mistake, and predicted Abby would refuse to wear it the day she turned six.

'Hello, sweetheart,' he greeted her.

'Hello, Daddy. Can I have some orange juice, please?' she asked.

'Er, sorry, we don't have any until we go shopping,' he apologized. 'How about some milk instead?' he suggested, then poured out a glass and watched her drink it dowm thirstily. 'What does your mother most like to eat for breakfast?' he asked. Abby considered the question for a moment, frowning in concentration.

'Those curly bread things,' she said finally, and it was Matt's turn to frown. Then his brow cleared.

'Croissants?' he guessed, and she nodded.

'Mmm. And posh jam,' she added. Conserve, Matt translated silently.

'Tell you what – why don't you go and get dressed – *quietly*,' he stressed. 'And then we'll go shopping and take Mummy breakfast in bed – okay?'

'Why is she still in bed? Is she poorly?' Abby asked, still harbouring fears for Tessa's health.

'No, not at all. She's just tired. She didn't get much sleep last night,' Matt explained, and was unaware of the note of smug satisfaction in his voice until he caught his daughter looking at him curiously. 'The traffic noise kept her awake,' he added hastily.

They left Tessa a note lest she wake while they were out – even that small task became a lengthy process since Abby insisted on signing her name and adding dozens of kisses.

Eventually, they arrived at the nearest supermarket, where bread was baked on the premises. Matt bought still-warm bread as well as croissants and the raspberry conserve which Abby assured him was Tessa's favourite, and then decided to stock up on groceries they would need for their week's stay while he was there.

He had noticed before that, when he was alone with Abby, other women tended to try and mother the pair of them. Today was no exception, as if he couldn't possibly manage the mundane task of the weekly shop without maternal guidance! He wasn't sure whether to be amused or affronted by the unsolicited advice on how best to cook trout, or by the kindly suggestion that he stick to instant coffee granules instead of purchasing coffee beans.

He turned a blind eye to Abby popping biscuits and sweets into the trolley, until she overreached herself, literally, trying to grab a packet of ice-cream snowmen from the back of a freezer cabinet and went headlong

311

inside it! The upper half of her body disappeared completely; only her legs, kicking furiously, could be seen.

Matt, his ribs aching with suppressed laughter, pulled her out and silently set her back on to her feet, pretending not to notice the expression of outraged embarrassment on her face.

Tessa awoke slowly, emerging gradually from a blissful dream. She became aware first of the delicious aroma of freshly brewed coffee and newly baked bread and sniffed appreciatively, beginning to feel hungry. Slightly, disorientated, she glanced around at her unfamiliar surroundings. Ah yes, Matt's flat. Matt's bed . . .

She sighed happily and stretched luxuriously; her whole body tingled with remembered delights. She looked up as the door opened slightly and Abby poked her head round to see if she were awake.

'Hello, sweetie.' Tessa smiled sleepily.

'We've been shopping,' Abby announced. 'A nice lady wanted to help Daddy . . .'

'Oh yes?'

'Mmm. Why aren't you wearing a nightie?'

'I was hot during the night,' Tessa said hastily, pulling the quilt up over her breasts.

'I'll second that,' Matt drawled meaningfully, grinning at Tessa as he walked in and placed her breakfast on the bedside cabinet. She blushed furiously, then returned his grin.

As one fun-filled, happy and loving day followed another, Matt couldn't help but notice how Tessa blossomed away from Stafford House, back in the city, and began seriously considering a life away from Drake's Abbot for the three of them.

But, when he broached the subject with Tessa, she surprised him by turning down his offer to live permanently in London.

'You've agreed to take over running the estate from your father,' she reminded him. 'And we can't uproot Abby again. She loves her new school already, and she would miss your parents, not to mention Lollipop and Flynn.'

'Point taken,' Matt nodded, realizing, to his shame, that he had not considered anyone's wishes but his own when he had first decided to take over Tessa's and Abby's lives. Tessa had been in a coma at the time, he tried to excuse his hasty actions, but he wasn't feeling at all proud of himself, and now wanted to make amends.

'But you're not keen on living at the Dower House, are you?' he asked.

'You've spent so much money on it,' Tessa prevaricated.

'That doesn't answer my question . . . or, perhaps it does,' he realized. 'How would you feel about a place in Ashminster?' he suggested. 'You wouldn't feel isolated, Abby could continue at school, and it's near enough to Drake's Abbot for her to visit my parents and ride her pony regularly.' Tessa smiled gratefully.

'I think I'd love that,' she nodded.

'Great. I'll get on to an estate agent mate of mine, and see if he can fix us up quickly,' Matt said.

They continued enjoying their first holiday as a family, re-visiting the sights of London. Matt hadn't

313

been to places like the zoo or Madame Tussaud's for years, but loved Abby's excitement and wonderment in every new experience.

They took her out with them in the evenings, too, partly because they had no babysitter, and partly to ensure that she slept soundly throughout the night! Abby was enchanted by the show *Riverdance* and promptly forsook ballet in favour of Irish dancing, whereupon she, as Matt complained good-naturedly, proceeded to 'kick the hell out of the furniture' in her attempts to re-enact the role.

Matt had obtained the special licence required for a speedy wedding, and they were due to be married on Thursday. Matt couldn't wait; he was as impatient as a kid longing for Christmas. His life, pre-Tessa and Abby, now seemed arid and pointless: it was hard to believe he had once thought himself fairly content with his lot.

They had told Abby, who was delighted, but otherwise it was a secret. Matt, still angry with his parents over their lack of trust in Tessa, was in two minds whether to invite them to the ceremony, although Tessa felt he should.

On Wednesday afternoon, while Tessa went to have her hair done for the wedding, Matt took Abby to the zoo, despite Tessa's heartfelt warning that she would want to bring all the animals home, or, at the very least, release them from their cages.

Abby especially loved the chimpanzees, and laughed delightedly at their antics, but then proved her mother right by asking Matt if the monkeys could come and live at Stafford House.

'They could sleep in the stables with Lollipop and Flynn,' she told him. 'Grandpa wouldn't mind, would he?'

'I'm sure he'd be thrilled,' Matt said drily, imagining his father's reaction. The irony was lost on Abby, and she thought she was winning her case. Hope and pleading shone in equal measure from the brown eyes fixed unwaveringly on Matt.

He became aware that he was actually trying to conceive a way for a miniature zoo to be set up in Drake's Abbot and took himself sternly to task. He had always considered that parents who queued overnight outside shops each December in order to buy the latest craze in toys were idiotically over-indulgent. No doubt this coming Christmas would find him doing the same thing, he realized ruefully, just to see the look of delight on her face when she unwrapped the coveted gift.

However, he put those thoughts aside and concentrated on the problem in hand. He showed her the signs outside the cages which indicated the animals were sponsored by members of the public.

'What does "sponsored" mean?' Abby's brow furrowed.

'Sort of adopted,' he explained. 'They pay the zoo money to help take care of them.' If he had harboured any hopes that that would mollify her, he was quickly disabused of the notion!

'Well, I think that's horrid! If they adopt them they should take them home, not leave them locked up here,' she declared indignantly. Matt couldn't think of an adequate reply.

'I don't think they're allowed to do that,' he said lamely, passing the blame on to the zoo authorities.

* * *

That evening, they all dined out at a restaurant near Matt's flat. The staff knew Matt from his bachelor days, when he had frequented the place with various women, but accepted his new-found family with aplomb.

Abby, who had taken to eating at expensive restaurants with a speed and enthusiasm that rather alarmed her mother, had quickly become something of a pet with the waiters. She was always very adult and on her best behaviour, and obviously enjoyed being treated as if she were a grown-up.

The wine waiter solemnly presented the bottle of coke she had ordered for her inspection, as he had shown Matt his choice of wine. Abby, copying her father, just as solemnly nodded her approval, then tasted a tiny amount before rather imperiously indicating he could fill her glass.

Matt watched her with amusement: she was such a delight; loving, funny – often unintenionally – bright and inquisitive. He could barely remember a time without her. Or Tessa. He reached under the table and squeezed her hand. In a little over twelve hours, they would be man and wife . . .

He had phoned his parents just before they had left the flat; partly because Tessa wanted him to, and partly because he needed his mother to dig out Tessa's passport for a surprise honeymoon. He had come across the document while sorting through her papers when she was still in a coma, and remembered seeing it. It was still valid, although she hadn't used it since returning from Cyprus six years earlier.

After dinner, he had to carry a sleeping Abby back

316

to the flat. She hardly stirred when Tessa undressed her, and snuggled down into her sofa bed with a small sigh of contentment. Matt watched her for a moment, then drew Tessa into the privacy of their bedroom.

'I'm so proud of her. Although I can't claim any credit for her development,' he conceded. Tessa glanced at him sharply, but there was no reproach in his voice or his eyes and she relaxed.

'Why were you so sure you were her father?' she asked him curiously. 'You told the hospital staff, the day of the accident, but you couldn't have known, not until you found her birth certificate.'

'I wasn't at all certain,' Matt said slowly. 'I first thought I might be when I realized you had lied about her age, but I didn't know for sure.'

'So why did you take her to Drake's Abbot?' Tessa asked, puzzled. 'Why did you take responsibility for her?'

'Oh, Tessa, why do you think I did?' Matt asked softly, drawing her closer to him. 'She is so like you, almost a clone. I bet you were just like her when you were that age. I wanted to take care of her, for you, because she was your daughter. I'd have loved her and looked after her no matter who had fathered her,' he said truthfully.

'Oh, Matt, I do love you,' Tessa said fervently.

'Good. Because I adore you,' he told her, lifting her hand to his mouth and nibbling gently at her fingers until she felt the familiar stirring of desire. Always, her whole body responded to the lightest, most casual caresses he bestowed upon her, and she involuntarily leaned towards him, wanting more.

'I . . . I think I'll stop taking the Pill,' she said, thinking that was the best wedding gift she could bestow on him.

'No, don't do that,' he said, to her surprise. And to his own, actually: he had expected to leap with joy when he heard her say those words.

'No?' Tessa pulled back a little to gaze into his eyes. 'I thought you wanted us to have a baby?'

'I do, very much,' he said slowly. 'But not yet. I don't want to share you,' he suddenly realized. 'Much as I love Abby, I sometimes find myself almost resenting the time and attention she needs from you. I never seem to have you all to myself for more than a few hours.' He paused. 'God, that sounds selfish,' he said, a little shamefaced.

'No, it doesn't.' Tessa smiled slightly, recalling how, only a few weeks earlier, he had been practically ordering her to provide him with another child, as if that were her only value to him. How he had changed! How we both have, she amended, for she discovered she wasn't as relieved by the postponement as she would have been a while ago.

She leaned happily against him, resolving silently not to wait too long to give him a baby. After all, he had missed out on changing nappies, pacing the floor half the night with a teething, fractious child . . . it simply wasn't fair to deprive him of such experiences!

Evelyn arrived in London for the register office ceremony accompanied only by Ricky, who had returned unscathed from his pot-holing expedition.

She began to talk, very quickly, and flitting from one

318

subject to another, to gloss over the rather lame excuse that George's arthritis was too painful for him to make the journey.

'Poor George, he hardly got a wink of sleep last night. And he's so stubborn, won't take painkillers . . . How lovely you look.' She kissed Tessa's cheek, then stood back to admire the hastily bought pale pink suit, far plainer than the elaborate outfit yet to be completed by the dressmaker in Drake's Abbot for the church service.

'Hello, darling, what a pretty dress!' Evelyn continued, hugging Abby. 'Have you had a wonderful time? I've missed you so much.'

'I'm still going to be a bridesmaid,' Abby informed her, returning the hug and bestowing a rather sticky kiss on her cheek.

'I know; isn't it exciting? You are naughty, Matt,' she scolded, turning to her eldest son. 'Giving us no notice, I mean. I couldn't tell Helen – she is in New York for a few days. She and a group of friends always go to New York Christmas shopping,' she explained to Tessa, whose brows rose in astonishment and disbelief. Three thousand miles to go Christmas shopping? That seemed rather extreme, even for someone who enjoyed shopping as much as Helen and her friends.

Ricky grinned at the expression on Tessa's face, then stepped forward and, mindful of Matt's somewhat frosty look, kissed her chastely on the cheek.

'You look wonderful,' he told her sincerely.

'Thank you. I'm so sorry about getting drunk last week,' she apologized. 'I can assure you it's not something I do very often!'

319

'No problem. You had a lot on your mind,' he said easily. Which reminded him of the rather odd comment Belinda had made. He had remembered it, or at least he thought he had, but he'd had other things on his mind when she had made it! However, she was one of those who had accompanied Helen to the States, so he'd had no opportunity to question her about it.

He glanced at his brother, hesitated, then gave a mental shrug and decided to stay silent. Why spoil his day with what was probably nothing to worry about? The marriage was a *fait accompli* – or would be in thirty minutes: any childish, spiteful attempts to cause trouble between Matt and Tessa would cease, he thought, with misplaced optimism, never guessing how much he was underestimating the enmity directed at Tessa.

Evelyn normally felt a register office wedding was about as spiritually uplifting as a trip to the dentist, but unexpectedly found herself fumbling for a handkerchief as they exchanged vows. Matt looked so proud, so happy. And Tessa adored him, one could see it in her eyes. The rather prickly, defensive I-can-manage-by-myself shell had crumbled away completely.

And, of course, her gaze rested fondly on Abby, who was unusually quiet and solemn. The icing on the cake, Evelyn thought. She tilted her head sideways and surreptitiously scrutinized Tessa's figure, or, to be precise, her stomach. It was disappointingly flat; she had rather hoped this early wedding meant a second grandchild was already on its way . . .

To celebrate, Evelyn insisted on taking them all for a very expensive lunch which, she lied, unblushing and unashamed, was George's idea. What did a little white lie matter if it promoted peace and harmony in the family? she thought. And they were now certainly all part of the same family. No longer need she fear that Tessa would take Abby away.

'Are we all called Stafford now?' Abby asked, echoing her grandmother's thoughts.

'Indeed we are,' Evelyn confirmed. 'Isn't that wonderful, darling?'

'Mmm.' Abby nodded, accepting it without question, as she had accepted the change in plans regarding their future home. When asked for her opinion on living in Ashminster instead of at the Dower House, she had merely looked from Matt to Tessa and asked if they would still all live together. Assured that they would, she had relaxed and shrugged, perfectly content.

Now, Matt drew her on to his lap and hoped she would be as accommodating with his plans for a brief honeymoon. Evelyn had found Tessa's passport and passed it to him secretly, and, in his jacket pocket, he had two air tickets to Paris and reservations at one of the best hotels the city had to offer.

'Is it okay with you if I take Mummy away for a couple of days?' he asked, ultra casual. 'You'll go back to stay at Drake's Abbot with Grandma and Uncle Ricky for the weekend, and we'll collect you from school on Monday and then move into our new house.'

'I'll come riding with you,' Ricky offered. Abby smiled at him; she hardly knew him, but his resemblance to Matt endeared him to her.

'Oh, yes, do come,' Evelyn urged. She had been disappointed, if not surprised, to hear of the move to Ashminster. Even before the shoplifting incident she had felt Tessa would prefer the bustle of the town to

321

the solitary splendour of Stafford House or the Dower House.

'We'll bring you back a present,' Matt added, quite prepared to resort to bribery!

'Okay, you can go' Abby conceded graciously, after what seemed an interminable wait to Matt, but which was only actually a matter of seconds. 'What will you bring me back for a present?'

Tessa and Matt had a blissful, if brief, honeymoon in Paris. Tessa phoned Stafford House each morning and evening to check on Abby, then, once assured that she was well and happy, devoted all her time and attention to her husband. Husband. What a terrific word!

The hotel was the ultimate in luxurious living; the suite lavish and comfortable, the food and wines excellent, the staff discreet and helpful.

Paris was supposed to be for lovers in the spring, of course, but was beautiful in autumn, too. The weather treated them kindly; the days were cool, but sunny and invigorating, and Tessa finally felt fully fit and healthy.

They wandered, hand in hand, along the ancient streets, shopping and sightseeing, and, in the evenings, dined on one of the many boats that slowly sailed along the Seine, with the city lit up on both banks of the river.

'We'll come back again, often,' Matt assured her, as they reluctantly took their leave on Monday morning. 'Are you happy?'

'You know I am,' Tessa smiled at him. 'So happy it's almost scary,' she confessed. 'I feel no one is allowed to be this lucky.'

'You deserve it, and more.' Matt hugged her. Tessa smiled and nodded, but surreptitiously crossed her fingers lest a malicious fate was watching and listening.

But it wasn't fate that had her in its sights, but a woman of flesh and blood, pushed over the edge by the news of the premature wedding.

CHAPTER 17

Tessa loved the rented house in Ashminster as soon as she saw it. It was conveniently close to St Hilda's School and to a small arcade of shops which provided day-to-day items, saving a trip to the centre of town. It was also within easy reach of the main-line railway station, giving speedy access to central London.

It was a three-storey Edwardian red-brick house set in large, well-established, beautifully maintained gardens and, whilst spacious, was not on the huge scale of Stafford House or even the Dower House, and Tessa felt immediately at home as she wandered through the rooms.

It had been fully modernized, with sparkling new kitchen and bathrooms, yet had retained much of its original character. Tessa even liked the décor and the furniture which the present owners had left behind.

'I grew up in a house very like this,' she told Matt.

'I know,' he said quietly, reminding her that he had indeed tried to find her after his tour of duty in Bosnia. But, by then, she had sold the house and moved away. She bit her lip and looked away, briefly regretting again her past actions born of pride. Matt guessed what she was feeling and moved to hug her tightly.

324

'The house is ours for the next six months, at least,' he told her, for the owner had a six-month contract to work abroad, with a possible extension after that time.

'If we like living here we'll make him an offer to buy,' he added, a short while later, watching Tessa's expression of delight as she inspected her new home.

'Will he sell?'

'If the price is right,' Matt said cynically. 'Come on, let's go and collect Abby.'

Abby was thrilled to see them, as if they had been away for months instead of days, and greeted them both with hugs and kisses, and didn't even ask about her present until bedtime. The clockwork and very life-like monkey, which performed acrobatics on a trapeze when wound up, rendered her speechless with delight.

As the days passed, they all settled very well in the house that rapidly felt like home to them all. Abby visited her grandparents often – or perhaps she visited Flynn and Lollipop – Tessa was never quite sure which was the greater attraction and thought it better not to ask!

A week after returning from Paris, Matt stayed home alone to babysit Abby while Tessa drove to Drake's Abbot for a fitting with the dressmaker. The 'proper' wedding, as Evelyn continued to call it, was only a couple of weeks away: after the church service, to which the entire village had apparently been invited, there was to be a huge reception at Stafford House. They intended to spend their first Christmas as a family in their new home, and then Matt planned to take both Tessa and Abby away on a skiing holiday.

Matt put Abby to bed, listening to her chatter and reading a story with her before she fell asleep. He stayed in the room for a while, standing at the window and watching for Tessa's return. Before long, he saw her car indicating her intention to turn into the driveway, and, with a last glance at Abby, he quietly left the room.

The bathroom looked as if a bomb had hit it after Abby's bath, and he hurriedly tidied up before heading downstairs to greet Tessa.

'There's some food in –' He stopped. 'Tessa?' He checked the downstairs rooms, but there was no sign of her. Perhaps it had been the neighbour's car he had seen? 'Tessa?' he called again, feeling unaccountably uneasy. He walked back into the kitchen: it was empty, and he turned to leave, then caught the sound of a car engine running.

He retraced his steps and entered the utility room, from where a door led into the garage. He opened it and immediately began to cough as exhaust fumes poured into the room.

'Tessa!' He fumbled for, then snapped on, the light switch, but nothing happened. However, the light from the utility room was sufficient for him to see inside the garage, and his heart almost stopped when he spotted her lying on the garage floor, seemingly lifeless, her head near to the deadly fumes pouring from the exhaust pipe.

'Christ!' The poisoned air caught at his lungs and eyes as he dashed forwards. He picked her up and carried her towards the main garage door, leading to the fresh night air. He struggled to open it for what seemed an age, then it burst open abruptly and he half-fell on to the gravel driveway. Eyes streaming, fighting for breath, he tried to turn Tessa over, desperate to give her whatever oxygen he could.

'Let me do that.' Someone shoved him unceremoniously out of the way and Matt, recognizing calm efficiency in the voice, staggered to one side, coughing and wiping at his eyes. Someone else hurried inside the garage and switched off the car's engine. A rather eerie silence descended.

'I've called for an ambulance.' This time, a woman's voice, kind and concerned.

'Tessa,' Matt managed to gasp.

'She's breathing; her pulse is steady, if a little weak,' said the first voice, still calm.

'Thank God.' Again, Matt had to wipe his eyes, but now they were tears of emotion. He had thought it was a dead weight he carried; had really thought he had lost her. Again. And, this time, for eternity.

He tried to rise, needed a helping hand, and fell to his knees beside her. In the harsh light from the street lamp her face looked too pale, bloodless, her eyes closed. Matt clutched her hand tightly, trying to give her his strength, and looked up with relief as the sound of the approaching ambulance cut through the night.

The man who had first to come to their aid spoke to the paramedics, talking urgently as they quickly and carefully transferred Tessa on to a stretcher. Matt, watching, had a sense of *déjà vu*. Was this his fault, too? Would she have been better off if he had not entered the coffee shop that day and taken over her life?

'She's got a nasty bump on her head, too,' the man continued. 'And that chap needs treatment, in my opinion. He breathed in too many fumes.'

327

'I'll be okay,' Matt said hoarsely. He felt dreadfully sick, but how much of that was due to the exhaust fumes and how much to fear for Tessa he couldn't tell.

'I'm coming with her . . . oh, God. Abby!' He had almost forgotten about her. He glanced around wildly, and saw the woman who had called the ambulance, and dimly recognized her as a neighbour.

'My little girl is in the house – still asleep, I hope. Could you possibly stay with her until I can phone my mother and get her over here?' he asked urgently.

'Of course I will. Abby, isn't it? I spoke to her and your wife yesterday morning. If she wakes up, I'll just tell her you had to go out,' she said soothingly.

'Thank you. Thank you all,' Matt said, his gaze encompassing the entire group who had gathered, some merely to watch, but most to help.

He clambered into the ambulance, was handed an oxygen mask and then pushed aside while they tended to Tessa. He sat as near to her as possible and watched closely for any sign of returning consciousness, or even some colour to her cheeks. He couldn't bear it if he lost her. If he had to tell Abby . . . He closed his eyes and swallowed convulsively. Suddenly, something Tessa had said recently struck a chord. 'Loving someone makes you vulnerable.' He clearly remembered his too-confident reply: only if it's unrequited, he had said. How wrong he had been.

'But however could it have happened?' Evelyn asked, bewildered, when Matt phoned her from the hospital.

'I don't know,' he replied, rather shortly. His head hurt abominably and he was desperately worried about Tessa, who was still unconscious. Right now, who the hell cared how it had happened? 'Can you go and stay with Abby?'

'Yes, of course. I'll leave right away. Call me as soon as you have any news,' she said, and disconnected.

She, too, had a sense of *déjà vu* as she set out to take care of Tessa's child while Tessa was unconscious in hospital. She just hoped there would be a similarly happy outcome, although hopefully, please God, they would not have another almost unendurable nine days of waiting. She dreaded to think what lasting effect that would have on Abby.

Matt sat alone in the hospital waiting-room, his head in his hands, his stomach churning with fear and nausea. He hadn't prayed for years, but he did now. If not for me, dear God, then for Abby. Please don't let my daughter lose her mother . . .

He felt a gentle hand on his shoulder and looked up, both fearfully and hopefully, expecting to see the doctor who was caring for Tessa. Instead, he found himself staring up at his father.

'I'm sorry, son,' George Stafford said quietly. They locked glances as further, unspoken, words hung in the air. Sorry for making her feel unwelcome, sorry for driving her out to a place where she had suffered an accident . . .

Matt was too weary and worried to bear grudges and nodded briefly. George sat down, rather awkwardly, for his arthritis was painful, and stayed perched uncomfortably on the hard chair provided by the hospital. Penance, he told himself. He'd already tried consoling himself with the thought that the same thing could just as easily have happened at Stafford House, but knew it wasn't true. For one thing, in the isolation of Stafford House, away from vandals and joyriders, they very rarely bothered locking away their cars.

'Do you know what happened?' he asked.

'No, I don't. I think she must have fainted, or fallen and hit her head when she got out of the car,' Matt replied, rather vaguely. The 'how' still didn't seem important. Besides, he couldn't bear to think he might be partly responsible by letting her do too much; first the busy week in London, then the trip to Paris and, since their return, managing a large house without staff to help out. He knew she had wanted to get away from Stafford House, but at least she had been able to rest there whenever she felt tired. He had been so sure she was fully recovered; she seemed so happy and full of life . . . oh, God. He squeezed his eyes tightly closed and began to pray again. George, sitting quietly by his side, did the same.

It was after midnight before Tessa recovered consciousness, and immediately wished she hadn't. She felt dreadfully sick and her head hurt as much as it had when she had first awoken after being knocked down by the London bus. What hit me this time? she thought dazedly. A truck? She pulled at the oxygen mask covering her nose and mouth, not realizing what it was.

'Don't do that,' a soft voice remonstrated, and even softer hands took hers and held it. 'It's there to help you. Try to relax and breathe deeply.'

George saw the doctor approaching first and nudged Matt, who raised his head so quickly he cricked his neck. The smile on the doctor's face reassured him somewhat and he got to his feet.

'She's awake?'

'Yes, and there doesn't seem to be any permanent damage from the carbon monoxide. But she does have concussion, which we will need to watch carefully for a while, but I think she'll be able to go home in a couple of days.'

'Oh, thank God!' Matt expelled a pent-up breath. 'Can I see her?'

'Yes, but just for a few minutes, and then you both need to get some sleep.'

'I'm fine,' Matt said dismissively.

'I'll phone your mother and then wait for you here,' George told him.

'That's not necessary, but thanks for coming. I appreciate it,' Matt said sincerely.

'You'll need a lift home,' George reminded him.

'Oh.' Matt had forgotten he had no car, and, besides, he was too impatient to see Tessa to waste time arguing with his father. 'Okay, thanks.' He smiled briefly, then followed a nurse to Tessa's room.

'Tessa!' The stricken look on his face caused her to burst into tears and he moved swiftly to gather her into his arms. 'Don't cry, darling, you're going to be fine,' he assured her brokenly. 'But, in future, switch off the car engine before you close the garage door – okay?' He strove to speak lightly, but his voice was harsh with the fear he had felt for what seemed an eternity.

Tessa frowned, trying to remember something, but the image on the edge of her consciousness slipped away as anxiety for Abby rushed to the forefront of her mind. Again, she tugged at the oxygen mask.

'Abby? Is she all right?'

'She's fine, she slept through the whole commotion,' Matt said soothingly. 'My mother's at the house now. I'll tell Abby in the morning.'

'No, don't.' Tessa clutched his arm. 'She already worries about me too much. Tell her . . . tell her I took the early train to London to do some shopping.'

'Are you sure?' Matt frowned slightly.

'Yes. Let her have a happy day at school, and maybe I'll be back home before she is,' Tessa said.

'I doubt that, but . . . oh, okay.' He decided to go along with what she asked. He hated lying to Abby, but perhaps it would be in her best interests. He could tell her when he collected her from school in the afternoon and bring her straight to visit Tessa, who would hopefully be much better and be able to reassure Abby that this was not a repeat of what she had endured a couple of months earlier.

A nurse entered the room, looked pointedly at her watch and then at Matt, and replaced Tessa's oxygen mask. She still clung to Matt's hand and, ignoring the nurse, he pulled up a chair and sat down beside the bed.

'I'm staying here until she's asleep,' he said firmly. 'Close your eyes,' he added to Tessa. She obeyed gladly, feeling ill and exhausted.

Matt watched her, wincing when she turned her head on the pillow and he saw the lump and surrounding abrasions she had sustained in her fall.

Tessa had almost drifted off to sleep when the memory that had eluded her earlier returned in full force and she wrenched off the oxygen mask.

'Matt!' Her shout intensified the pain in his head as well as her own.

'What's wrong?' he asked, reaching for the buzzer to summon medical help.

'I don't need a doctor – I need the police!' she said wildly. 'The car engine – I *did* switch it off. I did, Matt, I remember,' she said urgently, gripping his arm. 'Then I got out of the car, turned to lock the door, and . . . someone hit me!'

'Hit you? A mugger,' Matt guessed, fury erupting in him at the thought.

'It wasn't a mugger.' Tessa shook her head. 'Not an ordinary one, anyhow. I –' She stopped speaking for a moment, almost gagged. 'I smelled that perfume again, a split second before I saw stars!' She stared at him, her eyes huge with shock and fear.

'Are you sure?' Matt asked: despite the warmth of the hospital room, he could feel goose-flesh pimpling his arms.

He pulled Tessa into his arms and held her tightly, his mind racing. He had smelled nothing other than the acrid fumes pouring from the exhaust pipe, and had noticed no one lurking while he had been watching for Tessa's return. Was it time to call in the police? Tessa's fear was certainly genuine, but he was forced to question if it was based on reality. He really did not know the answer: however, what he could do was reassure her and ensure her safety.

'I'm scared, Matt,' she faltered, clinging to him. 'Who hates me?'

'Try not to worry; I'll get to the bottom of this.' He kissed her cheek and then, still holding her close, reached for the phone. He checked the number he required and then dialled, waiting with mounting impatience as it rang interminably at the other end.

'Saul? It's Matt Stafford . . . what? Who cares what time it is? You provide bodyguards – right? I want twenty-four-hour protection for my wife . . . what? Yes, it was rather sudden,' he smiled at Tessa. 'Someone apparently disapproves of our marriage, to the point where they are willing to hurt her. She's in Ashminster General . . . I don't give a damn if the staff like it or not. I want a minder here as quickly as possible . . .' He ended the call finally and noticed that Tessa had already lost some of her anxiety.

'A bodyguard? I feel like a film star.' She smiled weakly. 'How do you know these people?'

'They're all ex-Army; one of the partners is a friend of mine,' he explained. 'They'll take care of you when I'm not around. I'll stay here until the cavalry arrives, so you can relax and get some sleep,' he told her firmly.

Tessa nodded and felt sufficiently reassured and protected to do just that. Matt left the room briefly to tell his father what was happening, asked him to ensure Evelyn didn't tell Abby about her mother being hospitalized, and sent him home.

At five o'clock a tough-looking, wiry ex-soldier and martial arts expert arrived and introduced himself as Geoff Rawlins. Matt outlined the situation – from Tessa's point of view; he could see no advantage in expressing any doubts. He stressed that the assailant was probably female and that not even someone in nurse's uniform should be allowed into Tessa's room unsupervised.

'I'll be back soon, but I must go and see my daughter,' he said, wishing he could split himself into two parts. Tessa was at least sleeping peacefuly, so he refrained from touching her and, with Geoff Rawlins sitting on guard outside her door, he made his weary way outside.

He decided that a walk home might clear his head and his thoughts, and the cold air did revive him somewhat after the stuffy, overheated atmosphere of the hospital. As he approached the house, lights were already blazing from both upstairs and down, indicating Abby had awoken early, so he paused outside for a moment to school his features before going inside.

The garage door was still open, and Tessa's car stood innocently where she had parked it. He hesitated, then averted his gaze, unwilling to enter. He would check it out later, not that he was hopeful of discovering anything meaningful. If someone had been lurking in the shadows, waiting for Tessa to return, they were hardly likely to have conveniently left behind a business card . . . *if* there had been someone. He sighed. Surely a mugger was a more probable suspect, seeing the garage door open and acting on the spur of the moment? And perhaps Tessa's earlier fears had later added the false memory of the perfume she associated with danger?

He sighed again and shook his head wearily, knowing he was too tired to make sense of even a simple problem, let alone this nightmare. He needed coffee, food, and a hot shower before attempting to unravel the mystery.

He unlocked the front door and walked in, plastering a broad smile on his face as Abby, clutching a piece of buttered toast in her hand, ran towards him.

'Hello, Daddy!' she greeted him brightly.

'Hello, sweetheart.' He swung her up into his arms for a hug and glanced over her shoulder at Evelyn as she emerged from the dining-room.

'Why did Mummy leave so early?' Abby enquired, pulling back a little to look into his face. Her clear gaze, so innocent and trusting, dried the lie on his lips, yet surely it would be even worse to witness the dimming of her happy smile? He was relieved when his mother spoke up for him.

'The shops are so busy this near to Christmas,' she said quickly. 'It's much better to go early and avoid the crowds.'

'Oh.' Abby nodded and thankfully accepted the explanation without further comment. 'Can I go and watch TV?' she asked.

'Yes, okay.' Matt gave her another hug, then set her down on her feet and she scampered off. 'Thank you,' he said fervently to his mother, and she grimaced slightly.

'I didn't like doing it, but I must admit I was relieved when your father warned me not to tell her what had really happened. School's the best place for her today, Matt,' she added comfortingly.

'I know.' He nodded.

'I'll have a word with the headmistress, though,' Evelyn continued. 'Just in case the news is already doing the rounds,' she explained, at Matt's look of enquiry.

'Right.' He nodded again.

'I'm so glad Tessa's going to be all right, but you look exhausted. Go and get some sleep,' she urged.

'Yes, I think I will,' he agreed.

'And let me collect Abby from school and take her home with me,' she suggested.

'Postponing the evil moment of telling her the truth?' Matt smiled slightly. 'Yeah – why not?' He decided the longer Tessa had to recover before Abby saw her, the better.

He intended only to rest for an hour before returning to the hospital, but, once he stretched out, fully clothed, on top of the bed, he fell instantly into a deep slumber.

Evelyn, George and Helen lunched together at Stafford House and, naturally enough, the conversation was dominated by what had happened to Tessa.

'Is she unlucky, or just plain careless?' Helen asked flippantly.

'Oh, hush, I feel awful about last night,' Evelyn confessed. 'I thought she was being rather neurotic, all that fuss over nothing, claiming someone was sneaking into her room, stealing her ring. And as for thinking someone shot at her when she was walking in the woods! Well, I didn't believe that for a minute.' She shook her head slightly.

'Don't be so hard on yourself,' George said, reaching across the table to pat her hand. 'Even Matt didn't take her seriously at first. And there's no actual proof that she was attacked last night – she could easily have fallen, or fainted, and hit her head. If Matt was convinced she was in danger he'd have called in the police to investigate properly, not just hired some of his Army cronies to look after her.'

'I know, but Matt said she was very definite about someone hitting her last night,' Evelyn reminded him.

'Well, if that's true, it was probably a random mugging, not a personal attack on Tessa. As for the shooting, I agree with Matt; that was a local after pheasant – Tessa's presence was a coincidence.'

'I hope you're right.' Evelyn glanced guiltily at Helen; they'd had a rather bitchy conversation about that particular episode. Helen avoided looking at her and instead addressed George.

'How does Matt explain away the note?' she asked.

'Which note?' George frowned. 'I haven't heard anything about a note.'

'The one warning – oh, it doesn't matter. I must have misunderstood,' Helen said quickly.

Evelyn stopped eating and slowly put down her knife and fork, staring at Helen, first in incomprehension and then in mounting horror and disbelief.

'Excuse me,' she muttered, and hurried from the room, running up the stairs and into her bedroom.

She tugged open the cupboard door and began scattering her rather extensive collection of handbags all over the carpet in her haste to find the one she had used on one particular day some weeks earlier.

She cast her mind back feverishly, trying to remember what she had been wearing as a clue to which bag she might have been carrying. How stupid! She could remember the incident clearly; she had driven Tessa's car for the first time . . . of course! She had worn a blue suit; could recall thinking it almost matched the colour of the paintwork. Now, which shoes and bag? she mused.

Finally, she found the bag she sought and, in contrast to her earlier haste, delved slowly, reluctantly, inside. She was almost sorry to find the

338

crumpled note she had found on the windscreen of the car and forgotten about until now. With shaking fingers, she unfolded it and smoothed it out. I WON'T MISS NEXT TIME! The printed words leaped out at her and she closed her eyes briefly, as if she could shut out the sight and thereby banish the memory. But she couldn't, of course.

'Oh, Helen, what have you been doing?' she muttered.

With a heavy heart, and even heavier footsteps, she returned downstairs. She placed the note in front of Helen.

'Why?' she asked simply.

'Er, would you believe – a joke? A bad one, I admit, but at the time you agreed that she was being hysterical over nothing,' Helen pointed out calmly, evidently not too perturbed at being caught out.

'What's that?' George frowned. Silently, Evelyn passed him the note.

'I found that on the windscreen of Tessa's car a couple of days after the shooting episode,' she told him. 'I didn't make the connection at the time and forgot all about it. I only kept it in my bag because I couldn't find a litter bin to throw it away.'

'I was in Ashminster and saw her car,' Helen put in. 'I didn't know you were driving it. Okay, I'm sorry! It was stupid –'

'And cruel,' Evelyn interrupted.

'Yeah, okay.' Helen shrugged. 'But, as she didn't even read the bloody thing, I can't see what you're making such a fuss about!' she said disgustedly. Evelyn and George glanced at each other, then at Helen.

'Are you responsible for anything else that has upset her?' George asked sternly.

'Of course not. Why would I? I was just fed up with all the attention she and Abby were getting and decided to give her something to really worry about,' she said petulantly. 'Matt was much better off with Belinda.' She stared unflinchingly at George and he sighed, but sat back.

'I do hope you and Belinda haven't been conspiring to break Matt and Tessa up.'

'Of course we haven't. That note was written on impulse, a stupid one I admit, considering what happened to her last night. But Tessa doesn't even know about it, so where's the harm?'

'All right, we'll forget about it,' George decided. 'I don't see any point in telling either Tessa or Matt about it,' he added, glancing at his wife. She hesitated, then reluctantly nodded her agreement.

'Very well, I won't mention it to them,' she promised. But I'm going to talk to David, she added silently. She had never been able to control Helen, and George had never shown any inclination to do so, so her husband would have to take on the task. She also decided to phone Ricky; they were only a year apart in age and he probably knew how Helen's mind worked better than anybody else.

They dropped the subject, but, after lunch, when Helen and George had gone out to the stables, Evelyn phoned David. He was working at home at Grange Farm and she arranged to call in on her way to collect Abby from school.

Matt was appalled to wake up and discover he had slept for most of the day. He felt as if he had let Tessa down but, when he phoned the hospital, he found she was

340

feeling much better and was quite cheerful despite being told she would have to remain in hospital for at least one more night.

'I'll be over just as soon as I've had a shower,' he assured her.

'What about Abby?'

'My mother's picking her up from school and taking her back to Drake's Abbot,' he told her.

'Good.' Tessa relaxed.

'Tessa? About last night . . . do you still think you were attacked? Or could you have hit your head on something?' he asked.

'I . . .' She hesitated: she had been sure, but in the clear light of day it all seemed so unlikely. 'I'm sure I switched the engine off,' she said, but with a note of doubt in her voice. And renewed tension, Matt thought.

'Okay, don't worry about it,' he said quickly. 'Is Geoff Rawlins looking after you?'

'Yes, he's great,' Tessa said warmly. 'Although he keeps frisking one of the nurses!' she giggled.

'Only one?' Matt grinned.

'Yes. She doesn't seem to mind, though; she keeps coming in here for the flimsiest of reasons!'

'It sounds as if you're all having a better day than I am,' Matt said drily. 'I'm coming to join in the fun!'

He felt much better after a hot shower and a change of clothes, and wolfed down sandwiches Evelyn had thoughtfully prepared before she left with Abby that morning. After several cups of strong, black coffee, he felt ready to confront and overcome any problems.

However, he still had to brace himself before entering the garage: despite the door being open, the acrid smell of the exhaust fumes still hung in the air. He glanced around, but nothing seemed out of place, nor could he see anything on which Tessa could have hit her head. It seemed just as it had when he had come out last evening to open the door for Tessa . . . hold on! The light! It had worked when he had entered that first time, but not when he had returned in search of Tessa.

He glanced up at the socket – it was empty! His skin crawled as he realized that someone had removed the bulb, and then lain in wait for Tessa, probably hiding behind his car, ready to pounce after Tessa had switched off her headlights. He swallowed; not a random theft, then – if that were so, his Mercedes, or its stereo, would have been the target.

He looked around the garage again, this time searching for the missing light bulb, and spotted it at once, lying innocuously on the work bench. He returned briefly to the house and then carefully transferred the bulb to the small box. Gotcha! Unless the assailant had worn gloves . . . He grimaced at the thought of that probability, but presumably clothing fibres or other minute pieces of evidence would be detectable to experts. If he needed more proof that the attack was not a spur-of-the-moment mugging, he caught sight of Tessa's handbag on the floor, still complete with wallet and credit cards.

He was halfway to the police station when the truth hit him with an almost physical blow and he realized what a blind fool he had been. He slammed on the brakes and pulled over to the kerb, thinking furiously, trying to recall and date every incident and reviewing them in the light of what he now suspected.

When his mobile phone rang, he ignored it, then picked it up in case it was Tessa. It wasn't; it was Ricky.

'I can't talk now,' Matt began impatiently, then he frowned. 'Belinda said what? God, how awful.' He grimaced. 'Thanks, Ricky, but I'd already worked it out for myself.' He paused to listen again, then, 'I don't think I have much choice, do I? I have to stop her, and that means going to the police.'

CHAPTER 18

'Mrs Stafford?' Geoff Rawlins poked his head around the door. 'There's a Mr Warrender here to see you – do you want to talk to him?' He lowered his voice. 'I think he's been drinking,' he added. Indeed, David had been drinking: what Evelyn had told him had shocked him to the core, and the confrontation he'd just had with Helen had shocked him even more. He had decided that Tessa deserved to know the truth.

'Oh? Yes, he can come in,' Tessa decided. She was rather bored, and was wondering what had happened to delay Matt. He wasn't at Stafford House, for she had just spoken to Abby, who was staying there overnight for the important task of helping Molly bake Christmas puddings, and had fortunately assumed Tessa was still in London.

'I'll leave the door open slightly,' Geoff said, somewhat doubtful about letting the visitor in to the room. He nodded to David and pointed to a chair that was visible from his own vantage point outside the room, then left and sat down, able to watch David without intruding on the conversation.

'How are you feeling?' David asked, rather stiltedly.

'I'm fine, thanks to Matt,' she said warmly. 'He saved my life.'

'Oh, Matt the hero!' David sneered. 'I should hope he did save your life considering he's to blame for putting you in danger!'

'What on earth are you talking about?' Tessa faltered, glancing nervously towards the door and immediately gaining comfort from the solid presence of her bodyguard. One shriek for help and he would be in the room in a flash.

'Don't be alarmed, Tessa.' David had seen her worried look towards Rawlins. 'You're the last person I'd want to hurt. We're fellow sufferers, you and I, both in love with members of the Stafford family!' he said bitterly.

'What do you mean? Have you had a row with Helen?' Tessa guessed. 'What does that have to do with Matt and me?'

'You really don't know, do you?' he mused. 'Still, why should you? They kept me in the dark for years.'

'In the dark – about what?'

'What everyone has failed to tell you, Tessa, is that Helen is not George and Evelyn's natural daughter. They adopted her when she was twelve years old – worst day's work they ever did. George doesn't see it that way, of course, he's always doted on her. I think Evelyn saw the potential danger in the situation, but not until it was too late.'

'What danger?' Tessa whispered, fighting down a terrible premonition and feeling her heart begin to pound heavily with dread.

'Helen and Matt,' David said unemotionally, but the linking of their two names, as if they were a couple, made Tessa feel sick.

'Matt's quite a bit older than Helen and no one thought it untoward that she should hero-worship the older brother she had acquired – I gather she used to follow him around much as Ricky did. Matt was away a lot while she was growing up, first at boarding school and university, and then in the Army. I don't know this for sure, but I guess he came home on leave one time and suddenly realized she had become a beautiful, desirable young woman . . .' he droned on, but Tessa heard the words as if from a great distance; her head had begun to throb and waves of nausea swept over her.

'It was Helen,' she whispered. 'But . . . weren't you two on holiday while I was in hospital? It can't have been Helen who came into my room.'

'It was. I tackled her about it earlier and she admitted it. Yes, we were away when you had the accident, but we returned the day before you left hospital. She heard about you and Abby, and that Matt intended marrying you. It was a great shock to her; she thought he was happy enough with Belinda – and Helen knew that would never become a serious relationship.'

'But . . . Helen married you,' Tessa told him, as if he didn't already know that. His lips twisted into a grimace.

'I'm extremely wealthy.'

'So is Matt,' Tessa pointed out. Some of the numbness had disappeared and she found she could think more clearly. 'If Helen is adopted, there is no reason why she couldn't marry Matt, if that's what he wanted,' she said, with mounting confidence. 'It's not illegal for adoptive brothers

346

and sisters to marry, is it? After all, there's no blood tie.'

'It's not illegal, no, but there *is* a blood tie,' David told her, dashing her hopes. 'They're cousins and Matt felt they are too closely related to risk having children.'

'Cousins marry all the time,' Tessa objected. 'Obviously Matt didn't want to marry her and said that to let her down lightly,' she decided.

'I'm afraid it's not as simple as that,' David sighed. 'You see, Helen *is* a Stafford. Her father was George's younger brother, and he married Evelyn's sister.'

'So, they're cousins . . . twice,' Tessa said.

'Yes, they have different parents but the same grandparents. Helen was prepared to ignore it – she doesn't want children anyway, not even Matt's, I don't suppose,' he added bitterly. 'But Matt thought it would be too great a risk. And he wanted children.'

'And now he has Abby,' Tessa said slowly. 'If . . . if I were out of the way, he would have his child, and be able to have Helen as well . . .'

'Yes,' David agreed. 'I suspect that's what has been tormenting her. You almost died in that road accident; she must have thought she and Matt were so close to getting what they wanted.'

'Are they . . . ?' Tessa shuddered, then looked at David searchingly. 'Are they lovers?'

'I honestly don't know. Probably in the past, but my guess is they aren't now – Helen wouldn't be behaving as she is if she thought she still had Matt at her beck and call,' he said shrewdly. 'She thought she could scare you off before the wedding, but then she returned from New York to discover you and Matt were already married. That prompted the attack on you last night –

she knew you'd gone, alone, to the dressmaker and went to your house to . . .' he hesitated, substituted 'kill you' with '. . . confront you.'

'She's admitted she attacked me?' Tessa gasped.

'Yes.' David nodded. 'She's not even very repentant, either. She feels sure I won't betray her to the police.'

'You might not, but I bloody will!' came Matt's furious voice from the doorway. 'How dare you come here and upset my wife with this nonsense?' he asked angrily, glaring at David while moving to take Tessa into his arms.

'Matt!' Tessa clung to him.

'It's all right, sweetheart. I love you; I'd have wanted to marry you with or without Abby, you know that. I'm going to get rid of Helen once and for all, and I'm desperately sorry I didn't guess earlier what trouble she was causing. I finally figured it out, almost too late. And Ricky called a while ago – my mother told him what had happened to you and he decided to pass on something Belinda said to him.' He paused, then added uncomfortably, 'Apparently Helen asked Belinda what I was like in bed. Belinda thought it was rather odd, and it rang alarm bells with Ricky. It's a pity he didn't tell me before, but I'm hardly in a position to criticize anyone for being slow on the uptake,' he said ruefully.

'So Helen doesn't know what you're like from personal experience,' Tessa realized joyfully, hardly hearing the rest of his words.

'Of course she doesn't!' Matt drew back a little, obviously shocked that the thought had even occurred to her. He glanced over at David. 'I've just been over to your place – where is Helen? The sooner she's behind bars the happier I'll feel.'

'She is. Behind bars, I mean. I locked her in the attic,' David said grimly.

'I'm glad to hear that.' Matt relaxed slightly. 'But that's only a temporary measure. She damn near killed Tessa last night and she is not going to get away with it. Nor is she going to have an opportunity to try it again,' he declared. David looked at him, his eyes narrowed.

'Do you expect us to believe that you're totally blameless in all this? That Helen's made it all up?' he asked sceptically. Tessa glanced apprehensively at Matt, cowardly wishing David hadn't asked – she was quite happy to believe it was all Helen's doing.

Matt sighed heavily and raked his fingers through his hair.

'I didn't hear very much of what you said to Tessa, so I don't know what Helen has told you . . .'

'Well, let's hear your version of events,' David suggested, rather snidely, implying he expected to be told a pack of lies. Matt subjected him to a hard look, but bit back his anger, since it was obvious David was deeply hurt by whatever he had learned from Helen.

'Helen's natural mother died when Helen was just a baby,' he began, 'and her father – my uncle – worked abroad for most of each year, so Helen always spent a lot of time with my family, and she came to live with us once she started school because her father wanted her to be educated in England. Then, when he died some years later, my parents formally adopted her.' He paused to gather his thoughts, aware of the other two hanging on to every word.

'She and Ricky were a pain,' he continued, 'forever following me about and wanting to do whatever I did. They're much the same age and were inseparable for a while, not that I took much notice of them other than to referee the occasional fight. I had my own life, my own interests and friends. They were just a couple of silly kids.'

'Sure,' David said impatiently, 'but that was when you were all children. What's important is what happened when Helen grew up.'

'That's the trouble – Helen never did grow up,' Matt snapped. 'She's a spoilt little girl who dreamed up a silly, romantic idea of a tragic love affair and apparently became obsessed by it. It was a schoolgirl fantasy, nothing more than that. Nothing ever happened to lead her to believe I cared about her in a sexual way. Nothing,' he repeated, ignoring David, his eyes boring into Tessa's. 'You do believe me? Trust me?' he asked urgently.

'I . . . yes,' she faltered, and saw the flash of pain, quickly masked, that her hesitation had inflicted. She gripped his hand tightly. 'I'm sorry, I do trust you. I know you love me, but David said –'

'David only knows what Helen has chosen to tell him – which I imagine was a pack of lies,' Matt said angrily. He stared at David. 'Just what did she tell you? I bet she didn't admit I rejected her?'

'She said you loved her, but that you considered the blood tie was too close to risk having children,' David said slowly, and Matt swore so viciously that Tessa flinched.

'Sorry, sweetheart,' he apologized, then turned back to David. 'And you repeated that garbage to Tessa?

Why? You were hurting so you figured you'd share the pain,' he said disgustedly.

'I thought she deserved to know the truth,' David said defensively. Matt swore again.

'The truth!' he spat.

'So – you didn't want to marry her? You weren't in love with her?' Tessa forced herself to ask.

'Good God, no!' Matt said emphatically. 'I barely knew she existed; I certainly never thought of her in that way, and assumed she had come to her senses. In fact, I'd forgotten the whole sordid episode, and . . . it *was* more than ten years ago,' he added, sensing David's continued skepticism.

'What exactly *did* happen ten years ago?' David asked.

Matt sighed, embarrassed even now by the event, the memory of which he had long since banished to the deepest recesses of his mind.

'I came home on leave to discover she had developed a crush on me – a case of absence making the heart grow fonder, I suppose. She and some of her schoolfriends had been writing to me and a couple of my fellow officers – silly letters, but it's always nice to receive post when one's away from home for any length of time. The girls sent, er, sexy photographs – not nude or pornographic,' he hastened to add, 'just pictures they'd taken of each other in swimwear while on holiday. Perhaps that should have sounded a warning bell, but it didn't. In fact, I assumed she probably fancied one of my friends,' he said, rather helplessly.

'Go on,' David said tersely, when Matt paused, obviously reaching the part of the tale he didn't want to remember. Or to relate.

'Well, I came home on leave, and Helen was fussing over me a bit, putting flowers in my room and such like. She even baked me a coming-home cake, which again I thought was a gesture to impress whichever of my friends she had her eye on . . .' He paused again and closed his eyes briefly; he really did not want to remember what had happened next, Helen coming to his bedroom, declaring her love . . . He shuddered.

'I was appalled when she finally spelled out to me what she wanted. I told her it could never happen, perhaps a little too bluntly, and she became extremely upset, almost hysterical, threatening suicide.' He shuddered again. 'God, it was horrendous. She was so upset, and I felt guilty – not because I had ever encouraged her,' he added quickly, 'but because I hadn't realized sooner what was going on inside her mind. So I tried to make her feel better about it all and I admit I did cite the blood tie as one of the reasons why we could never be together. With hindsight, that was a mistake, I should have been cruel to be kind: obviously that excuse merely fed her fantasy.'

'Then what happened?' Tessa prompted. Matt shrugged.

'That was it, so far as I was concerned anyway. She sulked but generally kept out of my way, for which I was grateful,' he said feelingly. 'I returned to my barracks a week later and we were sent out to Germany for the rest of that summer on NATO exercises. I was busy and put the whole unpleasant episode out of my mind.'

'Helen didn't,' Tessa said bluntly.

'No.' Matt sighed. 'Apparently not. But I was sure she had. I was home again, briefly, that Christmas, and there was never a hint that she still harboured any infatuation for me. As the years passed, she had dozens of boyfriends and she never showed a hint of hostility towards any of the girls I brought home,' he said, looking and sounding very much the bewildered male, Tessa thought, with an inner smile.

'She probably sensed they were only temporary,' David said shrewdly.

'Perhaps.' Matt shrugged. 'Then she married you and I – well, I just never gave it another thought. Even when she began bitching recently, I didn't realize just what was on her mind. She's always been the old man's blue-eyed darling and I assumed she was resenting the time and attention he was bestowing on Abby!' He shook his head at his own obtuseness.

'How many people know about this?' David asked suddenly. 'I gathered from Evelyn that she and George had suspicions, nothing more.'

'Yes, I've never discussed it with either of them, but I think Helen did ask my father about the blood tie,' Matt said, then added slowly, 'I once mentioned it to Ricky, but not in any detail, just that she'd had a crush on me; I thought he ought to be warned, in case she turned her fantasies in his direction. As for Helen . . . I doubt she's told anyone. Why do you ask?' He narrowed his eyes suspiciously at David, guessing he wanted to cover it all up.

'You haven't involved the police so far, have you?' David asked.

'Not yet, no,' Matt admitted.

'Can we come to some agreement to keep it quiet?' David suggested hesitantly.

'No way,' Matt said flatly.

'Hear me out, please?' David looked beseechingly from Matt to Tessa. 'Helen doesn't deserve any mercy, but she isn't the only one who will suffer if there's a court case. We all will. The tabloids love this sort of scandal, and there are a lot of people who will think you were at least partly at fault, Matt,' he said steadily. 'You were older, male – if Helen has any sense, she'll claim she only acted as she did towards Tessa because you betrayed and rejected her. You won't come out of this with any honour.'

'My shoulders are broad enough to bear any amount of unfounded gossip,' Matt said dismissively.

'Maybe yours are,' David agreed. 'But what about Tessa? And Abby? This type of scandal doesn't die down quickly. People will remember it for years and, sooner or later, someone will take delight in telling Abby about it. And don't forget the effect it will have on your parents. They'll come in for a lot of criticism, too – people will whisper that they allowed you to abuse your young cousin . . .'

'You've made your point!' Matt snapped irritably. 'But the fact remains that Helen tried to kill Tessa! We're not going to forget about it just because Helen now says she's sorry!'

'Well . . .' David prudently forbore to mention that, so far, Helen hadn't actually shown much remorse, mostly chagrin at being caught out! When he had challenged her, she had been defiant and tearful, with barely a hint of an apology, and he sensed the latter had been a belated, deliberate ploy once she realized she needed his help.

'If you'll agree, I'd like to take Helen away from here. As you know, I only bought Grange Farm so she

354

could remain near your parents . . . or perhaps near you,' he bit out, and struggled to compose himself. He wished he could hate Helen, but he couldn't; he still loved her and wanted her. But on his terms now, if Matt and Tessa would agree to his plan.

'Before I met Helen, I never intended settling in England and I've always wanted to return to Australia. Helen has always refused to consider it. She's not in a position to refuse now,' he said, with savage satisfaction. Matt and Tessa exchanged glances; she shrugged slightly, she was willing to let Matt decide. Strange, but she felt quite calm about it all, and not just because Helen was currently locked in the attic! She hadn't imagined an enemy; it had been real, and the problem would now be resolved, one way or another.

'That sounds okay,' Matt conceded grudgingly. 'But there's nothing to stop her getting a flight back here at some time in the future. You can't watch her for every minute of the day,' he pointed out.

'I'll confiscate her passport, and cut off her money supply,' David said promptly. 'I'll also take her out to show her my family's sheep farm in the outback, and she'll be left there permanently if I even suspect she's thinking of causing you any trouble. Given that choice, she'll settle down in Sydney,' he said confidently: the farm would horrify Helen – there were no shops within three hundred miles! 'If she does give me the slip, well, it's a twenty-four-hour flight and I promise to let you know immediately so you can have the police waiting for her to land. However, I think that's a remote possibility – if I get her out of this scrape, I intend keeping her barefoot, pregnant and extremely busy looking after me,' he added grimly. Matt's brows rose.

'That's the first time I've heard you talk like a stereotypical Aussie male,' he commented, with a slight smile.

'Oh, I can be as macho and insensitive as the next bloke,' David said. 'I've been too soft with Helen, but that's all about to change. So –' he looked squarely at Matt, as if sensing his was the dominant role '– it's your decision – does Helen go to trial, or to Australia?'

'I want to talk to Helen first,' Matt decided. 'And I want a signed confession, as insurance against her returning to England.'

'Of course,' David relaxed, recognizing probable capitulation in the proviso.

'Tessa?' Matt turned to her.

'I just want it to be finished with,' she said truthfully. 'She can't hurt me if she's in Australia, can she? And the publicity of a trial would be horrendous,' she shuddered. 'David's right about that. I hate to think what it would do to your parents, especially your father. He almost had a fit when he thought a member of the family had been caught shoplifting! He . . . Oh!' she looked at David. 'Did Helen put that bracelet in my bag?'

'Yes, I'm afraid she did.' He sighed. 'I think her plan, if such deranged, haphazard actions can even be described as such, was to make life uncomfortable for you here. She just wanted you to leave, or for Matt to send you away. She didn't plot to harm you, Tessa,' he said earnestly. Matt snorted his disgust and disdain.

'Last night she lay in wait for Tessa, hit her over the head and deliberately switched the car engine back on! That can hardly be described as "making life uncomfortable".'

'No, well –' David shifted in his seat '– she thought she had plenty of time to scare Tessa away before the wedding. I imagine it was a great shock to her to hear you had married while she was in New York, and she overreacted,' he said, aware of how lame it sounded.

'Did she shoot at Abby and me that day in the woods?' Tessa asked suddenly.

'No,' David assured her. 'That was just a, to her, happy coincidence. One more thing to make you feel unwelcome and uneasy about staying at Drake's Abbot.'

'But she did come to my hospital room?'

'Yes,' he admitted unwillingly.

'And I actually asked her if it could have been Belinda!' Tessa groaned, and remembered how Helen had seemed amused by her questions.

'Yes. And you also told her you could only identify the woman by her perfume,' David reminded her. 'Helen stopped wearing it immediately, but carried some in her bag and sprayed some in your room at Stafford House a couple of times.'

'And in the cloakroom of the restaurant where we had lunch,' Tessa realized slowly.

'What else has she admitted to doing?' Matt asked tightly.

'Well . . .' David was reluctant to repeat Helen's gloating list of crimes, but he figured it was better if Matt heard it from him, not Helen. 'She put a photograph of you and Sue Dalton in Tessa's room. And she also took your ring,' he added to Tessa. 'But she realized there would be one helluva fuss about that, and also, of course, she would never be able to wear it, so she replaced it.'

'And she left some perfume behind,' Tessa said, remembering that awful day when she had accused Sue of theft. Matt's anger, although justifiable, had frightened her badly. 'I really thought I was losing my mind,' she shivered. Matt held her even closer and stroked her hair until the trembling stopped.

'I'm sorry, David, but Helen can't just walk away from this,' he said angrily. 'She's caused too much pain.'

'I can't stop you turning her over to the police, but I'm begging you not to,' David said. 'Despite her faults, I still love her,' he added simply. Matt sighed heavily and looked enquiringly at Tessa.

'I don't want revenge, or even for her to be punished,' she said slowly. 'I almost feel sorry for her, but I can't spend my life wondering if she'll ever again plot to hurt me. Or Abby.'

'Abby?' Matt was startled.

'Yes. I think you were right when you said Helen was jealous of your father's affection for Abby, and I'm sure it was Helen who broke that porcelain – Abby kept saying it wasn't her fault, and I thought she meant it was an accident, but now I think Helen broke it and blamed her.'

'My God, she's sick,' Matt said, remembering Abby's distress over the breakage.

'Agreed. She needs treatment, not punishment.' David pounced on that. 'I'll see she gets psychiatric help in Australia, hospitalization if necessary,' he promised. 'Don't do anything hasty, Matt. Once you report this to the police, there'll be no going back.'

'Yes, I know that. I'll come and talk to Helen before I decide what's best to do,' Matt said, his distaste at the

358

thought of confronting Helen evident in both his expression and his voice. 'I might as well get it over with now,' he added, and moved reluctantly away from Tessa. 'You'll be okay, sweetheart? I'll leave the bodyguard in place for now, so you can sleep more easily.'

'Thank you, but I'm fine, honestly.' She reached for his kiss and tried not to cling, reminding herself that she was perfectly safe, that Helen was locked up and would soon either be on her way to Australia or to jail. She'd put her money on Australia, for she doubted Matt could bring himself to involve the authorities in what was essentially a family matter. He would resent the interference, the probing questions, and would hate even more the distress an investigation and trial would cause his parents.

'Okay, let's get this over with.' Matt glanced at David and the two men left the room.

Matt paused briefly to speak to Geoff Rawlins's replacement, and then followed David out to the car park. They drove separately to Grange Farm, and Matt braced himself to face Helen as they entered the house.

They climbed the stairs in silence, up two flights to the largely unused attics. They were unheated and, as David unlocked the door, he expected to find a cold, tearful and dejected Helen. Which proved how little he knew her, he just had time to think before she sprang at him, her fingers curled into claws, her long, expensively manicured nails raking his face and aiming for his eyes.

'You bastard!' she screamed. 'How dare you! You'll regret this! You –'

'Stop it, Helen!' David grabbed her wrists and pulled her arms behind her back. Then she spotted Matt and changed from virago to victim in a second.

'Help me, Matt,' she pleaded. 'He's gone crazy! He's accusing me of hurting Tessa.'

'Cut it out,' Matt said curtly. 'We know what you've been doing. The only question now is whether or not you go to jail,' he told her sternly.

'Jail?' Helen repeated uncertainly, as if the possibility had never occurred to her.

'David wants to take you to Australia instead,' Matt said, and she relaxed.

'Really? I thought we had stopped sending criminals to Australia!' she drawled. 'Not that I am one, of course,' she added quickly.

'Helen! You are in big trouble!' David shook her roughly, afraid she would antagonize Matt into calling the police. 'You could have killed Tessa last night!'

'But I didn't do anything,' she said, all wide-eyed innocence.

'I have the light bulb you removed from its socket. I bet your fingerprints are all over it,' Matt said, watching closely for her reaction. There was a flicker of doubt, he was sure, then she smiled triumphantly.

'No, they aren't,' she said confidently.

'You wore gloves.' Matt sighed. 'There will still be forensic evidence to convict you,' he said, sounding more positive than he felt.

'Bastard!'

'Calm down, Helen!' David ordered, dabbing at a deep scratch she had inflicted on his cheek. 'We'll go downstairs and discuss this rationally.' He took her arm and kept a firm hold on it as they descended the stairs, Matt one step behind them and keeping a close eye on Helen, half expecting her to make a bid for escape.

'I need to go to the bathroom,' she said sullenly, jerking to a stop on the landing and turning towards the bathroom.

'Not that one – use the one in our room,' David said grimly, pushing her in another direction, for the room she had wanted to use had a window with an easy drop down on to the conservatory roof and then to the ground.

'I'll wait downstairs,' Matt muttered uncomfortably. 'Just make sure she doesn't grab her passport or credit cards and run,' he added warningly. Helen gave him a mocking little smile.

'You know me so well, darling,' she drawled meaningfully, and David shot Matt a look full of renewed suspicion. Matt sighed: if he had still needed convincing that mud would stick, David's attitude, even accounting for his natural desire to believe his wife, was proof enough of what conclusions the outside world would draw if this mess was made public. He hated to see Helen escape scot free after all the pain and distress she had caused, but he knew he would probably agree to letting David take her to Australia.

He waited at the foot of the stairs for the other two. Helen sauntered down first, and Matt stood back to let her enter the drawing-room first, thereby barring her route to the front door.

Many of David's prized antique porcelain figurines were dotted around the room and Matt remembered Tessa's suspicions that Helen had broken the Harlequin and blamed Abby.

'Did Abby really break that figurine – or was it you?' he asked abruptly. Helen merely shrugged and refused to answer, which was actually an admission in itself, Matt thought, fury welling in him again as he recalled Abby's sobbing over the episode.

'I've got an idea,' Helen said suddenly. 'Why don't we send Tessa to Australia instead?' she suggested. 'She'll be out of my way. You can keep your daughter, Matt. And me.'

'I don't want to keep you,' he said distastefully. 'I sincerely hope I never have to see you or speak to you again. And stop being so flippant!' he snapped, enraged by her calm demeanour – she was obviously confident that she wasn't going to be punished. 'You are so close to going to prison,' he warned her.

'Do you really think so?' she said musingly. 'Perhaps, but not for long. I think the jury would be extraordinarily compassionate, especially when I testify that you seduced me when I was fourteen . . . no, let's make that twelve – that would really cast you as the villain of the piece, wouldn't it, Matt?' she asked conversationally. 'And, when I also tell them that you encouraged me to frighten Tessa away; that you wanted to keep the daughter but not the mother . . .'

'How soon can you get a flight to Australia?' Matt turned to David, afraid he would throttle Helen if he listened to her insane ravings for much longer. The problem, of course, was that she had a valid point – few people would believe he had never laid a finger on her; she would be perceived as being as much a victim as Tessa.

'We'll leave England first thing tomorrow morning,' David said promptly. 'If I can't get a direct flight to

362

Sydney, we'll go to Paris and wait there until one's available.'

'Do it. But, before you go, make sure she writes down everything she's done, and signs it. And keep her under lock and key,' he added tightly.

'I will,' David nodded.

'You will not! You –'

'Shut up, Helen!' both men yelled in unison. She glared at them, but refrained from further comment.

'I'll see myself out – you watch her,' Matt said to David, and then walked out of the house without a backward glance.

After leaving Grange Farm, Matt headed first to Stafford House, to check on Abby. He couldn't face his parents, so sneaked in through the kitchen entrance and left a message with Molly stating that he would return to drive Abby to school in the morning.

His long sleep that day meant he had no difficulty in keeping awake throughout the night: despite the bodyguard, he couldn't rest, his gut instincts warning him that this wasn't over yet. He paced the hospital corridors, much to the disgust of the minder, who felt his capabilities were in doubt, and several times phoned David to check that Helen was still under lock and key at the farm.

He left the hospital at dawn, stopping off to shower and change, and grab a bite to eat before heading back out to Drake's Abbot. He drove Abby to school and promised, rather rashly and with fingers crossed, that her mother would be at home waiting for her that afternoon.

It was while he was on his way back to the hospital that the second shoe finally dropped. He snatched up his phone on the first ring.

'Matt, I'm sorry, she's done a runner,' David said tersely.

'How the hell did you let that happen?' Matt exploded; too late, he wished he had spent the night guarding Helen, not Tessa. But he couldn't have trusted himself to stay near Helen.

'She asked if she could say goodbye to your parents. I didn't see what harm it could do,' David said, rather defensively. 'She signed a full confession, handed over her credit cards and passport; I've even got her car keys . . .'

'So – is she on foot?'

'No, she's taken one of the horses. She phoned George, and he and Evelyn came over here. Helen was in the kitchen making coffee, with Evelyn, and suddenly dashed out. It wasn't until Evelyn came back into the drawing-room alone that I knew Helen had gone. I'm sorry, Matt,' he finished miserably.

'She can't go far on horseback, unless she has cash on her and is heading for the railway station,' Matt said, thinking out loud. 'Or she could have gone to one of her friends and asked them for money.'

'I'll start phoning round,' David said.

'I ought to call the police,' Matt countered.

'Give me a couple of hours. Please?'

'Very well,' Matt agreed reluctantly. 'Where are my parents now?'

'They've gone home, I think. I told them only that Helen and I had had a row about returning to Australia.'

'Two hours, then I phone the police,' Matt said, then disconnected.

He returned to the hospital to be with Tessa and, on

364

reflection, dispatched another minder to St Hilda's School lest it occur to Helen to strike at him and Tessa through Abby. He also phoned the headmistress and told her that under no circumstances was Abby to be allowed to leave with, or even speak to, her aunt. She hid her curiosity well, and he just hoped to God she would never need to know exactly what it was all about.

In just under two hours, David phoned again.

'It's over. Apparently she didn't wait to saddle up and tried to jump that wall at the bottom of Draper's Lane. The horse caught his foot in the cattle grid,' David said, his voice raw with pain.

'Helen?' Matt asked carefully.

'Dead.' David hung up, saving Matt the necessity of finding a suitable reply. He tried, but couldn't quite feel anything other than relief – even with Helen on the other side of the world, he would never have felt Tessa was completely safe.

The following hours, days and weeks were an ordeal for them all. George and Evelyn were devastated, of course, and Matt, Tessa and David agreed to keep the truth from them.

It was only at the inquest that Matt learned the identity of the horse Helen had been riding; it was the one he had suggested she rename 'Neckbreaker'.

EPILOGUE

A little over a year later, Matt and Tessa were at St Hilda's School to attend the nativity play being enacted by the children. Tessa had been somewhat surprised to learn Abby was even being allowed to take part again, for, the year before, she had caused a near-riot when she realized one of her fellow 'angels' had a bag of sweets, and a lot of pushing and arguing had ensued when the child refused to share!

However, not only was she allowed to take part; she had been promoted to playing Mary – presumably in the hope that the responsibility would make her behave, Matt had decided.

Tessa shifted uncomfortably in her chair: she was eight-and-a-half months' pregnant, but was becoming increasingly convinced that, if the kids didn't hurry up with their play, she was going to upstage the lot of them by giving birth! As yet, she had said nothing to Matt, afraid he would insist on taking her to hospital immediately, and she desperately wanted to watch Abby's performance.

She also felt it was very important for Abby to know she had been in the audience. The prospect of sibling rivalry was a real concern to Tessa, and she felt that

366

going off to hospital instead of watching the play would hardly endear Abby to the new arrival. After all, she was too young to understand that neither Tessa nor the baby had much choice in the matter!

'I'm sorry we're late,' Evelyn said breathlessly, as she and George entered the row of seats behind. 'The traffic's dreadful this near to Christmas, and we couldn't find a parking . . . Are you all right, Tessa?' she asked anxiously.

'Yes, thank you.' Tessa smiled brightly, then, as Matt turned away to speak to his father, she leaned towards her mother-in-law, and lowered her voice. 'I haven't told Matt, but I think we'll be leaving as soon as the play ends. Can you look after Abby?'

'Of course,' Evelyn said promptly: it was already arranged that Abby would stay at Stafford House for the duration of Tessa's stay in hospital. 'Are you –?' she broke off when Matt turned to listen. 'Is Abby nervous?' she asked instead.

'No, but she's still a bit miffed because Joseph does most of the talking!' Matt grinned.

'Those were the days,' George said wistfully, but with a kindly smile for Tessa. Their relationship had begun badly, but his love for Abby and Matt's obvious happiness in his marriage had gradually won him over and he was as thrilled as any of them about the prospect of a second grandchild.

Thankfully, a lot of healing had taken place over the past thirteen months: rumours had been rife, of course, but Helen was known to be a reckless rider and the inquest verdict had been accidental death. George and Evelyn had accepted that – rather too readily, Matt and Tessa thought, and they had never questioned why

Helen had been riding bareback, nor why she and David had planned such a hasty trip to Australia.

Also, they had never again mentioned the attack on Tessa, or asked why there was to be no police investigation. It was as if they guessed the truth, but didn't want their suspicions to be confirmed. David had returned to live in Australia after the funeral, but had written recently to tell them he intended remarrying in the New Year.

Tessa turned her thoughts and her attention back to the stage, wishing they would get a move on, convinced now that she had a production of her own to deal with very shortly!

So far, Abby seemed to be taking her role seriously, her only trouble that of preventing the doll representing Baby Jesus from sliding off her lap. She quickly solved the problem by gripping the doll firmly around the neck with both hands.

'I hope she won't try to hold her new brother or sister like that!' Matt murmured to Tessa. She smiled and nodded, thinking it wouldn't be long before they discovered just how Abby reacted to not being an only child. They had involved her as soon as the pregnancy had been confirmed, letting her choose wallpaper and furniture for the nursery, but her initial excitement had given way to uninterest as the months passed.

Tessa gave a heartfelt sigh of relief when the play ended, and was able to catch Abby's eye and blow her a kiss before turning to Matt.

'We have to get to the hospital,' she told him, as calmly as possible. Oh, God, he thought, but managed to suppress his panic and maintain a calm demeanour as he helped her outside and into the car.

368

He intended being present at the birth – at Tessa's request. For once, Matt agreed with his father – the husband's place was outside in the corridor, pacing, worrying and smoking, but he figured that his wishes were of no importance. After all, given the choice, Tessa would prefer not to be there, either! She had to be, therefore, so would he.

In the event, it was much quicker and easier than Tessa had dared imagine – she was even able to reassure Matt that it really wasn't so bad this time. Then, just when he was thinking this was the most horrific day of his life, his son was born and it suddenly became the most wonderful. Tiny, red, wrinkled and squawking, Matt thought he had never seen anything so precious. Then he looked at Tessa, flushed with exertion and triumph, her hair black with perspiration and he buried his face in her neck, too choked to speak.

He stayed until Tessa had been moved back to her room and fell asleep and, with reluctance, left his son who was also sleeping soundly. He must never forget that he had a daughter, just as precious, at this moment waiting anxiously for news of her mother.

Abby had been allowed to stay up late to help her grandparents decorate the Christmas tree – a task they had been saving for just this occasion. When she saw Matt, she almost fell off the chair she was standing on in her haste to reach him.

'Hey!' He swung her of her feet and held her close. 'Your mother's fine, and you have a baby brother,' he told her. George and Evelyn exchanged glances of delight, but, also mindful of Abby's feelings, carefully made little fuss until she had been put to bed.

Then George produced a vintage bottle of champagne and they toasted Tessa's health and that of the new arrival.

'To Harry Stafford.' They touched glasses.

'What a lovely Christmas this will be,' Evelyn said. The words, 'Unlike last year', hung in the air. They all thought of Helen for a moment, then simultaneously banished her from their minds without a word being spoken.

Tessa was watching the car park from the window of her room when Matt arrived with Abby the following afternoon. He had been back twice already, but Tessa had wanted to be up and dressed before Abby saw her, for the little girl had never quite lost her anxiety over Tessa's health.

She smiled as she saw Abby clamber, rather awkwardly, out of the car, carrying a bouquet of flowers almost as big as herself. She turned away from the window, placed Harry gently into his crib and then sat down some distance from him – a carefully thought-out manoeuvre, for she wanted her arms free to hug Abby in this first meeting with her brother.

She looked up as the door burst open and the bunch of flowers on legs hurled herself at her, as if they had been apart for weeks instead of just one night. Tessa held her close and listened attentively to her chatter.

Matt perched on the arm of her chair; he glanced towards his son but stayed with Abby and Tessa, also listening to Abby's chatter. Finally, Tessa raised her eyes to his and jerked her head slightly towards the crib: they had discussed this moment many times, but still Tessa felt apprehensive.

'Do you want to come and have a look at your brother?' she asked casually. Abby seemed to have no strong feelings either way, but allowed Tessa to take her hand and lead her over to the crib.

Tessa stood back a little, her hand reaching out and instinctively finding Matt's as they waited anxiously for Abby's reaction.

'What do you think of him?' Tessa asked softly, when Abby remained silent, peering uncertainly at the small bundle.

'He's boring,' she said dismissively. 'And he's ugly,' she decided.

'You looked like that when you were born,' Tessa told her.

'Did I?' Abby seemed disbelieving. 'Oh, well, I 'spect there's hope for him, then,'' she said, sounding exactly like George Stafford. Matt bit down hard on his lower lip.

'I expect there is,' Tessa agreed gravely, carefully avoiding Matt's eye.

'I don't know much about babies, either,' Matt said, hunkering down to Abby's level and putting his arm around her waist. 'We'll have to learn together, you and I, how to help look after him, won't we?'

'Mmm, yes.' Abby nodded at last, tentatively reaching out to touch the baby's curled fist and smiling when he gripped her finger with surprising strength. 'He can ride Lollipop if he wants to,' she offered, and Tessa kissed her.

'Thank you, sweetie, that's a lovely idea. I'm sure he'll enjoy that when he's a bit bigger.'

Matt leaned over to encircle his entire family in the strength and protection of his arms, kissing Abby first, then Tessa, and finally dropping a gentle kiss on to Harry's head.

'I love you all, so much,' he said softly. 'I must be the luckiest man in the world.'

THE EXCITING NEW NAME IN WOMEN'S FICTION!

PLEASE HELP ME TO HELP YOU!

Dear *Scarlet* Reader,

As Editor of *Scarlet* Books I want to make sure that the books I offer you every month are up to the high standards *Scarlet* readers expect. And to do that I need to know a little more about you and your reading likes and dislikes. So please spare a few minutes to fill in the short questionnaire on the following pages and send it to me.

Looking forward to hearing from you,

Sally Cooper

Editor-in-Chief, *Scarlet*

QUESTIONNAIRE

Please tick the appropriate boxes to indicate your answers

1 Where did you get this Scarlet title?
Bought in supermarket ☐
Bought at my local bookstore ☐ Bought at chain bookstore ☐
Bought at book exchange or used bookstore ☐
Borrowed from a friend ☐
Other (please indicate) _____

2 Did you enjoy reading it?
A lot ☐   A little ☐   Not at all ☐

3 What did you particularly like about this book?
Believable characters ☐   Easy to read ☐
Good value for money ☐   Enjoyable locations ☐
Interesting story ☐   Modern setting ☐
Other _____

4 What did you particularly dislike about this book?
_____

5 Would you buy another Scarlet book?
Yes ☐   No ☐

6 What other kinds of book do you enjoy reading?
Horror ☐   Puzzle books ☐   Historical fiction ☐
General fiction ☐   Crime/Detective ☐   Cookery ☐
Other (please indicate) _____

7 Which magazines do you enjoy reading?
1. _____
2. _____
3. _____

And now a little about you –
8 How old are you?
Under 25 ☐   25–34 ☐   35–44 ☐
45–54 ☐   55–64 ☐   over 65 ☐

cont.

9 What is your marital status?
   Single ☐   Married/living with partner ☐
   Widowed ☐   Separated/divorced ☐

10 What is your current occupation?
   Employed full-time ☐   Employed part-time ☐
   Student ☐   Housewife full-time ☐
   Unemployed ☐   Retired ☐

11 Do you have children? If so, how many and how old are they?
   _____
   _____

12 What is your annual household income?
   under $15,000 ☐   or   £10,000 ☐
   $15–25,000 ☐   or   £10–20,000 ☐
   $25–35,000 ☐   or   £20–30,000 ☐
   $35–50,000 ☐   or   £30–40,000 ☐
   over $50,000 ☐   or   £40,000 ☐

Miss/Mrs/Ms _____
Address _____
_____
_____

Thank you for completing this questionnaire. Now tear it out – put
it in an envelope and send it, before 31 March 1999, to:

Sally Cooper, Editor-in-Chief

USA/Can. address   *UK address/No stamp required*
SCARLET c/o London Bridge   SCARLET
85 River Rock Drive   FREEPOST LON 3335
Suite 202   LONDON W8 4BR
Buffalo   *Please use block capitals for*
NY 14207   *address*
USA

Scarlet **titles coming next month:**

FIND HER, KEEP HER   Judy Jackson

Daniel St Clair is everything Jess Phillips should avoid. She's a career woman – fighting to make a living in a man's world. Daniel, she tries to convince herself, is a pompous university intellect with a pretty face and a nice body! When Jess accepts Daniel's help, she gives in to the physical attraction between them. Why not? They're both unattached, intelligent adults . . . but Jess should have remembered that romance plays by its own rules and it plays to win!

THE TROUBLE WITH TAMSIN   Julie Garratt

Tamsin runs away from love but soon discovers that 'out of sight' doesn't necessarily mean 'out of mind.' She likes men – she might even be in love with one of them: cheating Patric Faulkner, lost love Vaughn Herrick, and the attractively menacing Craig Andrews. Then there is Mark Langham - the one person Tam can always rely on to be there for her. But Mark's patience is wearing thin, and it is only when she begins to lose him that Tam realises just where her true happiness lies. But is she too late for love?

JOIN THE CLUB!

Why not join the *Scarlet* Readers' Club – you can have four exciting new reads delivered to your door every other month for only £9.99, plus TWO FREE BOOKS WITH YOUR FIRST MONTH'S ORDER!

Fill in the form below and tick your two first books from those listed:

1. *Never Say Never* by Tina Leonard ☐
2. *The Sins of Sarah* by Anne Styles ☐
3. *Wicked in Silk* by Andrea Young ☐
4. *Wild Lady* by Liz Fielding ☐
5. *Starstruck* by Lianne Conway ☐
6. *This Time Forever* by Vickie Moore ☐
7. *It Takes Two* by Tina Leonard ☐
8. *The Mistress* by Angela Drake ☐
9. *Come Home Forever* by Jan McDaniel ☐
10. *Deception* by Sophie Weston ☐
11. *Fire and Ice* by Maxine Barry ☐
12. *Caribbean Flame* by Maxine Barry ☐

ORDER FORM

SEND NO MONEY NOW. Just complete and send to **SCARLET READERS' CLUB, FREEPOST, LON 3335, Salisbury SP5 5YW**

Yes, I want to join the *SCARLET* **READERS' CLUB*** and have the convenience of 4 exciting new novels delivered directly to my door every other month! Please send me my first shipment now for the unbelievable price of £9.99, plus my TWO special offer books absolutely free. I understand that I will be invoiced for this shipment and FOUR further *Scarlet* titles at £9.99 (including postage and packing) every other month unless I cancel my order in writing. I am over 18.

Signed ....

Name (IN BLOCK CAPITALS)..

Address (IN BLOCK CAPITALS)..

....

Town... **Post Code**..............................

Phone Number ....

As a result of this offer your name and address may be passed on to other carefully selected companies. If you do not wish this, please tick this box ☐.